'Having earned his spurs with some acclaimed histories of the RAF during the Second World War, Patrick Bishop turns novelist in this beautifully crafted love story'

Mail on Sunday

'Bishop writes an exciting aerial dogfight, rich in the telling detail that makes for authenticity. Yet this is a good deal more than a bloke's yarn, with well-drawn, convincing characters and plenty of love interest.'

Daily Mail

'Gripping . . . powerful descriptions of the air battles and life on a RAF station . . . equally good at capturing the mood in a rural pub, or a smoky, sweaty ballroom . . . The final, most thrilling, part of the book takes place in the aftermath of the D-Day landings in 1944 . . . a poignant end to an enthralling tale, and I hope not the last of Bishop's wartime novels.'

Spectator

'A measured, lyrical novel of remarkable scope and poise . . . replete with the realism and authenticity that are the author's hallmark . . . wonderfully evocative'

Damien Lewis, author of *Apache Dawn*

PATRICK BISHOP

A Good War

HODDER

First published in Great Britain in 2008 by Hodder & Stoughton
An Hachette Livre UK company

First published in paperback in 2008

1

Copyright © Patrick Bishop 2008

A CIP catalogue record for this
title is available from the British Library

ISBN 978 0 340 97900 6

Typeset in Plantin Light by Hewer Text UK Ltd, Edinburgh
Printed and bound in the UK by CPI Mackays, Chatham ME5 8TD

Hodder & Stoughton policy is to use papers that are natural, renewable
and recyclable products and made from wood grown in sustainable
forests. The logging and manufacturing processes are expected to
conform to the environmental regulations of the country of origin.

Hodder & Stoughton Ltd
338 Euston Road
London NW1 3BH

www.hodder.co.uk

In memory of Marek Adam Polanski 1948–1979

PART ONE

I

Soon after Montcharles the rain started. It fell in fat, heavy drops that danced on the hot road. Gerry flicked on the wipers, slow, then fast, but the rain overwhelmed them. It was no good. He pulled over into a lay-by under a stand of beech trees.

'Best to stop a bit. It won't last long.'

The woman next to him said nothing. The rain drummed on the roof with tropical fury, coursing down the windscreen and turning it into a distorting lens so that nothing was visible through the glass except a green, aquarium blur. The din emphasised the silence inside the car. Gerry felt a clammy intimacy descend. He took the yellow Michelin map from the pocket in the door. Number 68. Niort-Châteauroux. He traced a line along the thin black track of back road through the hamlets and villages – Saint-Hilaire, Chapelle Marie, Bresse – to their destination. Thirty more kilometres until they reached Vercourt. Soon the map's abstractions would turn into bricks and mortar. He sighed and reached down for the lever beside him and pushed it down so that the seat slumped back. He always forgot how much he hated returning, always told himself never again, always went. He took a packet of small cigars from his blazer and gestured for permission towards the woman, who smiled back in a little ritual of assent.

He puffed for a few minutes in silence. Then, as quickly as it had started, the rain let off. A shaft of watery light split the cloud and the damp green and khaki of the trees and fields began to take shape through the glass.

The woman squeezed his hand. 'It's never as bad as you think it's going to be.' Gerry nodded. He started the engine and they pulled out on to the glistening road.

It was noon when they reached Vercourt. There was bunting stretched across the square, tricolours interspersed with Union Jacks. A sky-blue banner with the cross of Lorraine and the dates 1944–1984 picked out in gold hung from the wrought-iron balcony of the mairie.

Every time he returned, the place had changed a little more. Forty-five years ago the square had been paved with cobbles, ground smooth and shiny by centuries of cartwheels so that the stones gleamed in the light of a strong full moon. At some time in the 1960s the municipality had covered them with tarmac and painted lines to mark parking spaces. Already, beneath the tar skin, the old, hexagonal stones were pushing through.

Forty-five years ago the only businesses on the square were the baker's, the butcher's, the café and the hotel. The rest of the square was made up of narrow houses, with heavy stone lintels framing the windows and flat, grey concrete façades, relieved in summer by splashes of red from the geraniums in the window boxes. Once, he had stepped inside one of the houses, and could remember the dense, dark quiet and the mingled smell of polish, cooking and Eau de Javel cleaning fluid.

Half the homes had been turned into shops and businesses now. There was a mini-market, a hardware store, a building society, a newsagent's and a hunter's armoury with shotguns, rifles and broad-bladed knives with bone handles displayed in the window below a mounted boar's head.

The café was still there. It had changed hands several times but sentiment or superstition had preserved the name which glowed now in a flowing neon script but in the old days was painted in signwriter's three-D on a warped board. L'Espérance. Hope, thought Gerry, as he saw it again, and he brightened slightly.

The Auberge de la Vienne had also survived and prospered. It now had the kind of lacquered antiquity that made it worth a detour as an overnight stop for holiday-makers heading south. Gerry parked behind a Volvo estate car with a Belgian number plate, just by the short path that led to the creeper-covered porch. They got out, stretched and looked around. It was hot and still and quiet. Gerry heard a cough, soft and habitual. Someone was watching them from the shadows of the porch. A large man in his late sixties with a lined and pouchy face stepped out of the shade and walked slowly towards them with his arms held out in greeting.

'You're early,' he said. 'Come in. The boy will bring your bags.' He raised the woman's hand to his lips, then gently pushed her away to arms' length for an appraising look.

'Moira,' he said.

'Hallo Alain, darling.' She brushed a kiss onto his cheek.

Then he dipped down to fold Gerry in a brief embrace and Gerry smelled cigarette smoke and cologne.

Alain led them through the stone door, hung with AA and Logis de France badges, and into the flagged hall. There were tapestries on the wall and swords and pikestaffs, wooden coats of arms and singed-looking parchment maps of the region. 'I've put you in room seven again,' Alain said, holding out a heavy iron key.

Moira took it. 'I'm going to leave you boys alone for a while,' she said, and stepped onto the broad staircase behind the young man and woman who were carrying the bags upwards.

Gerry watched her mount the stairs. The weary grace he had noticed when he first met her and which she had carried through life was heavier now.

Alain moved behind a carved wooden bar that sat in a corner of the hall. He pulled at the handle of a stainless-steel door that opened with a satisfying *thock*, exhaling a gust of coldness, and brought out a bottle of champagne.

The wine boiled into the glasses.

'Not bad, eh?'

For a moment Gerry thought he was talking of the champagne, but Alain was gesturing around the antique-lined walls of his domain. 'It's getting better all the time. It will go on getting better too. Here's to the future.'

Gerry said nothing and drank. The champagne was dry, almost peppery. The big man looked at him and laughed. 'Don't look so worried. What's the matter with you? The war's over. You're here to enjoy yourself. Everything has been taken care of.'

They had been given the best room. Moira lay face down on the bed, her head buried in the heavy counterpane. The silk print skirt settled over her limbs, emphasising the length of her legs and the narrowness of her hips. Her scent, the scent that he'd badgered the RAF boys to bring back from special operations in France in the early days, hung faintly in the air. He felt a rare stirring of desire and sat down heavily on the bed, running a hand tentatively over her bottom.

'Pissed already, darling?'

She did not say it unkindly. Gerry rose from the bed. 'Early days yet,' he murmured.

Up from the square floated a noise of revving and grinding gears. He moved to the window. A small coach was swinging round in front of the hotel. The driver seemed to be having trouble manoeuvring. There was a fierce sigh of air brakes and the engine stopped.

The door of the coach snapped open and one by one a line of elderly men and women lowered themselves, hesitantly, onto the road, clustering at the side of the vehicle to wait for their bags. They all seemed to be talking, and their voices reached up to the window like the chatter of starlings. The women were in floral dresses and pastel cotton blazers, with round straw hats crowning identically permed, grey heads. The men wore blazers with badges sown lumpily on the breast pockets, white shirts and block striped ties. Grey slacks flapped above broad-fitting brown shoes, bought from newspaper advertisements that vaunted their comfort and cheapness.

Gerry looked down. He felt the same queasy fluttering in his chest as he had done at the start of a big show. He glanced in the mirror and smoothed his hand through the ridges of wavy hair. It was more grey than black now, but it was still mostly there. He took his blazer from the hanger and buttoned it over his white cotton shirt. He raised first his left foot, then his right, and polished the toe-cap of each already gleaming shoe on the back of his charcoal-grey flannels. For a moment he held himself stiffly in front of the long mirror, arms pressed to his side. Then he swivelled away from the image and walked firmly out of the room and down the corridor.

They were crowded into the hall when he got downstairs, the men already at the bar, the women standing in a huddle discussing some drama of the journey. Alain moved among them with a magnum of champagne. When they were all filled, he tapped a fingernail against his glass and the talk faded.

'Let me explain the programme before we all get too comfortable,' he said. 'There's a long day ahead of us. We will have a light lunch here.' He looked meaningfully at the men. 'That means going easy on the wine.' There was a chorus of good-natured boos.

'At three o'clock there will be a ceremony in the main square where your party will be officially welcomed by the commune of Vercourt. Next there will be a speech in response by Major Gerald Cunningham.' He waved at Gerry who was standing unnoticed at the foot of the stair. 'From there we shall make our way by foot to the war memorial. Transport can be laid on for those who don't feel up to it. Then back to the mairie for the *vin d'honneur* and dinner.'

Alain hurried away towards the kitchen and chatter flooded the room. The men moved towards Gerry. 'Hallo boss. You beat us to it then?' The speaker was slight, red faced with an extravagant helmet of very white hair.

'Hallo Roy.' Gerry nodded around the group. 'Spider, Mark, Frank. Yes, Moira and I decided to make a holiday of it. Stopped over in Paris and after this we're heading down south. How was the charabanc?'

'It was a bloody nightmare,' said a wiry man with a long, horse face. 'You think the coach operator would run to a karsy given the number of prostate cases on board.'

Gerry smiled. 'Same old Spider, always bloody moaning.'

They all laughed, and Gerry laughed with them. He put his arm around Spider's shoulder and guided him towards the dining room.

After lunch they filed out into the square. The wives stood behind a red velvet rope in front of a stage, rigged up from scaffolding poles and planks and swathed in red, white and blue crepe. The men took up their places in the middle of the square. They had pinned up their medals and pulled on their faded old service berets. The weight of the medals pulled at the blazers, spoiling the martial effect. An order sounded from the platform and they shuffled to attention.

From the corner of the square came a discordant blaring that after a few bars took on the ragged but recognisable form of the 'Marseillaise' and the band of the local fire brigade marched in. On the tribune stood the mayor, flanked by Alain and a thin woman who appeared to be the mayor's wife. The mayor cleared his throat and, through a whistle of feedback, began reading from a sheet a speech full of French abstractions, *Honneur, gloire, fidélité* . . . Gerry felt his attention drifting away. The mayor went on and on. The sun glanced off the windows of the square. Far away a dog was barking. Then the droning words stopped and it was his turn.

He half walked, half marched across the tarmac and mounted the steps, which were tacked with faded red baize. At the top he stumbled slightly. Alain threw him a look of mild alarm. No one else seemed to have noticed. He steadied himself and strode to the microphone, feeling the eyes of everyone on him.

It was the speech he had made at every one of the ten-yearly gatherings, as vague and formulaic as the Frenchman's. 'Monsieur le Maire. Ladies and Gentlemen. Comrades. We gather here once again today, a little older and a little sadder, to mark the memory of tragic events.' A little breeze picked up, rustling the leaves and the bunting.

'Forty-five years ago this village, along with the rest of France, was locked in a struggle, a struggle to the death, with the forces of darkness and evil. On one side was the might of Nazi Germany. On the other a gallant band of Frenchmen and Frenchwomen, helped in a small way by the force of which I am so proud to have been a member.

'We were different people with different backgrounds and different ways of doing things.' He lifted his head and looked around. 'At times it wasn't easy. There were moments of despair; long moments when it seemed that the night would go on forever. But we shared a common hope, a belief in justice and humanity. In the end that counted for more than their tanks and their machine guns.'

Gerry lowered his voice. 'We should thank our good fortune or our God for every day that has passed since then. We should never forget that we are the lucky ones. As we celebrate we should never forget those we left behind. The dead, who are not here today, but who will always be with us . . . Let us remember them for a few moments in silence.'

The only sound was the rustle of the bunting in the breeze. Gerry stole a look around the square. His men looked like soldiers again. They stood rigidly to attention, their faces set hard, sealing in their feelings. The band sat immobile on small wooden seats, staring ahead. Behind the velvet rope, some of the women held handkerchiefs to their eyes. Gerry noticed that a few strangers, neither veterans nor locals, were standing behind them. They seemed embarrassed, standing awkwardly as they waited for the emotion in the air to be discharged.

Then the bandsmen were on their feet again, loading themselves up with their instruments. They struck up a march and stumped out of the square with the mayor and the VIPs and the veterans and their wives falling in behind. The parade shuffled up a long street of flat grey, houses that petered out into beet and maize fields. The road began to rise, leading them towards a wood. Gerry was sweating a little and there was a tightness in his chest. Moira was finding it hard to keep up. The procession turned a bend in the road and there it was. You could drive past it without noticing it, a low, rough monument almost hidden in the pines and oaks at the edge of the forest. The marchers lined up in front of it. The white stone was flecked with moss. It showed a young man, naked, clinging with one hand to a cross of Lorraine with almost erotic fervour while the other pointed to the inscription, *Pour Ceux Qui Sont Tombés Pour La Liberté*. At the side of the monument was carved a list of names. Until now the events had passed in a somnambulant fuzziness. That morning he had tried to put something inside him to protect him, a cold pillar of indifference that would support him through the day, but as he read the names the furnace doors of the past swung open and he felt his numbness dissolving and tears pricking his eyes.

A young priest began talking but Gerry heard nothing. He was matching the names to the faces, remembering the frightened eyes above the mud-stained tunics, the panic and the shouting and the patter of bullets in the leaves. The words of the priest broke in. He seemed to be taking a long time. He was young and he spoke in a low, solemn voice, portentous and quietly dramatic, and Gerry felt a stab of anger. What was this pious bullshit? What did he know?

By the time it was over he was crying. In all the years he had been coming here this had never happened. The grief came up in little jolts that he could not hide or disguise. Faces were turning towards him. He felt ashamed. Moira put her arm around his waist and turned him away from the group and back down the road towards the village.

When they reached Vercourt, they saw Alain standing on the steps of the mairie at the corner of the square. He saw them and motioned them over with glass-raising gestures. Gerry hesitated. 'Go on, darling,' Moira said. 'I'll be there shortly.'

Alain led him into a panelled hall where trestle tables covered with white tablecloths were set out for dinner. On each stood big, unlabelled bottles of red wine. Alain poured two glasses and handed one to Gerry, who drank half of it at once.

'I had to leave before the end,' he said. 'How was it?'

'I don't know how many times I can go through with this, old son,' Gerry said.

Alain poured again. 'You'll go on doing it until you drop down dead. You know that. Everyone expects it of you. You can't let them down.'

In twos and threes the veterans and their wives drifted into the hall. They stood among the tables, holding tightly onto their glasses and talking softly, waiting for the last formalities to end. Some local people arrived, but they spoke little English and the veterans no French and, after smiles and handshakes, they stood in huddles on their own.

At last the mayor stepped up onto a small dais that looked like a pulpit in the corner of the hall. He made a short speech, then called for his glass to be filled, holding it rigidly in front of him as if examining it for impurities. 'To Freedom and Comradeship,' he said loudly.

'Freedom and Comradeship,' they answered back, with the fervour of children being dismissed from class. The hard benches scraped back and they sat down in a rumble of conversation. Six young women appeared with tureens of onion soup and ladled them into thick, white bowls. The guests spooned away hungrily.

Then the bowls were cleared away and the waitresses appeared again with steel, oval dishes of salmon and sorrel sauce. They ate without pause for an hour. The salmon gave way to plates of beef and pungent wood mushrooms. Then came the cheeses – chalky chèvre; orange rounds of Reblochon; crusted slabs of Pont l'Eveque – served on beds of straw and vine leaves.

They were men and women of appetite who, every day of their lives, expected to sit down to three square meals, but at the end they were defeated and the apple tarts were barely tasted when they were taken away.

By now the magnums of red wine had been emptied and replaced and emptied again and tall bottles of pale, gold spirit appeared on the tables.

Clouds of cigarette smoke climbed into the rafters. The veterans began changing places, settling down into little groups to trade anecdotes polished by forty-five years of repetition. Gerry was tipsy now, from the wine and from the knowledge that the day was almost over. He was sitting at the head of one of the long tables with the mayor on one side of him and Moira on the other, insulating him from the company of his comrades. Moira tipped some of the yellow spirit into his glass. 'Go on,' she smiled. 'They're waiting for you.' Gerry rose and moved down to the middle of the table where Roy and Spider and Mark were sitting, laughing as another old story came to its familiar conclusion.

Spider looked up. 'Hold up, you lot, the boss has arrived.'

Gerry stood over them, swaying slightly. 'Someone shift your bum so an old man can sit down,' he said.

Spider patted the space beside him. 'Come on, sir. You climb in here.'

At last Gerry felt at ease. The electric chandeliers had been turned off and candles placed on the tables. In the buttery glow, creased skin became smooth and broken veins disappeared and dentures lost their counterfeit gleam, and for a while the light gilded the guests, turning them into characters in some classical tableau, warriors and their women, celebrating victory.

He could not linger too long. It was his duty to talk to everyone before the night was out. He got up, waving down the protests, and moved along the table, shaking hands, swapping stories, recalling those who had died since the last encounter, feeling from each man and woman a charge of affection and respect. Then there was only one table left to visit, hidden in the shadow at the alcove at the end of the hall. Gerry finished the story he was telling to a gratifying burst of laughter and excused himself. As he approached the last table, he realised he need not have bothered. They were not veterans at all, but a group of local Frenchmen and - women and some guests from the hotel. By now Gerry was drunk. He felt invincibly happy, as if the wine and the admiration and the goodwill had been pumped straight into an artery. His eye was caught by a striking middle-aged woman with dense, black hair chopped severely into the nape of her neck. He climbed carefully over the bench and sat down next to her.

'I am Gerry Cunningham,' he said thickly. 'Who, beautiful lady, are you?'

She said nothing. A man's voice answered in an accent that was not English.

'She's my wife, Gerry.'

Gerry turned towards the dimness of the corner of the alcove from where the voice had come. The alcohol and the euphoria lifted. Gerry heard his own voice, slow and heavy as if supplying the phrase needed to fulfil a prophecy.

'Where do I know you from?'

The man leaned forward into the candlelight. 'You know me from here, Gerry. It's me, Tommy. I've come back.'

2

Later, when he tried to remember, it was the smell of things that brought it back: the scent of honeysuckle and white clover in the field where they waited; then, inside the cockpit, the canvas and leather of his harness and the stink of hot oil and metal and aviation spirit gusting from the engine. Finally, in the cool of the evening, when the day's fighting was over, the hoppy tang of spilled beer, cigarette smoke and a certain woman's perfume.

It was hot that summer. Every day seemed warmer than the last. The sun leeched colour out of the land, turning the trees and grass a milky green and the cornfields a tawny, lion-hide tan.

That morning, the sun seemed to have risen specially early, beating down hot on the tarpaulin covers of the lorries that took him, at eight o'clock with the other pilots, from the house to the base then out to the dispersal areas where the Hurricanes were parked in the blast pens, noses tipped eagerly up, waiting for them. They were tired, numb with a weariness that never quite lifted, and he was hungover. No one ever felt much like talking at that hour. They walked to the shade of the hedgerow that ran along the edge of the field, and stretched out on their backs on the springy grass.

Adam lit a cigarette and closed his eyes. He could hear the soft chatter of the ground crew sprawled underneath the planes and a wood pigeon cooing in the distance. Soon he was falling, toppling into oblivion that came up to meet him like a black velvet cushion.

For a while he dozed, floating luxuriously in and out of consciousness. Then a hand bell was ringing, faintly at first but growing louder, and the air filled with the bass throb of engines. He wrenched himself awake. The others were on their feet, jogging forwards, heads down, parachutes bumping absurdly against the backs of their legs, towards the aircraft whose propellers were already spinning invisibly in the shimmering air. He stumbled upright and ran towards his Hurricane, the last in the row, the ground crew waving him towards them like spectators at a race. He caught his foot in a hump of grass, lost his balance, righted himself, ran harder. The first Hurricane was moving off, jolting over the turf towards the tarmac. He reached his aircraft and hauled himself up onto the wing root, swung his right leg into the cockpit and dropped down on top of his parachute wedged into the steel bucket of the seat. The aircrew jumped away. He pushed on the rudder bar and eased open the throttle and the aircraft bounced forward on to the runway.

He plugged in the headset and Buxton's grimly cheerful voice filled the earphones.

'There's a bloody great swarm of them heading our way. Angels twenty, everyone, and listen out.'

He lined up behind Whitbread's Hurricane, and watched it race away. The runway stretched ahead of him, rising slightly in the middle. He eased the throttle lever forward and released the brakes. The aircraft bounded away, the ridges of the concrete beating under the wheels, faster and faster, then suddenly there was nothing and he was in the air. As he left the ground he twisted his head around looking for the enemy aircraft, but the serene, airmail-letter-blue sky was empty. With one hand he reached down and cranked the handle that wound up the undercarriage. Then he lifted his fingers to the oval gold medal of Our Lady of Czestochowa at his throat and said the prayer. 'Please ask God to give me one more day.'

His heart thumped and his mouth was dry and sour. He opened the throttle wide and pulled back the control column, watching the altimeter loop steadily as he pushed the Hurricane upwards. He tucked in behind Whitbread. The rest of the squadron were ahead of him and higher, crawling upwards towards the thin wisps of cirrus that hung at 20,000 feet.

He glanced down at the unfurling land. He was over Chichester. The white stone spire of the cathedral reached up out of the drab rows of brick and tile. Then came a muddy estuary, veined with channels, and beyond that the sea, a deep inky blue in the morning sun. A thermal cushioned the weight of the machine as he crossed the chalk cliffs of the Isle of Wight. The land below looked dreamily at peace. Tiny figures stirred in the fields, women, old men and young boys, doing the work of the sons and husbands and brothers who were off at the war. Among the corn sheaves someone straightened, looked up and raised a hand in salute.

Buxton was banking and turning, straining for the height that would bring them level with the Germans. They swung back towards the shore. Ahead were the green upholstered Downs he could see from his bedroom window. A windmill stood out on the side of the highest hill, hung with terracotta tiles that glowed in the sunlight.

His eyes stayed stuck to it for a second. Perhaps this would be his last sight of earth. He pushed the thought aside, quickly made the sign of the cross and jerked his head round, searching the sky again for signs of the Germans.

Still there was nothing. The infinite blue around him was empty. Then he saw them, straight ahead, maybe ten miles off, stacked in neat rows, the size of insects at this distance. He could not count them all. There were dozens. As they got closer they got bigger and he saw the crooked wing line of Junkers 87s, Stukas and, alongside them, shoals of sleek Messerschmitt 109 fighters. He felt a line of sweat crawl down his spine and settle in the small of his back. He began humming to himself, a stupid song of childhood, as Buxton's voice spilled into the headphones: 'Corks in, boys. Here they come. Tally-ho.'

The Germans seemed to be heading directly for the aerodrome, whose runways lay spread out invitingly on the flat coast ahead. As they clipped the north headland of the small island that lay before it, the lead machine dropped yellow signal flares and the formation split into groups. The largest kept on towards the aerodrome. The air around him was full of fighters from all the base's four squadrons – Hurricanes mostly, but he could see Spitfires too, climbing rapidly, clawing for more height.

It was clear now that they had been scrambled too late. The Stukas were almost above the base and preparing to dive. They were slow and ugly when they were flying straight, but when they dived they became almost beautiful. As they approached the target they seemed to stop for a moment before tipping over, one by one, falling from an invisible cliff, slanting down almost vertically as if the pilot was trying to bury himself deep in the Sussex earth, but at the moment when it seemed there could be no recovery, the nose of the aircraft came up, a dark shape tumbled from the belly and the Stuka climbed away. Adam watched, feeling curiously removed, as dirty brown smudges of flak from the Bofors anti-aircraft on the ground blossomed around the cascading bombers, and geysers of mud and debris climbed silently up from the airfield in cypress-shaped columns. Then there was no distance between him and the spectacle and he was part of it and German aircraft were sliding across the air in front of him.

He felt for the milled edge of the safety catch on the firing button and thumbed it open, releasing the lever to drop his seat to get the maximum protection from the engine block in front and the armour plate at his back.

The fear that he felt like a fluttering bird inside his ribcage had left him, and in its place a cold excitement was mounting as he looked around for a target. With their bombs gone the Stukas had lost their menace; they looked slow and vulnerable, foxes weary from the henhouse romp, limping for the sanctuary of home. They turned for France, struggling for height to escape the bursting flak. Below, to his right, he could see a straggling line of five, lumbering in a diagonal towards the sea, and he pushed gently on the control column, taking the Hurricane into a steady, shallow dive. But, as he closed on them, he saw two Messerschmitts flying protectively towards them. He was sure they could not see him. They were five hundred feet below and he had the sun over his right shoulder, which would make him invisible to them until it was too late.

The dappled green camouflage gave them the look of a predatory fish of river or lake, like the pike he had once seen hauled out of a pond near his old house at Novo Polje, streamlined and glistening with a slash of a mouth that ran a quarter the length of its body.

He eased forward more sharply on the stick, man-oeuvring the nose of the Hurricane onto the nearest Messerschmitt. It flew on oblivious, gradually filling the whole space of the reflector sight. He held his breath and laid his thumb on the dimpled black plastic firing button. At 250 yards he squeezed. The lines of yellow tracer from the eight Brownings raced away and the nose bucked slightly with the recoil.

The fire streamed brightly onto the cockpit and the engine cowling of the Messerschmitt. He felt a strange intimacy, as if he was bound to his victim by the line of bullets. He pressed down again, feeling the solid platform of the Hurricane shuddering with the pulse of the guns. Sunlit shards of shattered Perspex flew up and scattered in the wake of the Messerschmitt as it rolled slowly onto its back. Then the nose dropped and it fell into a vertical dive, smashing, in a great column of spray, into the sea.

The sky was suddenly empty. The Stukas and the other Messerschmitt had vanished. He was soaked in sweat and frightened again. He had killed a man, his first ever. He was struck by the absurd thought that the Germans would now be seeking him out to punish him. The fight had carried him far away from the land and there was no friendly fighter in sight. He twisted his head around, trying to get his bearings. Then his fears were fulfilled as yellow lights twinkled past him, disappearing into the blue ahead. He gave a yelp of terror, and threw the Hurricane to starboard then immediately back to port in a sharp, diving turn. Something dark loomed over him then disappeared out of his vision.

He glanced frantically round. His body was bunched and knotted, anticipating the thump of pain. But his part of the sky was empty once more.

Away to the right he could see a handful of dwindling black dots, the Stukas and Messerschmitts running for home. The only sign of the fighting now was the looping tracery of vapour trails, already feathery at the edges as they sank into the oceanic blue of the sky.

He let the tension seep from his muscles and pulled down on the spade grip of the control column to swing back towards the shore. As he turned, a shape appeared flying high and to his right, and he saw a straggling Messerschmitt, doggedly holding a heading for the distant French coast, running as fast as he could before his fuel ran out. He was tired and nervous and was about to leave it alone when he thought again, *If I don't kill him today he might kill me tomorrow.*

He pulled up the Hurricane's nose and the silhouette of the German flitted across the hatching of the reflector sight. He fired a burst but he was too close and the bullets overshot, glittering past the propeller. The pilot saw them and pulled his machine hard to the right to climb away, all thoughts of saving fuel gone. There was no point in chasing him. A Messerschmitt would always out-climb a Hurricane. Instead he aimed a long burst ahead and to the right of the Messerschmitt, keeping it concentrated there, hoping that the German's course would carry him into the focus of the fire.

Then he saw debris tumbling in the Messerschmitt's slipstream and the aircraft suddenly lost speed, so that it seemed that it was being hauled back to him on an invisible cable. For a second he thought he was going to overtake it, but he throttled back hard and the German was comfortably under his guns. He eased on the column, feeling all the power of the Hurricane concentrated in the trembling stick, and manoeuvred the sight onto the canopy of the Messerschmitt. He pushed on the firing button, a short, ranging volley at first, then a long sustained burst that punched into the hood, tearing it away from the cockpit. The pilot's head rocked forward and back like a violently shaken doll's. Then something vital seemed to leave the plane. It fell gracefully away, slipping sideways through the sky towards the ridged calm of the sea, trailing a thin banner of white smoke. He watched fascinated as the waves came up to meet it. For a moment it seemed that the laws of gravity were suspended and the aircraft would settle dreamily above the swell. But then a wing dipped and caught a wave top and the Messerschmitt whipped, cartwheeling forward, through a curtain of spray, turning and turning until it finally settled on the seething water.

When he got back, the base was burning. He flew low once over the aerodrome, looking for somewhere to land. The two big hangars were blazing. The water from the fire-crew hoses was turning to steam before it reached the flames. The runways were pocked with craters. He did a circuit and put down on the one that was damaged the least. As he landed he had to zigzag to avoid the holes. He taxied over to the dispersal area, pausing to let the fire tenders and ambulances race past. All this had happened, he found himself thinking abstractedly, while he had been in the air. It took him a few moments to connect the events.

When he reached the blast pen, a clutch of Hurricanes was already parked. He counted them. There were twelve including him. Everyone in the squadron had made it back. Two aircraftmen climbed onto the wing and pulled back the canopy and he climbed out.

He recognised one of the ground crew, a lean, curly-haired man his own age called Hennessy, who wore a polka-dot silk handkerchief knotted around his neck above overalls that were shiny with grease.

'How did you do?'

'Pretty good. I got two definites.'

Hennessy whistled. The crew crowded round.

'What were they, sir?' one of them asked.

'ME One-O-Nines.'

They cheered as if they had shot them down themselves.

'Well done,' said Hennessy. It seemed to Adam that he was looking at him for the first time with respect.

'We'll take good care of the kite. It'll be ready to go as soon as you need it.'

'Thank you.'

He felt his legs wobble as he dropped down from the wing. Whitbread was walking towards him, undoing his helmet and running his hand through blond hair that was plastered to his scalp with sweat.

'So Adam. Get amongst them?'

'You bet.'

'Go on then.'

'Two definites.'

'Balls. Maybe by Polish arithmetic. What you mean is one possible but pretty unlikely.'

Adam smiled. 'Piss off. How about you?'

'One definite: a Stuka. The thing practically ran into me. I couldn't bloody miss.'

They both laughed, suddenly exhilarated with the relief of having survived.

'Come on,' Whitbread said, pulling his Mae West over his big head. 'Let's go and hear what that bugger Buxton has to say.'

There was no more flying that day. The runways were out of action and several of the radar stations were damaged. If the German bombers came back later there would be no one, at least from the Kingsmere base, who would try to stop them. The pilots did not hide their relief. They had been flying for six straight days, three or four sorties a day, and were dazed with exhaustion.

Adam settled into the back of the lorry that would take them back to the house and as he closed his eyes was immediately back in the air again. That morning, for the first time in his life, he had killed someone. He did not know what that meant, or if it meant anything at all. He lay back against the jolting wheel arch of the truck and fell asleep.

3

The lorry took them through the dozing countryside, then turned through flint gateposts to drop them in front of a pillared entrance. Updyke House was large and unevenly proportioned, built of flint and brick and covered with creeper and ivy that licked around the sash windows. The hall was cool and dark, panelled in oak and paved in marble. The pilots clattered up the broad staircase to their rooms.

Adam's room was a servant's room with a single bed, a wardrobe, a broken-springed armchair and a table. There was a print on the wall of a hunting scene, with stout men clinging to horses, flying over hedges and ditches. The window was open and the white gauze curtains shifted gently as he closed the door. He went to the window and looked out. The air was tainted with the smell of burning petrol drifting over from the base, and he could see oily drifts of smoke rising over the fields. Over to the left, in the middle distance, the plain rose abruptly, swelling into downland. To the right, the dull green of countryside ended in a neat, straight line giving way to the sea.

The breeze from the sea fingered the curtains. The bedsprings groaned as he sat down and pulled off his flying boots. He went to the wash-hand basin and tried to coax some lather from a gritty bar of soap. The water felt cool on the taut skin of his face. He examined himself warily in the square of glass over the basin, looking for signs of change. But he looked just as he had that morning: the same hard blue eyes, dirty blond hair and bony beak of nose, red from the sun. He rubbed the rough towel over his face, tossed it on the armchair and lay down on the narrow bed. The room was bare but he liked it. The British pilots had tried to make their lodgings more homely, with inscribed oars and college photographs, but he had nothing to soften the barracks feel of the room. Everything he had was lost, back in Poland. All he had managed to salvage was the leather coat he had worn at the flying school at Deblin and which made him look like a Nazi, a few framed pictures of his parents and sister and a silver flask his grandmother had given him on the day he was commissioned into the Polish Air Force.

When was that? A year and a half ago? The memory already had a shadowy remoteness. What came after was real enough, though. He often returned in his mind to the frantic, hopeless week of the invasion, camping in pine forests, taking off from hayfields in the high-winged, slow, pathetically armed P 11s for sacrificial encounters with the Luftwaffe. Half the time they had no aircraft. When he did fly he never expected to come back, never dared to think of a future beyond the hot harvest days of smoke, flame and exhaustion. And one morning there were no more planes and no more petrol and they had fled; by car and then by foot over the border to Romania, to weeks of dodging border guards and policemen and living on scraps and charity until he found a place on a steamer sailing from Balcik to Beirut. He had stood with the other Poles on the deck of the SS *Patrice* as it pulled into a November gale on the Black Sea, tears mixing with the salt spray as their voices lifted and carried over the grey waves to the fading coastline.

> 'Poland is not lost forever . . .
> March, march Dombrowski from Italy to
>   Poland . . .'

In Beirut, life briefly got better. A Frenchman looked after him and twenty of his comrades, bought them food and clothes and paid for a passage to Marseilles. A message from General Sikorski was waiting for them, welcoming them to France. They were taken by train to an aerodrome in Lyons. And then, nothing. The French had no interest in them, privately absorbed in their own approaching nemesis, but acting as if the war would never come to them. They sat through the winter on the damp banks of the Rhône, drinking when they had the money and getting on each other's nerves. At last the French gave them uniforms, dark blue scratchy serge, and, after five months, planes that several of them got killed in learning to fly.

Then one May morning it had happened all over again. The aerodrome was attacked without warning. They had never even got off the ground. A few weeks later it was over. Adam had been moved to an airfield near Sedan where the Germans were crossing the

Marne. He flew five sorties in a lumbering Caudron, protecting British Fairey Battles as they tried to bomb the bridges. After two days his unit was ordered by the Polish HQ to move to Bordeaux. The roads were choked with civilians and drunken, despairing troops. They offered their guns to the Poles in return for bottles of wine.

They left Bordeaux in a coal ship, the *Alderpool,* with bombs falling around them. Three days later, on 21 June 1940, they landed in the rain in Plymouth. There had been a month at a training camp near Blackpool, a flying test with an RAF examiner, a few weeks learning how to handle a Hurricane. Then, ten days ago, a posting to Kingsmere, to 404 Squadron Fighter Command, flying and fighting almost every day. And today he had managed to kill his first German.

He was hungry. He got up from the bed and put on his tunic, slipped his feet into his only pair of shoes and went downstairs. He crossed the hall, past the massive stone fireplace and the matching suits of armour that guarded it, into the large, high-ceilinged room that served as the mess, and through leaded French windows that opened onto a balustraded stone terrace. The pilots were gathered by a trestle table that was shaded by a cedar of Lebanon and a monkey puzzle tree.

Adam walked over to where Whitbread was standing next to Miles Miller-Morton, a short, slightly stout young man with smooth pink skin and blond, almost yellow hair. Miller-Morton was a good pilot; after Buxton, the best in the squadron. A small group stood around him listening with various degrees of attention.

There was Bealing – uncouth, ungainly, a Londoner who even Adam could tell fell outside the social orbit of most of the other pilots; Jerry Westerham, a dapper boy with good looks and wary eyes who laughed a lot and said almost nothing; Frizell, good-natured, clumsy and barely formed, and Crouch, impatient, doggedly loyal to his hero, Buxton. And last, the least noticeable, hanging hopefully on the edge of the group, was his countryman Ted Sobinski; Ted of the mournful moustache and the spaniel eyes and the soft pot belly, who he remembered dimly from the Deblin days as the owner of a motorcycle that he took to Warsaw on unsuccessful girl-chasing forays. Adam had hardly spoken to him since he arrived at Kingsmere a few days after him. He said hallo to him now.

'Jak sie czujesz, Tadeusz?'

'Niezle.' He smiled wanly. 'Alive, at least.'

Miller-Morton looked round at the interruption. He had a dimpled beer mug in one hand and a cigarette in the other, and his tunic hung open showing a flash of red satin.

'Ah, here's Tomaszewski,' he said banteringly. 'What's this I hear about you claiming you got two today?'

'It's not a claim,' Adam said, a little too loudly, he realised. Miller-Morton made him feel like a foreigner. 'It's a fact. '

'No one's calling you a liar, old man.' Miller-Morton flapped his arms placatingly. 'I did too. Only Stukas, mind you. But other people saw mine. Didn't you, Peter?'

Whitbread smiled and took a sip of his beer. 'Don't you get fed up shooting lines, Miles? But if it makes you happy, yes, I did see you knock one down. At least I think it was you. Could have been anyone though, really. It's so bloody confusing.' He looked at his watch. 'Can't we talk about something else? Like how we're going to spend the rest of the day?'

Morton-Miller was willing to change the subject. 'What about going up town?' He addressed himself to Whitbread and Westerham, making it clear that the others were not included.

'To do what?' Whitbread seemed unenthusiastic.

'No, come on. It will be a hoot. We could start at Delvano's, or the Troc. Bite of supper. Then the early show at the Windmill. Finish off at the Café de Paris.'

'Bit of a trek. Just for a piss-up.'

Miller-Morton resumed his persuasion but suddenly no one was listening. Buxton had arrived. He stood by the French windows, glancing around with a rigid, humourless smile. The pilots stopped talking.

'Don't want to break up the fun,' he said, removing an unlit pipe that jutted from his jaw. 'I just thought you would want to know how we're faring, after this morning's fun and games.'

They turned towards him. Now he had everyone's attention, Buxton began in his cold, jaunty voice. 'The score sheet looks something like this. We did well this morning. Twelve enemy probables, mainly JU Eighty-Eights but two ME One-O-Nines as well.' He looked over at Adam. 'We've our Polish friend to thank for those.'

Someone – Frizell? – gave a half-hearted cheer but was shushed into silence.

'There's no cause for self-congratulation, though. Far from it. They still got through. They destroyed five Blenheims on the ground and one of the new night fighters. You saw what the base looks like. The big Belfast hangar's gone and so has the hospital and the mess and half the workshops.

'The runways should be serviceable tomorrow – if the ground crews pull their fingers out. They'd better be. Because we can be damned sure the Germans will be back.'

He paused and looked around, stabbing the air with the stem of his pipe. 'It's very simple,' he said. 'This is really a very old-fashioned form of combat. It's a matter of attrition. We have some advantages – we're fighting from our own ground. But otherwise we're pretty well equal. Whichever side wins will be the one with the greater stamina or the greater skill. I think we've shown that our pilots and planes are as good as theirs. It will really come down to a question of who can soak up the punishment the longest.'

He glanced challengingly around. 'That's all. Enjoy your break. It may be the last for a long time.'

'Cheerful bastard, Buxton,' said Whitbread as he filled a mug from the small barrel balanced on the trestle table. 'I might join you in London after all, Miles. On the eat, drink and be merry principle.'

Miller-Morton seemed delighted.

Whitbread looked at Adam. 'What about you? Celebrate today's successes?'

Adam thought for a moment. He had only been to London once. But a great tiredness weighed down on him and Buxton's speech had depressed him.

'Not today, thanks. I'm going to get some kip.'

But when he lay there naked under the cool starched cotton sheet he could not sleep. The images of the morning kept crowding his head. He remembered the German pilot jerking under the blows of the Brownings, the wall of spray as the aircraft cartwheeled across the waves. At three o'clock he got up and dressed. He thought of writing a letter but there was no one to write to. His mother was dead. His father and sister he had left behind in Poland. He had heard nothing of them for six months. Perhaps they too were dead. If not, they were intangible and invisible, swallowed up in the night and fog of Greater Germany.

Adam went downstairs and walked through the house, then out of the front door and up the drive, not sure where he was going. At the gates there was a path, more of a cart track, running alongside the flint wall that enclosed the house and garden. He followed it, skirting a cornfield, until it joined a narrow, metalled lane that wound between high banks and hedges. There were no signposts. They had been taken away to confuse any German agents who might be roaming the Sussex countryside. When he had first heard of this precaution it had made him laugh. Now it made him think about the awaited invasion. The battle in the air was the preliminary. When the air force was swept away the ships would come and then the tanks. He had seen two nations crushed within the last year.

The Poles had gone down under the first blows. It had not been their fault. They had courage but no guns. The French had held out a little longer. They had guns but . . . no, he did not want to think of the French like that. An image returned of unshaven infantrymen reeling in the roads, begging the Poles to take them with them on the lorry to Bordeaux.

And now it was Britain's turn. No one seemed to talk about the meaning of the war. In the pubs and teashops and barracks they discussed trivial things: rationing, gas masks, the blackout, the price and availability of beer, as if unaware of the great steel mace that was swinging down on them. His short time at the RAF training school had left him with no clear idea of whether the British military had the heart or the skill or the means to resist the stroke when it fell. His instructors had been mild men who never spoke of victory or heroism, and whose rare displays of enthusiasm were inspired by flying technicalities. Possibly it was all a great bluff and beneath the insouciance there was the same trembling terror of what was to come that he had seen so often across the Channel. Or perhaps this blitheness was real, the outward manifestation of an inner dullness and stupidity that blinded the British to the horrors that lay ahead.

It was quiet among the fields and hedges. The frantic violence of the morning seemed very far away. Adam passed a pair of low cottages that seemed too tiny for humans to live in, then the fields ended and he came into a street of pebbledashed terraced houses that turned into a parade of shops. There was a butcher's, a teashop and an ironmongers. A pile of sandbags was stacked along the post office wall. Outside, two young women had parked their prams by a bench and were sitting talking in the sun. They smiled at him, taking him by surprise. Somehow he had thought himself invisible. Belatedly, too late for them to notice, he smiled back. The encounter pleased him. He went into a tobacconist's to buy some cigarettes, even though he did not need them.

He glimpsed the sea at the end of a side street and walked towards it. A sign on the promenade warned: 'DANGER: Persons are prohibited from walking on the beach and foreshore.' Coils of barbed wire glinted dully in the sunlight all along the length of the front. Here and there stood pillboxes and gun emplacements, with long-barrelled cannon that looked as if they dated from the last century poking out to sea. Despite the obstacles and prohibitions, something was happening on a section of the beach. Groups of men in coarse brown uniforms were standing in rows with rifles with fixed bayonets sloped on their shoulders, while a short man with sergeant's stripes shouted at them. In front of them, twenty or so yards distant, was a kind of gibbet from which hung a stuffed sack surmounted by what looked like a deflated football. Someone had painted on eyes, a grinning mouth and a nose, and a toothbrush moustache.

One of the men stepped out of the line and lowered his weapon and began trotting towards the dummy, emitting at the same time an unconvincing yell. On reaching the gibbet he began to poke at the dummy, which swung back and forth as if eluding the jabs, its smirking features seemingly enjoying the encounter.

The sergeant swore and bustled forward to seize the rifle from the recruit. Then he squatted in a menacing crouch and launched himself, screaming, at the dummy, which he skewered and slashed, emptying half the stuffing. The men laughed and cheered until silenced by a shout from the sergeant. Another recruit was called forward to perform. This one managed a full-blooded war cry and plunged the bayonet enthusiastically into the dummy's straw guts.

Adam walked on, towards the pier that jutted out from one end of the promenade, past cafés and fish-and-chip shops and a closed amusement arcade. Set back a little from the front was an old hotel with a pillared entrance and velvety lawns. Several camouflage-painted Jeeps were parked outside. Their drivers, dressed in ill-fitting khaki and oversized green berets with black cockades and silver badges, were lounging and smoking, cupping the butts in the palms of their hands after each drag, then looking around with shifty, darting glances. On the terrace, four or five army officers sat at a table drinking beer. He walked up to the entrance and they nodded to him as he passed.

The lobby was dark after the bright sunshine. Plants stood in glazed pots on the oriental carpet and there were two large engravings on the wall of Highland cattle, heads lowered, drinking at sundown at the rim of a mountain lake. A cardboard poster stood on a sort of easel in the middle of the floor. Adam read: 'Bristol

Hotel Ballroom, Alberton. Dance to the sound of the Miff Smith Dance Band. 8 p.m. Fully Licensed Bar Until 11.30 p.m. Admission 3s. HM Forces 2s.' Pasted diagonally across a corner was the word 'Tonight!'

'Can I help you?'

A young woman was standing behind the reception desk. She was wearing a blue blouse with and had thick, copper-coloured hair that flicked up in points under her rather square jaw.

'Just looking at the poster, thanks.'

'You're one of the RAF boys.'

'Yes, over at Kingsmere.'

'You're foreign.' She made it sound as if she had made a pleasant discovery.

'Polish.'

'Welcome to Alberton.' She said it with a touch of irony.

'Thank you.'

'Now, you will come, won't you?'

'To the dance?'

'Of course. And you're going to bring lots of lovely boys with you.'

'It sounds like an order.'

'Then you should jolly well obey it.'

They both laughed.

'I shall certainly do my best.'

'Eight o'clock then.'

'Eight o'clock.'

Adam was smiling as he trotted down the Bristol steps and along the path where some army officers were climbing into their Jeeps.

'Heading for Kingsmere?' one of them asked.

'Yes.'

'It's on our way. Jump in.'

'You know, I don't think I will. It's such a lovely day.'

'Suit yourself.'

There was an exchange of words that Adam could not hear and a burst of laughter. The Jeeps drove away. Were they laughing at him? He decided he did not care. He took the road out of town. Quickly, the narrow, identical houses and shops thinned out and he was in the country. At a bend in the road he came across what looked like an old barn with a blackboard outside advertising tea and cakes. He sat down at a metal table and a girl of about fifteen with thick round glasses and disconcertingly heavy breasts that showed through her print dress came out. He ordered a cup of tea and a cake and sat back.

She emerged five minutes later with a cup and a plate with a slice of cake.

He broke off a bit and put it in his mouth. It tasted quite good.

As he was finishing his tea he heard an aircraft some way off. Its engine note was uneven, throbbing and fading. He looked up. Not far off a twin-engined aircraft with black crosses on its wings was limping towards him. On a recce mission, he thought, flying over to assess the day's damage. It was clearly in trouble. The engines seemed to be cutting out, and it was losing height. After a minute something fell from the fuselage and tumbled through the air until a white streak appeared behind it that blossomed into a parachute. Adam left some coins on the table and set off in the direction where he calculated the German would land, a few cornfields away.

When he got there others had beaten him to it. Climbing over a stile he saw two men, agricultural labourers by the look of it, in the corner of the field. A hay cart with a mountainous horse between the shafts stood nearby. As he got closer he saw that one of the men was gripping a pitchfork in an aggressive posture, like a medieval halberdier, while another, older man, held a scythe. A big German was lying on his back in the stubble, still harnessed to his parachute. His face was smeared with oil and he looked scared. The three glanced round as Adam arrived.

'What's going on?'

'We've captured a Jerry,' said the man with the pitchfork, grinning.

'I can see that. Stand back.'

The German struggled up onto his elbow.

'Don't you move!' The man with the scythe planted a boot on his chest and pressed him back onto the ground.

'Stop that please.'

They drew back reluctantly and Adam squatted down beside the man, first unbuttoning the flap on his revolver holster.

'Are you hurt?' The man looked bemused. Adam tried to remember the German.

'*Sind sie verletzt?*'

'*Mein Knochel.*' The man rubbed his ankle.

'Können sie gehen?'

'Ich werde es versuchen.'

The German tried to get up but again the old man with the scythe pushed him back.

'It's OK,' Adam said. 'You've done your bit. I'll take over now. There's a café over there. Why don't you go and ask them if they've got a telephone and, if they have, then call the police.'

The old man looked reluctant.

'Who are you anyway?' he asked nastily. 'You don't sound like an Englishman.'

'Go on, Cyril,' the man with the pitchfork said. 'Do what the officer says. We'll take the Jerry over to the road.'

The old man hesitated, then reluctantly tossed his scythe into the back of the hay cart and jogged off across the field at surprising speed. They helped the German to his feet. Adam released him from his parachute harness and asked him his name and which unit he was from. He told him he was Leutnant Wilhelm Kohler. Then he shut up. His ankle was sprained not broken. He put his arms around Adam's shoulder to hobble across the field. He was a big, bony man with high cheekbones and jug ears. He made slow progress. Every time he stopped, the labourer growled and poked at him with a pitchfork. When they reached the road the German was sweating. They sat down at the café. The big-breasted girl stood goggling in the doorway, then she disappeared inside and came back a few minutes later with a camera. The two labourers moved behind the German's chair and stood to attention. The camera clicked.

'One for luck,' said the man with the pitchfork.

'That's enough,' Adam said. 'Please could you now bring us some tea?'

He gave the prisoner a cigarette. Whatever fear the German felt had gone. Now he looked depressed and disgruntled. Adam guessed he had been on a reconnaissance flight, sent over to assess the results of the morning raids, but when he tried to question him the German pretended not to understand. Adam began to dislike him. He had possibly just saved him from death, from being cut to ribbons by farm hands; not the sort of knightly end that a young Luftwaffe airman would wish for. Now he wished he had left him to the peasants. It was, after all, the fate of many a Teutonic knight, toppled from the high saddle that raised him above the herd, pinned down by the weight of his now useless armour, awaiting a dagger thrust through the visor from some scavenging peasant picking over the battlefield.

His thoughts were interrupted by a car driving up fast. The doors opened and four uniformed policemen holding revolvers jumped out.

'Don't move,' shouted the leader, levelling his gun at the table.

'Please. Don't shoot,' Adam said. 'He's harmless.'

The policemen looked disappointed. Two of them moved cautiously to the table and placed hands on the German's shoulders.

'Easy now, mate,' the leader said, 'you're coming with us.'

'Hang on a minute.' The girl from the café was standing in the doorway with her camera. 'Just one more snap.'

The policemen looked at her, blankly. Then they straightened their uniforms, arranged themselves around the prisoner and looked towards the camera.

4

When Adam got back, the house seemed empty. There was no one in the hall and thick beams of sunlight slanted through the leaded windows, making buttery squares on the marble. He walked out onto the terrace. It was deserted except for a black labrador sleeping stretched out on the flags in the late afternoon heat. He could hear music, a thin, beseeching violin, coming from the garden. He walked down the stone steps and across the lawn, past an ornamental pond covered with lily pads to a grove of yew trees.

Buxton was sitting, short legs stretched out, eyes closed, on a wooden bench, listening to a wind-up gramophone. Adam stood immobilised, wondering whether he had been seen. He was turning to go when Buxton's eyes opened.

'Tomaszewski. What are you doing here? Why aren't you off enjoying yourself?' He made it sound like an accusation.

'Don't know, sir.'

Buxton sat upright. 'Come over here and sit down. And call me Brian.'

Adam went reluctantly over to the bench. There was a silence that Buxton showed no signs of breaking.

Adam noticed a book lying face down on the bench. 'What are you reading?' he asked.

'Oh that. Nothing.' He seemed slightly embarrassed. 'Just some cheap thing I picked up.' The cover showed a woman with smeared lipstick and a torn dress being restrained by a man with a gun.

'And the music?'

Buxton brightened. 'Ah, that's a bit more highbrow. But you should recognise this.'

Adam pretended to listen to the swooping old-fashioned notes, while Buxton looked expectantly at him. 'I'm sorry. I don't know it.'

Buxton seemed disappointed. 'You should. He's one of your lot. A Pole. Hang on.'

He got up and stopped the disc. 'Here you are. *Légende*. By Henryk Wieniawski.'

'Oh yes.' He had never heard of him. 'Nostalgia and pathos. I should have known it was a Pole.'

Buxton looked at him blankly then gave his cheerless smile. He picked up his pipe. 'You speak English pretty well. Not even much of an accent. Not like some of the others. Learn it at school?'

There was no getting away now. 'Yes. We did French mainly, but I had private lessons in English. My mother was an Anglophile. Perhaps that's not the right word. She loved Scotland. Her maiden name was Maklinska. She claimed she was descended from a man called Maclean who came to Poland as a soldier a long time ago. She wanted me to go to study in Scotland for a year, but then she died and the war came.'

Buxton's pipe bobbed as he gripped it hard in sympathy. 'Sorry to hear about that.'

He went back to the gramophone and put on a dance tune. How old was Buxton? Twenty-seven or twenty-eight? Only a few years older than Adam, yet he seemed to belong to another generation. He came back and sat again, smoothing dark, Brylcreemed hair back from his bulbous forehead.

'I have a great deal of sympathy for your people,' he said. 'You've already been through it. We've got it all to come. It may not look like it to you, but no one's under any illusions. A chap said it on the radio the other day. He said if we let the Nazis in then it will mean that the laziest loudmouth in the workshop will be given the power to kick us all up and down the street. I reckon that says it all.'

Adam nodded. Buxton fell silent.

After a while he said: 'It's not easy, you know. Leading young men up there to die every day. Some of them have less than twenty hours' flying time in a Hurricane or a Spit, no practice at dog-fighting or aerial gunnery – and we send them up. No choice really. We either throw everything into the fight or we give up. It's a question of which side's supply of young men runs out first.'

He looked at Adam warily, as if he felt he had said too much.

'Anyway, you're a veteran. Practically an ace after today.' He held out a hand. 'I haven't congratulated you properly. Well done. Now go off and enjoy yourself and don't have too much beer tonight. I fear tomorrow's going to be a big day.'

*   *   *

In his room, Adam thought about the evening ahead. The girl at the hotel was pretty in a wholesome way. He liked the look of her. But what did her invitation mean? Had she taken an instant fancy to him? That hardly seemed likely. He had heard that English girls were more forward than Polish girls, but they had only spoken for a few minutes. Probably she was just being friendly to a lonely foreigner. In either case it would be good to have some companions to drink with if he had no luck with her. He would try and round up some of the others when they gathered for a drink before dinner.

By six o'clock he was feeling restless. He had a bath in pleasantly lukewarm water. He shaved for a second time. He spent some time in front of the mirror, combing back his dark-blond hair, arranging a strand to fall across his forehead. His mother had told him he was handsome, pointing out when girls glanced twice at him in the street, but he never really believed it, wanting to be darker and taller. In the showers at Deblin, at the end of one of the sadistically arduous training marches, he envied the fuzz on the chests of the older students. Even now his body was smooth, but there was hard muscle under the skin.

He tore open a paper parcel and put on a clean shirt. His uniform needed pressing and cleaning. He was shabby; a thin, shabby Pole. He picked up the silver hip flask engraved with an eagle. He usually carried it with him, as a memento, a talisman of his identity, rather than for any practical purpose. This evening, though, he put it back on the table. His old life, he realised, seemed as remote and unattainable as the planets he steered by at night. Poland, real Poland, had ceased to exist for him. Poland had become an idea.

The blurred exhaustion of the last few days had lifted. He felt like getting drunk. He was glad there would be others who would feel the same way. He went downstairs and through the house to the terrace. Bealing, Frizell, Crouch and Sobinski had already taken up position next to the barrel.

'Crouch is angry with me' said Sobinski, smiling, when Adam joined them.

'Oh. Why?'

'Tell him, Crouch.'

Crouch looked sulky. 'The subject's closed,' he said.

'All right, I'll tell him. He says I'm a bad sport.'

'What have you done?' Adam asked.

'Well, in my opinion, I haven't done anything.' Sobinski took a sip of beer. 'But Crouch says I've—' he felt for the phrase, 'let the side down.'

'Get on with it, for God's sake,' said Bealing, jovially.

Sobinski shrank back in mock fear. 'All right, all right. Anyway, this morning when we were coming back we saw a Jerry on the end of a parachute.' He took another mouthful of beer.

'And what happened?'

'Well, the funny thing was that he seemed to be OK, floating down like a feather. Then all of a sudden— ' he raised his hand and mimed a rapid descent accompanying the movement with a diminuendo whistle, 'he fell like a stone. Or a bomb.'

Bealing laughed.

'It's not bloody funny,' said Crouch.

'What isn't?' asked Sobinski innocently.

'You know damn well. There's a way of doing things. I don't know what you're used to, but shooting parachutists is not on. Not in the Royal Air Force anyway.'

'But I didn't shoot him.'

'Yes, but you altered course to fly over his 'chute, which amounts to the same thing.'

Sobinski's bantering manner evaporated. 'Be careful.' he said.

Crouch's face reddened and his small blue eyes glinted with anger. 'I'll say what I like, thank you.'

For a moment it seemed possible that Crouch was about to hit Sobinski. Then Bealing broke in. 'Lay off it you two. You're supposed to be on the same side.'

'I would have thought that you might have backed me up. You know what Buxton said about fighting according to the rules,' said Crouch, switching his anger to Bealing.

Bealing sighed. 'Why don't you piss off and annoy someone else,' he said mildly. 'All we're doing is having a quiet drink.'

'I think I might do that.' Crouch moved off to another group which had formed by the window, attaching himself awkwardly to the edge of the circle which failed to open fully to admit him.

'He's a bit of an arse,' Bealing said. 'But he's all right really, if you can be bothered to make the effort to get to know him.'

From somewhere inside the house a dinner gong boomed. Adam glanced at his watch. It was already seven o'clock.

'Coming in?' Bealing asked.

'I don't know. I was going to a dance in Alberton. But it starts at eight.'

'Oh that,' said Bealing. 'Miff Smith. I used to go and see him in London. There's no point getting there before nine. Best to have a few sherbets beforehand. Let's grab a bite and head off.'

They ate dinner quickly. Like all the meals he had eaten since arriving at Kingsmere, it was good. They had fresh tomato soup, then grilled sole followed by roast chicken. There was even wine, first a German Gewürtztraminer, the subject of some ponderous jokes, then a claret. Bealing explained that the food and drink had probably been donated by grateful local farmers and shopkeepers.

'Nothing too good for the RAF,' Frizell said, rolling the wine around his glass before swallowing it noisily.

They slipped out before pudding arrived. Frizell and Sobinski came with them.

'How are we getting there?' Adam asked.

'Don't worry about that,' Bealing said. 'Pool transport's provided.'

A brand-new, racing green Riley drophead was parked in the stable block. Frizell climbed into the driver's seat, started up the engine and reversed out.

'Smart car,' Adam said.

'Nice, isn't it?' Bealing said. 'It's not Frizell's, though. It belongs to some bloke they sent us straight from training school. He drove down in it one morning about a month ago. Present from the proud parents. An hour later he was in the air. And fifteen minutes after that he was dead. We've got to use it while we can. His brother keeps threatening to come down and take it away.'

Frizell revved the engine, sending out clouds of blue exhaust smoke that drowned the sweet scents of the evening. Sobinski climbed over the door and dropped into the front seat. Adam and Bealing sat on the boot, holding on with their legs.

'Chocks away,' shouted Frizell, and shot off down the drive, almost jerking Adam and Bealing out of the car. It was getting dark and a big moon hung in the violet sky above the Downs. Adam felt recklessly happy. They pulled out into a lane and soon joined a main road empty of traffic. In less than ten minutes they were on the outskirts of Alberton. There was a pub at the corner of a crossroads.

'Beer stop!' shouted Bealing over the noise of the engine. Frizell swerved into the car park and pulled up sharply. They climbed out. Inside, the pub was almost empty. It had dirty white walls and a dark brown ceiling stained by years of tobacco smoke. The only decoration was a few posters on the wall advertising cigarettes, pale ale and stout. Two almost identical-looking middle-aged couples sat in lugubrious isolation at two small tables along the wall of the bar. The men wore dark suits and sat mechanically raising and lowering cigarettes and beer mugs. Their women sat silently opposite, hands folded in their laps, lips set in a firm, stoical line. Placed before them were glasses shaped like chalices. One of the women nudged her husband and twitched her head in the direction of the new arrivals.

'Bit of a dump,' Frizell murmured.

'A pub is a pub,' said Bealing. 'Four pints of bitter, please landlord.'

The old man behind the counter pulled on the truncheon-like lever that pumped the beer and lined up four glasses of brown, sudsy liquid on the bar. Bealing raised his in salute.

'Cheers, m'dears. All the breast.'

He put it to his lips and drained the pint in four or five gulps. Then he slapped some silver onto the wet counter and made for the door. 'Buck up,' he said. 'There's at least three more boozers between here and the Bristol.'

Five hundred yards later, Frizell stopped the car again outside a Tudor-style building set back from the road. There was a sign outside in the shape of a playing card and the words, 'Knave of Hearts'.

They pushed through two sets of double doors and into a long, low room bathed in dim red light. Around the edge of the room were booths, like railway compartments, where the shadow thickened. There was a piano in the corner at which a man in his forties wearing a plum-coloured jacket was playing a slow number dating from the preceding decade with bored proficiency. Bealing led the way to the bar and sat down on one of a row of circular stools covered in red plush.

'Four pints please, love,' he said to the lavishly lipsticked blonde woman behind the bar.

She shook her head as if he'd made some outlandish demand. 'Sorry, boys. We don't do beer. Just cocktails.'

She held out a drinks list, designed like a playing card, which Bealing studied, frowning.

'All right then. A Grand Slam,' he said after a pause.

'That will put hairs on your chest,' said the barmaid in a low, movie-star voice. 'What about you boys?'

They ordered the same. The drinks came in tall glasses and tasted of cough medicine. In a few minutes they were finished, so they ordered another round, which Sobinski paid for. As the barmaid handed him his change, he took the opportunity to squeeze her fingers. She squealed and pulled her hand away.

'You're a fresh one,' she breathed.

'Bit early for that,' said Bealing. 'So you can tell us now, Ted. Did you or did you not deliberately croak the Kraut parachutist today?'

Sobinski was swaying slightly by now. He gave a sly smile.

'It's a trick we learned in Poland. You fly over and something happens. I don't know why.' He repeated the mime of a plummeting parachute and gave the falling bomb whistle.

This time no one laughed. Sobinski looked belligerently around. 'What's the matter?'

'Nothing's the matter,' said Bealing.

'Yes there is. You think this is a game. Crouch and the rest of you think that you can fight this war according to some set of rules. There are no rules. You'll see that soon. Tell them Tomaszewski.'

Adam looked at Sobinski's red, sweaty face, at his unconvincing moustache and his double chin that made him look more like a waiter than an airman.

Yet he knew he was good, a real fighter. He was a good pilot and a good hater, the ideal combination. Sobinski was right. Hate had yet to harden in the souls of the British.

Bealing and Frizell were waiting. 'OK,' Adam said. 'In the first few days, when a German baled out we left him alone. The Germans, though, did things their way. They came back and finished you off if you jumped. We lost three of our squadron like that. So we started shooting them, too. Or just flying over the parachute, which is easier.'

'And you?' Bealing asked.

'I never got the chance.'

Bealing blew out a plume of smoke. 'Don't get me wrong, Ted. I'm not having a go. I don't see there's much difference in how you kill someone, whether it's roasting them alive in the plane or buggering up their parachute. Crouch, for some reason, thinks differently.'

'Crouch is a schoolboy,' Sobinski said thickly. 'Why should I have to explain myself to him?'

Bealing laughed his easy laugh. 'Gloomy bloody Poles.'

He looked around the gathering, at Frizell who was staring with a glazed expression at the barmaid, and Sobinski who had retreated into a defensive silence.

'The party seems to have gone a bit flat,' he said. 'Let's get to the Bedford before all the beer and crumpet disappear.'

5

It was dark outside. Frizell drove slowly but erratically, cursing the absence of street lights. They stopped at a sandbagged Air Raid Precautions post for directions and the warden leaned out and pointed them towards the hotel. The street in front of the Bristol was lined with a variety of military and civilian vehicles. Frizell parked the car with difficulty and they walked along a path at the side of the hotel towards the ballroom.

'Got to piss,' said Frizell, blundering into the shrubbery.

'See you inside,' Bealing called to him. They took their place in a small queue behind a group of other servicemen, some wearing the same floppy berets that Adam had noticed on the drivers loafing outside the hotel earlier in the day.

A middle-aged woman sat behind a table at the entrance. They paid their two shillings and walked in. The tide of noise, heat and smoke was overwhelming. It was a big ballroom, capable of holding five hundred people, and it was already very full. At one end stood a bar, besieged by a wall of men in brown and slate blue serge, who strained towards it, holding up beer mugs and glasses in supplication to the white-jacketed barmen.

Along the sides, at intervals of a few feet, were round tables, where small groups of men and women sat on flimsy gilt chairs, leaning over to shout at each other over the noise. The dance floor was packed with entwined couples, circling like cogs in an intricate piece of machinery, each individual revolution contributing to a much bigger rotation that swung like the sweep hand of a watch, slowly around the room. Above the dance floor a giant ball stuck with square shards of mirror scattered doubloons of light over the heads and shoulders of the dancers and lit up the rolling banks of smoke sent up from the glowing cigarettes that winked in the gloom below.

Rising over the roar of talk and the rumble of feet on the sprung floorboards, dominating the dancers and spinning them looping round the floor, was the sound of the band. They were grouped on a stage, four or five feet high, that jutted out into the crowd. Eight of the musicians were lined up in a row behind oblong wooden boards inscribed in copperplate script with the name of Miff Smith. On either side of them sat a drummer and a pianist.

In front and facing the band, imprisoned in a cone of limelight, crouched Miff Smith himself. He was small and delicate-looking with high cheekbones, a trim purse of a mouth and a folded quiff of chestnut hair. Unlike the band, who wore dinner jackets, he had on a dove-grey suit, a dark shirt and a pinkish tie. One hand was jammed into his trouser pocket, while the other, directing the tempo, bobbed up and down as if trying to suppress an invisible spring.

He moved to the end of the number, a fast-ish foxtrot, then brought it to a close in a surging roll of drum and cymbal with a downward swipe of his arm. There was a cheer from the dancers and the musicians stepped back and pulled cigarette packets from their jackets, evidently taking a break. In the sudden silence Adam felt the blood singing in his ears.

'Time for a drink,' Bealing announced. 'Ted, why don't you fight your way through that scrum? Adam will go next. We'll take it in turns.' Sobinski seemed to welcome the opportunity to demonstrate his membership of the company and set off, his broad shoulders working like a spade, digging his way through the crowd.

'In the meantime . . .' Bealing produced a hip flask, unscrewed the top and handed it to Adam who tilted it back, tasting whisky.

'Fat chance of picking up anything tonight,' Bealing continued. 'There must be three blokes for every girl. Nothing for it but to get properly pissed.'

Adam had been examining the crowd, randomly at first, then systematically. The women stood out from the drab groups of men like flowers in a cornfield. He worked from table to table and through the couples clotted around the edge of the dance floor waiting for the band to start up again. Then he saw her, the girl from the hotel. She was sitting next to a dark-haired woman at a table close to the bar on the far side of the room, together with four or five uniformed men. As his eyes fixed on her, she seemed to feel it, for she looked up and glanced around.

Adam thrust up his arm and waved vigorously, willing her to look at him.

'Who are you waving at?' Bealing asked. Adam ignored him and raised both his arms in an urgent semaphore, but she stopped looking about her and turned her attention back to the table.

'Who is it?' Bealing demanded. 'Don't tell me you know one of the popsies. Why didn't you say so before?'

'I don't know her,' said Adam defensively. 'I just met her for a second this afternoon.'

'Well, what are we waiting for?'

Bealing set off across the dance floor, which was beginning to fill up as the musicians finished their break and picked up their instruments ready for the next number.

Adam followed, just as the band struck up again. The tune was clearly a favourite. The opening chords were recognised immediately by the crowd, who clapped and whistled. At every table, men reached forward to grab a partner. Adam pressed ahead but couples were pouring onto the floor, begining their slow, spinning circle. Through the press of people he could see the girl from the hotel nodding to someone, pushing back her chair and getting to her feet, holding out her arm to be taken, being led into the crowd by a smiling man in army uniform who steered her into the thick of the dancing, his hand resting on the small of her back. Another man was speaking to the dark-haired woman. She too got to her feet, more reluctantly it seemed, and was escorted into the swirling crowd.

Adam was alone among the couples. He pushed towards the wall where Bealing was standing sipping from his hip flask. He winked at Adam and held out the flask, but he shook his head, leaned back against the cool wall and looked back towards the stage.

Miff Smith was facing the crowd, his head cocked before a ridged microphone that looked like a hand grenade. Behind him the tune unwound, sweet and sentimental, the drummer's brushes pushing the beat along like the slow padding of a big cat on the jungle floor.

'Seems like you know this one already,' the singer murmured and the crowd clapped again. The music paused for a second; then he set off in a soft, unctuous tenor:

> 'By an old, old cottage
> Down a shady lane
> There's an old, old wishing well
> Where we'll meet again
> Autumn days are coming
> Spring seems far away
> And the drums of war are beating
> When they'll stop none of us can say
> But I can still hear the splash of the penny
> That I tossed in that quaint old well
> And I knew at the moment so long ago
> That we'd love again some day'

The crowd picked up the song gently on the second verse, crooning the words to themselves as they leaned into their partners' shoulders. Adam felt a pricking behind his eyelids. He glanced at Bealing who was staring at the singing mannikin on the stage, all his gruff casualness gone, replaced by an almost reverential solemnity. As the song moved into the last chorus, Miff Smith stood back and let the crowd take over the singing. The noise swelled up as heartfelt as a hymn. The couples clung together but individual intimacy had gone. In its place was a feeling of universal complicity that linked everyone equally – the musicians and the singers, the dancers with their shuffling manoeuvres and the pensive drinkers – in a conspiracy of shared sentiment. Adam felt it with the rest of them, an overwhelming, tender melancholy.

Then the music was over. The last notes took a time to die. The dance floor emptied in a slow, eddying whorl. Adam felt alone. Bealing had turned away from him and was tilting once again at the hip flask. He looked for Sobinski but he was hidden in the throng at the bar.

'Hallo there.'

Adam turned around. It was the girl from the hotel, smiling and flushed from the dancing and the heat, one coppery strand of hair sticking to her forehead.

'Hallo.'

She took him by the arm. 'I've been looking all over for you. Come and join us.'

'What about me?' Bealing asked, feigning dismay.

'You too. Everyone's welcome.'

The table was full up when they reached it. At their approach the men stood up, scraping back chairs, elaborately making a place for the lady.

'Come and sit over here, Pam, next to me.' The girl's dancing partner was pointing to the chair next to him. She moved obediently across, and he pulled out the chair with a flourish, like a waiter seating a favourite customer.

He wasn't tall or short, about the same height as Adam, with glossy, dark hair swept back from a high, square forehead, a long straight nose and flat cheek-bones. He was carefully dressed in a well-fitting tunic with captain's pips on the shoulders and a polished Sam Browne belt. The effect was old-fashioned, as if he did not belong to that decade – or even that century. He glanced towards Adam as if he was just noticing his presence.

'You're out of luck, brother,' he said. 'We seem to have run out of chairs. Why don't you shove along and find somewhere else to sit?'

The woman sighed. 'Don't be a pain, Gerry. These boys are friends of mine. Now why don't you introduce yourselves and I'll go and find some more chairs if no one else will.'

Two of the other men at the table stood up hurriedly and, apologising, gave up their seats to Adam and Bealing before going off in search of replacements. Adam took his chair and drew it up to the table.

'All right then,' the soldier said, 'who are you?'

Adam and Bealing introduced themselves.

His manner thawed, and the casual hostility was replaced with an equally easy warmth. 'Well, I'm Gerald Cunningham, London Irish Rifles, and these are . . .' He went round the table, listing the other men in a brisk way that suggested that they could not possibly be interested in remembering any of them.

Adam turned to the copper-haired girl. 'And you're Pam? I forgot to ask you at the hotel.'

'That's me. Pamela Sutton. And, as beastly Gerry isn't going to do it, can I introduce Moira Fleming?'

This was the first chance Adam had got to look at the other woman close up. She had dark brown hair, very thick, chopped square at the back so the nape of her neck was left naked and vulnerable. She looked at him, cool and direct. Adam never noticed people's eyes. Hers were the colour of granite, a bluish grey. There was a slight sharpness to her features: vixenish, thought Adam. She smiled, no more than politeness. Adam smiled back and glanced away, knowing that he would want to look at her again very soon.

'Right, what are we all having? 'Gerry looked round genially and slid his wallet from inside his tunic. 'Roger, go and get the drinks will you?' He patted Moira's arm. 'She'll have an Americano.'

A young man with a thin moustache stood up and went around the table taking the orders.

'We've got some coming, thanks,' Bealing said. 'On the other hand, there's no sign of Ted. I'll have a pint of bitter.' Adam ordered the same.

Gerry turned his full attention on them like a lighthouse beam flicking out of the darkness.

'You must be over at Kingsmere,' he said. 'It's taken a hell of a bashing lately. You boys are doing a fantastic job. You won't mind me saying that it's a great improvement on your performance at Dunkirk. We kept hearing how you were knocking lumps out of the Luftwaffe. There were very few actual sightings, though. From where I was standing, anyway.'

The other soldiers laughed.

'I was in that show,' said Bealing casually. 'We were there all right, whether you saw us or not. If you don't believe me, perhaps you should talk to the families of some of the pilots. The ones who didn't come back, I mean.'

'Christ, I didn't mean it like that,' said Gerry. 'I was just pulling your leg. Let's change the subject. Have a fag.' He held out a silver case which sprang open like a conjuror's prop revealing two rows of fat cigarettes.

'What about the ladies?' Bealing asked solicitously.

'I'm all right, thank you,' said Moira. 'But thanks for asking.'

Bealing and Adam took a cigarette from the case and lit up. The officer with the moustache returned with a tray of drinks. The music had started up again, but softly, and there were fewer dancers on the floor. They settled down around the table.

'We're based over near Chichester,' Gerry said. 'We've been there since June after getting out of France. We're getting a bit fed up, to tell you the truth. You're fighting the war on your own at the moment. For us it's just training and more training with no sign of another show in sight. Most of it is a bloody waste of time.'

'Tell them about the unarmed combat, Gerry,' said the officer with the moustache eagerly. Gerry laughed. 'All right then. The girls have heard this one so I'll keep it short. The other day they'd run out of things to make us do, so someone came up with the idea of an unarmed combat course, throttling the Hun with your bare hands and that sort of thing. Me and my platoon were first on. The guy running the thing was one of those sadistic PT types who look as if they were born wearing a vest and rugger shorts. Anyway, he pointed to one of my boys and ordered him to come at him and try and hit him. Well, he did as he was told and, surprise, surprise, two seconds later he was on the deck with blood pouring out of his nose.'

Gerry's army companions murmured disapprovingly.

'Then the thug ordered someone else to have a go and repeated the performance. So it went on. Eventually my turn came. I tried to warn him that I knew something about the noble art, having boxed a bit at school, but he just ignored me, prancing about like one of those prints of bare-knuckle prizefighters. Anyway, I'd twigged that he always threw the same punch, a sort of right cross. So I just ducked under it and hit him with a right uppercut. He went down like an ox in an abattoir.' Gerry took a long drink as the table laughed. Adam laughed too. There was something attractive about Gerry's show-off bumptiousness. It had a juvenile freshness, almost a sort of innocence, that rendered it tolerable. Bealing was laughing too.

Adam became aware of a slight commotion behind him. 'Hey ho,' said Gerry, 'who's this?' Adam turned around. Frizell was standing leaning with one hand against the wall, red faced, breathing hard.

'Dearie me,' Bealing said, 'I wondered where you'd got to. And where the hell is Ted? I think I'd better get you home.' Adam got up to help but Bealing motioned him to sit down. 'No point in everyone's evening being ruined,' he said, rolling his eyes meaningfully in the direction of Pam. 'You stay put.'

Adam felt a flicker of guilt but suppressed it easily. He was enjoying himself. The air was charged with possibilities, and the banal smell of smoke and beer and scent made the hall as strange and exotic and dangerous as an opium den. Gerry's spirit was infectious. For the first time since the war began, Adam felt as young as his years.

Bealing put his shoulder under Frizell's arm. For a moment it looked like an idealised scene of comradeship on the battlefield.

'Try and enjoy yourselves as best you can without me,' he said as he led Frizell away.

'Time for another dance,' Gerry announced. 'May I, Pam?' Pam looked across at Adam and then at Moira as if seeking their approval. 'I take it that's a yes?' Gerry said. 'Adam, perhaps you . . . and Moira?'

'Of course. That is, if she wants to dance.'

'Why not?'

She ground out her cigarette, stood up and walked onto the dance floor. She was taller than he expected and came up to his forehead. He took her right hand in his left hand, and placed the other cautiously around her, resting it on the middle of her back. He felt bare flesh, warm and slightly damp, and the bony ridge of her spine. He pulled his hand away quickly and let it settle again at the top of her bottom, which he was thankful to feel was covered by her dress. She chuckled; a dark, chocolatey sound.

They set off, taking up their place in the great revolving wheel of dancers. She moved fluently. He could hear her humming along with the tune, and every now and then a stirring of the air would bring her perfume into his nostrils. Somehow he imagined it was her own smell, her essence, something that came from inside her. The dance came to an end.

'Would you like another?'

She shook her head.

'No. Let's go and sit down.'

There was no one at the table now. She took a cigarette from a box in her purse and put it to her lips, making no move to light it. Adam struck a match and she ducked her head to put the cigarette to the flame. As she inhaled she looked up at him, and he saw something kindle in her eyes. She blew out a plume of smoke and smiled.

'You don't say much,' she said.

'Neither do you.'

'If we're going to be friends, we'll have to make a bit more of an effort.'

'Are we going to be friends?'

'Oh yes.' She said it without guile, a simple assertion.

'You go first.'

'No, you. I'm no good at talking about myself and I'm sure your story is much more interesting than mine.'

'All right then.'

Over the past year Adam had recited his history many times; to hostile and incredulous officials at borders and checkpoints, to French and British recruiting officers, to the functionaries of the nation-in-exile to which he belonged. He had pared down the story to a bare catalogue of facts. Mechanically he began to list them, but she soon interrupted him.

'I'm not interested in that. Tell me about where you grew up and what your parents are like, and whether you've got a girl.'

'This could take a long time.'

'We'll have time. If not now, then later.'

So Adam began talking. The hall was starting to empty now and the band was playing soft and low so there was no need to shout. He described the house among the trees in Nowo Pole. He told her of his mother with her sallow face and thick bun of hair and her melancholy moods and his father with his riding boots and horses and vodka and the little sister he adored and the farm that never made any money and the priests at the local school and the day that he decided to become a pilot.

'I want to hear all about that,' she said.

'I was eleven, almost twelve. It was autumn, in the late afternoon. I was playing on my own in a field behind the house when I heard a droning noise in the sky. I knew what aeroplanes looked like, of course, from pictures in the newspapers, but I had never actually seen one. And suddenly there one was, an old-fashioned biplane, coming towards me over the trees, silhouetted against the sunset. He had engine trouble and was looking for somewhere to land and he put down in our field. I remember the plane coming towards me, bumping over the rough ground and stopping a few yards away from where I was standing. It was as if it had been looking for me. The plane had an open cockpit. The pilot got out. He was wearing a helmet and goggles and a long leather coat that reminded me of the pictures of medieval knights in my school history book.

'He was an air-force pilot from the airfield at Toruń, which was the nearest big town. I took him to my father who gave him a drink and insisted that he stay with us that night. My father seemed very proud that he had landed in our field and treated him with a respect I had never seen him show anyone before. I decided then that this was what I had to be.'

She seemed delighted with the story.

'It was fate!' she said. Again, it sounded categorical, certain, an exclamation. 'You believe in fate, don't you?'

Before he could answer there was a burst of laughter. Gerry and Pam were back at the table. They seemed bright with excitement. 'Whose turn is it to get the drinks?' Gerry asked cheerfully, but in a way that implied that the duty lay with Adam.

'I think it must be your turn by now,' Moira said firmly.

'Aye, aye, skipper.' Gerry saluted facetiously. 'Coming right up.' He bounded off towards the bar.

'You seemed to be enjoying yourself out there,' Moira said to Pam.

'Gerry's such a good dancer.'

'Gerry's good at everything he does. It gets quite boring sometimes.'

Adam heard the sharpness in her voice. 'I'll go and give him a hand with the drinks,' he said. They both protested, each pressing him to stay put, as if wishing to enlist him as an ally.

'I'll be back in two minutes,' he said, and walked over to the bar. The crush around it had thinned out. Gerry was just paying. Adam stood at his shoulder.

'Thought I'd give you a hand,' he said.

'That's nice of you. Though I don't know that it's a good idea to leave the girls on their own in present circs.' He smiled conspiratorially. 'I got you another pint.'

They walked back. The women were sitting silently.

'Looks like the party's over,' Gerry said. 'Let's knock these back and get on our way. I've borrowed a motor. I can drop you off if you like.'

The car was an old five-seater Ford with a tattered canvas top. Gerry sat in the front with Moira and Adam got in the back with Pam.

'Don't you stay at the hotel?' he asked her.

'No, I've got a little cottage just outside Chichester. It's blissful right now but I don't know what it will be like in the winter.'

'Does it have a wishing well?'

They all laughed. Gerry began singing Miff Smith's hit in a loud voice, slurring and bending the words in a parody of the crooner's cockney intonations and inserting obscene additions.

He kept it up all the way to Updyke. They pulled up by the gates. Gerry reached back and levered open the back door. 'Here we are. So long, brother.'

The women said perfunctory farewells. Adam stood watching in the darkness as the car pulled away. He could not see whether Moira had waved to him or not.

6

When Adam woke up his mouth was dry and he could taste the beer from the night before. The curtains were open and outside the sun was rising hot and bright over the fields. Going downstairs he heard the clatter of plates and cutlery and the laughter of the orderlies laying the breakfast places.

He took a place at one of the long refectory tables. A boy servant returned with a jug of coffee and some rolls, butter and marmalade. He chewed the soft, doughy bread, enjoying the saltiness of the butter and the bitterness of the oranges, sipped the coffee and thought about the previous night. Something had happened to him. He had spent the last year almost entirely in the company of men. He had met a few women, had a few stories, as they called them in France, but these encounters had left no mark. There had been a woman he'd met on a train between Cluj and Bucharest, a small, mute blonde who had taken him back to her flat in the Calle Victorea. There was a picture by the side of the bed of a man in uniform: her brother, she said, but he knew it was her husband. He left the following day before she woke up. In Lyons there had been a prostitute who slept with him for nothing, and on leave in Paris a woman he had met behind the counter of a Polish welfare association who had put him up for a week in her tiny flat at the top of six flights of stairs. She was Jewish, of Polish parents, not pretty but kind. After a few days it had felt stifling and illicit, as if he was making love to his mother, bringing certain bad luck. Yet she had probably been no more than five years older than he was. Again, he had slipped away without a farewell. Whatever guilt he felt evaporated as soon as he saw his leave companions at the bar where they held their daily rendezvous.

He knew men, particularly the men he had fought alongside, and got drunk with. They had a familiar weight and value. The women of the previous evening had been unlike any he had encountered before; the first he had felt he wanted to do more than merely show off to, or to fuck. They had been confident and strong, handling their sex with a sureness that he could only think of as masculine. Perhaps that was it. Perhaps he was attracted to them because they were like men.

One by one the other pilots were arriving in the dining room. He saw Sobinski and called him over. 'What happened to you?'

'I couldn't find you after I got the drinks so I drank them myself. Then I met up with someone I knew at Northolt. After that I don't remember.'

Bealing appeared and sat down opposite. 'Any luck?' he asked, grinning.

'None at all.'

'Captain Gerry seemed to have his hands full. It's not right, a bloke hogging two birds in a time of national crisis. Doesn't he know there's a war on?' He poured himself some coffee.

'Which one did you fancy?'

Bealing's cheery vulgarity annoyed him, yet it was this question that had kept him awake for a time after he went to bed. He felt he knew the women from somewhere and now he remembered where. They belonged to the dream world of his adolescence. These were the sort of women that came into his head as he lay in his bed at the house in Nowo Pole or on his bunk at Deblin, soft and warm and graceful, who would make love with a quiet fervour and lie damply alongside you in the aftermath, sharing with you the singing silence and tasting the sadness. Women to fall in love with.

'There's a lot to be said for both of them,' Adam said matter-of-factly. 'Can you pass the bacon, please?' Bealing shut up.

While they were eating, Buxton appeared, urging them to hurry up.

For a few hours Adam had forgotten about the war, but now it crashed back into his consciousness, obliterating thoughts of Pam and Moira. They hurried outside to where the lorries were waiting on the gravel to take them to the base. It was going to be a very hot day. The haze was already building up over the cornfields, which were dotted with haycarts, with big, blinkered horses between the shafts, flicking their tails at the flies.

At Kingsmere, gangs of labourers were at work on the runway, emptying wheelbarrows of rubble into the bomb craters. The pilots gathered in the briefing room. Buxton seemed in a bad mood. The good weather meant the Germans were bound to come in force, he said. Heavy raids were expected all along the coast, starting at any minute. They were to move out to the dispersal areas at once.

He climbed into a van with Whitbread, Westerham and Miller-Morton; they were driven to the edge of the aerodrome, where the Hurricanes had already been pushed out of the blast pens. Aircraftmen in boiler suits fussed around the aircraft, making last adjustments.

Whitbread walked over, pigeon-toed and stooped, and offered his pack of cigarettes to the aircraftmen. The others fetched deckchairs from the hut and settled down to nap. Whitbread stretched out alongside Adam.

'How was your big night out?' Adam asked.

Whitbread smiled and glanced over at the other two who seemed to have already dozed off.

'Pretty good all in all. But I'm knocked to the wide this morning.'

He closed his eyes and settled back. Then he sniggered.

'What is it?'

'I'll tell you about it later.'

'I want to hear now.'

'All right then.' Whitbread lit a cigarette and exhaled extravagantly.

'Miles is going to be a film star.'

'What?'

'It's true. Listen. The evening started off as a pretty standard piss-up, doing the rounds of the West End. We booked into the Strand Palace, had a few drinks, went to a show at the Windmill, had a few drinks, had a bite to eat, had a few drinks. It was all a bit tame really and we wondered why we had to come all the way up to town just to—'

'Have a few drinks.'

'Precisely. Then someone, I think it was Tony, suggested we go on to the Café Royal. There was someone that he liked playing there, or supposed to be. When we got there, there was no sign of them, but we decided to hit the bar nonetheless. I don't know if you know the place. It's all red plush and turn of the century, very much home to the brown hat brigade.'

He drew on his cigarette.'Anyway, there we were sitting at the bar, a bit glum, when I noticed a type sitting in one of the booths looking over at us, or more accurately at dear old Miles. A few minutes later the barman informs us that the next round is free, courtesy of the mystery benefactor in the corner. We raise our glasses in gratitude and next thing he's slid over and is sitting on the bar stool next to us, or rather to Miles.

'He looked familiar, but I couldn't place him. Miles, though, got him at once. "Aren't you Ivor Savage?" he said, and the guy admitted he was.'

'Who is Ivor Savage?' Adam asked.

'Ivor Savage is a theatrical bod. Plays, musicals and that sort of thing. Anyway he apologised for staring at us but said that his interest was purely professional. He'd just been asked by the Air Ministry to produce a propaganda movie and he was looking for some genuine flying types to put in it.

'Miles was in seventh heaven. It turned out that he knew all Savage's stuff and had bunked off school to come up to town to see them. He'd even acted in *Tender Triangle* in some amateur production. Played the part of the doomed youth who falls in love with the housemaster's wife.

'Well, after that we might as well not have been there. Savage spent the rest of the evening regaling Miles with tales of life behind the footlights. He finished up by saying that he was going to approach the Ministry on Monday to request permission to put Miles in his film.'

'And will they give it?'

'Who knows? But you have to admit he's perfect for the glamour-boy role.'

They looked over to where Miller-Morton half lay in his deckchair, legs stretched before him, ankles crossed, his mouth half open, a trace of saliva glistening at the corner of his mouth.

For a while they sat, smoking and reading newspapers. Westerham woke up and suggested that they kick a football around but it was too hot. An orderly came over the grass with a tea tray. Despite Buxton's forecast, the base seemed unusually quiet.

The telephone bell rang in the hut. Adam tensed, waiting for the order to scramble, but instead the clerk leaned round the door and called Whitbread over. After a few minutes he walked back, shaking Miller-Morton out of his sleep.

'Looks like there's nothing much doing after all that. Sector wants us to fly patrol for a bit.'

'What does that mean?' Adam asked.

'Just stooging about over the Channel shipping, keeping an eye out for Jerries,' Whitbread said. 'Let's get going.'

They took off and climbed to 15,000 feet, lining up abreast in a loose formation fifty or so yards apart, with Whitbread, the flight leader, just ahead. The tightness of the cockpit was comforting. The static of the radio telephone hissed soothingly in his ears, overlaying the noise from the engine. Below the sea was flat, a dark, slaty blue, shading into brown as it reached the shore. The Channel was busy. Merchantmen and their Royal Navy escorts were scattered over the water, the white chevrons of their wakes the only sign that they were making progress.

They flew for fifteen minutes northwards up the coast, then swung back and down. The scene seemed imperturbable, the white smoke rising from the funnels of the ships in the Channel, the creamy cliffs rising on either side of the narrow sleeve of water, glowing in the sunshine, the insect progress of cars and lorries crawling along a road. Adam found his attention wandering and brought it back sharply into check, shifting his gaze systematically around the sky, left and right, down and up, checking the rear-view mirror. Survival meant vigilance; endless, reflex checking of the instruments, the weather, your position in the sky and its relation to other aircraft, and constant judgements about speed and height. In peace, unrelenting concentration was enough. In war you needed a higher alertness, an animal wariness that sounded the alarm when your senses told you there was nothing to fear. Without the instinct you did not live long. But the only way to acquire it was to survive.

Adam thought back to the dead pilot whose car they had borrowed the previous night. Bealing could not even remember his name.

Since they had taken off, Whitbread had said nothing except to reverse their course to fly back down the Channel. Now his voice filled Adam's earphones.

'I can see something. Nine o'clock low.'

Adam looked down and to his left. Far off, a shape was just visible against the blurred conjunction of sea and sky, approaching from the coast of France. It looked like a single aircraft but not of a type he could recognise.

'Watch my arse,' Whitbread said. 'I'm going down to take a look.'

He banked and turned, getting the sun behind him, and set off in a shallow descent towards the aircraft which was now on a course towards a convoy of half-a-dozen freighters being shepherded up-Channel by a small warship. They kept their formation, Whitbread at the front, Miller-Morton, then Westerham to his right, and Adam on his left. In the messes and the bars, much time was spent trying to decide which formation would allow the best chance of killing and the best hope of being killed. The tactics taught before the war prescribed a 'vic' configuration, an arrowhead of three aircraft, which theoretically enabled each aircraft to cover the other. In practice it provided a degree of security only for the leader, leaving the back two vulnerable to the 'bounce', the sudden descent of an enemy out of the great blind spaces above. Everybody knew the vic was a bad formation but no one could think of a better one.

As it got closer, the enemy aircraft was taking on a shape. It had a long, glassed-in nose and two engines, probably a Heinkel bomber. But where were its fighter escorts? Adam squinted into the sky above but there was nothing there. He felt a flutter of fear. Perhaps they were already behind him and even now he was framed in the sights of an unseen Messerschmitt.

He spoke to Whitbread, trying to suppress the nervousness in his voice. 'Peter from Adam. I can see the Heinkel but where are the rest of them?'

There was a pause, then Whitbread's voice came back. 'I don't know. We can't just leave him there though. I'm going in. Hold back and for Christ's sake watch me.'

The Heinkel seemed to be interested in the convoy, swinging round astern of it as if preparing for a bombing run. As it lined up, Whitbread lowered his Hurricane into a comfortable trajectory above and behind. Light twinkled from the gun ports of his wings and tracer began to curl around the bomber, occasionally sparking on the fuselage.

It looked like a straightforward kill. But now fire was coming from another direction. Feathery puffs of brown smoke were blossoming around the Heinkel, rocking it off course. Adam looked down towards the small Navy escort. On the front deck he could see the barrels of an anti-aircraft gun pistoning, pumping flak into the path of the Heinkel and the Hurricanes pursuing it.

'Shit.'

Whitbread's voice broke over the R/T. Adam could see him slewing across the sky to his right, away from the bursting flak but away too from the Heinkel, which was climbing and turning back towards the French coast. Now the bursting Bofors rounds were clustering in the air in front of him. He pulled back sharply on the control column and felt the Hurricane flatten, then the nose came up and the grey shape of the escort skidded underneath him. He climbed and turned, searching the sky for Whitbread and the others, but there was no one there. In the space of a few seconds, calm had returned to the scene. He felt the tension of his body as it began to relax from the involuntary bunching and stiffening that always came with moments of fear, as if this could ward off bullets or hold the aircraft in the air. Low and on the right, something was moving. It was the Heinkel, almost over the coast now. It was not alone. A Hurricane was on its tail and firing, but too far back to have any effect. The guns were aligned to converge into a funnel of fire at 400 yards. The Heinkel was at least half a mile ahead, untroubled by the tracer dying harmlessly in its wake.

Adam decided to head for home. He tried to put the aircraft into a tight turn but the Hurricane was slow in responding. He looked out at the port wing. Part of the aileron had been shot away, presumably by flak from the Navy ship. It was a nuisance, slowing him down and reducing his manoeuvrability, but not a disaster; not unless he was bounced on the way back to base. He tried to raise Whitbread on the R/T, but there was no response. That could mean several things. Whitbread could have gone down, or his radio was out of action, or Adam's radio was broken. He called up Miller-Morton but got only silence. That meant it was his radio. He ran his eye over the instruments. Everything looked normal. There was enough fuel to reach home comfortably. He set a course for Kingsmere, pointing the nose of his Hurricane at a stretch of the coastline where the green was smudged with brown and grey, the bricks and mortar of Alberton. It was eleven o'clock. Pam would be at work in the Bristol, fresh and welcoming behind the reception desk, setting the thoughts racing of the men in uniform who would be crossing the threshold wanting a pot of tea or a glass of beer. For a moment he considered flying low over the hotel and showing off, waggling his wings, but he dismissed the thought. It was the sort of thing Miller-Morton would do.

The pier was ahead, its scrolled iron rusty and festooned with barbed wire, its planks warping after a year of war and neglect. The hotel passed under his starboard wing, then the roofs and gardens of the little villas and bungalows, then corn stubble. He pulled the lever that depressed the flaps and felt the air dragging the Hurricane down. He lowered the wheels and heard the bang as they locked into place. Beneath him the earth speeded up. He passed over a road, then a row of elm trees that stood at the edge of Kingsmere's main runway. He pulled back on the throttle, and for a moment the Hurricane hung there, as if reluctant to leave its element, then its three wheels touched lightly on the tarmac, lifted, then settled again, this time for good.

Adam braked and pressed left on the rudder bar to bring the aircraft over to the perimeter and the flight's dispersal area. The ground crew was waiting for him. He cut the engine, slid back the Perspex hood of the cockpit and levered himself out. There was no sign of Whitbread or Miller-Morton. One of the ground staff started poking with a screwdriver at the damage to the port wing.

'How did you get this?' It was Hennessy. He spoke confidently, with no trace of the deference that Adam had noticed among some of the other ground crew.

'I'm not sure. I think it was flak from a Navy boat that was firing up at the plane we were chasing. What do you think?'

Hennessy pulled away some shards of blackened aluminium exposing some tattered wiring. 'It's hard to say,' he said. 'But the aileron is going to take some work – two hours I should say. That's if we've got the part.'

'I'm going to need a replacement radio as well.'

They ducked under the nose of the plane. Hennessy poked two fingers into a hole that had punched through the skin, exiting out of the top of the plane in front of the cockpit.

'Looks like you were very lucky there. Six inches further back and you'd,' his voice rose an octave, 'be talking like this.' The other aircrewmen laughed. 'Anyway, come back at three and we'll see what we can do.' He walked away. Adam felt as if he was being dismissed.

Judging from the number of aircraft parked around the perimeter, nothing much was going on and the onslaught predicted by Intelligence had yet to fall on them. He picked up a bicycle lying on the grass and pedalled over to the base offices to report to Buxton. He found him in his office reading a newspaper, which he put down hurriedly at the sound of Adam's knock, as if he was ashamed to be caught engaged in such an unmartial activity.

'How'd it go?' he asked.

'We went after a Heinkel but then we got caught in a lot of flak put up by a Navy escort. I lost touch with Whitbread and Miller-Morton.'

'Well, we've heard nothing.'

Buxton picked up a telephone and spoke to someone, requesting news. In the silence that followed, he sucked on his unlit pipe and gazed rigidly through the window. Adam heard a snuffling noise. He had not noticed the black labrador that was lying dozing behind Buxton's desk.

A tinny voice sounded from the earpiece and Buxton began nodding, a motion that sent the pipe jerking up and down. He replaced the receiver.

'They're both OK, it seems. Whitbread received some damage and put in at Hawkinge, up the coast. Miller-Morton ran out of fuel and crash-landed in a field.' He frowned and gripped the bowl of his pipe. 'What about the Heinkel?'

'I can't be sure, sir, but it looked OK to me.'

Buxton made a grunting noise conveying disappointment. There was a long silence.

Somebody had to say something. 'My machine was a bit damaged too, sir.'

'What?'

'I got a bit of flak in the port wing and the radio is U/S. It will only take a couple of hours to put right.'

Buxton nodded then, and as if with a great effort looked at Adam. 'What about you then? You all right?'

'Fine, sir.'

'Good show.' Buxton smiled and nodded again. 'Good show.'

There was a long pause. 'I'll be going then, sir.' Adam saluted.

'Thank you Tomaszewski. Leave the door open.'

Adam was struck by a thought.

'Could you spare me for a little while, sir? While my machine's being repaired? I really do need to try and replace some lost kit.'

Buxton did not look up. 'OK, if you must,' he said. 'Off you go.'

The few hours of freedom sat like gold coins in his pocket waiting to be spent. His first thought was to find Pam. It was not yet one o'clock. He would take the bike and cycle over to Alberton and surprise her at the hotel.

He retrieved the bicycle, which he had left propped up against a wall outside Buxton's office, and set off. He rode for twenty minutes through the heavy midday heat along roads that were almost empty, until he reached the Bristol. He climbed the steps and walked into the cool of the lobby. It was dark after the bright sunshine and he paused to look around. A shadowy figure was moving behind the desk. He smiled in anticipation.

'Pam?' he said.

The figure turned and he caught an impression of spectacles and hair scraped severely back.

'Excuse me. May I help you?'

A middle-aged woman, perhaps the same one who was taking the money at the ballroom door the previous night, was smiling helpfully at him.

'I'm sorry.' The English habit of relentless apology was catching. 'I was looking for . . . Pam.'

'I'm afraid you've just missed her,' the woman said. 'Miss Sutton has just stepped out for lunch.'

'Do you know where she went?'

'She didn't say. But you're very welcome to wait if you wish. She'll be back within the hour.'

He went outside and sat at a table on the verandah. A maid brought him tea. He sat smoking cigarettes, feeling the heat of the sun, listening to the humming of the bees in the garden and smelling the heavy scent of roses. He closed his eyes.

He heard footsteps coming up the path and sat up. She was wearing a pale green cotton dress and a yellow straw hat and carrying a shopping bag. She saw him straight away and waved with her free hand.

'You,' she said, climbing the steps and sitting beside him. She took off her hat and wiped a hand across her forehead.

'Shouldn't you be up there?' She pointed skywards.

He felt himself grinning. 'They kindly gave me a few hours off.'

She was pink from the heat and he could see tiny drops of moisture at the roots of her coppery hair. She poured some tea into his cup and took a sip.

'Have you recovered from last night?' she asked.

'Was I that bad?'

'Just kidding. Your poor friend must have felt dreadful this morning, though.'

'Frizell?' He had forgotten about him.

'Anyway,' she said heartily, plonking down the cup. 'I had a whale of a time. We should all get together again soon.' She stood up.

'Are you going?' he asked, trying not to sound disappointed.

'I'm afraid so. We've got a job to do as well, you know.'

He stood up, formally, as if a senior officer was leaving the company.

'Will you give me your telephone number?' he asked.

'Ring me here,' she said. 'Alberton 321. It's easy.' She picked up her hat and shopping bag and waved, curling her fingers in a vaguely flirtatious farewell, and stepped into the hotel.

The verandah suddenly seemed very empty. He looked at his watch. There was at least another hour before he had to be back at the base. He collected the bike and wheeled it down the path and along the front. He caught a glimpse of himself in a shop window that was crisscrossed with sticky tape against the bombs: a shabby Pole, pushing a bicycle. She had been friendly enough. But that was, of course, how she saw him. He glanced down at his creased and baggy uniform. He had to do something about his clothes. There would be shops in Chichester. He had money. A month's wages were sitting virtually untouched in the breast pocket of his tunic. He would try there.

He cycled down a suburban street then out into the fields. Now and then he passed a cottage and wondered whether it was the one that Pam lived in. In Chichester he dismounted and wheeled the bike along narrow pavements. The pubs had their doors open to relieve the heat, and the scent of hops spilled out into the streets. He went past a butcher's shop and smelled the sawdust and heard the thud of a cleaver. Then he saw a window filled with hats and socks and a headless dummy wearing a tweed jacket. He went in. The shop was fitted out with dark wood shelves and drawers and a middle-aged man was standing behind the counter. He would have to wait for the quartermaster to provide him with a new uniform. In the meantime he could try and relieve his threadbare appearance with a touch of luxury. He asked to see some scarves and the man pulled out a mahogany drawer. He liked the first one he saw – heavy silk, dark blue with small white diamonds stitched into the weave, just like everyone else had. He knotted it loosely round his neck, enjoying the cool touch of the silk, and looked in the mirror. It suited his dark-blond hair. He smiled at his reflection. He chose some handkerchiefs in silk and cotton, some socks and underwear. Then, as an afterthought, a pair of yellow wash leather gloves. The man wrapped up the goods. Adam handed him two five-pound notes, took a few coppers in change and went out. Further down the road he found a shoe shop where he bought two pairs of brogues, one in brown suede, the other in black leather. He put the bags in the pannier on the front of the bike and pedalled back through the town, his time and money spent.

The base was still quiet when he got back. He cycled round the perimeter to the blast pen where his Hurricane was parked. Two mechanics were standing with spanners and screwdrivers at the trailing edge of the port wing, attending to the ailerons, which were waggling up and down. He saw Hennessy's curly head poking above the lip of the cockpit.

'What's going on?' he asked of no one in particular.

'Hallo there,' Hennessy said. 'I think we're almost done. I'm just testing the controls to see nothing's sticking.'

'What about the radio?'

'Had a bit of luck. A couple of spares just came in this morning. It's been fitted.'

'Very impressive.'

'All part of the service.'

Hennessy levered himself out of the cockpit. He had a lean, rubbery body whose lines showed through his overalls. He looked good in the Hurricane, as if he belonged to it.

'Cup of tea, sir?' One of the mechanics held up a vacuum flask.

'Thanks.'

Adam sat down on the grass and sipped the tea. It was very sweet, with the custardy taste of evaporated milk. He pulled his cigarettes from his tunic and offered them round. Hennessy sat down next to him, then stretched out on his back, spreading his arms and legs like a starfish. He lay there with his eyes closed and his cigarette gummed to his lower lip. For a few minutes nobody spoke. Then Hennessy rolled over on his side and hoisted himself up on an elbow to look at Adam.

'Where are they putting you officers up, then?' It was an unexpected inquiry.

'Over at Updyke. It's a big house about three miles away.'

'You mean like a stately home.' It was more of a statement than a question.

'What's that?'

'You know, a castle, that type of thing.'

'I wouldn't say that.'

'But nice?'

Adam agreed that it was a pleasant place to live. He knew that he had no choice but to ask the next question.

'And where have they put you?'

'Oh don't worry about us. We're in some tents over on the racecourse. Very nice too, it is. Like being back in the bleeding boy scouts.'

The others cackled softly, a mildly subversive sound. Hennessy puffed lazily at his cigarette.

'Do you mind me asking you something?'

'Go ahead,' Hennessy said.

'Didn't you ever want to fly a plane yourself, rather than just looking after them?'

'*Just*,' Hennessy said scornfully, 'I like that *just* . . . The fact is, I can fly a plane. I had a pal at Hendon, a flight sergeant, who taught me. He said I had an . . . aptitude.' He used the word as if it meant a lot to him. 'But I bet you any money you haven't got a bloody clue what goes on inside an engine.' The mechanics murmured in agreement.

'You're right,' Adam said. 'Well, I know the theory, but it's true I couldn't work as a fitter or a rigger. But if you can fly, why didn't you become a pilot?'

Hennessy chuckled. 'Don't make me laugh. Me, Terry Hennessy, who left Abbey Wood Technical School at fourteen with a certificate in carpentry? You don't understand the RAF.' He paused. 'It's different with the Poles, isn't it?'

'What do you mean?'

'I knew some Poles at Hendon. Fitters like us. They seemed to have some . . . standing. Their pilots treated them like equals. I'm not saying they're all toffee-nosed bastards here. Most of the pilots are OK. But there's a fair few . . .'

Adam began an evasive reply but Hennessy seemed to have lost interest in the subject and got to his feet.

'Anyway, we've got another job on. Do you want to check the controls to make sure nothing's binding?'

Adam did as he was told. He manoeuvred the control column and the ailerons responded smoothly and obediently.

'You've done a very nice job,' he said, climbing down.

'Thanks,' Hennessy said, flipping away his cigarette. 'So long.' He set off across the field with the entourage of mechanics following respectfully behind.

Adam reported back to Buxton that the Hurricane was serviceable again, to be told that there was little likelihood that any serious German attack would materialise that afternoon. Buxton told him to go back to Updyke where he would later be addressing all the pilots on what they could expect the following day.

'It's Sunday tomorrow,' he said. 'You may have forgotten that. One does tend to forget which day of the week it is. I don't think the Jerries are going to regard it as a day of rest.'

At Updyke Adam lay on his narrow bed listening to the rustling of the trees outside his window. He fell off to sleep thinking about Pam and Moira. At six he woke again and went downstairs. There were pilots already on the terrace, including Whitbread and Miller-Morton. He went over, anxious to hear what had happened. They were standing apart from the rest by the stone balustrade that ran the length of the terrace. Whitbread looked up as he approached. They seemed to have been arguing and Miller-Morton looked flushed and sulky.

'Good,' said Whitbread decisively. 'Now that Adam's here we can have a proper post mortem, if that's the right word.'

'What happened?' Adam asked.

'Well, you saw me latch on to the Dornier,' Whitbread said.

'I thought it was a Heinkel.'

'No, a Dornier,' Whitbread said testily. 'It was a Dornier on a recce flight, that's why there was no fighter escort. I thought I had him cold. Then those idiots in the escort opened up and I had to break off. I knew straight away that some flak must have hit the engine because I could smell fuel. There was nothing for it but to head for home. I was obviously very vulnerable. If there were Jerries about I wouldn't be standing here now. But I was more worried about running out of juice and having to ditch.

'Well, I thought, at least if that happens, my wingman here,' he jabbed his thumb at Miller-Morton, 'will be able to look out for me and radio over my position. But when I looked around he'd gone.'

'Where was he?' Adam asked dutifully.

'He went after the bloody Dornier, leaving me to fend for myself.'

Miller-Morton shook his head slowly, a ponderous mime of good-natured disagreement, but Whitbread went on.

'It's pathetic,' he said. 'It's the most basic rule in the book. The first duty of a wingman is to look out for his leader.'

'Now look,' Miller-Morton said reasonably. 'I resent what you're saying. I didn't know you'd been hit. You looked perfectly all right to me. I was just doing the job. You know. Knocking down the Hun.'

'Save the stiff upper lip stuff for your bum-chum Savage,' Whitbread said. 'You're not in the movies yet.'

Miller-Morton flushed. 'I don't follow you,' he said quietly.

Whitbread laughed. 'This is priceless. Don't tell me you don't know.'

'Don't know what?'

'That Savage is a raving pansy.'

'Don't be ridiculous,' Miller-Morton said coolly. 'He's as normal as I am. It's another one of your delusions, like this business that I let you down today.'

'Well,' Adam said pacifically, 'at least we're all here and in one piece.'

After dinner, Buxton asked for the radio to be switched on. They sat talking quietly as Crouch twiddled the knobs of the receiver, searching through the static for the BBC. Eventually, out of the hissing, a man's voice emerged, plummy and conceited. He was talking about Adolf Hitler.

'We should not have liked him to come before we were ready to receive him, but we are quite ready to receive him now and we shall really be very disappointed if he does not turn up. We shall assure him that he will meet with that welcome on our shores which no invader has ever missed. This was to have been a week of German victory. It has been a week of British victory instead.'

No one laughed, or even smiled.

Buxton got up and switched off the radio. 'Well, you heard the information minister,' he said. 'I wish I could be quite as confident as he is . . .' He paused. 'But it's true that so far we've been holding our own. The Germans have had a fair go at us and so far we've been giving as good as we get. Today was funny. Not a single scare, flap or diversion. It would be nice to think that it's all over and the Jerries are beaten. I have to tell you I think they are merely catching their second wind. All the signs are that they are preparing something really big, something that we haven't seen before. And the chances are that they are going to throw it at us in the morning. Get to bed early, gentlemen. Tomorrow is going to be a long day.'

7

But as the morning wore on nothing happened. They sat in the briefing room, smoking and chatting quietly, waiting for news to come in from the radar stations. Adam was feeling unlucky, the way he did some days without knowing why. The bird was fluttering in his chest. He sat with his head hunched, adrenaline pricking in his blood, willing the scramble order to come and the waiting to be over.

The fear was beyond his power. Whatever valves and switches controlled it, opened and shut independently. With that knowledge, courage and cowardice meant little.

Towards midday, reports started to arrive from other airfields. Just after eleven, fighters on patrol over the Thames Estuary intercepted a Messerschmitt 110 flying at 31,000 feet on what appeared to be a reconnaissance mission and shot it down. At midday the radar station at Dover warned that German aircraft were building up over the Pas de Calais in the heaviest concentrations yet seen. The message came down from the controller at Group Headquarters near London that every serviceable aircraft should be ready to fly within thirty minutes. At 12.30 the first Spitfires were scrambled, joined a few minutes later by another 70 fighters from squadrons around the capital, to face a force of about 300 bombers and escorts that were approaching the Kent coast.

In the briefing room, the Kingsmere pilots could only follow the battle through the occasional bulletins issued by Buxton, who shuttled back and forth to the base operations room. The first attack had been aimed at Biggin Hill. A force of 60 Heinkels met little resistance, as the defending fighters were unable to break through the escort of 40 Messerschmitt 109s, and the anti-aircraft gunners on the ground were under orders to hold their fire for fear of hitting British aircraft. Despite the clear run, most of the bombs fell on the runways and the nearby woods and did little damage that could not be easily repaired. Then they heard that another force of Heinkels had attacked Kenley, in Surrey, to the south of London, destroying three of the four hangars and wrecking the station headquarters.

It seemed certain that the coastal fighter stations would be next. Trucks took them out to the dispersal areas.

Just after two o'clock, four swarms of German aircraft were picked up on the radar approaching Kingsmere and they scrambled. Buxton ordered the squadron to climb to 15,000 feet and circle the base, ready to hit the bombers as they arrived. Adam touched his Madonna and said his prayers. Now he felt calm as he climbed behind Whitbread, following Buxton's lead as he took them out to sea, turning back to circle behind the aerodrome to gain enough altitude to be able to swoop down out of the sun onto the Germans.

The landscape below was familiar now: the brown fringe of the sea turning to white as the water met the pebbly beaches; the green of the shoreline broken here and there by the red roofs of the bungalows and little houses; then, behind that, the billowing Downs.

The squadron was flying in four 'vics' of three, loosely in line astern. Buxton was in the lead with Crouch, his wingman and Whitbread's section tucked in closely behind and to the right.

As they swung around to face the sea once more, they could make out the shapes of the German aircraft as they approached the coast. There were four distinct groups, dark flecks against the increasingly hazy blue of the sky. They were moving at the same height, at about 15,000 feet. At this altitude, at this speed, they would very soon be flying into each other. But now the German aircraft altered course. Two of the formations shaded off to the right while the third and fourth moved to the left, a heading that took them east of the base. Adam could see what they were now, Junkers 87s and the twin-engined 88s, escorted by Messerschmitt 109s.

He watched the 88s heading south and west, and saw the first sticks of bombs falling from the belly of the lead aircraft, tumbling anti-clockwise. He could guess their destination: an airfield close to the big naval base at Portsmouth. Soon pillars of white and brown smoke began to climb silently from the ground.

To the left, he saw a group of about 25 Junkers 87s – the Stukas – and their fighter escorts forming up off the shore.

Buxton's voice broke into the earphones.

'Buxton to squadron. It looks as if they're heading for the Turling radar station. We can catch them on the dive. Let's go.'

The Stukas appeared to be throttling back, preparing to launch into their almost vertical descent. It was the moment when they ceased to be sluggish and ungainly and took on a lethal sleekness. But it was also the moment of their greatest vulnerability. The Messerschmitts that had shepherded them across the sea were unable to cover them effectively during their dives and stood back, resuming their guard once they had pulled out.

Buxton led the squadron at about 20 degrees to port of the swarm of Stukas' line of flight as they lined up ready to plunge at the radar station. Adam picked out a Stuka placed third in a row of bombers in line astern, calculating that it would come into his sights just as it tilted into its dive, but as he closed on it the pilot seemed to sense his intention and dropped down the sky, anxious to deliver his bomb and get back up among the protective thicket of Messerschmitts as quickly as possible.

Adam tried to follow, but the angle of the dive was too much for the Hurricane. He knew that if he forced the aircraft into too steep a descent he would risk stalling. Unlike the German fighters, whose Daimler-Benz engines had fuel injection, the British Rolls-

Royce Merlins had float carburettors which starved the engines of petrol if the machine went too close to the vertical.

As he pulled away, he glanced reflexively over his shoulder. There were three rapidly growing specks in the air behind him. He put the Hurricane into a tight turn but then he heard a drumming of explosions and he felt the tailplane shunt violently to the left and the control column being wrenched from his hand. The aircraft was bucking and yawing. He turned the aircraft on its side and pushed the nose hard down, so that he was flying as if propped up on a wingtip with the sea rushing beneath his left shoulder a few hundred feet away. He knew he could only maintain this position for a few seconds before his senses jammed and he would pile the plane into the water below, as hard as concrete at this speed, or into the rising ground ahead. He flipped the plane upright again but a glance in the mirror showed that one of the Germans was still with him. He dropped the nose, pressing the aircraft almost flat against the surface of the sea, knowing that the slightest brush against the water would send him cartwheeling over the surface in an explosion of spray; just like the Messerschmitt he had finished for two days before. A small fishing boat lay dead ahead, its mast poking right up into his line of flight and white, astonished faces staring straight at him from the deck. He pulled hard back on the stick and braced himself for the shock of the mast gouging into the belly of the Hurricane, but the boat sped underneath and he was in clear air again.

The German was hanging back, waiting for Adam to climb again as he would have to do if he was to avoid the houses along the beach, so as to get in a good, long volley. He was almost certainly dead if he was caught with a sustained burst now. Even if he was not killed outright by the bullets, he would die in the subsequent crash, or fall to his death. Parachutes did not open below a thousand feet and he was flying at nearer fifty. The beach was rushing towards him. He recognised Alberton pier to the left and the stucco-fronted houses and wrought-iron balconies of the boarding houses that stood behind the promenade. He remembered there was a road that was wider than most, a sort of boulevard that ran into the front a few hundred yards to the right of the pier.

There was gap in the line of buildings ahead and he aimed for it, raising the nose of the Hurricane so it would just clear the lip of the promenade and the fortifications ranged along it. There it was, just to the right, a break in the buildings with a pub on one corner and a red brick church on the other. He aimed the Hurricane at the gap and felt the houses and the stunted, pollarded trees close around him. The bowed front windows of the semi-detached houses seemed to be brushing the tips of his wings. He had an impression of net curtains and the backs of dressing-table mirrors. In front of him he saw a woman flinging herself to the ground, two children sitting on a brick wall and an old couple staring up in terror.

The Hurricane seemed to be flying itself. He dared not touch the control column for fear of sending it smashing into the bricks and tiles rushing past his wings. Then he saw the road was bending away to the left and there was nothing for it but to climb. He pulled back on the stick, steeling himself for the arrival of the bullets. Nothing came. He glanced in the rear-view mirror but the Messerschmitt had disappeared, having apparently reached the limit of its fuel.

From here on he was safe. He let out a shout of joy. He closed his eyes for a second or two and felt the Hurricane buoying him up. He turned the aircraft for home.

The base seemed to have escaped attack. To the left he could see fires burning between the crumpled poles and sagging wooden radio receiver tower at Turling radar station. Beyond, the ground over the Fleet Air Arm station at West Huston was boiling with flame and smoke and it looked as if the bombers were still coming in.

Adam radioed the Kingsmere controller to announce he was about to land and was told to refuel and rearm ready to take off again immediately. He taxied over to the blast pen, where a crew of aircraftmen he had not seen before swarmed around the Hurricane, prising off the hatches over the machine-gun ports and feeding in belts of ammunition, while a fuel bowser pumped aviation spirit into the tank. He pulled back the canopy, released his harness and climbed out onto the wing to look at the damage. There were two fist-sized holes on the port side, towards the back of the fuselage, where cannon shells from one of the Messerschmitts had struck – exiting almost opposite, leaving slightly bigger holes but doing no damage to the control wires that ran to the elevator and rudder; and a spattering of machine-gun strikes: nothing to keep the machine from flying again straight away.

A breeze was picking up and he suddenly felt cold. Looking down he saw that sweat had drenched through his tunic, leaving dark blue patches on his chest and under his arms. Other aircraft were landing. He noticed Whitbread's Hurricane putting down and waited for him to arrive. The cockpit canopy slid back. Whitbread's hands went to the chinstrap of his helmet and peeled the monstrous ensemble of oxgen mask earphones and goggles away from his face. His cheeks were red from the heat and his hair was pasted onto his scalp.

'You OK?' he called over the noise of his engine. Adam nodded and put his fingers in his ears. Whitbread cut the engine and hauled himself out.

'We're going to have to try harder to stick together,' he said. 'I lost you after five minutes.'

'I didn't do it on purpose.'

'I suppose not. You had me worried though. Have you seen any sign of Miles?'

'No, I lost him the same time I lost you, which was as soon as the show started.'

'Well, it's not over yet. Try and stay a bit closer this time.'

They got back into the Hurricanes and fired up the engines. Two aircraftmen lay across the wings of their tailpanes as they bumped back to the tarmac, to stop the wind getting under them and tipping the noses forward. Whitbread took off first and Adam followed him. The haze was thicker now and building up. Whitbread led him towards West Huston. The fires had got bigger and a massive coil of black, oily smoke wound up from the ground. The raiders were departing. Beyond the base, just crossing the coast, a group of three Stukas were climbing hard having dropped their bombs. Whitbread's voice came over the radio. 'These will do.'

He set his Hurricane into a shallow dive calculated to bring him on to the Stukas at an angle that would allow him to take his pick. Adam's job, according to the tactical manual, a work that had long been overtaken by the realities of combat, was to guard his leader against fighter attack on the approach, carry on the attack if he broke away without downing his victim, then resume flying protectively behind him.

The rear gunner in the middle of the formation was the first to spot them, and he opened up wildly, his shots curving away, the glowing phosphorus of the tracer dying out before the Hurricanes got into range. The others must have noticed the approach but held their fire. The sensible thing to have done was to have engaged the last Stuka in the line but, for some reason, Whitbread chose the middle one.

He approached cautiously and began stitching fire from the tail along the length of the fuselage until the bullets reached the cockpit, playing on the long hooped steel and plastic cockpit cover. There was no response from the rear gunner who, Adam supposed, was now dead or out of ammunition. But fire began floating towards them in brief, accurate bursts from the forward Stuka. Most of it was directed at Whitbread, but Adam felt a rattle of bullets on his wings. There was no opportunity to fire back, for Whitbread was blocking his line of fire, so he opened up on the middle Stuka instead. For a few seconds both the Hurricanes' guns were hammering on the nose and cockpit of the Stuka, then Whitbread broke away to the right. There was smoke already curling from behind the dive bomber's propeller and Adam thought he could see yellow licks of flame coming from the engine cowling. With Whitbread out of the way, the gunner in the lead Stuka now had a clear line of sight on Adam's Hurricane and he felt another flurry of machine-gun fire striking the leading edge of his starboard wing. The middle Stuka was in trouble now and slowing down. The rear dive bomber in the formation began steadily to overhaul it, until it was flying alongside. As it passed he saw the pilot wave from the cockpit to the crew in the stricken plane.

Adam felt an odd pang at this gesture of solidarity. The Stuka was never going to make it back to France. At the rate it was losing height it would crash in a mile or two into the Channel where, if its pilot and gunner had survived, the ordeal of fire would now become trial by water. He made the sign of the cross. All pilots of single-engined planes had a horror of large stretches of open water.

He left the Stuka limping for home and swung over to the right, searching the sky for Whitbread's Hurricane. There was no sign of it. He turned towards the shore and as he did so Whitbread's voice come over the radio.

'Red leader to Adam. I'm going back.'

'Adam here. What's the problem?'

'I'm leaking coolant. The engine's overheating. What do you want to do?'

Adam checked his gauges. He had another fifty minutes' flying time and enough ammunition to make it worth hanging around.

'I'll try and find the others, wherever they are.'

'OK.'

Now the skies around Adam were bare. Once more he marvelled at how the air filled and emptied with dreamlike swiftness, and at the way in which – at a supreme vantage point – you could be blind to the things going on a few hundred feet away from you. He radioed his whereabouts back to Kingsmere and was given a heading that would take him to where the rest of the squadron were still airborne over the sea, south and east of the base. But when he got there they had gone, and all that was left was a skein of blurred vapour trails. Below, the sea was running stronger, the white caps of the waves coursing north up the Channel, driven on by the southwesterly wind. Over the land, great turrets of cumulus were forming, stacking up in sultry piles in the hot, humid air above the Downs.

He moved out over the Channel, passing a long convoy of freighters butting southwards through the waves. He decided to head northeast in the hope of coming across the rest of the squadron. If he failed to find them soon he would loop round to cross the Kent coast at Dungeness and set a course west to Kingsmere.

The cloud was thickening fast, coming down over the land like a protective blanket, shielding the bases and the radar stations from the eyes of the bombers. He dropped down to get beneath it and soon saw the long shingle spit of Dungeness and its striped, pepper-pot lighthouse ahead. Tattered banners of cumulonimbus draped themselves across the cockpit as he banked to port and moved over the land.

He dropped again to get below it, and a monstrous shape loomed on his right, huge and grey, far too big to be an aeroplane. It was a barrage balloon. Where there was one there would be others. The only way out was upwards, to climb as quickly as he could above 5,000 feet, the ceiling at which the balloons were tethered. But even as he made his decision he felt a violent shock on his port side that sent the Hurricane lurching sideways. The balloon cable had sliced through his port wing tip.

Now the only way was down. He looked around for other balloons. There was nothing ahead, but that did not mean that they were not there, hidden in the cloud overhead like the one that he had collided with. He nursed the Hurricane earthwards. The wonderful responsiveness was gone. He tried to compensate by trimming the elevator and rudder, but it was no good. The Hurricane was swinging all over the sky. He would never be able to make it back to Kingsmere. He felt a fool. It was just the sort of carelessness that Buxton hated.

He looked around for somewhere to put down. Ahead he could see some woods, and between them a long strip of grass. He levered down the flaps and lowered the undercarriage, dropped over the trees and lay the Hurricane as gently as he could on the grass. The plane raced over the rough surface, bounded up as if struggling to get back into the air, then rolled to a halt.

He could not work out where he was. It did not seem like farmland, for the grass strip had been carefully cut and tended. To his right a hundred yards away he could see a pit that appeared to be full of sand, and at the end of the strip the grass changed colour, becoming a vivid, almost emerald green. He climbed down and began examining the damage to the wing tip. While he was doing so there was a rustling among the trees. He looked over and saw a middle-aged man, dressed in tweed plus fours, a diamond-patterned pullover and a flat hat, examining him cautiously from the trees.

'Just checking,' he said in a soothing, apologetic voice. 'Couldn't tell whether you were friend or foe. You can't be too careful.' He looked back towards the trees. 'You can come out now dear,' he said. 'He's one of ours.' A woman wearing a felt hat and a tweed skirt that matched her husband's outfit emerged from the shadows.

'Bring the clubs.'

She dipped back obediently and retrieved a long leather bag with metal shafts poking from the top.

'The caddy just hopped it as soon as the fireworks began,' the man said. 'It's been quite an afternoon here.'

There had been dogfights over the links all afternoon, he told Adam on the way to the clubhouse, and now there was Adam's crash landing.

'I don't think the West Kent will ever see anything like it again,' he said.

Inside the clubhouse, Adam asked for a telephone and was directed to an office. His rescuer asked him what he wanted to drink.

'A pint of bitter will do fine.'

'Oh, you've got to have something stronger than that,' the woman said. 'Leave it to me.'

When he dialled the Kingsmere number he got only a squealing electric monotone. Either the base communications had been damaged or the connecting lines were down. The best thing was to try and get back to Kingsmere as soon as possible and organise the retrieval of his Hurricane from there.

He walked back into the bar. A group of golfers were standing alongside it, feet propped nonchalantly on the brass rail, discussing their rounds. A few of them looked at Adam in his stained tunic and Mae West, then turned back to the group.

Adam sat down at a table by the window with the woman. The man returned with the drinks, three balloons liberally filled with brandy, and put one in front of Adam.

'I know you're not a member, but they were prepared to make an exception in your case,' he said.

'Well, cheers.' The brandy made a fiery descent into his stomach, warming and relaxing him.

'Take a look at this.'

His host was pointing at a framed document hanging on the wall nearby. 'Had to adjust the rules slightly to take account of wartime conditions.'

Adam read:

West Kent Golf Club. Temporary Provisions.

(i) In competition, during gunfire or while bombs are falling, players may take cover without penalty for ceasing play.

(ii) A ball lying in a crater may be lifted and dropped not nearer the hole without penalty.

(iii) A ball moved by enemy action may be replaced as near as possible to where it lay.

The regulations continued in meticulous detail. Adam had never played golf and had no idea of the rules. It was hard to tell whether this was a ponderous joke or a serious attempt to adjust to the demands of war.

Adam raised his glass. 'Very good,' he said and smiled, hoping this response covered both possibilities.

His host smiled back.

'Got to have rules,' he said. 'Now, how are we going to get you back . . . ?'

They found a map. They were about 30 miles from Kingsmere. The local telephone line appeared to be working, for his host was able to call the taxi rank at a nearby railway station, and twenty minutes later a black saloon arrived at the clubhouse door. Adam said goodbye to the couple. The group at the bar took no more notice of his departure than they had of his arrival.

He slipped onto the worn and cracked leather of the back seat and watched the countryside go by. It was hot, but the nature of the heat had changed. The soporific warmth of the past days had given way to something baleful and threatening. There were few other vehicles on the road. He noticed some army trucks, and several times they were overtaken by army motorcycles and sidecars mounted with machine guns. In the fields on either side of the road, motor-tractors were churning through the corn rows trailing harvesters.

When they had been driving for three quarters of an hour, they rounded a bend and found themselves at the back of a short queue of cars, sitting patiently with their engines turned off. Ahead, some sort of checkpoint had been thrown across the road. Adam sat for a while, listening to the intermittent song of a bird in the hedgerow and the buzz of insects, smelling the hot earth and the petrol fumes. From the direction of the roadblock he could hear voices, rising in pitch, getting angrier. He opened the door and walked to the front of the queue.

The roadblock was manned by several men of varying ages, dressed in scratchy, serge khaki uniforms and carrying rifles. On their arms were bands proclaiming them to be members of the Home Guard. With them was a policeman. They were listening to a respectable man in a dark blue suit whose wire-rimmed spectacles gave him the look of a bank official. He too had a band on his arm with the words 'Civil Defence' stitched onto it.

The policeman was talking to him. He had removed his helmet because of the heat and had cropped grey hair, a closed, immobile face and slightly crossed eyes that gave him a challenging, belligerent look. When he spoke it was with a formulaic politeness, which failed to conceal a threatening insolence.

'I'm sure you are who you say you are, sir, but I have orders not to let anyone through without the right documents.' He paused. 'A man in your position ought to be able to understand that.'

Behind, the other motorists were growing impatient and one of them gave a brief toot on his horn.

'Now, if you don't mind just standing to one side, sir.' The policeman motioned the next car forward and began examining the driver's papers.

'What's going on?' Adam asked.

The Civil Defence official noticed him for the first time.

'I'm trying to get to West Huston to report on the damage there and help organise the relief operation but they simply won't let me through. They say this armband isn't enough.'

'Haven't you got any other identification?'

The official looked embarrassed. 'I left it at home. The problem is that someone saw some parachutes earlier – probably a German aircrew baling out – and the word has gone out that a full-scale invasion is under way. The Home Guard told me that they have instructions to look out for Germans.'

Adam laughed. 'Maybe I can get you through.'

When Adam approached, the policeman seemed impressed by the air-force uniform and came to attention, snapping a salute. 'Where are you trying to get to, sir?'

Adam explained.

'Come to the front of the queue,' the policeman said. 'We've got to do what we can to help the real fighters.' He threw a glance at the civil defence official.

Adam signalled the taxi driver to come forward. The sight of this favouritism had a dramatic effect on the six or seven cars in the queue; their drivers began sounding their horns and shouting half-heartedly at the policeman and the Home Guard. Adam seized the moment.

'I wonder if I could have a word, officer?'

They moved to the side of the road.

'This chap,' he nodded towards the official, 'is obviously wrong to be out and about without his proper authorisation. But I think he is telling you the truth. I think it might be better to let him through.' He looked straight into the policeman's badly aligned eyes. 'It might save a lot of trouble later on.'

There was another burst of honking as the policeman reflected. 'I see what you mean, sir.' He paused. 'All right, then.'

He turned towards the Home Guard men manning the barrier and called out in a grudging voice. 'Open up. Let 'em through.'

The official got in with Adam and told his own driver to follow on. In the back of the car he told him what he knew about the day's events. The first raids of the day had produced mixed results, with Biggin Hill getting off lightly but Kenway suffering badly. The communications had been put out of action for several hours, which had disrupted the reporting system that was vital if the controllers were to direct the fighters effectively.

The second wave of bombers had dropped their loads virtually unmolested on two air bases west of Kingsmere, but had done little serious damage as there were few aircraft on the ground. The attack on Turling had wrecked one of the 240-foot wooden receiver towers, but the radar cover was still more or less intact. The worst destruction had been at the Fleet Air Arm base at West Huston, where there had been hardly any anti-aircraft guns deployed. In the confusion the all clear had been sounded just as the bombers were arriving.

The car arrived at a town clustered on top of a low hill, dominated by an operatic castle that he remembered passing in the train to Chichester less than three weeks before. They could see the smoke from West Huston reaching up into the sky, the oily black staining the creamy mattress of cloud that now made a canopy over the land.

'Must have hit a fuel dump,' the official said.

Adam told the driver to go faster. They were stopped a few hundred yards from the entrance to the airfield by a fire tender blocking the road. The official thanked Adam and hurried on. Adam told the driver to wait and followed him. Just by the gates he saw a body covered by a blanket lying on the grass verge. He walked past it. The blanket was brown, the roughly woven issue they gave the soldiers. The two legs sticking out from underneath it were pale, almost white. They were a young woman's legs, bare and stockingless. The delicacy of her ankles was emphasised by her clumsy high-heeled shoes and her toenails were painted bright pink. A choking pity rose inside him. He wanted to see her face. He glanced furtively about him but there was no one around. He lifted the top edge of the blanket delicately, fearful of what he would see, and glanced down. She was still a girl, with a mass of dark hair, curly and glossy, and a pale oval face touched with freckles on her cheeks. Her mouth was painted, inexpertly, in the same shade as her toenails. She had a dreamy, vacant look, as if she was sleeping with her eyes open. He ducked down and pressed his lips to her cheek. It was warm still and smelled of talcum powder. Then he covered her over again and walked up the road to the driveway that led into the base.

He was angry now, appalled at the contemptuous carelessness of the destruction. To the right of the drive some civilian houses had been caught in the blast of a bomb that had landed in the front garden, digging a crater 15 feet across. Part of the upper storey wall had been blown in, exposing a bedroom with flowered wallpaper, a double bed and a chest of drawers that had been torn open and the clothes strewn around the room. Next door the wall had been peeled away to reveal a lavatory and a basin, exposing the life of the inhabitants in all its intimate banality.

He walked further up the road. Two firemen emerged from a mound of bricks carrying a bundle between them. The body was burned almost to charcoal. The only sign that it had once been human was the teeth grimacing out of the blackened skull. They lay it down alongside two other corpses, brown and shrivelled like mummies.

He found the civil defence official by a huddle of buildings at the edge of the airfield. He was looking through the partially demolished gable end of a Nissen hut that had been used as an ablutions block. He was staring at a bath in which lay a young man wallowing in blood tinged water. Adam put a hand on his shoulder and led him away through the still burning fires.

8

That evening Adam went with Whitbread and Bealing to a pub on the Downs. Whitbread drove them in Miller-Morton's MG. Its owner was in hospital recovering from burns sustained in a crash-landing.

Adam sat wedged in the gap behind the seat, listening to the talk in the front.

'Poor old Miles,' Whitbread said as they raced through the warm, insect-laden air.

'Still, the glamour-boy looks are unimpaired. It was mainly his hands. He'll be off for a couple of weeks. It'll give him a chance to learn his movie lines. He'll be back in no time.'

'Shame about Wildblood,' Bealing said.

'Yes. Mind you, he took one of the bastards with him.' Wildblood, a shy Canadian, had been killed in a mid-air collision with a bomber. His death was an accident. Very little was remembered of him. There was not much more to say.

The British pilots were superstitious when it came to the dead, as if talking about them might hasten their own doom. The Poles were different, always remembering the day's casualties in the evening's drinking.

The pub was already full of servicemen. They found places in a beer garden in the back. It was sultry, threatening thunder. Frizell was standing in a corner with Ted Sobinski, who was red in the face and swaying slightly on his stout legs. He was surprised to see Buxton sitting at a table next to a stack of wooden beer crates, smoking his pipe and twisting the stem of a glass of tomato juice. Crouch was sitting next to him, hunched attentively.

Whitbread looked over and cackled. 'You don't often see Brian Buxton on licensed premises. He never touches a drop.'

They walked across. Buxton was friendly, almost effusive.

'Won't be much flying tomorrow if the weather keeps up like this,' he said.

They glanced skywards, through the green-black lattice of branches and leaves, to the stacked piles of cloud.

'If it stays this way there'll be nothing for the Luftwaffe to aim at.'

Crouch made a thwarted, grumbling noise, as if the thought of not being able to get to grips with the enemy for 24 hours was unbearable to him, then looked towards Buxton for approval. Buxton seemed not to have noticed. He looked at his watch, tossed back his tomato juice and made to go.

'I'll come with you if you don't mind, sir,' Crouch said, rising to join him.

They sat down in the vacant places. Adam went inside to get the beer. It was a cool, clean place with white-painted wood panelling halfway up the walls and a horseshoe-shaped bar with engraved glass panels running around the top. He gave his order. The counter was made of densely grained wood and was slick with spilled beer. He began to trace patterns in the wet, as he waited for the barman to return with the drinks; first an aeroplane, then a swastika, finally a heart.

'Penny for them, brother.'

He looked round. Gerry Cunningham was standing there, smiling.

'Hallo,' said Adam, surprised at how pleased he was to see him. 'Can I get you something?'

'No thanks, I'm just on my way to the gents.'

He seemed a little drunk. Adam noticed a scrap of ribbon on the pocket of his tunic that had not been there on Friday.

'What's that?' he asked.

'It's my MC. Came through today. I got it for Dunkirk. I've been celebrating a bit already. The fact is, though, I'm feeling a tiny bit blue.'

'What's the matter?'

'Oh, it's nothing to do with me,' Gerry said. 'No, I've just had to break the news to one of my boys that his girl's been killed. He was on guard duty over at West Huston and she was on her way to see him when the raid came in. She was an Irish girl – came all the way over from County Mayo.' He fumbled for a cigarette.

'They found her stripped naked by the blast. I've seen that happen a few times. The strange thing was, there wasn't a mark on her. Fortunately someone chucked a blanket over her. I don't imagine her old

mother would have liked to think of her like that, lying there in the buff with a lot of English blokes around.'
Adam had already forgotten about his encounter with the dead girl. He was about to say something when the drinks arrived. Without asking, Gerry picked up one of the thick glasses and took a gulp of beer.

'The chap was naturally very cut up about it. But then, so was I. It's the old Oirish sentimentality in me coming out, I suppose.'

He turned away. 'Tell you what, when you've delivered those, come and have a chat. I'm over there in the corner.'

Adam went back to the garden with the drinks. He was pleased to have bumped into Gerry. He felt drawn to him, despite all his cockiness, in a way that he was not to Whitbread or the other fliers. Perhaps it was the melancholy streak. The Irish were meant to be like the Poles. Anyway, if he was here, Moira and Pam might be with him.

'I've just bumped into a pal,' he told Whitbread and Bealing. 'I'll be back in a bit.' He returned to the bar, picked up his drink and found Gerry sitting with his legs stretched out at a table next to a fireplace, contemplatively smoking one of his fat cigarettes.

'I'm glad you came back,' he said. 'The truth is I was hoping to bump into you again and would have tracked you down if you hadn't popped up tonight. I must admit my motives are not entirely honourable, but I'll tell you about that in a minute.'

He sat there for a minute in silence, puffing on his cigarette. The beer glass was almost empty. 'I can't help thinking about that girl,' he said. Then he began reciting in a slightly curdled voice:

> 'Deal on, deal on my merry men
> Deal on the cakes and the wine
> For whatever is dealt at her funeral today
> Will be dealt tomorrow at mine.'

The verse seemed to have the effect of a magic incantation, dispelling his gloom. Gerry brightened up again.

'That's enough of the bloody Irishry.' He put a hand on Adam's shoulder and fixed him with a comradely look. 'Adam, Adam, how are you? Tell me the news from the front. Do you know something? Adam doesn't suit you. It sounds too old, as old as the bloody hills. What's your surname again?'

Adam told him.

'Tomaszewski. Right, from now on you're Tommy, to me at any rate. Gerry and Tommy, we're going to be very good pals. The joke is that Gerry is really a Paddy and Tommy is really a Pole and we're both fighting for the good old British.'

Adam laughed.

'Where's the harem tonight?'

'Don't you worry about them, they're fine. In fact they should be here soon.'

Adam felt bold. 'Which one of them are you actually with?' he asked.

'Now that's a tricky one,' said Gerry, a delighted smirk breaking out on his face. 'I suppose you could say that Moira is the official Cunningham consort but that Pam is coming up fast on the rails.' He leaned forward conspiratorially. 'That's where I thought you might be able to help me out.'

Without ever knowing it, Adam had been hoping for something like this. He had thought hard about the two women but had reserved his judgement about which of them would win the golden apple. He had met Pam first, so she had had more time to take root in his fantasies. He liked her big frame and her copper hair and good nature. She was what he expected an English girl to be. He imagined what she would be like in bed. Boisterous, he thought, slightly clumsy but enthusiastic. The other one, with her slightly sharp features and dark, dense hair looked more like a certain type of Polish woman. She looked deep, but whether that was real or not he did not yet know.

Gerry dropped his voice. 'Here's the thing. As I say, I'm pretty keen on young Pam. The problem is that I'm not making much headway because Moira never lets me out of her sight.'

'And you want me to, what, create a diversion, take her off your hands, while you try to fuck Pam?'

Gerry sat upright and pushed both hands forward, palms open, in a gesture of outraged propriety.

'Tommy, please, where did you learn such language? No. Well, maybe, yes. Really what I want is the opportunity to get to know her a bit better. Then we'll see what happens from there.'

Adam thought for a moment. It seemed to him that he could only win. He would have an opportunity to see more of both of them. If the subterfuge was to work, they would have to spend time together. If he decided on Moira he was in a strong position to win her, a shoulder to cry on after Gerry's treachery was revealed. On the other hand, if he preferred Pam, it would not be too late to snatch her back from Gerry.

He believed he was Gerry's equal in charm. He found himself surprised at the easy cynicism of his thinking.

Gerry was still going on. 'I suppose you think I'm a bit of a swine.'

'Yes.'

A flicker of what seemed like genuine hurt clouded Gerry's luminous eyes.

'I mean, yes, I'll do it,' said Adam quickly.

'You will?'

'Of course.'

Gerry looked relieved. Then shifty. 'Now I don't want you to think I'm greedy,' he said piously. 'I've been seeing Moira for a bit and she's a great girl. But it's wartime. Who knows what's going to happen? It would be a bloody shame to go to your maker without ever having known what it was like to . . .' He trailed off.

He paused then slapped Adam on the back. 'That's that, then. Let's have another drink.'

They talked for a while about the war. Gerry had dropped his bantering rudeness about the RAF and spoke admiringly of their performance, of which he and the rest of the regiment had a grandstand view at their camp near Chichester. He talked, with a few strokes of sketchy detail, about his army career. He had worked for a wine shipper in London and joined the Territorials after Munich. He had been commissioned soon after the war broke out and moved up quickly.

'I must admit when the war broke out I saw it as a stroke of luck,' he said. 'War's a great opportunity for blokes like me.'

As Adam ran through his own story he saw Gerry's eyes flicking over his shoulder. He smelled perfume, Moira's perfume.

He turned round and she smiled down at him. 'Hallo, Adam.'

'No,' Gerry said, 'he's called Tommy now. I'm insisting on it.'

'What does Adam say?'

Adam shrugged. 'I don't mind.'

'I'll see whether it grows on me.' She sat down. 'Get me a drink please, Gerry. A gin and It if they've got it.' Gerry jumped up, eager and attentive.

She ignored Adam for a few moments, delving in her handbag for a packet of cigarettes, then looking expectantly towards him for a light. He felt slightly ashamed at not having a lighter like the dull gold one that Gerry plied constantly, and produced a box of matches instead.

She bent to catch the flame and looked up at him at the moment the tobacco caught fire, just as she had on that first night at the Bristol. Was it an affectation or an unconscious habit?

She blew out a plume of smoke. 'I've been thinking about you,' she said.

'Really?'

'I've been thinking about all you RAF boys. It's hard not to with what's been happening right over our heads for the last few days. How much longer do you think it can go on for?'

Adam was disappointed at the neutrality of her interest. 'I don't know,' he said rather sulkily. 'I just do the flying.'

Gerry appeared at the table with a tray of drinks. 'Look who I found,' he said brightly. Pam was standing beside him looking almost unnaturally fresh and healthy in a dusty pink skirt and a white blouse.

'Surprise, surprise,' said Moira, coldly, then in a more welcoming voice, 'Hallo Pam.'

The challenge that lay ahead seemed to have sobered Gerry, for he was now fussing around in a state of barely suppressed excitement, showing elaborate concern for everyone around the table.

The women took little notice. For a while they devoted themselves to Adam, asking him in detail about the fighting of the last few days. He felt placated and answered at length, taking care not to appear too boastful. From time to time Gerry tried to join in, but his efforts were ignored and he lapsed into silence.

While Adam talked, he looked closely at them both. When listening, Pam had an absorbed sort of look, head on one side as if drinking up every word that was spoken. It was touching, but in other circumstances it might be irritating.

Moira sat back, hands folded over her flat stomach, looking at him with her sceptical, blue-black eyes. She had on a dark blue silk shirt and a single string of big red beads. Her bare arms were brown, dusted with fine dark hair. At that moment she looked like Gipsy royalty. He realised that he knew nothing at all about her.

Gerry was starting to get restless.

'Can't we give the war a rest for a bit?' he asked good-naturedly. 'Tell us what's been happening down at the Bristol, Pam.'

Pam began to describe a dinner that had been held by some businessmen in a private room at the hotel the previous evening.

'The manager was off for the evening so he asked if I would supervise. One of the guests took a bit of a shine to me and offered me a lift back to the cottage.'

'Oh yes?' Gerry said.

'But before we set off he made it clear that he expected to be asked in. He said that – because it would mean using up his precious petrol coupons – he would have to know it was worth his while.'

'The rotter!' said Gerry delightedly. 'And this is the civilisation we're fighting to defend. It makes you sick. Come on everybody, drink up.'

Adam had had enough beer and was thinking of switching to whisky. As he was deciding, he saw Bealing and Whitbread coming.

'We were wondering who the pals you ran into were,' Bealing said.

'I was just coming to get you,' Adam said, a bit embarrassed.

'Don't worry,' said Whitbread, 'we're here now.'

They sat down. Gerry squeezed up on the settle to make room. He placed Whitbread between himself and Moira and put Bealing on the far side of Pam. For a while Adam found himself outside the conversation. Moira made Whitbread welcome, asking him about himself and his exploits and listening carefully to his halting replies. On the other side Bealing, Pam and Gerry were now laughing and chatting easily. They seemed three of a kind, locking smoothly into the casual human meshings of wartime.

Gerry was determined that everyone should feel the lighthouse beam of his charm, turning to Whitbread and asking him earnestly about some aspect of the fighting.

After a while, Moira and Adam drifted out of the circle of chat. They sat in silence enjoying the complicity between two people who did not talk much. Then Adam said:

'It's your turn.'

She gave her chocolatey chuckle.

'My grandmother used to say that interrogation was not conversation. She was brought up to think it was bad manners to ask questions.'

'What else did she say?'

'Oh, lots of things, most of which would make life impossible if you took them seriously.'

'So you had a grandmother, we've established that.'

'She was a fierce woman. I don't know why I speak about her in the past tense. She's still very much alive, though I haven't seen her since I was sixteen, when Mummy and I went to Africa.'

'What made you come back?'

'The war. It may not look like it, but I wanted to do my bit.'

Adam remained quiet, sensing that too much prodding would stop the flow of information.

'The trouble is that I haven't discovered yet what I'm best cut out for. I tried some of the ministries but they tell me I haven't got any qualifications, at least not the ones they want. I've put in for the WAAF and the ATS but I'm still waiting to hear.'

Adam noticed that she had made no mention of Gerry. As if sensing this absence, Gerry's voice broke in, delivering the punch line of a joke, which was followed by the laughter of Pam, Whitbread and Bealing. They listened a while to the neighbouring chatter. Gerry was conducting the group like an orchestra, creating a sort of minor conversational symphony. He had started off wanting to monopolise Pam, but Adam could see that he had now lost interest in that and was devoting himself to the bigger audience.

Moira was looking at Gerry now. There was a glint of scepticism in her eyes but also affection and a sort of slightly unwilling admiration. She saw Adam looking at her and gave an indulgent shrug.

Suddenly he wanted the evening to end. There was nothing more to be gained that night and to carry on would only risk losing the ground he had made. Moira started talking to Whitbread again. Soon the hilarity became subdued. Adam was saved from suggesting that they leave by the voice of the barman calling time.

As they were leaving, Gerry took him to one side. 'Give me your number,' he said. 'I gather from your chums that the weather situation means there's probably nothing doing tomorrow, in which case we could get together.' He threw a glance in the direction of the women who were talking together. 'All four of us.'

9

In the morning, as the forecasters had predicted, the cloud still hung low and thick and the Germans mostly stayed away. Twice, they sent formations towards the coast. The first, a large fleet of Messerschmitt 109s, the controllers judged to be a provocation aimed at tempting the British fighters into the air where the swarming Messerschmitts could whittle the numbers down, and the stations were ordered to ignore it. Then a medium force of twin-engined Junkers with fighter escorts was picked up on the radar heading for Southampton, but a squadron other than Adam's was ordered up to see it off.

In the middle of the afternoon the pilots of 404 were told they could return to Updyke. When Adam arrived there were telephone messages waiting, from Pam and Gerry, each asking for him to ring as soon as he got in and leaving separate numbers. He wondered which of them to call first. Not Gerry, he thought. He felt slightly ashamed of himself for having fallen in with the half-formed conspiracy of the previous evening and was determined not to be dragged further into Gerry's plans. His calculations concerning the women now seemed shabby and unworthy, demeaning to them and to himself. He remembered Moira's clever, sceptical eyes and imagined her contempt had she known of his conversation with Gerry, just before her arrival.

He would ring Pam.

He dialled the number and a stagy female voice announced he had got through to the Bristol Hotel.

'Pamela Sutton, please.'

'I'll see if she is available.'

A minute passed.

'Hallo.' Even in this single word she managed to sound friendly and cheerful, thought Adam, even though she could not have known who was on the line.

'It's Adam.'

She gave a little cry of pleasure.

'So you got the message. I was just about to ring you again. Gerry told me I had to twist your arm and make sure that you came along.'

'What are you planning?'

'Gerry had the idea we might all go for an early evening picnic up on the Downs. Can you come?'

'I'll have to check.'

'Call me back soon.'

Ashford gave him permission to stand down at five and he rang Pam back to tell her. She sounded delighted. 'We'll be by at five to pick you up, then.'

He had an hour to kill and went upstairs to lie down on the narrow bed, feeling the coolness of the dense cotton sheets under his bare back, smelling the comforting scent of wax polish. Someone had put flowers in the room – not his orderly, he imagined, maybe a maid who had been kept on when the civilian owners left the house. He felt touched. He was anxious not to fall asleep in case he missed the rendezvous. After a while he got up and went down the long corridor to the bathroom and climbed into a deep enamel bath. He mixed the water to the exact temperature of his blood and felt his flesh melt into the water, relaxing him, clearing his mind from the tension of a day of waiting.

Back in his room he opened the wardrobe. The new clothes he had bought in Chichester were sitting there untried. The blue silk scarf with the diamond design hung on the brass rail inside the door. He put on trousers and tunic, and a clean shirt and a pair of the long socks he had bought at the haberdasher's. He pushed his feet into the brown suede brogues, and checked the effect in the mirror. Then he reached for the scarf. It slithered away from the rail, heavy and cold. He knotted it loosely round his neck and went downstairs.

Five was striking on the clock in the hall. He walked out onto the terrace. The thunderclouds were rolling away eastwards and the haze was thinning. He heard a car engine and saw Gerry's saloon come round the bend in the drive. The top was down and Pam was driving. She had on a headscarf and dark glasses like an actress in a film magazine. Gerry and Moira were sitting in the back. Pam sounded the horn when she saw him and gave an extravagant wave.

Adam climbed into the passenger seat and they set off.

'I managed to scrounge some food but no booze,' Gerry said.

'Where are we going?' Adam asked.

'Who cares?' shouted Pam exuberantly.

'Where the mood takes us, brother,' said Gerry, 'but preferably somewhere near a pub.'

They took the road that led up towards the Downs. The sunshine had driven away the haze and shimmered on the tawny stubble of the cut corn. They passed through a hamlet of flint and brick houses and a tiny, ancient church standing alone in a field. They rounded a corner and came by a pub set back from the road.

'Hallelujah,' said Gerry. 'Pull in, Pam.' But when he tried the door it was locked and there was no sign of the landlord when they went round to the back.

'Let's stop here anyway,' Moira said. 'There's a path over there that looks as if it leads onto the Downs.'

Gerry opened the boot and pulled out a small canvas bag, which he held up triumphantly.

'Grub!' he said.

They crossed the road and climbed over a stile and onto a rutted track. Deep summer lay on the countryside. The smell of baking earth rose from the cut fields. The track rose steeply, taking them into the shade at the edge of a copse. The path was dappled with scattered sunlight and the woods exhaled coolness. Presently the trees closed in around them, making a green, glowing tunnel. The path still climbed. The sun filled the top of the tunnel with molten gold light.

When they emerged from the trees they were on the flank of a gently curved hillside. In front of them stood a windmill. Adam was sure it was the one he could see from his bedroom window at Updyke. He had flown over it several times. It was a blunt cone of warm red brick, surmounted by a white weatherboard cap, with four sails from which the canvas had been removed.

'It's not used any more,' Pam said. 'They've taken away the machinery that used to grind the corn.' She sounded solemn. 'It was a ruin until a few years ago. Then the chap who owns the land had it restored as a memorial to his dead wife.'

They walked towards the windmill. There was a slight breeze that dried their sweat and soughed through the bare sails, making them groan on the rusty axle. Gerry strode over to the lee of the windmill and flopped down, spreading himself luxuriously on the grass. Then he sat up and opened the canvas bag, pulling out paper bags turned greasy and transparent from the melting butter in the sandwiches, and some apples and chocolate bars. At the bottom of the bag was a tartan rug, which he spread out on the ground over the pellets of rabbit dung.

They lay on their backs listening to the rustling of the wind, the creak of the windmill sails and the sound of their own breathing, gazing up at the last wisps of cloud leaving the sky.

'You'll be flying tomorrow, Tommy my boy,' Gerry said gently.

Pam sat up suddenly.

'Let's eat,' she said. She began unwrapping the packages and laying the sandwiches down on the paper.

'We've got chicken, beef and cheese and pickle by the look of it,' she said. 'Dig in.'

Adam picked up a chicken sandwich and took a bite. They chewed in silence.

'It's not the same without a beer,' Gerry said after a while. 'I'm going to nip back down to the road and see if that pub is open yet.'

Moira shook her head. 'It'll take ages. Why don't you just enjoy the food? We can have a drink later.'

'No, I'm a perfectionist,' Gerry said. 'If I don't wash it down with a beer I'll regret it for the rest of my life.' He stood up. 'I'll be back before you know it. I could do with a hand, though. Pam, would you be an angel?'

Pam looked doubtful. 'It's a bit of a trek.'

'Think how good it will taste when we get back,' said Gerry coaxingly.

She got to her feet, miming resignation. 'Oh, all right, then.'

Moira reached over and picked up the canvas bag. 'You'll need this, won't you?'

'Oh yes,' Gerry said. 'Good thinking. OK then, see you both in a tick. Leave some food for us.'

They watched them set off down the hillside.

'Do you think that was deliberate?' Moira asked.

Adam felt startled. 'What?'

'It doesn't matter.'

She lay back and folded her hands behind her head. The action drew her breasts into peaks. She was wearing slacks and Adam found himself staring at the slight swelling under the cloth where her legs joined. She seemed to feel his eyes on her, for she turned over onto her stomach with one deft movement like a seal, but now he was presented with her narrow hips and the line of her underwear denting her buttocks and he felt desire, hot and chemical.

He was trembling. He had free will. He could lean forward now and run his hand down the nubbled ridge of spine that he had brushed against at the dance. He imagined tracing his fingertips along the nerve endings, making her gasp and shiver, then moving down to caress the rise of her rump before pushing her gently onto her back, cupping her head and drawing her mouth to his, tasting the shocking warmth and wetness of her tongue.

She seemed to stiffen slightly, then relax, as if she was preparing herself for his touch. He could hear the seconds passing in loud, thumping beats. Then it was too late. She moved again, the same deft, instinctive action, and sat up.

'Let's walk about for a bit until the others come back,' she said.

They walked slowly, round and round the crown of the hill, and she talked. This time there was no need to prompt. She painted in her story in swift, economic strokes. Her grandfather had been a Glaswegian businessman, risen to riches after starting out as a bank clerk, by a combination of industry and two audacious gambles. He married, young, a schoolteacher, and they had one child, her mother, Jean.

Jean was brought up in a gloomy house on the Clyde. Her father collaborated in her escape by paying for her to pass a summer in London on the fringes of the Season. There she met her future husband who was home on leave from the trenches of northern France. He was older than her and grander. By the time he left they had an understanding. They married on his next leave and Moira was born just before the Armistice. Peacetime was hard on him. War had shored him up and money and comfort and leisure undermined him, revealing the fragility of his personality. He killed himself when Moira was four years old and her mother had taken her off abroad, first to Paris where they spent several years, then to Kenya where she passed most of her girlhood and adolescence.

She softened as she described their life in a suburb of Nairobi. They were rich but life was rackety, filled with drunken adventurers and melodramatic women, the seediness and destructiveness of it all masked by the sunshine and the overpowering vitality of the land around them.

In the summer of 1939, when the war became inevitable, they sailed back to Britain. They took a house in London. Then she met Gerry.

'It was last New Year's Eve,' she said. 'I was doing the rounds of the nightclubs with a group of . . . well, not friends exactly, but people I was going around with. It was after midnight and beginning to be a bit of a bore. Just as I was thinking about getting someone to take me home, I felt a tap on the shoulder and there was Gerry asking me to dance.' Her face softened.

'He wasn't the Gerry you know now. He was in uniform and he danced very well and looked the picture of the dashing soldier, but he seemed nervous and uneasy. He told me later that he was on his own and was just about to go when he saw me. He spent the last money in his pocket on buying us both a drink.' She smiled at the thought of it and hurried on.

'Well, we saw a little bit of each other after that. He took me to the movies – we went Dutch as Gerry was so hard up. After that he went off to France. We didn't get together again until after he got back from Dunkirk.'

Moira stopped speaking, as if she felt she had said enough for the time being and the rest would have to wait. She began asking Adam to identify features of the landscape that rolled out on all sides beneath them, but apart from the military installations and a few obvious landmarks, he could tell her little. 'We really need Pam here,' she said. 'She knows what everything is.'

'How come?'

'Her father and mother live round about here somewhere,' replied Moira vaguely.

In the stillness, voices carried. They heard Gerry and Pam several minutes before they emerged from the trees carrying the canvas bag, clanking with bottles, between them. They seemed very young and healthy and innocent, as if they had sprung from one of the railway posters advertising seaside destinations.

Gerry pulled out big brown flagons of cider and beer, which foamed out of the necks as he unscrewed the black stoppers.

'We'll have to drink from the bottles,' he said. 'Ladies first.' Moira took a cider bottle and, holding it with two hands, tilted it so that it poured into her mouth, gulping to keep up with the flow, then snatched it away, twisting to avoid being splashed by the froth.

'That's the girl,' Gerry said.

They ate and drank, then lay there feeling the early evening intensity of the heat, as if the sun were making a last effort before closing down for the day. The musky smell of wild thyme hung like dust in the air.

'Moira says you can point out all the local beauty spots,' said Adam to Pam. She feigned modesty and embarrassment, like a little girl being asked to do her party piece. Then, after a suitable amount of cajolery, she gave in, and made them stand up and led them again around the top of the hill, identifying churches and manor houses, naming the winding rivers and the stout stone bridges. She showed them where the grass was striped greener in a distant field and explained these were the traces of a Roman road that led all the way to London. She spoke as if what she was telling them was important, no longer eager to please. Even Gerry forgot to be facetious.

'It all looks very bland and chocolate-boxy at first glance,' she said, 'but the more you see of it the more you realise that it's full of old magic. Look over there.'

She pointed across to a neighbouring hill, which was unnaturally round and domed and crowned with a straggling line of beech trees. 'That's Hanger Hill. It's been a fort since prehistoric times. You can see why.

You could spot your enemies coming ten miles away. The Romans took it over when they invaded. Then the Saxons. They've found all sorts of amulets and idols up there. They say that if you run round it backwards you can summon up the devil.'

As she spoke, one of the last clouds remaining in the sky passed in front of the sinking sun, and for a moment the shadow fell across Hanger Hill, turning if from dusty green to a faded blue. Then the cloud was gone and it glowed innocently again in the light that bathed the rest of the countryside.

They all noticed, but no one said anything. Then Gerry spoke.

'The drink's all gone,' he said.

It came out strangely, not as a statement of fact but as if he were uttering a biblical metaphor signifying the pitiful impermanence of all that lives and breathes on the earth.

'It's not the end of the world,' Pam said gently.

'Oh, but it is.' Gerry shook his head. Moira moved towards him suddenly, with concern in her face.

Gerry got to his feet. 'It is, it is. Tommy will tell you that.'

Then he flung back his arms and declaimed:

> 'But, fill me with the old familiar Juice,
> Methinks I might recover by-and-bye!'

They laughed, out of relief, not amusement.

'Let's pick up the empties and find a pub,' said Moira.

★   ★   ★

It was Gerry's idea to go to the Knave of Hearts. 'Got to see a man about a dog,' he said mysteriously. There were several other cars lined up on the asphalt car park. They left the light of the dying sun and pushed through the swing doors and into the dim, red glow of the bar.

'Hallo, Janey,' said Gerry to the blonde woman behind the bar.

He raised a hand in salute to the bored pianist, who managed to wave back without disturbing the progress of the chords he was planting lazily on the keyboard.

'My shout,' Gerry said. 'I'll bring you the list.' He returned with a giant playing card. Moira ordered promptly, a gin fizz. Pam insisted on reading out the fanciful names of the various cocktails and conducted a debate with herself over which one she felt like having. While she did so, a well-dressed middle-aged man came in and slipped with predatory lightness into one of the railway-compartment-like booths that lay along one of the walls. He saw Gerry and raised his eyes in a barely noticeable signal of greeting.

When Pam had made up her mind, Gerry took the orders. Adam watched him at the bar laughing with the barmaid. Then he returned with the drinks.

'Cheers, everybody,' he said. 'You carry on. I've got a little business to conduct.'

He walked over to the booth and slid in alongside the well-dressed man. 'Well, that's the last we'll see of Gerry for a while,' Moira said, taking a sip of her drink.

'What on earth do you think they're talking about?' asked Pam.

'I've no idea, but if you find out, do let me know,' Moira said. 'Forewarned is forearmed.'

'What do you mean?' said Pam, laughing.

'It's just an expression. I don't know why I said it.'

The women seemed to have accepted, for the moment at least, the ambiguities of the situation. In Gerry's absence, though, the conversation was halting and awkward. They looked to Adam to amuse them.

'What's the worst thing to have happened to you since you came to England?' Pam asked. 'Apart from meeting us, I mean.'

'Fish paste, probably,' said Adam. They looked interested and attentive, waiting for the joke.

'When we got off the boat at Plymouth there was a stall at the quayside where some women in green overalls were waiting with tea and sandwiches. We'd never had English tea before. It was completely different to Polish tea, dark brown like wood and thick with milk and sugar.

'The sandwiches were filled with pink stuff. We had no idea what it was. No one would eat them. Then they told us it was fish paste. We were given them everywhere we went after that.'

There was a pause.

'You Poles are too finicky,' Pam said decisively. 'There's nothing wrong with fish paste. It's an aquired taste, like caviar.'

Moira gave a short, approving laugh.

Adam felt foolish. He prickled with resentment at Gerry for leaving him alone with them and exposing his inadequacy as an entertainer. He searched his mind vainly for something to say to retrieve the situation.

The door opened again and two men in army uniform with lieutenants' pips on their epaulettes came in and walked over to the bar.

'I know them from the hotel,' said Pam. 'Shall I ask them to come over and join us?'

'Please don't,' said Moira quickly. 'But don't let us stop you from going and saying hallo.'

Pam looked doubtful.

'Well, it looks as if the party's almost over anyway,' she said, and walked over to the officers.

Moira looked across at him and smiled. 'You're looking very sulky,' she said. Her hand darted out, and tugged at the scarf around his neck. He felt the colour rush into his face.

'Silly boy,' she said. Then her hand was back on her lap.

Adam noticed that Gerry was leaving the booth now, but instead of coming straight over to join them he went to where Pam stood at the bar with the two new arrivals. Even at that distance he could see that he was taking charge of the situation, placing his arm under her elbow and leading her back to where Adam and Moira sat.

'What are you doing letting her escape?' he said sternly to Adam.

Pam giggled.

'I'm sorry about that,' Gerry said, waving his hand in the direction of the now-empty booth. 'Just a bit of business that couldn't be put off. Now you have my undivided attention. But before we do anything, let's get some more drinks. I believe it's your turn, Tommy.'

When Adam got back he found a small package sitting on the table in front of his chair.

'What's this?' he asked.

'Go on, open it,' Gerry said.

He tore off the paper. Inside was a plush box, the sort that came from jewellers' shops. He opened the lid revealing a flat, streamlined cigarette lighter.

'It's a Ronson,' said Gerry. 'Same as mine, except mine's gold.'

Adam took it out and snapped it experimentally a few times.

'That's very kind of you,' he said.

'Turn it over,' Gerry commanded.

He did as he was told and carved in the silver metal in curlicued script were the words, 'To Tommy from Gerry, August 19, 1940'.

'Got a chap at the camp to engrave it,' Gerry said.

Adam tugged a cigarette from the box in front of him and ceremoniously inserted it between his lips. Then he snapped on the lighter and applied it with a flourish to the tip.

'I'll think of you every time I light up,' he said.

The women laughed, a gratifying sound.

The pianist was joined by a bass player and a guitarist; a few couples were moving around the dance floor. Presently the two soldiers at the bar came over and asked Pam and Moira to dance. The women looked across at Gerry, wordlessly seeking his permission.

'All right then,' he said indulgently.

When they were gone he sat back in his chair, legs stretched out in the same philosophical pose he had struck on the pub settle the previous night.

'It was really very generous of you,' Adam said.

'The lighter? Oh, it was nothing. Life's short. We've taken a shine to each other.' He waved a hand, mock theatrical. 'Who knows where the winds of war will blow us?'

He looked at Adam. 'How long do you think this show will go on?'

It was the question that everybody asked.

'I don't know. All I do know is that it can't last much longer. It's too exhausting for both sides. It's a matter of attrition. They send over their bombers and fighters. We go up and chop some of them down, and we get chopped down in the process. One day one side will run out of planes. Or courage. Then it will end.'

Adam had barely thought of the battle since setting off on the picnic. He had noticed how during long periods of fighting some kindly valve of the brain periodically opened, and an amnesiac balm trickled over his raw nerves, sealing out the fear and anxiety. Gerry's words brought the war back.

He watched him sitting there, leaning back, the long fingers of his right hand sweeping alternately glass and cigarette to his mouth, dark eyes burning under his glossy hair.

He was talking about his war now. He spoke with a low seriousness, all jocularity gone, like a business-man describing the emergence of a new and exciting market.

'I'm beginning to realise I'm in the wrong outfit,' he said. 'Us infantry types are pretty redundant at the moment and, the way I see it, there isn't going to be another European show for ages. It's too late for me to jump ship and try another service. The thing is to try and get in on the ground floor when they open up another front elsewhere.'

Adam's attention began to wander and Gerry, sensitive as ever to the mood of his audience, changed the subject.

'How are you getting on with Moira?' he asked solicitously.

'Very well. She's . . .' He couldn't think of a word that conveyed his confused feelings; nor, he realised, did he wish to reveal them even if he could establish their identity.

'She's what?' Gerry demanded.

'Special,' Adam said.

'Yes,' Gerry said carefully. 'That's a good word. And what about Pam?'

'She seems very nice. Clean, sort of.'

'Christ,' said Gerry. 'You must be able to do better than that. She's a peach. But, you know, I do see what you mean. Very much the English rose, the type that chaps like you and me like to pluck.' He smiled, one conspirator to another.

'In fact I think I'll have an opportunity to get to know her better pretty soon. I've got to go up to town in the next day or two. I thought I might take Pam along to keep me company. What do you think?'

Adam wanted the conversation to stop. The assumption of complicity made him uneasy. He glanced around the bar, bathed in the unearthly red glow of the concealed lighting, the ambiguous figures grouped in the shadows on the plush banquettes, the drawling laughter and the insolent tempo of the band. In that moment the Knave of Hearts seemed full of danger, more perilous than the sky. Suddenly he wanted to be back at Updyke with Bealing and Whitbread and old Ted Sobinksi, with a pint of beer from the keg in his hand, talking about tactics and joining in the ragging. He stood up and Gerry, as Adam knew he would, put a hand on his arm.

'You're not going. It's early days yet.'

'I said I'd be back. We've got a briefing.'

'What, at nine o'clock at night?' Gerry sounded scornful. Then he added more solicitously, 'Was it something I said?'

'No,' Adam said firmly, 'the fact is I'm whacked.'

'I'm not suprised,' said Gerry. 'Well, you run along and get a good night's sleep. And Tommy . . .' He fixed him with a look of disconcerting sincerity.

'Yes?'

'Take bloody good care of yourself, won't you?'

He walked towards the door. To his relief, Moira and Pam were still being steered around the small dance floor by their two admirers. Gerry could explain his departure. Adam looked back at him. He was sitting with his feet stretched out, gazing into space, seeing things that only Gerry could see.

10

They were scrambled early that morning, and climbed straight to 25,000 feet, with orders to circle the base and to wait for a big force of fighters and bombers that was forming up over northern France. It was very cold at that height, and inside his new wash-leather gloves Adam's fingers were numb on the spade grip of the control column.

The raiders soon appeared, a swarm of black flecks against the watery blue of the early morning sky. Buxton lead them head-on towards the pack. Adam followed in Whitbread's wake, a numb desperation slowly grasping him as the insect dots grew wings and bright lines of fire reached out from the swarm and drifted towards him. He was too close to Whitbread to fire back. He was sure Buxton was leading them into a huge aerial collision; then a few seconds before they closed the German formation disintegrated. He was aware of a great growling of engines and a shadow flashing past him, then the air was miraculously empty again.

He realised he was holding his breath, and he let it out in a rush, feeling his heart banging madly inside him. He put the Hurricane in a slow turn back towards the coast, while scanning the skies for the others.

By time he saw the Messerschmitt it was too late to break, but he tried anyway, pulling the Hurricane into a shuddering turn so tight that the gravity forces dragged the blood from his brain and he almost blacked out.

The German kept up with him comfortably. Adam heard the ripple of his machine guns as he put in an exploratory burst, and the sledgehammer thudding of cannon rounds.

Then something seemed to explode inside the cockpit and his face was drenched in petrol and the machine was on its back and he was hanging from his straps and plunging, vertically it seemed, towards the sea.

To his surprise he found himself thinking clearly. He could do nothing to stop the Messerschmitt, but he could do something to reduce the chances of being roasted alive, for the cockpit was awash with fuel and his uniform was steeped in the petrol and coolant and the tiniest spark would set him on fire.

Calmly, he flipped off the fuel pump and opened the throttle to empty the carburettor, and a few seconds later the engine cut out. He switched off the ignition. He was falling fast. The air-speed indicator was off the clock at 350 miles an hour. He pulled back as hard as he could on the control column, but the elevators were locked tight in the blast of rushing air and it took all his strength to wrench the stick back a few inches. But gradually the angle of his descent smoothed out and the needle on the speed dial fell back and at 15,000 feet he was almost level, gliding down in a shallow, powerless descent.

He looked around for somewhere to land. When he had been bounced he had been turning towards land, but now he could see he was on a course parallel with the coast. He started to turn to landwards and as he did so he saw the Messerschmitt again, overhauling him on his port side. He was only a few yards away. He could see the fish-scale gray-green camouflage on the oil-streaked fuselage and the Mickey Mouse mascot painted on the side, and he could see the pilot, the indifferent eyes above his sallow cheeks, surveying the Hurricane to assess the damage before peeling away for a second approach.

The next attack would kill him. He had to bale out, quickly. He had never made a parachute jump before. He turned the Hurricane onto its back but as he did so the Messerschmitt opened up again and the machine began shaking as if it was rocked by a giant hand, and there was another flash and spurt of flame and he blacked out. When he came to, the Hurricane was spinning out of control again. The altimeter showed he was at 10,000 feet. His head was split with pain and the left side of his face was numb. He put his hand up to touch it and felt a gash in his cheek, running from his ear to his mouth. His oxygen mask and microphone had been torn away from his helmet. There were bullet holes in the cockpit canopy and the inside of the Perspex was coated in a fine red spray; it was his blood, he realised, whipped up by the wind whistling through the holes in the cockpit.

He slid back the canopy and again rolled the machine onto its back, so he was hanging from his straps.

He felt upwards for the pin that locked the harness to the seat and tugged hard. It came away cleanly. But instead of tumbling clear he fell only a few inches, so that his head and shoulders were caught in the blast of the slipstream, which flung him back into the cockpit.

He was dangling upside down. He reached up to try and identify the strap that was holding him prisoner and found that one of his leg straps was hooked round the lever that raised and lowered his seat. He tore at it but it was held tight by the weight of his own body. His only chance was to regain control of the aircraft. He swung the Hurricane upright. He was down to three thousand feet. He glanced around and saw he was heading out to sea again. At this height there was no hope of gliding back to land.

The Messerschmitt seemed to have gone. The sea was coming up to meet him. The uniform flatness of the surface grew corrugated and ridged. He knew what would happen. At the first touch the water would tear at the machine, sending it tumbling and spinning, then closing over it with terrible swiftness. He tightened his straps to prepare for the impact.

He brought the Hurricane down as evenly and gently as he could manage. He was lucky. The belly of the machine glanced off the top of a wave so that the aircraft skipped in a long arc like a skimming stone before landing once again in a blinding flurry of spray. Immediately the nose of the Hurricane dipped down and the sea swamped into the cockpit. Adam's fingers fumbled with the catch to release his straps and felt them spring free, but now he found that the weight of the sea on the elevators had pressed the control column against his stomach, so he was wedged tight in his seat.

He could feel the tail of the plane tipping up, digging the nose deeper into the water. A wave loomed ahead and the sea slid over his head. He pushed at the stick with a desperate, focused frenzy. It was solid. A memory broke in of a childhood picture book and a knight tugging at a sword embedded in a rock. He had often imagined the nightmarish totality of the immobility; the contoured grip of the sword handle, the unyielding grip of the stone on the steel.

He braced his two hands on the control column's spade handle, summoning the leverage of every available muscle and tendon, channelling the power through his rigid forearms, but the stick was locked.

So this was how he would die, he thought, wedged in the bucket seat of a sinking Hurricane with a joystick jammed between his legs. It seemed inevitable and natural. He felt a profound calmness take hold of him and he stopped pushing. The water now seemed benign and caressing. The easiest thing would be simply to open his mouth and let it flood into his lungs. He closed his eyes feeling no fear or curiosity about what lay ahead, only a mild regret at not having experienced more of the life he was leaving. His hands closed around the stick, feeling the familiar curve of the safety catch and the dent of the firing button. Instinctively his thumb pressed down on it. There was a muffled eruption of noise and the cockpit jerked back. Suddenly the stick slid forward with glutinous ease. He braced his hands on the side of the cockpit and pushed

down and kicked out and found himself soaring upwards in a cloud of bubbles. His head broke through
the surface and he gulped in a lungful of air, but was
immediately pushed back under by a rising swell and
he felt the bitter salt in his throat and windpipe and
kicked desperately with his feet to hoist himself above
the wave to take another frantic draught of air. At the
same time he pulled on the toggle on his webbing and
the Mae West hissed and swelled around him, holding
him up in the water while he coughed and gasped,
filling himself with delicious air.

When he was breathing normally again he tipped his
head back and looked up at the placid sky. He had
never thought he would see it again. It was empty. For
a while he hung there, rocking gently, looking up at the
sun, listening to his own breathing, feeling the simple
wonder of living.

It did not last long. Slowly the exhilaration subsided
as he calculated the odds on being rescued. No one, as
far as he knew, had seen him go down. Each passing
swell bore him up and gave him a glimpse of the land, a
brown and green smudge on the horizon, only a few
miles distant, but too far away for any onlooker to be
able to see him and report his position accurately. He
knew that the longest he could hope to survive – even
in the late summer sea – was four hours before the
coldness of the water finally drained away his body's
warmth.

He conjured up fantasies to keep his spirits up. He
imagined himself arriving out of the blue in the mess
that evening, the surprise on the cheerful faces of

Whitbread and Bealing, the back-slapping and the jokes and the drinking. Each swell of the waves brought him back in sight of the coast to where Updyke lay, just behind the line of pebble and scrub. The sea raised and lowered him. He thought of Gerry and Moira and Pam with a yearning fondness, all the reservations of the previous night gone.

The cold was taking hold of him, clutching at his toes inside his fur-lined boots. He kicked his legs and felt blood creeping into his his feet, but within a few seconds of stopping the water resumed its grip and his feet were numb again. After a while, what life he felt was concentrated in his brain and in the cavity of his chest where his lungs were filling and emptying in ever shallower breaths.

Drowsiness rolled over him. Death was coming. When he closed his eyes he could see it. He was in a huge room, like a hangar. In the corner was a ball that seemed to be made out of the pale clay they used at school to make models and pots. It was rolling towards him, getting bigger and bigger, and something was impelling him towards it. He moved forward slowly, attracted and repulsed at the same time, and as he did it grew and grew until the ball was towering above him, almost filling the limitless emptiness of the room. He knew that with one more step it would roll over him and he would sink into its clammy bulk and be instantly absorbed and forgotten. For a long second he struggled to wrench his brain back into consciousness. Then with a cry of terror he was out of the room and back in the cold sea with the indifferent sky over his head and trembling as much with fear as with cold. He could hear himself whimpering. He noticed movement from out of the corner of his eye and he turned his head. A gull was hovering a few feet away, paddling its wings, ugly black legs trailing beneath it, watching him with its cold, primeval eyes. It was then that he began to pray.

II

He was sitting in front of a fire, wet and naked, drying off after his bath in a tin tub large enough to float in. His mother came in with a big towel and wrapped him in it and rubbed him roughly so the old cotton scratched his skin. The fire was in the kitchen, a big room with flagstones on the floor. Then he was in a cot in the corner of the kitchen. The adults cast big shadows as they moved past the flames.

Sometimes a doctor loomed overhead. He felt the cold press of an instrument on his chest, then heard the doctor whispering with his mother and father at the door. It seemed to be always night-time. He was very hot, sweating so much that the sheets they wound him in were soaking a few minutes after they touched his body. At other times he trembled with a cold so deep that neither the fire nor the blankets could drive it out of his bones.

Then he was waking up, cool and exhausted. His mother was leaning over him, kissing his cheeks and his forehead. She smelled sweet and milky. She told him he could have anything he wanted from the toyshop in the town. He wanted a miniature sword that had been hanging in the window. He sensed her joy at his recovery and decided to be bold. He remembered the big globe, slanted on a spindle and coloured with the countries of the world, that had always sat at the back of the shop, unsold because of its high price. He wanted that too. She smiled and kissed him again.

'He's awake now.' It was a woman's voice.

Adam opened his eyes. A young woman was leaning over him. Behind her stood a short, bristly man in a white coat. He stooped down to take a look at him and Adam smelled tobacco on his breath.

'You're a lucky man,' he said in a brisk voice. 'Do what she tells you and you'll be back flying in no time.' He retreated with the nurse to the door. Then she came back and began fussing around the bed, plumping pillows.

'Can you sit up?'

He tried but felt paralysed with weakness. He shook his head.

'Are you hungry?'

He shook his head again.

'It doesn't matter. You're going to eat something.'

She went away and came back with a steel bowl of soup. She put it down on the bedside table, then moved to the bed and placed a skinny arm under him and deftly hauled him upright.

'That's better.'

She spooned the soup into his mouth. His lips were trembling. It was a broth with pearl barley in it, the sort of thing he would eat at home. Every now and then as he took another sip she said 'Good boy', as if he was a child.

Finally he asked: 'What happened?' It came out as a croak.

She turned her thin face towards him. 'Some fishermen found you. They thought you were dead.'

He nodded and lay back. She rearranged the pillows.

'Do you want the light on?' He only just noticed that it was dusk outside.

'No thank you.' He was tired, drifting away again.

'Good. Well, you just get some sleep. If you want anything there's a bell at the side of the bed. There's always someone here.'

He was walking with his mother in the garden, the first time he had gone out of doors since the illness. His mother took his hand. In the other he held the toy sword from the shop. Summer had arrived in the time since he had fallen sick. He smelled the sweet wallflowers. They were planted in a row under the kitchen window, yellow and red and they moved in the breeze. His mother pointed at them and talked to him. He felt the hilt of the sword in his hand and he swung it quickly, twice, sending up a flurry of petals and leaves.

'Adam!'

His mother squealed and stooped to pick up the severed stalks. Behind him he heard a man laugh. He felt himself being scooped up and the sandpaper scrape of his father's cheek on his. His father swung him up and placed his open hand under his feet.

'Attention!'

Adam remembered the game. He stiffened his legs and his father hoisted him up on one hand, as if he were balancing a stick. He laughed and his father laughed too. He kept his arms tightly by his side as his father manoeuvred him through the air. He was dizzy but he knew he would not fall. His father was panting. His mother was standing by the flowerbed looking at them. She spoke some words. His father put him down and walked over to her. He put his arm on her shoulder and tried to kiss her but she twisted away. Back inside the house she put the flowers in a vase on the kitchen table.

The door of the room opened. He saw a woman's head appear behind it. She was wearing a nurse's cloak and two red bands crisscrossed her breast. She looked at him for a few moments but said nothing and the door closed again with a soft hiss.

It was his first day at school. His father put him high on a brown horse he kept in the stable next to the house and walked alongside holding the halter. His mother followed, pushing his baby sister in a pram. After that he had walked the mile to the school on his own. There were twenty other boys in the class. They learned reading and writing in the morning and arithmetic and history in the afternoon. The teacher was a bony priest called Father Jan. Behind his desk stood a red and white flag and a framed photograph of an old man with a moustache.

At midday they sat in a dark hall with high latticed windows and ate black bread with creamy cheese and spring onions and drank milk. Tall trees waved outside the windows and sometimes when the wind was blowing they scraped and tapped against the glass.

In the summer they played in the fields of ripening corn around the school. Usually they played at war, with the Poles on one side and the Germans or the Russians or the Ukrainians on the other. They took it in turns, one side hiding amongst the dense stalks, the other crawling through the corn to attack.

In the winter there was no light to play in. It was dark by four o'clock and they spent the last hour of school undergoing instruction. The priest led them across from the schoolhouse to the church. Inside it smelled of paraffin from the heaters, and wax and stale incense. He liked the smell and the way the candles flickered on the grimy paintings of bloodshed and martyrdom that hung along the walls, making them glow.

He hardly heard what the priest was saying. Father Jan talked loudly, in a monotone, using the same words over and over. He had cropped, reddish hair and his black cassock was shiny and too tight for his bony body, as if it belonged to one of the altar boys. When he knelt to pray the boys could see the holes in the soles of his shoes. Once, he had told his mother he hated the priest. She scolded him and told him it was a sin. For a while he had sat in the front pew in the church during instruction, smiling at Father Jan every time he caught his eye, but Father Jan did not seem to notice and after a day or two he had given up.

One day, in the middle of winter, when Adam was eight, Father Jan had announced that instead of instruction they were to hear a talk from a visiting priest who had just arrived from South America. The next day the boys had filed into the school hall. At the back of the hall a broad-shouldered man was bent over a steel box. A strong beam of light shone out of it, lighting up a white sheet stretched above the stage. He looked up and smiled at the boys as they filed in. Adam noticed he was tall and heavily built, more like one of the farmers they passed on the way to school than a priest.

Father Jan told them that his name was Father Stefan and he was a missionary priest and that they should listen to him very carefully. The big priest fiddled with the steel box and an image appeared on the sheet. It was of a tall, white church made of wood, surrounded by palm trees. In front stood a group of dark-skinned boys and girls and in the middle of them was Father Stefan.

More pictures followed, of forested mountain ranges with smoke clinging to the peaks, of desolate-looking villages soaking under tropical rainstorms, of small groups with closed, pious faces kneeling in shacks. As the images appeared and disappeared, Father Stefan talked. He had come from a Polish village just like this one but had left his brothers and sisters behind and had gone far away. The land he travelled to was in the hands of soldiers who hated the church and jailed and tortured those who sought to spread God's word. At the beginning he had lived like a fugitive, moving from town to town, disguised as a worker, saying whispered Masses in makeshift chapels in the slums and administering the sacraments. Once when he was baptising a group of children someone had burst in to say that the police were on their way. There was no time to lose.

Rather than send them off unbaptised, Father Stefan had picked up the bowl of holy water and showered it over the lot of them. He laughed and the boys laughed with him.

Another time the police had arrived in the middle of Mass. He had run through the back of the house and jumped over a fence and into an alleyway, only to see an army patrol coming towards him. It looked like the end. Then he noticed a pretty girl hanging out her washing. Without speaking he seized her and held her in a passionate embrace until the patrol had passed by.

Father Stefan embroidered his stories with impersonations of the strutting soldiers, making the boys laugh with delight and excitement. At the end he grew solemn. His work was thrilling but it was dangerous and there were few who were willing to do it. If any of the boys felt drawn to such a life they should talk to their parents; then if they were still interested they should come back to him as he was staying on for a little while.

When Adam got home he told his mother about the priest and she seemed pleased. That night he dreamed of hot, corrugated-iron shantytowns, palm trees and small brown children. He saw himself scrambling out of windows and over fences, knocking down pursuing soldiers and policemen. Most vividly of all, he imagined himself standing in an alleyway kissing a young woman while an army patrol went by.

The next morning he told his mother he wanted to be a priest. She seemed surprised but happy. He was told to tell Father Stefan that she would like him to come to the house that evening to talk the matter over. He did not tell the other boys when he went to school. At lunchtime he followed Father Jan as he left the classroom and announced he wanted to see Father Stefan. Father Jan seemed delighted. For the first time that he could remember he saw him smile. He squeezed his arm with his bony fingers and led him across the yard to a brick house with a muddy yard and a smoking chimney where the priests lived. Father Stefan was sitting in an armchair reading a newspaper. He heard the news without surprise, as if it was what he had expected. He said he would go with him to meet his parents that evening.

In the afternoon, Adam stayed behind when the other boys hurried out of church at the end of instruction. He sat and looked at the altar, only just visible through the gloom that hung there even on the brightest day. He dropped onto the hard wood kneeler and tried to pray, staring at the pale, skinny figure hanging from the crucifix, suspended in the shadows of the altar. Sadness welled inside him. He wanted to cry, but not for the figure on the cross. He wanted to cry for Father Jan.

As he knelt there he heard a soft bang behind him as the church door closed. When he looked round he saw that he was on his own. Even the old women who were always there, muttering and clicking their rosaries, had gone. He felt scared. He tried praying harder, but the more he stared into the gloom the more hostile and sinister were the shapes he saw lurking within it. He had to get out. Slowly, looking straight ahead, he got to his feet and slipped out of the pew and began backing down the aisle step by step. He knew that he had to keep his eyes fixed on the altar. He knew that, as soon as he looked away, the demons who were hiding behind it would jump out and come leaping after him. Step by step he moved back until he felt the cold stone of the back wall of the church. He reached out for the door, pushed it open and stumbled out backwards into the freezing darkness.

A hand gripped his arm, hard. He shrieked and spun round. He saw a pair of sharp blue eyes staring down at him from under a shaggy fur hat. The rest of the face was covered in a dark woollen scarf. He was about to scream again when he heard Father Jan's muffled, concerned voice, coming from behind the scarf. His fright subsided. They went over to the priests' house to collect Father Stefan. As they walked down the lane towards his home, the frozen mud crackled under their boots. Father Stefan was in high spirits. He talked about his own school days and the tricks he had played on his teachers. Father Stefan asked him several questions but he answered sullenly and after a while the priest stopped talking. Eventually the house came into view, over the frosted fields, the lights poking through the bare branches of the trees. It was square and solid with faded yellow walls and green shutters. They passed through the stone gates and up the short drive. Father Jan pulled tentatively on the bell.

His father opened the door. He was dressed for riding in a whipcord coat and breeches, his thick legs packed into shiny boots. His flat, wide, face glowed red under the dark blond fringe. He showed the priests into the drawing room, then walked away, his boots clicking on the stone floor. His mother was sitting in an armchair by the fire. She stood up when they came in and offered them wine or tea or vodka. She seemed nervous and anxious to please them. Father Stefan took some wine, Father Jan, tea.

Father Stefan started talking. He spoke fluently, often gesturing in Adam's direction. Occasionally Father Jan added something in support of what the big priest said. After a while, Father Stefan got up from his chair and walked towards Adam's mother with his hand held out.

Then the door opened and his father walked in. He held a glass of vodka. He looked around, taking in the scene. His mother sighed and looked away. His father began to talk. He was smiling but Adam could tell that his words were angry. Father Stefan smiled too. He held his hands up in a gesture of surrender, and made as if to walk towards his father. This made his father even angrier. He threw aside his vodka glass, which smashed on the floor, and advanced towards the priest who backed away. His mother was speaking rapidly and earnestly to his father, pleading with him to stop.

Then Adam screamed. They all looked towards him as if they had only just noticed he was there. He ran out of the room and through the front door and out into the frozen fields. He ran and ran, the cold air slashing his throat and his lungs until he could go no further and he stood there panting, feeling the snot freeze on his face.

12

When he woke he was lying, bound tight by starched cotton sheets, in an iron bed in a room that was bare and white and filled with sunshine. A thin woman was standing with her back to him, looking out of the window. He began to remember the crash and the hours in the water.

'Nurse,' he said. The woman turned round. It was the same girl as yesterday.

'Good morning,' she said. 'Although it is only just still morning. You've been asleep for nearly fifteen hours. We'll get you something to eat, but first we're going to give you a wash.'

The door closed behind her with a gentle, pneumatic hiss, and she returned a few minutes later with bowl of hot water, a flannel, a towel and a wash bag.

'I can do that,' he said.

'You haven't seen yourself.'

She searched in the wash bag and retrieved a small mirror which she held out to him. His forehead was covered in thick cream and he had a thin gash running diagonally across his right cheek, the edges of which were held in a puckered line by spider's legs of black thread.

'It's not as bad as it looks,' she said in a kindly voice. 'There was a bit of burning on the forehead, and the scar will soon fade.'

She hauled him upright, then lathered his chin and began delicately steering a razor over his face, taking care not to get too close to the edges of his wound.

'That's better.'

She held out the mirror and he examined himself. He looked ridiculous. They had chopped off his hair at the front so it now stood out in a bristly ridge. Below that was the clownish smear of the burn cream. Then came the crude Frankenstein stitching on his cheek.

He started to laugh.

'What's so funny?' asked the nurse.

'Me,' said Adam, and this time she laughed with him.

She packed up the wash things, and left him a toothbrush.

'You can brush your teeth yourself. I'll be back with some breakfast. Bacon and eggs all right?'

He nodded and smiled. 'What's your name?'

She was very thin with a worried face.

'Mary.'

'Thank you, Mary.'

When she came back with the tray she said: 'You've got some visitors. Do you want to see them now?'

Adam thought for a moment that it was Bealing and Whitbread or some of the other pilots from the base, but at this hour they were almost certainly flying or at thirty minutes' readiness at the base.

'All right then,' he replied. She went out to the corridor then held the door open. Gerry and Moira walked in. He was dressed in his smartest uniform and his Sam Browne gleamed like a chestnut. He stood in front of the bed, in a shaft of sunlight, which made his hair shine like the flanks of a racehorse, holding his swagger-stick and his cap in front of him, head cocked solicitously.

'Brother, what have they done to you?' He turned to the nurse. 'OK if I smoke?' he inquired.

'As long as the patient doesn't mind.'

Gerry came over and parked himself on the edge of the bed, pulled out a packet of cigarettes and lit one with the heavy gold lighter.

'What happened?'

Adam told the story as well as he could remember it. 'How did you hear about it?'

'One of your pals phoned the camp. Bealing, I think. He said they'd be coming over later. I had to come straight away because otherwise I wouldn't get the chance.'

'Has something come up?'

Gerry looked as if he was harbouring some satisfying secret. 'I'm not sure yet,' he said carefully. 'I won't know until I've been to London. That's why I'm all togged up. I've got to go up to town to see one or two people about transferring to some new outfit they're setting up.'

'What sort of thing?'

'Oh, I can't tell you that. But I must say it sounds as if it's right up my street.'

Moira had hung back from the bed, standing in shadow behind the bar of light that slanted across the room from the window. He could barely make out her face.

He glanced at his watch. 'Look, I'm going to have to fly. I've got a train to catch. I'll probably be gone a few days, so the celebration will have to wait.'

He turned to go and Moira moved forward out of the shadows.

'We've got something for you,' she said, and went over to the bed and stowed a small bag in the side locker. 'It's just some fruit and magazines.'

'And a bottle of whisky,' said Gerry laughing. 'Don't forget the most important thing. Come on, darling.' He went to the door and held it open for her. Then he winked and waved towards the bed and then the room was empty, leaving only the smell of cigarette smoke and a ghostly trace of Moira's scent.

Adam tried to concentrate on the food in front of him, but he who was almost always ravenous no longer felt hungry. He sipped at a cup of grey, watery coffee. As usual, after any encounter with Gerry and his entourage, he felt unsettled and confused. Moira had barely said a word to him. Gerry had been friendly enough but seemed more excited by his meetings in London than by what had happened to Adam.

The nurse came back.

'It's a wicked waste you not eating that,' she said, looking at the half-finished plate of bacon and congealing fried egg. 'You shouldn't have asked for it if you didn't want it.'

'Don't be too hard on me, Mary,' he said, mock wheedling.

'Who were they?' she said, jerking her head in the direction of the door.

'Just a couple of pals.'

'Is she his girl?'

'Yes,' said Adam. 'At least she's supposed to be.' He paused. 'What did you think?'

'Of her? Oh, she's not beautiful. But she's got something.'

'And him?'

'Fancies himself, I should say.'

Adam laughed. 'I suppose that about sums it up, I suppose,' he said.

When the nurse left he lay back on the bed, bored suddenly. He leaned over and opened the locker to retrieve the bag. Inside were some apples and plums, four or five back numbers of *Lilliput* magazine and a flat half-bottle of whisky. Somehow he had been hoping for something more – a note or a card from Moira. A thin cloak of self-pity settled over him. He had been told about it, the survivor's blues, which moved in stealthily to take up position under cover of the initial satisfaction at having come through and left you wondering whether there had been any point in missing the rendezvous with death.

Moira's air of elusiveness now seemed irritating and affected. She had behaved as if she were royalty, graciously turning up to offer comfort to some anonymous casualty of the war. No more Moira when I get out, he told himself.

The doctor, a short, middle-aged man with hair the colour of iron filings, whom he dimly remembered surfacing through the delirium of the day before, came in to give him a swift examination, running his strong fingers over Adam's bones, clicking and grunting to himself.

'You'll be fine,' he told him. 'You just need a few days to get your strength back.'

After he had gone, Adam picked up one of the magazines and began to leaf through it. It was a jaunty, pocket-sized publication full of short articles by famous names interspersed with photographs, cartoons and jokes. The facetiousness and self-righteousness of it annoyed him and he tossed it on the floor.

He looked out of the window. He could hear, a little way off, the drone of a motor tractor cutting the corn, and the sighing of the wind in an unseen tree. It would be autumn before long, then his first winter in Britain. What were they like? Seamless days of grey, he imagined, none of the epic cold of a Polish winter. He wondered whether he would ever see Poland again. He had listened to the calls for sacrifice from General Sikorski and Winston Churchill without taking in the future they were sketching out. He was fighting because his temperament and upbringing gave him no other choice. Now the boundless enormity of the effort was revealed, a war without end, amen.

He drifted off to sleep again. He could smell apples and dreamed that he was lying under some trees in an orchard. Then the apples were mingled with a lemony scent that did not belong in the orchard but which he recognised anyway.

He opened his eyes and Moira was standing at the end of the bed, outlined against the sunlight. She was wearing a thin blue cotton dress and a cardigan that made her look vulnerable and adolescent. She walked over to him and brushed her lips against his cheek, then she stood back to look at him. He held her look. Her eyes had none of their usual mocking sparkle. There was a softness in them that he had never seen before.

'Oh, Adam,' she said. She sounded resigned to something.

'You came back.'

'Of course I did. When I saw you lying there this morning I just wanted to take you in my arms and hug you, but I couldn't.'

'You can now.'

She sat, gingerly, on the side of the bed. He struggled upright and tried to fold his arms around her. She slid her hands behind his back. For a moment they held each other. He felt her heart thudding against his ribcage, fast and hard. He put his face to the dark down that dusted the back of her neck, smelling talcum powder and youth and cleanliness, and tasted the slightly salty tang of her skin. She shivered and pulled his head away and turned it towards her so she was holding it between her two hands and gazing straight into his eyes. She put her half-open mouth to his. He closed his eyes tight. He could hear his own heart pounding now, and the blood pulsing in his ears. It was she who was kissing him. He wanted to regain the initiative. He shifted slightly sidewards in an effort to move her properly onto the bed, but as he did so he heard the swish of the door opening. They sprang apart.

Moira looked round and laughed, that low, smoky chuckle. 'Oh, it's only you,' she said. 'You gave us a fright for a moment.'

For a heart-lurching second, Adam thought it was Gerry. Then he saw the nurse, standing holding a tray. She put it down on the bedside table.

'I'll knock next time,' she said coldly.

When she had gone, Moira took his hand. 'What do you think?' she said.

'About this?'

'What else?'

'A few minutes ago I was thinking how much I hated you.'

'Because of the way I behaved this morning?'

'Yes. But it's funny how quickly one can change one's mind.'

He pulled her to him and they kissed again, without the tension of the first time.

She smiled. 'That was nice.' For a while they said nothing, and she broke off a piece of bread from the roll on the plate and crumbled it between long, strong fingers.

'They're letting you out tomorrow,' she said.

'How do you know?'

'I was talking to one of the doctors. Then they're giving you a few days to recover and you'll be back in the air next week.' She sighed and put her hand to his cheek. 'I'm going to take care of you in the meantime.'

'What about Gerry?'

'Fuck Gerry.'

He looked shocked and she laughed.

'I'm sorry, that wasn't very ladylike, was it?'

She got up from the bed. 'Now I'm going to have to leave you,' she said briskly.

He reached out and they held hands for a few seconds until she slithered her fingers away. Then she walked to the door and waved once and the door closed behind her with a long, hydraulic sigh.

13

The afternoon was marked out in the hourly arrival of cups of tea, ferried by Mary who had acted cool and formal since the visit. He tried to read, but the magazines bored him and Moira made constant incursions into his thoughts.

At about five o'clock he heard loud voices in the corridor and Whitbread and Bealing walked in. They pulled bottles of beer from under their tunics and settled on either side of the bed, making the springs groan.

'Got anything to drink this out of?'

Adam pointed to the locker. 'There are glasses in there. You'll find some Scotch too.'

Whitbread opened the bottles and the beer foamed out.

'Cheers, everybody,' he said.

They took a first, reverential swallow, swiping the foam from their upper lips with the backs of their hands.

'So what's the gossip?'

'You are, old man,' Whitbread said. 'They're all agog at your incredible escape. Buxton seemed quite worried about you. His stiff upper lip was almost trembling. When he heard you were OK he threatened to come down here to see you, but we told him the shock would probably be fatal.'

Whitbread's hand shook as he lit a cigarette. He could see from their faces they were exhausted.

'Bad day?' Adam asked.

'Uh-huh.' Whitbread nodded. 'We stayed out of it this morning but Four-O-Three got hit pretty bad. Partridge. Remember him? Lanky, with a moustache. He's gone. And Phelps, the New Zealander.'

There was a pause before Whitbread said quietly: 'Oh, and Ted Sobinski's missing.'

Somehow he had known.

'What happened?' he asked heavily.

'It was yesterday,' Whitbread said. 'Just after you went in. We were scrambled to intercept some bombers and escorts. There were only of a handful of them. For once there were as many of us as there were of them. Ted latched on to a Messerschmitt and was giving it a good squirt. Then we were bounced by a huge swarm of One-O-Nines coming out of the sun. We had no idea they were there. Buxton yelled at us to break but Ted just ignored him. The last we saw of him there were two on his tail and he was trailing smoke. Buxton wasn't best pleased.'

'There's a fair chance he managed to bale out somewhere,' Bealing said lamely.

'No, Ted's dead,' Adam said. He remembered his spaniel eyes and the soft moustache and his stubby legs, too short for him to swing up onto the wing root and drop into the cockpit with the same cowboy ease as the other pilots did.

'Did they give him the Messerschmitt?' he asked at last. That would have to be his monument.

'The int. officer made a bit of a fuss,' said Bealing. 'You know what they're like. No one actually saw it hit the ground. But in the circumstances we managed to get it put down to poor old Ted.'

'That's something, I suppose,' Adam said. He looked around. 'Where's the Scotch? I feel like getting drunk.'

Whitbread bent down to get the whisky from the locker.

'The news about Miles is worse than we thought too,' he said conversationally. 'Apparently the burns were pretty bad.'

'It looks like the Hollywood career's gone for a burton,' Bealing said, holding out his tumbler for the whisky. He raised the glass for a toast.

'Cheers. Here's to those of us who are still left. And to surviving the next few days until the new posting.'

'Why, what's going on?' Adam felt alarm.

'We're due for a rotation,' Whitbread said. 'The buzz is they're going to replace us with a northern squadron some time soon and we're moving to somewhere less exciting. Buxton says he'll fight it like mad but the brass seem to think we're knackered and it's time for someone else to have a crack.'

'But the northern squadrons haven't any combat experience,' Adam said.

'Not as a unit maybe,' said Bealing, 'but there are plenty of pilots who flew in France scattered about.'

They drank in silence for a while, finishing Gerry's whisky. Bealing produced a hip flask and they continued with that. The room filled up with cigarette smoke. Mary opened the door, smiled indulgently and closed it again. Adam felt an urgent need to go to the lavatory and climbed out of bed. He planted his feet experimentally on the linoleum floor, but when he took his first steps his legs gave way underneath him and he toppled over. Whitbread and Bealing caught him and hauled him upright, each putting an arm beneath his and helping him out into the corridor to the lavatory. He propped his head against the cool tiles as he pissed, listening to the slurred chat coming from outside.

When he got out he tried walking unaided, taking trembling steps like a man of eighty. They helped him into bed. Whitbread distributed the remains of the contents of his hip flask and extended his glass in a toast.

'To Four-O-Four. And getting Adam back.' Adam looked at them both and felt his eyes dissolving and his chin begin to wobble. He looked around for something to hide his emotion, and had to seize the edge of the sheet and hold it to his face.

'Steady on, old boy,' Whitbread said gently. Then he turned to Bealing. 'The patient is tired,' he said. 'And we have to get to the White Horse before closing.' He lifted his glass in a heroic pose.

Adam laughed with them. They shook hands. Bealing opened the window before they went to let some air into the smoky room. Mary came in and cleared away the saucers overflowing with cigarette butts and the froth-stained glasses. The visit seemed to have excited her. She spoke about his visitors as if they were film actors or crooners who had unaccountably descended on the hospital.

When she had gone he lay there, breathing in the air that drifted in through the window, carrying the damp smells of the night, and listening to the calling of a bird in the darkness.

He fell into a jerky sleep crowded with figures from the past and the present. He saw his mother and his father and the young faces of his fellow cadets at Deblin. Then he dreamed he was flying in a fantastic machine that was little more than a seat mounted on a pair of wings and he was soaring and diving over a beautiful island and tossing garlands and bouquets down onto the streets below. But now the engine was faltering and a weight was dragging the aircraft downwards and nothing he could do with the controls could get it to climb again. Then he saw a hand clutching at the edge of the wing, a plump hand with coarse hair sprouting from the knuckles. Then Ted Sobinski hauled himself onto the wing, sending the plane plunging sideways, and turned his sad face towards him shouting, 'Take me with you, Adam! Take me with you!'

14

Moira turned up early, sweeping efficiently into the room, pushing an empty wheelchair.

'I won't need that,' he said.

He was already bathed and dressed.

'Is that all there is to it? Can I just go?'

'I think you have to sign something.'

They set off slowly down a corridor smelling of beeswax polish. A woman in the almoner's office gave him a form to fill in.

'You're a free man, now,' she said.

Adam hesitated. 'I'd like to say goodbye to the nurse. Mary. Is she around?'

'Of course not,' the woman said, a touch scornfully. 'She's home at her mother's, asleep. She was here until four this morning, you know.'

'Tell her I said thank you.'

They stepped out onto the hospital's gravel drive. Moira led him over to a bright red two-seater car, an MG like Miller-Morton's, that stood parked at the verge.

'Whose is that?'

'Mine, of course. Don't look so surprised.' She tugged at the starter motor, jammed into first gear and moved off in a spurt of gravel.

'Where are we going?' He felt disoriented.

'I thought you'd better report to the base first, then if they've got no objections we should have the rest of the day to ourselves.'

At Kingsmere the guard at the barrier waved them through and he directed her towards the squadron office.

'I'll wait here,' she said.

Inside it was quiet. Everyone was out at the dispersal areas. He went to find Ashford, a non-flying administration officer who had looked after him when he arrived. He found him in his cubbyhole of an office. His grave face, lined like a ventriloquist's dummy, lit up when he saw Adam.

'Dear boy. I'm so glad to see you back. We've missed you, you know.' He looked perplexed. 'But we weren't expecting you so soon. I'd arranged for a van to pick you up at eleven.'

'A friend gave me a lift.'

Ashford nodded. 'Well, you're a free man, at least for a little while.' It was the second time that morning he had heard the phrase. 'The MO got the doctor's report and says you're to take it easy for two or three days before you can go back on ops. Have you got plenty to keep you occupied? Otherwise . . .' Adam stopped him before he could offer whatever suggestion he had in mind.

'No, honestly,' he said. 'I've got a heap of things to keep me busy.'

'Well you enjoy yourself.'

When he got out Moira was looking in the rear-view mirror and applying her lipstick.

'Everything OK?'

'Perfect.'

They swung out of the gate and onto the road. She drove quickly but unostentatiously and her reserve somehow emphasised the growling power of the engine. He didn't feel like talking and lay back against the leather seat, feeling the wind streaming through his hair, gazing upwards at the banner of leaves and branches unfurling overhead. They climbed up towards the Downs. She seemed to know where she was going. The road got narrower and narrower until she pulled up next to a stile and switched off the engine. It was quiet except for the rush of the wind in the high branches, and the air smelled of leaf mould – pungent and fertile.

She took his hand and led him over the stile and up a stony path that ran under the trees. The wood thinned out until they found themselves on a bare hillside. The wind was quite strong now. His legs still felt heavy and weak and he was glad when they reached the top.

'Do you recognise where we are?'

He looked around the hilltop, crowned with a straggling row of beeches.

'I don't know. I've never been here before.'

'But you've seen it. The other day when we were up by the windmill. Pam pointed it out. It's Hanger Hill.'

'The old fort.'

'Yes, where the devil appears if you run round it backwards. When she started talking about it, I wished I could go there with you. Alone.'

He did not want to think about Pam or Gerry. Now he found himself asking: 'Where is Pam?'

'Where do you think?'

'In London?'

'Yes.'

'How do you know?'

'I rang the hotel. They said she'd taken a few days off. Unexpectedly.'

He was not sure whether he was pleased that she knew.

'That doesn't prove anything,' he said half-heartedly.

'Oh come on. It's a bit of a coincidence, don't you think? Anyway, let's not talk about that.'

She took him by the hand and led him up to the crest of the hill, where they stood for a while, looking out over the scattered villages and farmhouses and the squares of farmland shelving down to the sea. Here and there were signs of human life – a tiny car crawling along a road, a woman putting out the washing in a cottage garden – that emphasised the remoteness of the hilltop.

The wind was shaking the tattered beeches, pushing and pulling their ragged branches to and fro in a mad semaphore. He felt the dark antiquity of the place, as mysterious as a pharoah's tomb. He imagined men in skins gathered round winter fires, legionary sentries scanning the land for a long-awaited supply column. He felt beneath his heels the compost of bones and branches, leaves and shit. It did not seem strange to imagine the devil living there. He wanted to leave.

'Can we go?' he asked. 'This place is starting to give me the creeps.'

She seemed surprised. 'Don't you like the view? But I suppose you spend half your life looking down from great heights. Oh well, let's go and find somewhere to get lunch.'

Walking back down the hill, something made him stop. Far out over the Channel a dogfight was in progress. At this distance all he could see was the looping tracery of the vapour trails and the golden filigree of tracer bullet arcing through the sky.

He felt her shivering. 'It's rather beautiful, isn't it?' she said.

'I suppose so. From here, anyway.'

'Do you feel guilty, not being there with them?'

She had glimpsed something.

'The funny thing is that I do, in a way.'

'Well don't,' she said firmly.'You're with me now. It's time to forget for a little while.'

They found the car and drove along a road that wound through the Downs until they rounded a bend and came to a pub of brick and flint, perched un-expectedly on a tree-covered bank. She parked in the yard at the back and they climbed up some stone steps to the front door.

'Did Gerry show you this place?' Why had he asked that?

'Actually, no,' she said coolly. 'But would it have mattered if he had?'

She was drifting away from him, back into that dreamy aloofness that shaded into condescension.

'You sit down,' he told her. 'I'll get the food.' The pub had leaded windows that filtered the sunlight into warm, coppery discs. The landlord was welcoming when he saw the uniform. Adam noticed some small wooden shields bearing the crests of several of the local squadrons mounted on the wall. There was not much food to choose from. He ordered plates of ham and cheese and bread, with pickled onions and walnuts and a pint of bitter for himself. He had forgotten to ask Moira what she wanted to drink. With Gerry she drank cocktails. He got her a half of cider.

He carried the drinks over to the table and placed the glass in front of her. She took a sip without comment. She looked at him and he saw a mocking spark in her eyes.

'Mister Moody,' she said.

'What do you mean?' he said defensively.

'Don't look so gloomy.'

'I can't help it,' he said. 'It's the price you pay for a passionate nature.'

The chill lifted. She smiled and reached across the table and touched his hand, just as the landlord arrived with their plates. He fussed sycophantically, laying them out, paying elaborate courtesies to Moira who accepted them tolerantly.

She ate steadily, forking in ham and cheese.

He told himself he should be happy. Instead he felt exposed and insecure. What were they doing there together? What did she want? Try as he could to dispel it, the shade of Gerry was hovering.

'Can I ask you something?'

'Of course.'

'Tell me more about you and Gerry.'

'What do you want to know?'

'You never finished the story. What happened after the fateful meeting at the nightclub?'

She seemed happy to talk.

'He was really very sweet,' she said. 'He came round the following day to the house. Mummy took an instant shine to him, I could tell. But it didn't stop her warning me that he was a bad lot and I'd be a fool to get mixed up with him.' She took a gulp of cider.

'At first I was just amused by him. He made me laugh and he was different from the other boys. I couldn't tell whether he really liked me or not or whether he just saw me as a good catch. We have money, and Gerry could never hide his interest in that.'

'Hasn't Gerry got money of his own?' Adam asked.

'Not a bean. His people used to, once upon a time. They owned a brewery in Cork, which turned out to be rather too much of a good thing. The men of the family drank their way through the Cunningham fortune years ago. There was enough to send him to school in England to get proper manners. But when I met him he was poor – as poor as a Connaught man, as he used to say himself.'

'He doesn't act poor,' said Adam. He thought of the dull gold lighter and the crocodile wallet, always well stocked with crackling white five-pound notes.

She laughed. 'I suppose I'm to thank for that.' She noticed his look. 'No, he's not a kept man, or anything. I helped him in a little scheme of his, that's all.'

'What was that?'

'I'd feel disloyal telling you.'

'It's a bit late for that, isn't it?'

Her eyes flashed anger but her voice was hurt when she spoke.

'You don't have to be nasty. We can stop now if you want.'

Adam felt stupid and cruel.

'I'm sorry. I don't know why I said that. Please tell me the story, I want to hear it.'

She looked away from him and ignored him for a few minutes, not eating any more, dragging on her cigarette. Then she began talking in a matter-of-fact voice.

'I've got some rather nice jewels. My grandfather gave lots to my mother when he was making a lady of her and she passed some on to me. Gerry was particularly interested in a diamond necklace and was always asking me how much it was worth. The answer was, I didn't know, but that it was insured for two thousand pounds. When Gerry heard about the insurance he got very excited. But he didn't bring the subject up at once. He worked up to it, at the same time doing his damnedest to make sure that I was well and truly smitten with him.'

'And were you? 'Adam asked.

'I don't know,' she said. 'Probably I was. Anyway, shut up, you're spoiling the story. Eventually he suggested his scheme. It was rather basic, really. He'd made a few inquiries. He had some pretty shady friends in those days – still does in fact. The plan was that I would hand over the necklace to him and report it stolen, then sit back and wait for the insurance money. We'd split the proceeds fifty-fifty. Once the fuss had died down I could decide whether I wanted to hang on to them or discreetly wear them again.

'I thought it sounded like fun. I didn't need the money, but Gerry did, desperately. He faked a break-in at Mum's. The police and the insurance people seemed a bit suspicious. So did Mother. But in the end it all happened pretty much as Gerry said it would.'

'What did you do with the necklace?'

She gave a sardonic smile.

'Well, it didn't take long before Gerry started dropping hints that it would be a good thing to get rid of it – I'd be uneasy every time I wore it, that kind of thing. He said he knew some crook who would pay him a decent price, though of course much less than what it would be worth legally. He took it away and came back with five hundred pounds for me. I've no idea how much he kept for himself.' She looked at him mischievously. 'You look shocked.'

'I don't know,' he said, shaking his head. 'It just wasn't what I imagined.'

'Oh, Gerry's a bit of a rogue all right,' she said. 'But there is something very endearing and loveable about him all the same. Very human, I suppose, is what it is.'

'What are you doing with me then?' He said it gently, out of real curiosity.

'I'm not sure I love Gerry any more,' she said. She drained her cider. 'Shall we go?'

He followed her down the steps. She was beautiful. His eyes fed on the dense dark hair and the startling nakedness of the long back of her neck, the slight swing of her hips and the curve of her rump as she dipped into the low car seat.

She started the car. He didn't ask where they were going. They drove through the dusty, green hedge walls of the lanes, past the tawny fields of corn stubble and the big loaves of stacked hay, until they came to a main road where she followed the sign to Chichester. The sunshine glanced off the brick terraces and semis on the outskirts of the town, showing up the dust on the windows and the stains on the concrete. The centre was almost deserted. The car rumbled over the cobbles as they turned into the cathedral close.

'These are my digs,' she said, pulling up in front of a handsome, cream stucco building facing the front door of the cathedral.

'I'd better go up first,' she said. 'Wait a few minutes then follow me. I'm in room twelve on the second floor.' She walked along the pavement, dappled with shade from the churchyard elms, and pushed open a panelled door. There was a gilded carving of an anchor on the roof of the building, and painted on a stone tablet below it were the words *Golden Anchor Hotel*. He had heard about it in the mess, the sort of place that officers went to celebrate birthdays or gongs.

He wondered how long he should wait. He counted to two hundred, then got out of the car. He pushed open the door and stepped into a dark hallway that smelled of wine and stale food. There was a coloured print on the wall of ruddy-faced squires sitting in high-backed wooden chairs in front of a roaring fire with long clay pipes clamped in their mouths, holding up ruby-tinted bumpers.

The staircase was directly ahead, broad and the colour of strong tea, with a stripe of red carpet. He walked gingerly up the creaking steps, looking around him like a burglar to see if anyone was about, but the place was empty. Room 12 was facing the street. He knocked. There was silence. He knocked again and this time he heard water emptying out of a basin and Moira's voice telling him to come in.

15

Moira stood in the middle of the room with her arms by her side. She was wearing a silk camisole, the colour of ivory. Her bare legs seemed thin and vulnerable below it. He walked over and put his arms around her and felt her arms reach up and circle his back. She turned her head sideways, laying it against his shoulder, comradely and reassuring. Then she pulled his head down to her mouth and began kissing him slowly and fervently. He backed towards the bed, kicking off his shoes and tugging at his clothes and lay down on it bearing her with him, but she pulled away.

'The curtains,' she said.

With two swipes the room darkened, then she was back by the side of the bed. She bobbed a sort of curtsey and her hands went to her hips, pulling down her knickers and throwing them aside. He glimpsed the patch of dark between her legs. Then she stretched out on the bed next to him like a cat in the sun. He dabbed kisses on her cheeks, her eyes, her lips, and slowly trailed his fingers over the cool silk of the petticoat, tracing the curve of her small breasts, sliding his hand over her ribcage to her flat stomach. He let it linger there for a few moments, then moved on, feeling the rough hair and the swell of flesh beneath the silk.

She flinched slightly, then sighed. He tugged at the hem, sliding it up over her hips. She made a purring noise and opened her thighs. They made love, solemnly at first, savouring each other's touch and taste, sampling each pleasure with the seriousness of connoisseurs. The first time he moved inside her she was modest, almost submissive, shifting slightly beneath him, stroking his hair and his cheek and whispering his name into his ear as he gently advanced and retreated. But gradually her restraint dissolved and she embraced him more greedily until, finally, she pushed him over onto his back and climbed on top of him, steering him into her, throwing her head back, moving slowly back and forth, half-rotating her hips and clamping him inside her. No woman had taken charge of him in this way before. At first he was intrigued and delighted, but after a while the novelty of her hot pressure on him gave way to disquiet as he looked up at her rocking to and fro, eyes half closed, lost in her own pleasure, as if she had forgotten he was there. But then she must have felt his look, for she opened her eyes and leaned over him and he could see the damp strands of hair on her forehead and her blue-black eyes fixed on his with a look of complicity, and he felt the fusion of flesh and nerves as if they had become one person.

They lay back, slack and dreamy, and she stroked his forehead and kissed his eyelids and he ran his fingers between her breasts and placed his hand softly, like a shield between her legs.

They drifted off to sleep. When he woke up the curtains were shuffling in the breeze, opening and closing to let the afternoon sunlight spill into the room. He sat up, gently, so as not to disturb her. She was utterly still, lying on her side, scarcely breathing. Some modest impulse had made her pull on her petticoat. The strap had fallen away leaving her shoulder naked and vulnerable. He pressed his lips to it and she stirred and said something unintelligible. He slipped from the bed and padded to the window. Her knickers were lying on the floor, a girlish confection of white cotton and broderie anglaise.

He pulled back the curtain a little. Outside, the town dozed in the heat. An old woman pedalled slowly by, underneath the window, the rubber tyres of her bicycle rippling over the cobbles.

'What are you doing?'

He turned back to the room and she was lying on her back, stretching luxuriously, showing her sharp elbows and the white undersides of her thin brown arms. 'Come back to bed.'

He obeyed. She nuzzled his ear, nipping and licking. He scooped her to him and they made love once more. Afterwards he drifted off to sleep again. When he woke he reached out for her, but the sheet had been pulled back and there was only a shallow dent in the mattress where she had been. He sat up and looked around the dusky room, suddenly anxious. But then he heard the slap of bare feet in the corridor outside and the door pushed open and she was standing there in a dark blue dressing gown holding a wash bag, pushing her hair out of her face and behind her ears.

'I thought you'd run away,' he said.

She sprang on the bed beside him and covered his face with kisses.

'Never,' she said between each kiss. 'Never, never, never.'

Then she leaned back and looked at him, jolly and businesslike.

'Sex always makes me hungry,' she said. 'What I really feel like now is a slap-up meal.'

He rose and went to the washbasin in the corner. There was a small mirror above it. He looked at his reflection, at the sheen of cream on his forehead and the blanket-stitching puckering his face, and marvelled that this woman had taken him to her bed.

'I look horrible,' he muttered.

'Don't be so vain,' she said. 'You'll do fine. Just get a move on, I'm starving.'

She insisted on the same subterfuge when they made their exit. 'You slip out first and wait round the corner. Then meet me in the dining room in half an hour.'

He did as he was told. He heard voices and the clattering of plates coming from down a corridor, but no one saw him leaving. He decided to go for a drink. He found an old pub near the market cross, with the name of the brewer engraved in the glass in the window, ordered a pint of bitter and sat down on a high-backed settle in the corner. The barman disappeared and the room fell silent except for the heavy tick of a clock.

He took a sip of the nutty beer and lit a cigarette. Moira would be getting ready for dinner, sitting at the dressing table, running a brush through her thick, resisting hair, parcelling herself into her underwear, hooking her head through whatever dress she had chosen. Would she be thinking of him, as he was about her? There was no knowing. That was part of her attraction, the way her coolness, bordering on indifference, suddenly gave way to passion.

He finished his drink and walked slowly back to the hotel. She was waiting for him in the empty dining room and beckoned impatiently towards him when he came in. She looked around for witnesses and, seeing none, stood up and kissed him quickly, darting her tongue into his mouth.

'I missed you,' she said.

'I missed you too.'

'Good. Now let's order quickly.'

An elderly waiter had materialised at the end of the room, leaning against a wall with his hands behind his back. She called him over and he arrived with two heavy leather-bound menus.

She read hers through quickly and snapped it shut.

'I want the crab and prawn salad followed by the sole.'

He was too preoccupied with her to study the menu and he ordered the same.

'And to drink we'll have a bottle of Puligny-Montrachet. Please bring it now,' she ordered with the offhand briskness of the settler. He imagined her on sultry nights on some colonial verandah, surrounded by sunburned men sweltering inside dinner jackets, eating and drinking while impassive black boys in fezzes waited on them from the shadows.

'Did you like it in Africa?' he asked.

'I loved it, at least for a while. I was still only a little girl when I went there but everyone treated me like a grown-up. Mummy was having a whale of a time so I was left to my own devices a lot.'

'Is that where you lost your virginity?'

'Don't be cheeky. But it was, as a matter of fact.'

The waiter came back with the wine, which he poured first into Adam's glass. He looked at her and she nodded back to him. He lifted the glass and let the cold, grassy taste roll over his tongue. He nodded and the waiter filled the glasses.

'I had this in France,' he said, anxious to show his sophistication. 'Anyway, go on.'

'It was a bit of a calculation, really,' she said, enjoying telling the story. 'I was seventeen and had never been kissed. The nuns at the convent taught us that all boys were rotters – not that I ever met any. One day I decided it was time I grew up. I picked someone out that I'd seen at the club.

'He was a bit of a bounder, a white hunter – and a pilot come to think of it – who was between wives. He was always hanging about the bar of the club trying to pick up commissions to escort safaris up-country. I started chatting to him, listening to his stories of being charged by elephants and so forth, waiting for him to pounce. The trouble was, he was frightfully stupid. He didn't seem to get the message at all and kept going on about rhinos and wildebeest. In the end I had to spell it out for him.' She took a sip of wine.

'He was perfectly sweet and efficient. When it was over he got quite sentimental and started telling me how fond he was of me. He didn't take it well when I told him I didn't want to see him again. I felt rather bad afterwards.'

She looked at him. 'What about you?'

He thought back to an outing to Warsaw at the end of his first month at Deblin and a bored woman who counted the money before she would let him leave the room.

'A trip to a brothel with my fellow cadets,' he said.

She laughed. 'I see. A traditionalist. And after that?'

'A few encounters; nothing that you could call a love affair.'

'Ah . . . love.' She clucked and shook her head.

The waiter arrived and shuffled around them, laying down the plates of crab and prawn and triangles of thin brown bread and butter. For a while she ate quickly and silently, taking frequent little gulps of the wine.

She pushed away the plate and looked up at him. Her eyes were glinting with an enthusiasm he had never seen before. She seemed almost excited. It made him feel slightly nervous.

'Are you enjoying this as much as I am?'

'Of course.'

'No really, Adam. Really and truly. I've been happy before, of course. But not in the way I am now and not in the way I think I'm going to be in the days ahead. It's going to be lovely. I'm going to make it so lovely for you.'

Her face clouded over with the earnestness he had noticed the first time he met her. 'You will let me, won't you?'

He pretended to think.

'All right then,' he sighed.

They both laughed. He splashed more wine into her glass.

They spent the rest of the meal taking it in turns to tell stories about their short lives. They were too absorbed with each other to bother very much with the food. She ordered a second bottle of wine. When the meal ended, he called for the bill, but she stopped the move with a faint shake of her head.

'Don't worry about that. It'll go on my account.'

It was still early. They went for a walk. It was cool out. They wandered along the lanes of the old town, holding hands. A full moon was rising, filling the dark streets with a light so bright that it cast a shadow. The blackout and the moon had turned Chichester into an enchanted place. They walked over cobbles that gleamed like bars of soft silver, through flagged alleyways smelling of lavender, until they came back to the cathedral. They sat down on a tombstone under a yew tree. The cathedral spire soared above them, a huge stone spear aimed at the disc of light glowing overhead. High above them droned a single-engined plane, mournful and mysterious. He looked up into the blue-blackness, studded with nailheads of starlight, but could not see it. He imagined the pilot looking down in his immense solitude at the moon-bathed land, watching the light shimmering over the wave crests on the Channel.

Moira lay on her back on the mossy stone, gazing up through the canopy of branches. He pulled her gently to her feet and held her tightly, feeling the steady thud of her heart beneath her thin cardigan.

She jumped as the bell struck the hour, splitting the silence into reverberating slivers of sound. She prised herself gently from his embrace. 'It's time to go back now, darling,' she said.

16

They made no attempt to be secretive going into the hotel. They passed a man in the entrance hall whom Adam took to be the manager. He was carefully dressed in a dark functionary's suit and had sleek black hair smoothed against his narrow head. Moira wished him goodnight, with a note of challenge in her voice, but he gave no sign that anything was out of the ordinary. There was something about him that seemed familiar.

'That's Mr Barron, the manager,' she said as he glided away. 'I expect he sees a lot of odd things these days.'

In the room, Adam sat down in an armchair while she went over to her dressing table and covered her face with cold cream, then wiped it off with quick, efficient dabs.

They lay in the wide bed talking for an hour before they made love again. She was eager to make a timetable for the days ahead, mapping out every hour like a schoolgirl planning the holidays. He tried to restrain her enthusiasm.

'I've only got two more days at most,' he said. 'There's nothing really wrong with me. I'm lucky to get any time at all. Most of the boys who ditch are back flying the following day.'

'That's why every minute has to count.' She leaned over and kissed him earnestly.

When he woke up he smelt coffee. She was sitting at a table by one of the windows, reading a newspaper.

'You're up.'

'I have been for hours. I didn't want to wake you. You were sleeping like a baby.'

He pulled on a shirt and trousers and went over to her.

'I ordered breakfast up here. If you're going to be shameless you might as well go the whole hog. There's eggs and toast and marmalade.'

She had covered over his scrambled eggs with a plate to keep them warm. He sat down and she went back to reading the paper. The main story on the front page was dedicated to an account of the air battles of the previous day, written in propagandist prose. The article carried the Air Ministry figures for the number of German aircraft downed, which were gratifyingly high, while the defenders' losses were negligible. He wondered whether the readers actually believed them.

She finished reading and put down the paper. 'To-day we're going to do some sightseeing. Then if it stays nice we'll find somewhere to swim.'

By the time they set off in the car it was sultry and hot, with clouds banked up in the thin blue sky like piles of snowy towels. She drove along a main road for a while before turning down a side road that wound past a stretch of reedy water then up through wooded hills before dipping down into a bowl of farmland.

'What's this?' he asked.

'Wait and see.'

She parked outside a farmhouse, told him to wait and went up to the door, returning a few minutes later with some keys.

'Come on.'

She led him across a field towards a cluster of low brick buildings that he had taken for farm outhouses. There was a wooden door set in the side of the biggest. She pushed the big, blunt key into the lock and it turned easily, then leaned on the door, which opened with a metallic groan. Inside it was dim. Some windows had been let into the ceiling, so the shafts of light, filled with dancing specks of dust, streamed down vertically.

'Look at this,' she said.

She was standing in a patch of sunlight, pointing at the floor, which he now saw was covered with a densely patterned mosaic. The centrepiece was a rose design in worn reds, browns and blues, surrounded by lozenges filled with swastikas.

'This was a Roman villa, once upon a time. It was discovered at the beginning of last century when a farmer was ploughing the field.'

She beckoned him further into the building to where a series of stone troughs and channels were set into the floor. 'This was a bath where they'd sit for hours after a feast, or what have you. But this is my favourite thing.'

She took hold of his hand and led him to a spot where the light streamed down vertically, illuminating a mosaic of the head of a young man, with curly black hair and a long, sardonic face, crowned with a horseshoe of olive leaves.

'He looks so interesting, doesn't he? The first time I saw him I thought I wouldn't mind marrying him.'

'When was that?'

'What, that I came here? Oh, a few weeks ago. I read about it and I was driving nearby so I thought I'd pay a visit. I've been back a few times.' She caught his look. 'On my own,' she added firmly.

She paused. 'It's a magical place. I wanted to come here one day with someone special.'

She looked so earnest and girlish. It was hard to connect her to the sophisticate of the previous night, blithely retailing the details of the loss of her virginity.

They walked out. The air was heavy with humidity and the atmosphere felt charged with electricity.

'This heat is ghastly,' she said. 'Let's find somewhere to swim.'

They descended from the downland, and when they reached the coast road took a turning that looked as if it led to the sea. The grass gave way to sand and they arrived behind a row of dunes. They parked and climbed up them, filling their shoes with sand, but when they got to the top they found they were cut off from the beach on the other side by coils of barbed wire.

'Let's follow it along,' she said. 'There's bound to be a gap somewhere.' They walked for a quarter of a mile before they found a breach in the wire, apparently left as an access point for maintenance of the beach defences.

'I hope it isn't mined,' he said.

She had brought a basket from the car, and took from it a large towel, which she spread on the gritty sand. She pulled her dress over her head then deftly removed her underwear and started off running towards the waves that were breaking feebly against the shore some hundred yards away. He undressed quickly and followed her more slowly.

As he arrived she scooped up water and flung it at him, laughing breathlessly. He ran towards her, stumbling through the shallows, until his foot hit a sharp rock half buried in the sand. The pain made him gasp. He hopped for a few steps then tumbled sideways into the water. He sat upright clutching his foot. She stopped laughing and came towards him, her face tight with concern. He could taste salt and for a moment he was back in the Channel, waiting for death.

'Are you all right?' She knelt in the waves beside him. His toes were grazed and were bleeding slightly. She held his foot between her knees to examine it, then she lowered her head and licked the wound. Her tongue felt hot against his skin. He pulled her up to him and they lay back in the eddying water, embracing, feeling the waves tugging and pushing them. Then she got up and ran away from him, before diving forwards, disappearing for a second to reappear with her hair sleek as an otter's against her head, carving through the water with strong, overhand strokes.

Adam followed her out, gingerly feeling his way over the stones, until it was deep enough to swim, then pushed himself cautiously forward. She swam towards him and clamped her legs around his waist so that he felt the strength of her thighs and he had to kick wildly to keep both their heads out of the water.

The water seemed to have intoxicated her. Her eyes were shining and she was breathless from the exertion and her giggles.

'I'll race you back to the shore.'

'What's the point, you're bound to win.'

She set off and he followed her, but she was already running up the beach by the time he was starting to wade ashore. When he reached her she was on her back, eyes closed, letting the sun warm her. The triangle of springy black hair looked shocking against the whiteness of her stomach. He lay down next to her, but felt restless and turned on his stomach to look around him. Behind them the beach gave way to scrub and stunted bushes. Adam looked idly at them, wondering how crowded the beach would have been at this time of year in peacetime. There was some movement in the bushes. A branch twitched. It could not be the wind, for even by the sea the air was stagnant and heavy. Perhaps it was a bird. Then he saw the glint of glass and metal catching the sun. He jumped up, full of anger and indignation, picked up a flintstone and hurled it at the shrub. A small, bespectacled figure in khaki burst from the undergrowth and scuttled away.

Adam ran towards him shouting, then he remembered his nakedness and stopped. Moira was sitting upright, looking at him in bewilderment. He realised how ridiculous he must look.

'What *is* going on?' she said.

'Some dirty bastard was spying on us from those bushes.'

She giggled. 'Oh let him,' she said. 'He's not doing us any harm, is he?'

His anger collapsed.

'I suppose not. Anyway, he's gone now.'

She pulled him down next to her and stroked his hair. 'You shouldn't get so worked up. You're not the jealous type, are you?'

He had never had to consider the question before.

'I don't know,' he said lamely.

He felt uncomfortable and pulled on his pants and trousers. She continued to lie there, unperturbed, looking even more naked now that he was dressed.

'Do you want to go?'

'Yes.'

'You old prude. All right then.'

She scooped up her things and hurried into them. Then, after towelling her hair briskly, she took him by the hand and led him back to the car, humming as she went.

She stowed the bag in the narrow space behind the seats. 'What shall we do now?' she said.

'You're in charge.'

'You really don't mind if I choose?'

'No.'

'All right then. I vote that we go up to town.'

'To London?'

'Yes, silly. We can get there in under two hours. Who knows when we'll have a chance to go there together again.'

The idea suddenly seemed inevitable. They stopped first at Updyke to pick up some clean clothes, then at the Golden Anchor, and soon they were on their way.

The countryside was bleached and brown, sated by the summer's sunshine. As they drove over the Downs, a breeze got up, lifting the branches of the birches that lined the road, revealing the white underside of their leaves like the flash of a dancer's petticoat.

Closer to town the traffic thickened. For a while they were stuck behind a line of army lorries, filled with young soldiers in coarse khaki, silently smoking and looking down at the pair of them with sullen, envious eyes.

They drove for miles down long dusty thoroughfares, past rows of identical brick houses and parades of shops and dusty patches of grass and stunted trees, until they came to a bridge and crossed the muddy river.

On the other side, the dreary terraces resumed. Then the streets broadened out and the buildings grew bigger and statues and monuments began to appear which Moira identified for him.

'Where do you want to stay?' she asked.

'I've no idea.' Adam's brief time in London had been spent at a gloomy, stucco-fronted boarding house in a treeless South Kensington street frequented by Polish exiles.

'Let's stay at the Pelham; it's cosier than the big ones.'

The hotel was a tall, redbrick town house, not far from Hyde Park. They were greeted deferentially by the woman at the reception desk, who took them to a large room on the first floor with a tiled and carpeted bathroom. Adam had never seen such luxury.

'Can I have a bath now?' he asked.

'Of course you can, darling.' It was the second time she had used the word.

He turned on the taps and steaming water gushed from their broad mouths, filling the huge bath in a few minutes. He climbed in and lay back in the water. The door opened and she came in and climbed into the bath opposite him.

Afterwards, she dressed carefully. She put on a dress of deep turquoise silk, then sat at the dressing table for half an hour applying make-up – more than he had ever seen her use before.

They started off in a bar in Jermyn Street where they drank cloying Brandy Alexanders. He suggested a play that he had heard the boys in the mess talking about, but she was hungry, so they moved on to an Italian restaurant she knew in Soho.

The streets and the bars were full of soldiers and sailors and airmen, and the swinging gas masks lent a martial air to the civilians. There was an atmosphere of suppressed excitement, as if a great adventure was about to begin. Moira seemed to share in it. 'Isn't this fun?' she said as they stood having a drink after dinner in the middle of the jostling crowd at the bar of the Savoy. Adam supposed she was talking about the outing, but she might as well have been talking about the war in general.

Moira seemed at home in the Savoy. The pianist in the corner nodded and smiled to her as they struggled through the press of uniforms on the way to the bar, and several young officers called over to her, but she just waved or blew them a kiss and ignored their invitations to come and join them. He caught a glimpse of glossy brown hair and broad khaki shoulders and for an icy moment he thought it was Gerry, but the soldier turned and he saw that it was not him, nothing like him. It was, he thought, just the sort of place where you might find Gerry. He was relieved when she complained of the crush and suggested that they leave.

They walked down the Strand and across Trafalgar Square, then along the Mall until they reached St James's Park. She was silent and absorbed, humming to herself, swinging their linked hands as they strolled, like a little girl.

'Did you have fun?'

'Yes. Lots.'

'Me too. I used to go out to places like that every night. I can't imagine how I did it now.'

They sat down by the lake. It was cool by the water and she shivered and he drew her to him.

'Kiss me, Adam.'

He kissed her slowly and deeply, feeling an urgency coming from her that almost amounted to desperation. She stopped suddenly and turned his head towards her. Even in the weak moonlight he could see the glitter of her eyes.

'Do you like me?'

'Of course I do.' He paused. 'And you? Do you like me? Really?'

In the thicket of reeds in the middle of the pond an unseen bird made a low, primeval squawk.

'I don't like you, Adam,' she said. 'I love you.'

He could think of nothing to say. She looked at him earnestly.

'Is that all right?'

He hugged her thin shoulders as he absorbed the shock of what she had just said. He felt a strange lack of elation. It had all been so fast and so easy. Could she really mean it? It had not taken her long to forget Gerry. How long would it be before she abandoned him?

Her face was pressed to his shoulder. Her breath felt hot against his arm as she lay against him, waiting for him to speak.

This was what he had wanted. Why was he not exultant? He remembered his blackmailing sulk of the day before and felt ashamed. She had not taken this thing as lightly as he had.

'Say something.' Her voice was low and expectant.

'You've taken me by surprise.'

'I've taken myself by surprise. I sort of knew it when I saw you in your hospital bed but I didn't want to admit it. Not until now.'

Her confession had disarmed her and now she sat there in her terrifying vulnerability. It was compassion he felt as he put his arms around her again.

'I'm glad you said what you said.' It sounded lame, inadequate. But it was all he could think of.

They listened for a while to the night noises of the park, the occasional cry of a bird and the rustle of the wind on the water. Then she tugged him to his feet and led him back through the darkened streets.

17

During the night he was woken up by the sound of a car crashing, just outside the window, as someone lost their bearings in the blackout. He could not get back to sleep. For a while he lay there, listening to the steady breathing beside him.

He propped himself on one arm and looked down at her. She looked so defenceless stretched out there, breathing softly through her half-open mouth. This thing was his, if he wanted it. At that moment, the doubts he had felt dissolved and he felt a glow of love. He bent down to press his lips to her cheek and she stirred and gave a murmur of alarm. 'Don't worry, sweetheart,' he said. 'It's only me. Go to sleep.' He lay back. In the distance, anti-aircraft guns thudded faintly.

Light was seeping through the gaps in the curtains by the time he finally went to sleep. He woke up feeling exhausted. She was already up, taking a bath.

'It's your turn to choose what we do today,' she called through the open door.

They spent the morning shopping. The way she was paying for everything embarrassed him. He was determined to buy her something from one of the expensive shops near the hotel. She protested at first when he told her to choose a present, but then submitted, sensing the needs of his pride. She picked out a silver watch, which was plain and pretty and one of the cheaper things in the shop. She hugged and kissed him in front of the assistant as if it had been the most expensive.

At noon she steered him into a bar in Jermyn Street. As they stood tasting the appley champagne, the sirens sounded. They followed the other customers out and down the street to a shelter in a cellar below a Victorian office block. It soon filled up with secretaries and middle-aged and elderly clerks and businessmen, who pulled on their gas masks and sat on the floor with their backs to the wall. Nobody spoke. It got hotter and stuffier. Adam was about to suggest leaving when they heard the rumble of descending bombs, some way away. Then the siren sounded the all clear and they dusted themselves down and emerged again.

The air raid had subdued her. He suggested they go to a matinee but she shook her head.

'No. Back to the hotel. If you don't mind.'

They spent the afternoon making love. She seemed melancholy. Once he looked down at her as she lay resting, the single strand of pearls around her long throat emphasising her nakedness, and thought he saw tears in her eyes.

Later she cheered up.

'I've got a suggestion for this evening,' she said as she sat at the dressing table smoking a cigarette and brushing her thick hair. 'But only say yes if you really want to do it.'

'Tell me.'

'Let's go and see Mum.'

'She's here?' That was unexpected.

'Yes, why shouldn't she be?'

'I don't know. I thought she might have gone back to Scotland or somewhere. Somewhere safe.'

'Mum likes a bit of adventure.'

They went for a drink beforehand.

'Who are you going to tell her I am?' he asked.

'I don't know. Someone I picked up in a pub. Don't worry, though, she's very broad-minded.'

She was her clever, metropolitan self again and he didn't like it.

She saw his frown.

'Gloomy old thing.' She kissed him on his sore forehead and turned serious.

'I suppose you might think it's a bit odd, me taking you to meet her. I just have a feeling that we can't put things off. I'm not suggesting anything drastic. Well, not right now, anyway. But there is a war on. Those bombs today. Here in London. We can't take anything for granted. We haven't got the luxury of hanging about.'

Her mother had moved to a modern block of flats behind Park Lane. They took the lift to the sixth floor and a maid let them in. Moira's mother was standing in the window with a cigarette in one hand, pointing dramatically in what at first seemed a theatrical pose. She seemed ridiculously young, scarcely older than Moira.

'Look,' she said. Across the park, the floodlights had been switched on and were raking the sky, illuminating the grey clouds stacked up overhead.

'Is this how it's going to be from now on?' she asked after they had been introduced. 'I imagine the excitement wears off after a bit.'

She had her daughter's mischievous laugh. He was pleased to see the affection they showed for each other, fussing over each other's clothes and jewellery, swapping gossip about family and friends, more like sisters than mother and daughter.

The sat down to eat and the maid wheeled in a trolley. Beneath the silver hood sat insipid fish and steamed vegetables, part of the régime, Adam supposed, that kept the hostess so young-looking. She talked generally – about the war, the situation in London, occasionally asking Adam a gentle question about his history and his life in the RAF, listening to his replies with quiet attention, adding an occasional shrewd observation. She asked him almost nothing about his personal life, yet he got the impression that he was being examined in some unobtrusive, almost undetectable way. As the evening wore on, what had been merely good manners gave way to genuine warmth. When she rose to go to bed at eleven, pleading tiredness, he felt he had passed some test.

She kissed Moira and held out her hand to Adam.

'Goodbye. Take care of her and yourself. We shall see each other again.' It was spoken in the same tone of voice as her daughter had once used towards him, as if it were a simple statement of fact.

They stayed on for brandy and coffee. 'You see, it wasn't too bad,' Moira said as the maid was clearing away the plates. 'Do you think I look like her?'

'Very much. But you act like her, too, or she acts like you, I don't know which.'

Sipping his coffee, looking round the room and calling the maid by her first name, he felt a pleasurable sense of belonging. He had been lucky. He looked across at Moira who looked unwaveringly back at him and smiled, a smile that seemed to set the seal on an unspoken arrangement. She ground out her cigarette and glanced at her new watch. 'Better get going,' she said.

On the way out he noticed a silver-framed photograph of Moira sitting on a sideboard. It had been taken, he guessed, about three years earlier. It was a bad likeness, softly focused and tilted at an angle to make her look like an actress in a film magazine.

'Do you like it?' she asked. He was on the point of saying that he didn't, but stopped himself, wanting to preserve the harmony of the moment.

'Yes,' he said. She picked up the frame and prised off the back and handed the portrait to him. 'Here,' she said. 'Mum won't mind.'

They slept in each other's arms. He woke up feeling happy and refreshed. He went downstairs before she woke, called the base and spoke to Ashford.

'Buxton wants to see you this afternoon,' he said. 'And there's a message passed on from Updyke. A Captain Cunningham called. He says he wants to see you this evening if you're free. Seven o'clock. At the Knave of Hearts.' Adam had almost forgotten about Gerry. He would have to tell him, of course, the sooner the better. There was no way of knowing how he would take it. He might accept the news with a shrug of his gambler's shoulders. Or he might flare up, standing on his warrior's honour. Adam would worry about that later.

They spent the morning lazily, eating breakfast in the room, going back to bed afterwards. She insisted on paying the hotel bill. After a lunch of steak and onions in a restaurant next to the hotel they set off.

On the journey back, people seemed to notice their happiness. A policeman directing the traffic around a broken gas main smiled and winked at Adam as they drove past. When they stopped at a red light beside a suburban underground station, an old woman selling flowers at the entrance noticed them and easily cajoled him into buying some roses.

As Moira drove he fixed his eyes on her, drinking in her looks and movements. He loved the straightness of her nose and the down on her ear lobe and the soft right angle of her jaw. He loved her efficient driving, changing gear and lighting a cigarette at the same time.

'Stop staring. You're making me feel uncomfortable.'

'I can't help it.'

'If I give you a kiss will you stop?'

'I'll think about it.'

She swerved suddenly off the road and onto a grassy verge and before the car had finished bumping over the rutted ground she had clamped her mouth on his.

When they had finished she said solemnly, 'Kissing's so much more intimate than making love, don't you think?'

'How do you mean?'

'Everything important in life goes into or comes out of your mouth. You need a mouth to eat with, otherwise you'd die. And to breathe with. And to talk with. If you didn't have a mouth you wouldn't be able to say "I love you." '

She fixed him with her candid, slaty eyes.

Why could he not say it? He searched his mind for some fervent phrase that would convince her of his feelings but which lacked the ringing absoluteness of those three, enormous words.

He took her look and held it but he felt she was gazing beyond his eyes.

'What's the matter?'

'I don't know. It's a big thing to say.'

'Yes, but easy if it's true.'

The ringing silence persisted. He took her head between his hands and said fiercely. 'You know I adore you, don't you? You know I would do anything for you?'

'That's not quite the same thing.' She smiled at him. He looked for a glint of the old mockery but he could see none there. She revved the engine and pulled back onto the road.

They drove the rest of the way hardly speaking. Just before Kingsmere she said in a neutral voice, 'I'll drop you off at the base. I'm going back to Chichester.'

She pulled up at the gates and he leaned over to kiss her. 'What about later?' he asked.

'Telephone me.'

'Can we have dinner?'

'If you wish.'

She gave him a wave and pulled away. He watched the narrow car as it dwindled down the lane, and the back of her head and her dark hair flicking in the wind, and heard the note of the engine, rising abruptly with each change of gear, getting fainter and fainter until the silence of the afternoon countryside washed over it and it was gone.

The sight of the utilitarian buildings of the base and the drabness of the uniformed men and women marching back and forth filled him with unease. He had barely thought of the squadron or what would happen to him when he got back. Buxton was in his office, pipe jutting from his yellow teeth, laboriously working on a pile of papers when Adam was shown in.

Eventually, after a minute or so, he removed the pipe and made a show of switching his attention to the next matter in hand.

'Recovered all right?' he asked gruffly. 'Any aches or pains?'

'None, thanks, sir.'

'Good.'

Buxton stood up and moved to the window and stared through the grimy square of glass.

'Normally you might have wangled another day's leave. But the fact is that things are moving pretty fast. We're moving on – the squadron that is. We're heading up north for a couple of months to some cushy posting. Then if I have anything to do with it we'll be back in the front line somewhere, here or overseas.' He looked over at Adam.

'Amid all this organisation they've decided to do some tidying up. All Allied pilots farmed out to RAF squadrons are to be transferred to their own units. I'm sorry, Tomaszewski, but that means that when we move on you won't be coming with us.' He paused. 'How does that strike you?'

His mind was blank as he tried to absorb the news. Bealing and Whitbread had told him the rumours but he had barely taken them in. He thought of Moira and the dying note of the car.

'I don't really know, sir,' he said eventually. 'I haven't been here long, but it already feels like home.'

'Yes, it's a pity that. We've liked having you here. But you can't really argue with higher authority, especially not in wartime.'

'What happens now then, sir?'

Buxton sifted through some of the papers on his desk and extracted a message.

'Here's the signal. It says that you're to report to Polish Air Force Squadron Three-O-Three at Northolt when we move on.'

'And when is that, sir?'

'Tomorrow.'

'Tomorrow?' he repeated stupidly.

'Yes, tomorrow,' Buxton said impatiently. 'You'd better get yourself over to Updyke and prepare for your departure.'

Adam walked numbly out into the afternoon sunlight. In a few minutes everything had changed. He had to speak to Moira. He went to the gate where a decrepit van was waiting at the gates, one of the transports used to ferry the officers back and forth from Updyke to the base. He got in and ordered the driver to take him to Updyke.

'I can't do that, sir,' he said. 'Our orders are that there have to be at least three passengers, on account of the fuel shortage.'

'Just drive the fucking car.'

Grudgingly, the driver started up the motor and drove with deliberate sedateness the few miles to the house. The main telephone was in the hall. Adam needed somewhere private. He shouted for an orderly who directed him to a little room, some kind of study, in a quiet corner of the house. He called the operator and asked to be put through to the Golden Anchor.

'Do you know the number, sir?' It was a middle-aged woman's voice, polite and unhelpful.

'No.'

'Well I suggest you look it up in the directory and give me a call back.' Before he could protest the line went dead. He searched round the room until he discovered a thin volume covered with estate agents' advertisements sitting on a chair. He flipped through the pages then lifted the receiver.

'Chichester 123.'

'*Please.*'

He paused.

'Please,' he said, humbly.

There was a series of clicks and whirrs until finally a ringing tone croaked in the earpiece. It sounded for a long minute until a man's voice, answered.

'May I speak to Miss Fleming?'

'I'm not sure whether she's available. I'll just go—'

'Look,' he said impatiently. 'It's an emergency. Just go and tell her Adam is on the phone.'

There was a silence and the sound of retreating feet. Then, to his relief, her voice came on the line.

She sounded concerned.

'What's going on? He said it was urgent.'

'It is. Well, to me anyway. I'm being posted away.'

'Oh no.'

'It's not far. Somewhere near London in fact.' He paused. 'But all the same, it gave me a bit of a shock and started me thinking about things . . .'

'Yes.'

'What I wanted to tell you was that I do love you and I want to be with you.'

'I'm glad you said that . . . Isn't that what you told me when I said the same thing?' She sounded cool.

'It's not a joke.'

'You don't have to tell me that, Adam.'

'Do you still mean what you said?' he asked, trying to suppress the anxiety in his voice.

'Yes, I suppose so.'

It was not enough. He waited for her to correct herself, say something reassuring.

There was a pause. Then she said, 'There's something you ought to know.'

'What's that?'

'Gerry's back. He left a message for me here.'

'Yes,' said Adam, cautiously. 'He left a message for me too. I'm meant to be having a drink with him later.' There was no reaction.

'I'm going to tell him about us. I'm going to tell him that we're in love and that we're going to get married.' Again there was silence.

'Aren't you going to say anything?' he demanded.

'What do you expect me to do? Wish you luck?' She sounded angry. He realised she had started to cry.

'It's all turned into such a bloody mess,' she said. She was sobbing, he realised. Then she stifled the sobs with a series of sniffs. When she spoke again she was businesslike.

'Sorry about the waterworks. It's just that this afternoon everything was so lovely and now it's horrid.'

'I know,' he soothed, 'I know. But it will all be over soon. I'll phone you as soon as we've finished, then I'll come and pick you up and we'll go out to dinner. Does that sound all right?'

'Yes, Adam.' She sounded as vulnerable as a child. He put down the receiver.

18

He sat in one of the red plush booths in the corner, nearest the door and furthest from the bar. The Knave of Hearts was empty. Seven came and went and but there was no Gerry. By half past seven he was starting to hope that perhaps he would not turn up. Just as he was preparing to go, the door swung open and Gerry stood there, framed in the fading daylight, peering anxiously into the rosy gloom. He saw Adam and raised his hand, waving slowly, then made a drinking motion indicating a first stop at the bar. He collected a drink and slid in beside him, an unlit cigarette between his lips. He reached for his pocket for a light but, before he could find it, Adam nervously picked up the Ronson that lay before him on the table and snapped it on.

'Nice,' Gerry said, 'where'd you get that?' He looked distant. Adam wondered whether he was already drunk.

'Sorry I'm late, chum,' he said. 'I had a million and one things to do before I could get away from the camp.' He took a drag on the fat cigarette. 'I've got a lot of clearing up to do, on account of the fact that I'm not going to be around here for much longer.'

He paused to sip his drink. 'Things went pretty well in London and I'm going to be on my way very soon. Nobody's said as much but I reckon it will be overseas. That's what I wanted to talk to you about.'

He glanced around the deserted bar then leaned forward conspiratorially. 'When I heard the news I decided to put my house in order. To tell you the truth I feel a bit of a bum. You probably twigged that I took Pam off with me on my jaunt to London. She's a nice girl and we had a bit of fun, but the fact is I spent most of the time feeling rotten about Moira – I hope you looked after her, by the way.'

Adam sat frozen as Gerry took another sip of his whisky. Then he let out a long, momentous sigh.

'The long and the short of it is, I've decided to marry Moira. In the circumstances I'd rather she didn't know about my little diversion with Pam.' He put his hand on Adam's arm. 'I can rely on you to keep mum, can't I?' He took another sip, then sat back triumphantly. 'Course I can. We're pals. Well, aren't you going to congratulate me?'

Adam sat for a second or two in silence.

'You're too late,' he said. 'I'm sorry.'

'What are you saying?' Gerry sounded confused. 'You mean she already knows?'

'No, not that – though she does, incidentally, although not from me. A lot's happened while you've been away. Moira and I are in love. If she marries anyone, it's going to be me.'

Gerry sat upright, taut with alarm. 'What the fuck are you saying?'

Their eyes met and locked, and they looked at each other as equals for the first time. Gerry breathed a long sigh.

He shook his head. 'You didn't waste much time, did you? Or her.' His eyes clouded with misery. 'All right then. What happened?'

Adam told the story in a few bare sentences. Gerry listened in silence. Then he said, 'Have you asked her?'

'Yes,' Adam said. 'In a manner of speaking.'

'And she's said yes?'

'More or less.'

Gerry gripped the table with both hands. 'She won't do it,' he said quietly. 'She can't. I love her and she loves me. You've made a mistake. Both of you.'

He stared at the varnished tabletop as if he could see her reflection in it.

Adam felt coldly happy at the consternation he had caused.

'I suppose you'll want to talk to her, but if I were you I wouldn't bother. Her mind's made up. It won't do any good.'

Gerry looked up, menacing suddenly. 'We'll see about that.' He drained his glass. 'Where is she?'

'I don't know.'

He stood up. 'You're a liar,' he said. 'Don't worry. I'll find her. I'll straighten things out. And when I do, you treacherous fucker, you'd better stay out of our way.'

Adam watched him go, almost tripping over a stool in his rush for the door. He waited a minute then went to the bar and asked for the telephone. The blonde barmaid nodded towards a door by the side of the bar where there was a cabin. He found some pennies, pushed them into the black box and dialled the number.

When someone answered he pushed a button; there was a ticking noise, then the same high voice, asking him with whom he wished to speak. He told him. Then he heard Moira saying, 'Give me that,' and she was on the line.

'Are you all right?' she said.

'Of course I'm all right.' His voice was calm and masterful. 'Listen, Gerry's looking for you. He's probably on his way to the hotel now. I have to warn you, he's pretty upset.'

'Is he?' She sounded nervous.

'Now, you don't have to see him, but I think he'll be hard to avoid. It might be better to get it over with. The question is whether you want me to be there.'

'I think I'd better see him alone. I think I owe him that.'

'OK. As you wish. Now I've got to go back to Updyke to sort out a few things. Will you phone me there as soon as you're finished and I'll come over and we'll forget this whole thing and live happily every after?'

'Do you promise?'

'I promise.'

They both paused, wondering who would be the first to break the thread of sound between them.

'Well, I'd better get going then,' said Adam. 'Tell me you love me.'

'I love you.'

He paused. Expectancy hung in the silence at the other end.

'Good,' he said. 'I love you too.'

There was a dry click as the receiver was replaced, then a low, electric burr that droned into infinity.

19

When Adam got back to Updyke there was a party going on. He heard a piano being played, badly, and the roar of voices coming from the mess. He went towards the study with the telephone to wait for Moira's call. But in the corridor he met Crouch coming out of the lavatory.

'Tomaszewski.' His voice slurred over the unaccustomed consonants. None of them could say it right. 'How the bloody hell are you?' His face was glowing, sheened in sweat. 'Come on,' he said, 'I'll get you a drink. Can't spend the last night at Updyke sober.'

Adam hesitated and looked at his watch. He needed a drink and she was unlikely to call for a little while yet. 'OK,' he said.

Crouch put his arm round Adam and steered him past through the press towards a trestle table covered with a beer-soaked sheet on which stood wooden barrels and bottles of whisky and gin.

He looked around the room. There were women in the mess, WAAFs from the base in uniform and lipstick, flushed with the attention they were attracting and laughing obligingly at the banter. Bealing and Whitbread stood by the piano, glasses clamped to their

chests, and Buxton and Ashford were talking to some
ground crew NCOs who appeared to have been invited
along to mark the end of the tour. Crouch came back
carrying two slopping mugs.

'Here you are. To Four-O-Four.'

'Four-O-Four.' They clinked their glasses together
and drank.

The faces round about were shiny, rosy with drink,
and the talk was loud and confident. He knew the real
meaning of the noise: it was the sound of relief at
having survived, and gratitude for the cushy few
months that lay ahead.

Crouch growled something. 'Hope it won't be too
long before we're back on proper ops again,' he said.
Did he really mean it? Adam looked at his small, close-
set eyes for some clue, but they revealed nothing.

'Got to keep buggering on,' he said thickly. 'Then
we can all go home.'

'Let's go and join the others,' Adam said. They
pushed through the crowd. Bealing was telling a joke
but broke off when he saw Adam. They grouped
around him, happy to see him again.

'Where've you been then?' asked Bealing. 'Give us
all the sordid details.'

'Just up to town, to stay with some Poles. It was as
boring as hell. It's almost more fun here.'

He thought of Moira as he told the lie. Gerry would
have reached the hotel by now. Would she have dismissed him straight away? No, she was too fond of him
to do that. She would have listened to him, tried to
comfort him, let him down gently. Perhaps she had

already rung, or was ringing now. He would never hear the telephone over the racket.

'Excuse me, chaps,' he said. 'Back in a minute.' He went out to the hall. A young orderly wearing spectacles sat behind the desk now.

'Been any phone calls in the last ten minutes?'

'No sir.'

'Would you have heard them if there had been?'

The young man patted the apparatus sitting hidden under the lip of the bureau. 'It's sitting right here, sir.'

'I'm Tomaszewski. If anyone calls you're to come and find me in there. It's vital. Understood?'

'Understood, sir.'

He looked at his watch. It was a quarter to nine. He went back into the mess and pushed his way to the drinks table. He felt like a Scotch. He uncorked a bottle and poured himself a half tumbler and took a mouthful, feeling a slight surge of nausea as it hit his stomach. A WAAF was filling a glass with gin.

'Hallo there.' She pointed at the red and white badge on his shoulder. 'Are you one of the Poles?' He smiled at her, miming incomprehension. She repeated the question slowly and loudly. He shook his head apologetically and walked back to the group.

'The question is whether we drink all night or try and get our heads down for a few hours before the off,' Whitbread said. 'What does Adam think?'

'It doesn't make any difference to me,' he said. 'I'm not coming with you.'

'What?' They sounded genuinely disappointed. He told them about the new orders.

'Seems bloody stupid to me,' Whitbread said. 'The squadron won't be the same without you.' Then he brightened up. 'At any rate, this calls for a toast.'

He disappeared, returning a few minutes later with a bottle of whisky. He sloshed some into Adam's glass, told the others to finish their beer, then passed the gulping neck of the bottle over their mugs.

He raised his mug and looked into the mid-distance. 'Here's to Adam. A bloody good bloke.'

'To Adam,' they replied. The glasses chinked dully. They talked for a while about the move, to a base in Scotland, a bleak station in the north near Thurso where they would be occupied flying routine patrols over the North Sea.

Adam was barely listening, his eye trained on the door for the orderly. At nine o'clock he came in, and looked around the room. Adam's arm shot up and he turned towards him, but he shook his head and went over to another officer.

'You expecting a call?' Whitbread asked.

'Yes,' Adam admitted.

'Something important by the look of it.'

'I'll tell you when it's over.'

He was on the point of confiding in him, but the gusting noise and the press of people discouraged him. The conversation slackened. Then Whitbread said: 'Why don't you call her? It is a "her", I take it.'

Adam smiled. 'You're right. I will.'

He left the music room, carrying his glass, and went to the study with the telephone. He called the operator who put him through to the hotel. The same man's voice answered. He remembered the sleek-headed manager – Barron. He was sure now that it was him.

'Is Miss Fleming there, please?'

'I'm afraid she's gone out for the evening,' he replied distantly. 'Can I take a message?'

Adam's mouth went dry and he felt dizzy with foreboding. He wanted to shout questions, demand details, but he stopped himself. 'No,' he said steadily, 'there's no message.'

Back in the music room a conga line had started up, and a train of men and women with blurred faces stumbled around the room, shouting along to the words of the song blaring from the gramophone. He pushed towards the drinks table. A young woman reached out from the line and tried to pull him into it, but he brushed her away. He filled his tumbler a little way up the glass and tossed it back in one gulp. The Scotch had stopped burning now. He splashed in another measure and downed it. He was drinking like a Pole. Instead of becoming clouded, his brain was getting clearer. He knew what he would do next. He would make one more phone call. Then he was going over there.

'I say, leave some of that for the rest of us.'

A young pilot he did not recognise was holding out his glass. Adam looked down at the whisky bottle in one hand and the tumbler in the other. 'Sorry.' He poured half a tumbler full and put the bottle back on the table. He looked at his watch. It was half past nine. He would give her until ten. He pushed his way back to the piano but his friends were no longer there. He looked around and saw Whitbread and Bealing, foolish, happy grins on their faces, hands on the wide hips of two WAAFs, swaying around the room in the conga line. The whisky tasted good. He finished the glass and looked around for more. Whitbread's bottle was tucked away under a chair. He helped himself. Each mouthful of whisky was giving him strength. He liked the confident way it marched into his stomach and out into his bloodstream. The room was getting hot, unbearably so. He shouldered his way through he crowd and out onto the terrace. The fresh night air hit him in the face and filled his smoky lungs. He clutched the stone balustrade to steady himself and looked up at the monkey puzzle tree silhouetted blackly against the moonlit sky. From the garden he heard a girl's laughter and a man's coaxing voice. He glanced back at the house, at the swirling figures glimpsed through the tattered blackout. He felt gigantic, heroic. He looked at his watch but could barely make out the time in the dim light. It didn't matter. He was going to phone again. He pushed open the French windows and stepped back into the room.

'Hey, watch it!'

He was treading on feet, stumbling against ankles. He put out a hand and grabbed someone's shoulder to stop himself falling. At last he was out of the room. He swayed along the corridor and sat heavily on the armchair next to the phone. It took a long time for the operator to answer. He moved his tongue experimentally around his mouth. But when he heard the operator's voice he could scarcely enunciate the simple words and he had to repeat them twice.

She put him through. The double note of the ringing tone bleated down the line five, ten, fifteen times, then the supercilious voice answered. This time he tried to sound more coherent.

'Miss Fleming . . . Moira. Is she back yet?'

'Yes, Miss Fleming has returned, but she has left instructions not to be disturbed.'

He began to argue.

'But this is Adam Tomaszewski here. Didn't she say anything about me?'

'No she didn't . . . sir.' There was insolence now in the voice. 'I suggest you ring back when you're sober.'

He put the receiver back in the cradle and sat back, his head reeling with the whisky and the confusion. He was not going to panic. She was probably upset. The meeting with Gerry had exhausted her and she had gone to bed early. She would want to see him though, he was sure of that. She had to see him. He got to his feet and walked uncertainly out into the hall. The orderly watched impassively as he stumbled down the stone steps of the front door and onto the gravel path. Over by what had once been the stables he saw some parked cars, gleaming in the faint moonlight. His brain seemed to be operating independently of his body. He moved by a conscious effort of will, translating the wishes of his head to his heavy limbs, placing one foot mechanically in front of the other, gulping in draughts of air in an effort to clear his head.

The first car was locked. The second was open but there was no key. The third, a bulbous Morris, was open and the key was dangling from the steering column. He started the engine. It was a long time since he had driven. He could fly a Hurricane but he was not sure he could drive a car. He turned the key and pulled the self-starter, which whinnied noisily for a few seconds. Nothing happened. He remembered the choke and pulled it full out. This time the engine roared, alarmingly loud. He jerked the stick into what he thought was reverse gear and let out the clutch. The car jumped forward into the stable door, throwing him painfully against the steering wheel. He tried again. This time the car hopped backwards over the gravel. He changed gear again. Then he was on his way. He heard the scrape of metal on stone as he pulled through the gates and out onto the road to Chichester. He fumbled at the switches, found the headlights and tried to focus on the road ahead. He fixed his eyes on a distant tree, hoping it would give him a bearing, but then he was seeing two trees, and the faint strip of paint in the middle of the road had duplicated itself so there were two parallel lines of dashes dividing the tarmac. He was wandering, drifting from one side of the road to the other. He put his hand to one eye and squinted and the world was singular again. The lane was rushing along underneath him, very fast it seemed. He looked at the speedometer. He was doing 15 miles an hour. The large illuminated clock on the dashboard said it was a quarter past ten.

He came to a crossroads and turned towards Chichester. The town was sleeping, with hardly a chink of light showing behind the blackout curtains. He steered cautiously down the main street and turned towards the cathedral. The hotel lay there, glowing white in the moonlight. He stopped outside the front door and got out. There was silence except for the sound of the wind in the yew trees in the graveyard. He felt sick with whisky and anticipation. There was no sign of life from the hotel. The windows were tightly shuttered and curtained, as if the inhabitants had left on a journey that would last for years. He tried the door. It was locked. He stepped backwards and looked up. The building was tilting and swaying before his eyes. He tried to work out which were the windows to Moira's room. He walked carefully over to the graveyard, reached over the wall and scooped up a handful of soft earth, then crossed back and hurled it at two middle windows. It pattered feebly against the wall and fell back in his face. He returned to the graveyard and found some pebbles. This time they cracked against the glass with such force that he thought he had broken a pane. He stood back and waited for a swirl of curtain and scrape of sash but there was nothing: silence, and the wind stirring the yew branches. The trees were whispering, trying to tell him something, repeating the same sibilant phrase over and over. His mind grasped for the meaning and for a moment he thought he had understood, but then the wind dropped and the trees fell silent and he sat down heavily on the moss-covered stone wall facing the hotel.

He got to his feet and moved unsteadily over to the front door. He leaned with one hand against the wall and with the other he raised the heavy brass knocker and brought it crashing down. The noise seemed immense. He heard it echoing down the hallway, rolling through the quiet, leaving eddying pools of stillness in its wake. But then the silence lapped back and enfolded the place. He knocked again, this time three insistent raps. Now out of the violated calm he heard slow footsteps. He leaned back against the wall, his head swimming. The door opened a quarter and Barron's face appeared at the gap. He looked unsurprised to see him.

'I was thinking we might have a visitor,' he said.

He jerked his head towards the interior and opened the door a fraction wider so that Adam could squeeze past into the hall.

He felt a flood of gratitude. He stepped into the hotel, slurring his thanks. Then a hand was at his throat and an arm slammed him against the wall and Barron's pomaded head was thrusting into his face.

'Where are you going, lover boy?' he hissed. His tainted breath filled Adam's nostrils and the cultured accent had gone. 'I told you the lady doesn't want to be disturbed. What are you, fucking deaf?'

He released his grip and twisted him round, wrenching his arm behind his back and propelling him back to the door which he pulled open. He shoved Adam onto the pavement, kicking at him as he sprawled forward.

He lay there looking up at the sleek head smiling down at him. 'I think sir has had a little too much to drink. If I was him I'd fuck off home sharpish. Before I call the Military Police. Or Captain Cunningham.' The door slammed shut.

Adam lay for a few minutes feeling the cold stone against the back of his head. Then, pulling on the mudguard of the car, he hauled himself to his feet and slumped into the seat.

Later he had no recollection of the journey home. He remembered turning into the drive at Updyke and sitting for a while in the car outside the stables and tasting the salt from the tears and the snot on his lip and wiping it off with his silk scarf and finding his way indoors. He remembered the worried look on Whitbread's face and the burning of more whisky as it descended into his stomach. Later he had a faint memory of hands tugging at his shoes and trousers and the cool of the cotton sheets.

The following morning he rang the hotel. A woman he had never heard before told him Miss Fleming had paid her bill and left the hotel an hour earlier. There were no messages.

PART TWO

20

Once again Adam was waiting for Koski, and Koski, as usual, was late. Still, it was no hardship sitting in the warm night, listening to the laughter at neighbouring tables and the distant tinkling of music. He called the girl over and ordered another drink. She returned with a sweating bottle of light ale, cold from the refrigerator, and emptied it into a tumbler so that the foam seethed over the lip. He looked up at her and smiled a thank you and she walked away with the tray tucked under an arm, her hips rolling under the tight wrapping of cotton sarong.

They came here most nights when they were waiting between trips. The Allied Victory Club consisted of three single-storey cement and breeze-block huts arranged around a courtyard planted with ragged jacaranda trees. In the day the trees shaded the round metal tables arranged on the sandy floor of the courtyard. At night the branches were strung with coloured electric lights. The club provided most of the social life that existed outside the base. In one hut there was a bar and behind it a large, refrigerated chest which was always stocked with beer from home. Another hut was a restaurant offering chicken and rice or lamb and rice.

The third was a sort of dormitory, to which the girls who hung around the place took their clients if there was nowhere better to go.

The courtyard was half full. Most of the customers came from the base. They sat around in small, relaxed groups, talking, smoking and sipping beer. There were a handful of white civilians in tropical clothing and a few black men who did business with them, over-dressed in European suits, chatting quietly under the glow of the patriotically arranged red, white and blue light bulbs. On the wall was a mural showing a bearded old man reaching out feebly towards a pretty whore, while her young and virile accomplice picked his pocket.

Adam had been there more than a year, now. The pilots were frequently told by distant superiors that their work was of the utmost importance to the war effort, but most of the squadron acknowledged amongst themselves that they belonged to the rear echelon. Some of them were veterans who had grown too old or too scared to stay on ops. Others were keen enough to fight but second rate, no use as killers and easy meat for the German pilots. The rest were crocks, whose disabilities disqualified them from returning to the front line.

Koski fell into the first category. Adam was in the last. It had taken them some time to diagnose the trouble. Shortly after he arrived at Northolt he started to notice a blurring in the top left corner of his field of vision. He was flying well enough – a definite and a probable in his first month with the squadron. But the loss of vision had nagged at him, installing a permanent fear that a Messerschmitt was lurking in the watery blur of the blind spot, which no amount of twisting and swivelling his head to scan the sky could dispel. One day, when he was flying as wingman to the squadron leader, they had been bounced. It had been his job to keep watch, but he had seen nothing until the tracer and cannon flowed around them and sent them running for their lives.

After that, he went to see the medical officer who sent him off to a specialist. There had been months of tests. In they end they decided that when he crashed into the sea he had damaged a small optical nerve. It did not stop him flying, but it was enough to get him taken off fighters. He had fought the decision, supported by his squadron leader and wing commander. But in the end higher authority confirmed the verdict.

There had been a spell as an instructor at a training school in Nottinghamshire. He knew that in effect his life had been given back to him and he should have been thankful, but instead he was bored and melancholy and got drunk a lot. When a Polish acquaintance offered him a job as a delivery pilot flying new aircraft from where they arrived by ship on the west coast of Africa to Egypt for the desert campaign, he took it.

It was hard work, and dangerous in its way. They never saw an enemy aircraft, but fatigue, the weather and teething troubles on the new machines ensured a regular toll in accidents and crashes. From Takoradi on the Gold Coast they flew for six days over jungle and desert, stopping each night at remote airstrips until 3,700 miles later they reached Cairo.

He had made the trip many times now. Tomorrow they were off again at dawn, flying a mixed consignment of fighters and bombers. Adam and Koski were piloting two of a new batch of Spitfires and would have to dawdle along in the wake of the bombers.

He began to wonder whether Koski was coming. The smell of the African night, of dust and spice and cooking fires, hung on the air. He was hungry. He had just called the girl over to order some chicken when Koski walked in. He was short and muscular with cropped, thinning blond hair and a quarrelsome look and was dressed in a sweat-stained cotton bush shirt and baggy shorts. When he saw Adam, his clenched face relaxed into a smile. He waved and flashed him a guarded thumbs up. Brushing by the girl, he whispered something that caused her to giggle, then stumped over to the table and sat down.

'Did you get them?' Adam asked.

'Finally. They are such bloody crooks.'

'That's the whole point, surely?'

'Don't preach, please.'

The drinks arrived and Adam took a long swallow of beer. 'Can I have a look?'

'I thought you didn't want anything to do with it.'

Koski took from his pocket a little square of stiff paper. He looked around and slid it under the table. Adam edged it out into the dim light and unfolded it carefully. Inside was a clutch of small, dull stones like dirty bits of glass.

'I thought you said they were diamonds.'

'They are, you fool. Dug out of the virgin earth of Africa. This what they look like before they're chopped and polished. Guess how much they're worth in Cairo?'

'About sixpence each.'

'Very funny. Well, you can laugh, but the proceeds of this trip alone will set me up in business once all this shit is over.'

Diamonds were Koski's latest obsession in his never-ending search for new ways to make fast money. The work brought many opportunities for trade. He had started off buying snakeskins from natives who waited at dusty stopovers in the interior, paying a few shillings for each one, then selling them on in Cairo for a few pounds. From that he had moved on to ivory bangles, and hideous fetish masks, which were surprisingly popular with Europeans in Cairo. Now it was uncut diamonds, smuggled out of the mines of South Africa by kaffir workers and sold for the price of a week's groceries to middlemen who passed them on to the Europeans.

Despite having only just started out in the diamond racket, Koski's restless mind was already working on a new scheme. The workers in the local gold mines regularly stole ore from the diggings but lacked the mercury needed to separate the metal. For weeks he had been talking about buying some mercury in Cairo, and getting someone to refine the gold for him.

They ordered chicken and more bottles of beer and Adam listened as Koski chattered about his schemes, the small blue eyes in his sunburned face darting around at the sound of any new arrival. Finally he saw who he was looking for. His face lit up and he signalled to a plump black girl, about eighteen years old, who crossed the courtyard and sat down with them.

Koski had been at the base when Adam had arrived fourteen months before. He was a peasant's son who came from a small village not far from Toruń. Adam had heard about him, a good pilot who had fought well in Poland and France and had caught the end of the Battle of Britain. Some time afterwards, the fire had gone out of him. Now he rarely talked about the progress of the war, only what he was going to do after it. Adam had disliked him at first. Then his honest greed and his unshakeable belief in his own survival became endearing. Gradually they became friends, to the surprise of a fastidious group among the pilots who guarded the social standards of the squadron.

Most nights, at the end of the desultory duties that engaged them while they waited for another batch of planes to arrive, they would go out drinking. Koski and his girlfriend Vicky were regular customers at the local shebeens. The three of them became a familiar sight, sitting in stuffy shacks, listening to the tinny music and drinking beer. Once, at the beginning Adam had gone off with one of Vicky's friends. An outbreak of clap that had decimated the base personnel put him off such cheerful, pagan encounters.

At first he had been slightly embarrassed at the amount of time he spent with Koski, and would accept an invitation to play cards or listen to music with one of the more conventional officers. But at the end of the evening he would find himself making his excuses and slipping down to the dirty old town to seek out his friend in the club or in one of the smoky, convivial dives.

The war was far away, glimpsed only hazily on the stopovers in Cairo. Even there, there was little feeling of danger and none at all of privation. The military lived a life of hectic and exotic sybaritism, far removed from the monochrome austerity of England. Once in a while he ran into Polish fighter pilots flying in the Western Desert and heard the news of old comrades, the deaths, gongs and promotions. It was a relief, though, when the evening drew to an end and he could return to the comforting routine of the delivery run.

The food arrived. Koski gave his plate of chicken to Vicky and ordered another one for himself. Adam ate his quickly then looked at his watch. 'I'm heading off.'

'What, already?'

'We've got a six o'clock start tomorrow.'

'So what?'

'Well, you two can stay. I'm going back.'

His motorbike was outside. He kicked it into life and climbed on and set off down the sandy coast road. The velvety sky arched overhead, studded with stars. A wind blew in from the sea, carrying on it the smell of decaying palm leaves and dead fish. The camp was only a few miles away. The guard barely looked at him as he swung in past the gate.

He bumped over the rutted concrete path that led to his quarters and stopped, hauling the bike onto its stand. His room was a breeze-block cell with a cool cement floor and an iron bed, over which hung a tattered mosquito net, yellowing and ectoplasmic. The only other furniture was a small table, upon which he had placed small, framed portraits of his mother and father, which had been smuggled out to him in a package from his sister in Poland. Ewa was living in the country near Warsaw with an aunt. His father had been last heard of living alone on the farm, solitary and drunk, if he interpreted the euphemistic language of the letter correctly.

The photographs were an act of piety. He rarely thought of his family any more. When he looked at the stiff figures there was no answering jolt of remembrance. For a while he had displayed a photograph of Moira, the film-star portrait that had sat on the sideboard at her mother's flat in London. One night, in a fit of drunken misery, he had torn it up. He could not bring himself to throw away the pieces and they survived, saved in an envelope, put away between the leaves of one of the small stock of unread books that he toted from place to place.

He had kept the letter, though, folded up in his wallet. It was written on the notepaper of the Golden Anchor Hotel and had caught up with him a few months after he arrived at Northolt. Occasionally, late at night, he would take it out and read it, though he knew the words almost by heart.

Dear Adam,
I know that I've done a terrible thing to you and I can't expect your forgiveness. If it's any consolation

*to you I'm feeling sick with guilt and misery. I am
too crazy now to even try to explain what has
happened. I don't even know myself.*

*Adam, darling, I meant what I said when I told
you I loved you, but I suppose I can't expect you to
believe that. The few days we had together will
always be with me and I think I will remember them
as some of the happiest of my life. One day when all
this is over perhaps we will meet again. In the
meantime, God go with you and protect you.*

There was no terminating endearment, just her
rounded, girlish signature.

Adam sat down on the narrow bed and the springs
groaned under his weight. He pulled off his desert
boots, his shorts and his shirt, and untied the mosquito
net, spreading it carefully so that it stretched over the
corners of the bed. No matter how carefully he arranged it, the mosquitoes always got in. He lay back
and listened to the wind shuffling in the palm trees
outside. He fell off to sleep but was woken some time
later by the noise coming from the cell next door as
Koski stumbled into his bed.

21

They landed at sunset at Kano. A morning storm and mechanical problems with two of the planes had delayed their departure from Takoradi until the afternoon. There were twenty-four aircraft in the formation and they flew in ranks in line abreast. The only diversion was the land below as it unrolled beneath their wings, green and lush and veined with rivers stained ochre by the mud from the rains.

Over the next three days the landscape grew rockier and more barren, until they were flying over blank desert. Now and then the air roiled with thermals that hoisted them up and dumped them down thousands of feet. Each day they landed before dusk and spent the nights in corrugated iron huts clustered at the edge of little airfields. The natives were always waiting for them, patient groups of men holding snakeskins and carvings and wooden shields and spears and, next to them, demure groups of girls in ragged cotton dresses, most of them barely past puberty, offering their bodies for two shillings. Koski had brought whisky and beer, and in the evenings after they had eaten their chicken and rice they sat round drinking and playing cards.

The night before they were due to set out on the last leg from Khartoum to Cairo, Koski took Adam aside.

'I just wanted to warn you that I won't be landing with the rest of you tomorrow,' he said.

'That sounds bad. Are you planning to crash?' Koski brought out a facetious streak in Adam.

Koski sighed. 'This isn't funny. Do you remember Foreman?'

He did – a delivery pilot killed when his Kittyhawk went into the desert just outside Khartoum.

'Well, I just heard that when they cleaned up his body they found his pockets were stuffed with diamonds. The station officers here told the military police at Cairo. One of my pals tells me they're planning to search us when we get to Heliopolis.'

'So what are you going to do?'

'I haven't worked it out yet. I'll probably develop engine trouble a bit short of Cairo so I have to put down somewhere else.'

'OK. Good luck.'

Next day they rose early. The last leg of the trip was the best. No matter how many times he made the journey, he was always filled with holy awe at the sight of the Nile carving its way through the rock and earth below, brown and muscular, the morning rays flashing off its surface as the river saluted the sun. You could see how the land worked. The richness of the narrow, water-nourished flood plain, thick with crops, which gave way abruptly to the exhausted yellow of the desert. From dawn, the fields stirred with the movement of animals and men, and the triangular sails of feluccas flitted on the water. They flew over scores of white-walled villages clinging to the banks, built from the crumbling mud of the shore. He imagined the children peering up at the black crosses crawling across the hard blue sky.

Towards Cairo the river edges grew more congested, and small towns appeared among the greenery of the plain. Adam heard Koski's exasperated voice coming over the radio.

'Yellow leader from Koski. I don't bloody believe it. The engine's playing up.'

The convoy commander, a morose squadron leader called Zaborski who sat apart during the enforced evening socialising, answered the call.

'What's the matter?'

'The temperature's going off the clock. But don't worry. I'm sure I can make it to Heliopolis.'

There were a few seconds of crackling silence before Zaborski came back.

'There's no point risking a machine. There's an RAF strip ten minutes away. Head for there.'

Koski blustered a little then agreed to give it a try. Adam smiled as he listened. Koski had managed to convey just the right mixture of frustration and resolution. He watched the Spitfire shift out of the formation and slope down towards the pale surface of the desert beyond the band of green.

Half an hour later they landed at Heliopolis. The aerodrome had grown in the years of war, gaining extra runways and acres of hangars and outbuildings. They trooped through the arrivals hut, hanging about while the squadron leader disposed of the paperwork. Adam noticed that three military policemen were standing in the corner, ostentatiously looking over the pilots as they stood chatting and smoking. They made no move to stop them, though, when they filed out and climbed into the buses that took them to where they were spending the night.

The headquarters of the Polish detachment was aboard a cruise ship moored near the centre of the city. After the squalor of the journey, the luxury seemed overwhelming. Adam signed in and was shown to an outboard cabin on the Nile side. He fell back onto the bunk, watching the reflection of the river rippling over the low ceiling. He had an hour of jerky, dream-laden sleep. Then he took his towel and wash bag down to the heads, shaved, and afterwards spent fifteen minutes letting the needle jets of lukewarm water sluice over him, easing the knots of tension out of his shoulders and rinsing the dust and grit from his hair.

Back in the cabin, he changed into the clean uniform he had brought with him. He knotted a blue silk scarf loosely round his neck and walked along the humming corridor and out onto the deck. The setting sun was hanging like a Chinese lantern over the stern of the boat. He sat on a bench next to a life belt, smoked a cigarette and watched the birds wheeling in the sky, darting and fluttering as they gorged on the evening insects. Around the city the sound of the evening prayer erupted in ragged unison from the towers of the mosques.

Most of the other pilots were already at the bar. Adam ordered a whisky and joined them. They talked for a while about their plans for the next few days, waiting for the converted bomber that would fly them back to Takoradi.

Adam asked if there was any news of Koski and was told he had made it down to the RAF base without incident and was on his way into Cairo. They drank for an hour, enjoying the feel of clean uniforms and the taste of whisky. There was a billiard table in the next room, and they took their drinks with them and placed them down on the bookshelves filled with thrillers and romances and played for a while. Then, singly and in pairs, the officers drifted away, to the cinema or to dinner or to catch up with Polish friends who were in town on leave. The battle of Alamein six months before had saved the city. Cairo was now a haven for the victors, a place for relaxation and the pleasures of peacetime. Adam declined invitations to tag along. He played a few trick shots he had been taught at Northolt, then wandered back into the bar and took up a place on a stool.

At about seven thirty, Koski walked in. He had shaved and bathed and he looked full of energy and mischief. He climbed onto the bar stool next to Adam, his legs dangling short of the brass rail, and ordered himself a large whisky.

'So,' he said, rubbing his hands, 'I managed to dodge them.'

'It was all a bit unnecessary,' Adam said. 'Nobody searched us at the aerodrome.'

'But they were there, weren't they?' Koski insisted. 'It was me they were after, I'm sure. Anyway, so far so good.' He patted his tunic pocket and raised his glass.

'What happens now?' Without really thinking about it he assumed that he would be tagging along with Koski while he conducted his business.

'Are you sure you want to come with me?' Koski asked.

'Why not? I haven't got anything better to do.'

'There could be a lot of hanging about. You know what it's like.'

'Well, I don't, but I'll take your word for it.' Whatever caution Adam might have felt was dissolving with the whisky.

'OK, well if you're sure.'

They finished their drinks and walked down the gangplank to where a line of gharries stood waiting. They climbed in and Koski showed the driver a piece of paper on which an address was written. They clopped along the corniche, the driver constantly flicking his whip at the scabby rump of the nag between the shafts, and over a bridge that led to Gezira Island.

The gharry turned into a quiet side street, lined with tall apartment buildings with green shutters and curved balconies, and stopped. Koski paid and the carriage clattered away.

'What is this place?' Adam asked.

'This is where I'm going to meet the man who can put me on to the buyer.'

'But I thought you'd have the buyer all set up?'

'It's not that simple,' Koski said vaguely. 'Anyway, come on.'

They climbed up four flights of stairs and emerged onto a broad landing. Light was coming from under the door in front of them and the sound of a gramophone playing dance music. Koski knocked. They heard the sound of shuffling feet and the door opened, revealing an old man in a red fez and limp cotton galabiya. His face was monumentally immobile.

'Yes?' he said, grudgingly.

'I've come to see Mr Swan,' Koski said.

'No Swan here.' The *sufragi* began shutting the door.

'Listen, old man.' Koski pushed his hand against the door and was shoving his way in when a weary voice came from inside.

'Who is it, Mohammed?'

'*Itneinn walad shar'a mashbouheen.*'

They heard a bark of laughter. Mohammed had clearly formed a bad impression of them. The door swung open. Framed against the light stood a spare, lanky man.

'Can I help you?' he asked brusquely.

'We're looking for Mr Swan.' Adam was starting to regret joining Koski's quest.

'Christ, not again. I don't know who this bloody Swan is. All I know is that he doesn't live here and hasn't done for ages.' He sighed and held the door open. 'I suppose you'd better come in and have a drink.'

He led them into a large high-ceilinged room with a wood-block floor and sparse furniture. The walls had been white once but now were yellow with cigarette smoke. The only decoration was a few pictures of society beauties torn out of magazines and stuck on the walls. They sat down on a sunken sofa with a grey, greasy line along the back where many brilliantined heads had lolled.

'Tell Mo what you want,' said their host. 'We've got most things.' They ordered whisky and sat apprehensively waiting for the drinks to arrive. Their host sat back in an armchair on the far side of the room and examined them.

'I'm Colin Cromarty, by the way. This isn't my place. I just camp here from time to time when I'm not in the desert. I'm sorry to disappoint you about Mr Swan. All I can offer you is a drink and the use of the phone.'

'There's a phone?' Koski was on his feet.

'Next door.' Cromarty extended a long arm. 'In the bedroom.'

Koski left and the *sufragi* returned with the drinks. Cromarty seemed to have lost interest in the visitors and returned to the book he was reading. He had a long neck, sparse gingery hair and a long sharp nose that gave him the look of a wading bird. Adam grew irritated at his self-absorption.

'What game are you in?' he asked. Cromarty put down his book and looked up.

'Difficult to say, really,' he said mildly. 'I'm with the Special Operations Service. The commander, in fact. We do a bit of this and a bit of that. Mainly stooging around behind the lines blowing things up. How about you?'

Adam explained. Cromarty listened, nodding, then resumed reading his book.

From next door he could hear Koski's wheedling voice rising and falling. He heard the clatter of the receiver being replaced and Koski came back into the room. He ignored Cromarty and sat down by Adam.

'I think we're getting somewhere,' he murmured. 'This bloody Swan is out of town, but I've got the name of another man. I've got to meet him in the Palmyra Club in three hours' time.'

'What are we going to do until then?' whispered Adam.

Cromarty looked up from across the room. 'The whisky's all right, isn't it? You're welcome to stay here if you wish.'

22

Cromarty went back to his book. The *sufragi* returned and filled their glasses and they sat talking in quiet, embarrassed voices for a while, sipping their drinks while they decided what to do next. There was the sound of footsteps and laughter on the landing. Mohammed moved to the door without waiting for the knock.

There were three of them, sunburned from the desert but dressed in neat uniforms. They greeted Cromarty respectfully, then sat down on the fragile dining chairs dotted around the room. Nobody paid any attention to Adam and Koski. They were all big men but one of them stood out. He was at least six feet four with an athlete's limbs and flat eyes sunk in a chiselled, primitive face. He crouched on one of the spindly chairs and lit a cigarette. Adam noticed his long thick fingers. They reminded him of the hands of a famous French sculptor he had once seen in an old newsreel, working over a block of marble.

'Where's the drink?' he said in a grating Ulster voice. 'I'm parched.'

Cromarty called for the *sufragi*. 'Whisky for Major Gibson, Mo.'

They were young. Adam was surprised to see that one of them was a sergeant. The second officer stood up and crossed to the gramophone and put on a scratchy record, then started spinning round the room, looping his arms as if embracing a phantom partner. After a few circuits he stopped.

'This song's ancient. Isn't there anything on the radio?'

Cromarty pointed silently to a set in the corner. The dancer fiddled with the knobs and the sound of a big band emerged through the whistling static.

'That's more like it,' he said, and continued his solitary dance. At one point he stumbled against Gibson's aggressively out-flung leg.

'Watch your step, pal,' he said, fixing him with his deep eyes. The dancer faltered and stopped.

'Uh-oh,' he said. 'Dougie's in one of his moods. I'd go easy on the firewater if I were you.'

'Sir.'

'Come again?'

'You fucking heard me. You address me as sir.'

The dancer threw up his hands and sat down. 'You can always rely on Dougie to make the party go with a swing.' He turned to the others. 'What's the plan for the evening?'

They began to work through various permutations of clubs, hotels and bars. The dancer turned his bland, blue eyes on Koski and Adam, as if noticing them for the first time.

'What are you fellers doing?'

Koski was evasive, but Adam took over, anxious not to waste the evening in hanging about waiting for Koski's contact.

'We've got a date later on,' he said, 'but in the meantime we're free. Do you mind if we tag along?'

'Sure. Why not? I'm Mark Minto, by the way, and this is Tony Lockyer. And that,' he pointed to the huge man balanced on the chair, 'is Dougie Gibson. Major Gibson, I should say.'

'Shhh.' Gibson held up a long hand.

'What?' said Minto.

'Listen.'

The dance music had finished and been replaced by the droning tones of a newsreader announcing a report from William Widdows, a visiting writer whose talents had been harnessed for the propaganda effort. A voice, flabby and cultured, came from the wireless.

'It's him!' Gibson roared. Minto and Lockyer started to laugh, but Gibson waved at them to shut up.

'Listen to the swine!'

They sat in silence while the broadcaster reviewed the progress of the war and looked forward to further heroism and sacrifice on the path to inevitable victory.

'What does that bullshitting bastard know about it?' shouted Gibson. 'He's never got nearer to the front than the bar of Shepheard's Hotel.'

'Oh dear,' Minto said. 'Dougie's off. It's always a bad sign when he starts going on about Widdows.'

Gibson was on his feet. He drained his glass. 'I'm going to find him,' he said quietly. 'Teach him a lesson.'

'It looks as if Dougie's decided the order of the evening's entertainment,' Minto said. 'Are you coming along?'

They trooped out of the flat and down the stairs, leaving Cromarty behind with his book. A line of gharries was waiting at the end of the street. Gibson commandeered the first one and ordered it to Shepheard's. Minto joined Adam and Koski in a second carriage.

They crossed the river, passing the barracks and the royal palace and the opera house, until they drew up outside the hotel. Gibson led the way, past some redcaps standing guard at the entrance and up the stone steps onto the large terrace. The evening was cool but it was crowded with drinkers, uniformed men and civilians, sitting around in wicker chairs. Gibson peered about him.

'Can't see the bastard,' he said, and strode towards the entrance. A small figure in a white galabiya and red fez moved into their path to stop them. He pointed regretfully at the three stripes on Lockyer's shoulder and at a sign at the doorway declaring that the hotel was out of bounds to other ranks.

'Fuck off, Abdul,' said Gibson and brushed him aside.

They marched into the vaulted lobby, dimly lit through a coloured glass dome and gaudily decorated in Moorish pastiche. The statues of two large-breasted women stood guard at either side of the staircase.

'Looks like a bloody brothel,' Gibson said. 'Where's the bar?'

The Long Bar was a large, high-ceilinged room, all dark wood and mirrors. It was thick with smoke and the rumble of masculine conversation. Gibson easily shouldered his way through the crowd and caught the arm of the European-looking barman.

'We're looking for the laddie from the BBC. Widdows. Has he been in?'

'You've just missed him,' the barman said. 'I think he was going to the Continental.'

'Fuck,' said Gibson. 'Give me a large whisky and a Stella, then ask them what they want.'

They sat down at a table. Gibson was starting to enjoy himself. 'Let's get these down us and get after him,' he said.

They set off along the pavement the short distance to the Continental. But when they arrived they were told that Widdows had stayed only a few minutes and gone on elsewhere.

'Might as well have a drink,' Lockyer said. They sat down. Gibson ran through the places where he might be found. 'We can try the Gezira next or the Turf Club. They're the sort of poncy holes he likes.'

Minto was showing signs of frustration.

'OK,' he said, 'but after that we'll have to pack in the manhunt. We're supposed to be meeting the others at the Kit Kat.'

The bar was quieter than the one they had left. A thin man with brilliantined hair was playing Cole Porter tunes on the piano. Gibson stared at him for a while before crossing the room to stand over him.

'Play "Lily of Laguna",' he said hoarsely.

The man looked up with terrified eyes and moved seamlessly into the lilting opening bars of the request.

Gibson chuckled. 'That's better,' he said. Instead of returning to the table he stood by the piano, with his head thrown back and his eyes closed, crooning along to the song.

'Who is he exactly?' Adam asked.

'Dougie?' Minto replied. 'Dougie's the leading light in the SOS. I don't know if anyone explained. We stooge around behind the lines blowing things up. He's destroyed more enemy planes than the RAF. And he's killed more Jerries and Eyties than most battalions. Some people say – not when he's around, of course – that he's not much better than a maniac and ought to be locked up by rights. I like to think of him as a Viking in the old berserker tradition: dumb and morose most of the time, but absolutely magnificent when fighting mad.'

The pianist finished the tune and looked timidly at Gibson. He nodded, and the pianist began it over again.

'This could go on for hours,' sighed Minto. He shouted across to the piano. 'Oy, sir. Widdows could be getting away. We ought to move on, pronto.'

Gibson snapped out of his trance. 'By Christ, you're right. Drink up. Let's get after him.'

At the Turf Club they were told that Widdows had left for the Gezira Club. At the Gezira Club they learned that he had gone back to Shepheard's. Minto shook with stifled laughter at each missed encounter, seemingly anticipating an entertaining explosion of rage, but Gibson took the bad news calmly. He nodded and his malevolent smile deepened.

'We've got the whole evening ahead of us,' he said in his discordant voice. 'Mr Widdows will see some action tonight, I will guarantee that.'

The carriages crossed back across the river and stopped outside the wrought-iron canopy in front of Shepheard's. The terrace was even busier than it had been earlier in the evening. They stood on the steps and surveyed the drinkers. Gibson was swaying now and breathing heavily. Minto nudged Adam and nodded towards a crowded table a few yards away.

'Oh my God. There he is.' It was easy to tell which one was Widdows. He was neat and pale, with dark brilliantined hair and hooded, appraising eyes. He sat back in his chair with his legs stretched languidly before him. He wore a well cut linen suit and smoked a cigarette through a long holder. He was talking to a circle of well-dressed civilian men and women, in the clipped, confident voice that Adam recognised from the radio.

Gibson had moved away and they could see him now talking to the terrace waiter who pointed in the direction of Widdows' party's table. Gibson turned away from him and edged between the chairs, his jaw clamped in a strange grin. On the way he dislodged a glass, which fell with a tinkling inconsequence amid the chatter, but it caught the attention of Widdows, who looked up to see a smiling giant with a major's crowns on his epaulettes striding towards him. He looked puzzled for a second, but a lifetime of celebrity had prepared him for such moments. A smile broke out on his face. He rose from his wicker chair and held out a hand.

Gibson's huge fist reached out as if to shake it. Instead it bypassed Widdows' grasp and clamped around his throat. A look of astonishment and hurt spread across Widdows' face. His hands moved up and scrabbled at Gibson's wrist. It made no difference. Slowly, with one hand, Gibson levered Widdows out of the chair so he was standing on trembling tiptoes, choking and gurgling for breath. A girl at the table squealed and there was a babble of male protests and the scrape of pushed-back chairs. Minto moved forward and grasped Gibson by the arm, but he was flicked away with an instinctive twitch of muscle. Gibson was still smiling but the malignity had departed from his face and he was gazing down on his victim with an expression that was strangely tender and benevolent. Then, as if on a signal, he hoisted him a few inches higher and dashed him down on his chair. Widdows fell forward, wheezing and clutching at his throat. The surrounding tables bubbled with horrified delight, uncertain whether or not this was some rough military joke. A woman fed Widdows some water, which he drank in desperate gulps. Gibson stood over him, looking down thoughtfully, then wheeled away, his interest already evaporating.

He put his arm around Minto's and Lockyear's shoulders and led them into the Long Bar. Adam and Koski trailed after them.

'The RAF can buy the drinks,' Gibson said.

He was amiable now, as if some duty had been discharged and he could relax. Koski went to the bar and they sat down on leather banquettes in a dark corner. They chatted about some past operation in which one of their number – whom they had given up for dead after a disastrous raid – had trekked for three weeks across the desert and arrived back at the training camp.

Adam countered with several stories of pilots who had been shot down over France and presumed lost who had turned up months later after arduous journeys over the Pyrenees. Gibson seemed mildly impressed. His voice softened and he started talking to Adam in an avuncular way, asking him about his life since leaving Poland and the whereabouts of his family. After a second drink, Minto was anxious to move on.

'We're meant to be at the Kit Kat next. We're meeting up with some of the chums. You boys are coming too, I hope?'

Adam and Koski were part of the gang now. They looked at each other. 'We've got to be at the Palmyra later on. How far is that?'

'They're practically next door to each other,' said Minto. 'Come on.'

23

They decided to walk to the club, making their way through the side streets that led down to the Nile. Gibson led them on, a massive figure, twice the size of the little men who dodged in their path offering them trinkets and women. Adam and Minto hung behind. When they reached the Anglican cathedral on the banks of the river, Gibson stood for a while at the stone parapet staring into the water. The river was in a hurry to get to the sea. Its long journey of accumulation was almost over. Soon it would be discharging its sweet water into the salt of the Mediterranean. The surface was patterned with whorls and eddies, like tattoos on a muscular arm.

They walked slowly, under the yellow, ragged palm trees, past lines of waiting gharries, hearing the clop and jangle of the patient nags as they stirred between the shafts. Gibson's voice drifted back to them, saying something that made Koski and Lockyer laugh.

'He can be quite charming when he wants to be,' Minto said. 'A bit of a misfit, but then we're a funny crowd. We've got all sorts, from belted earls to the sweepings of the Gorbals and the East End. You'll see when we get to the Kit Kat.'

'What's the party in aid of?' Adam asked.

'Nothing in particular. We think we're probably not going to be around here much longer. The North Africa show is practically over. It's a sort of end-of-term party before we head off somewhere new. It was Gerry's idea.'

Adam paused to light a cigarette, shielding the flame from the breeze coming in over the Nile.

'Who's Gerry?'

'Oh you'll love Gerry. He's one of the regiment's most colourful characters, out of a very strong field.'

The night had turned chilly. Adam heard himself saying. 'I think I might already know him. Has he got dark hair?'

'Yes.'

'And rather obvious good looks.'

'I hadn't thought about whether they were obvious or not. But he's good looking, or at least the girls in Cairo seem to think so.'

'Gerry Cunningham.'

Minto laughed. 'The same. Everyone knows Gerry. You don't seem too happy at the news. Do you owe him money?'

Adam managed a smile. 'If anything it's the other way round.'

He felt curiously unsurprised by the news. He knew they would meet again somewhere. In the first miserable months after it happened, he had spent almost all the time that he wasn't sleeping or flying an aeroplane thinking about her, or her and him together. He dreamed of revenge. He could tip off the police about the necklace fraud. He visualised the arrival of the detectives at the mess, the discreet conversation and Gerry's departure into the waiting police car under the embarrassed eyes of his colleagues.

Or Gerry would bring about his own downfall. He imagined receiving a telephone call from her hinting at distress, a clandestine meeting, the shaky recital of the stories of drunkenness and debt, then the feel of her again in his arms, the taste of the salt wetness of her cheek. Later would come the confrontation and Gerry's slinking exit, accepting of the justice of his defeat.

Or else, years later, he would glimpse them across a sea of uniforms at some reception, he in his tunic encrusted with the Virtuti Militari, his DFC heavy with bars, Gerry seedy, she faded, her fortitude fraying. She would look at him with hope. His eyes would send a signal back of complicity, sympathy, and . . . nothing more. Then the fantasy would subside, and even through the whisky he was able to laugh at the pathetic melodrama his imagination had concocted.

And now Gerry was sitting a few hundred yards away. Without setting foot inside the Kit Kat club he knew how things would look. He could see Gerry lolling back in the most comfortable chair, fat cigarette between his fingers, warming himself at the admiration of the men, and the inevitable women, who would be clustered around him. He foresaw the easy greeting, the hand on the back, the casual, blank annihilation of what had passed between them. They would drink together and the bitterness he nursed would soften and after he had gone someone would say what a nice chap

he was and Gerry would say, yes, charming, although
the extraordinary thing is he once had a crack at my
wife.

Adam stopped. 'Do you know, I don't think I'll join
you after all.'

Minto turned to him. 'What's the matter, old boy?'

'I'm feeling a bit under the weather, that's all. '

'Well, it happens to the best of us. It seems a bit
feeble, but suit yourself.'

Adam called out to Koski, who came back. They
stepped out of Minto's hearing.

'I'm leaving you to it.'

'Why?'

'Never mind. I just don't feel like it.'

Koski looked disappointed but accepted the validity
of the excuse. 'What about the meeting at the Palmyra?' he asked.

'That's your business.'

'But you promised.' He sounded like a disappointed
child. Adam relented.

'OK then. I might catch up with you there later. But
don't say anything to the others.'

Koski set off along the bank.

Minto called out: 'Goodbye Tomaszewski, I'll say
hallo to Gerry for you.'

He walked back along the riverside and sat on the
parapet with his legs dangling into the dark drop below.
Gerry, he guessed, would be pleased at the news of the
encounter. One side of him, Gerry's intermittent Irish
side, would regret the lost opportunities for sentimen-

tality that the reunion would present. But his ego would also be bucked by Adam's failure to appear, which he would take as evidence of remorse, or continued suffering.

A boy approached him offering some unintelligible service and Adam told him sharply to go away. He pulled out a packet of cigarettes, reached in his tunic for his lighter and clicked it alight. The action brought something back to him; something from the first time he met her. He remembered the dip of the head as she ducked for the flame, the quick look of thanks, the smoky Moira laugh. He had thought he could forget her, or at least wall up the memory of her in some place where it would never escape. But now he could see her again and melancholy bubbled up in him like a dark spring.

Another boy appeared. He shooed him off, more gently this time. He was only doing his job. He weighed the lighter in his hand, feeling the weight and coolness of the metal, then dropped it into the fast brown water below his dangling feet.

He felt like a drink. He turned down a side street. The paths were crowded with soldiers, most of them drunk, holding each other up, simulating uproariousness. He saw an illuminated sign advertising the Balmoral Bar and climbed a dingy flight of stairs. The bar was spacious. An attempt had been made to recreate the mahogany gloom of an Edwardian saloon, with dark stained wood panelling and framed engravings of long-bodied racehorses.

Adam sat down and ordered a Stella. The local beer came in long brown bottles with a badly printed yellow oval label. It could be delicious, or poisonous, depending on the conditions of the day or the tightness of the sealing. There was a momentary hiss of gas as the waiter levered off the cap. Adam signalled for him to pour and a reassuring cushion of foam built up on the golden beer.

The bar seemed to be popular with army NCOs. At one table a corporal was playing chess with a sergeant. At another a small group, smoking pipes and sipping Stella, were apparently engaged in a political discussion, for he heard the names of King Farouk and Nahas Pasha. He looked at them – hard, brown, serious men – and compared them with the self-consciously insouciant adventurers he had left. Then he thought of his own comrades: Zaborski, the punctilious squadron leader, trying to maintain his bearings when the compass of his life had been smashed; and Koski, doggedly obeying some evolutionary impulse which told him that if he could adapt to disaster he could survive and even prosper. But the war would not be won by them. Victory would depend on these men – sober, honestly calculating – and the world that lay beyond it would belong to them. The adventurers would go on gambling. The Poles would sink or swim. But it was the NCOs who would inherit the earth.

A clock chimed. He had almost forgotten the meeting with Koski. He finished the last of the Stella, asked directions from the barman and set out along the emptying streets. He found the entrance in between some shops in a parade next to the bus station. A fat man waved him down the steep stairs whose red carpet had been turned black by the passage of thousands of dirty boots. He pushed through a swing door into a surprisingly large room in which tables and chairs clustered round a small dance floor. The clientele were a mixture of Egyptians and soldiers of all ranks, most of whom seemed glazed with drink.

He looked around but could see no sign of Koski. He sat down at a table and ordered a Stella. The foam died quickly when the waiter popped the cap, leaving a pale scum. Somewhere a nasal-sounding violin started up and was joined by several others. Adam looked up. A small orchestra, made up of middle-aged respectable-looking men in suits, ties and fezzes, was now seated at the side of the dance floor.

There was a patter of applause as the belly dancer emerged from behind a curtain draped at the back of the dance floor. She was fat even by the standards of her calling, and her stomach slumped in folds towards her thighs. Her appearance provoked groans and whistles from the soldiers, but the Egyptians stopped talking to each other and pulled their chairs round to the stage and leaned forward eagerly to get the best of the spectacle. She stood with her hands spread out, so that the flesh hung in hammocks below her upper arms. The footlights at the front of the stage shone into her face, accentuating the already pantomime exaggeration of her make-up.

For a few bars she remained immobile. Then her hips started to stir and shudder, and her belly began to move with a lazy, circular motion that had the precision and power of the first few revolutions of a locomotive getting up steam. The Egyptians gave little moans of excitement. Slowly the music gathered pace and slowly she responded to it, keeping her hands and feet immobile but combining the gyrations of her belly with a thrust of her thighs so that all her energy was focused in her wobbling flesh. The music grew faster and faster. The Egyptians were shouting encouragement. The soldiers who had fallen silent were whistling again, but this time with emphatic approval, the eyes in their young, red faces sparkling with lust.

He felt a hand on his shoulder. 'I didn't know you liked them fat.' He looked up at Koski grinning down at him. 'I'll get them to throw her in for you as part of the deal.'

He signalled Adam to follow him and they stepped out into a corridor next to the stinking lavatory.

'I'm glad you came. You missed a good time. Your friend was very disappointed that you didn't show up. He wanted to know all about what you were up to, so I told him all the news. Anyway . . .'

Koski's interest in the affairs of others was quickly exhausted and he moved on to his own concerns. 'I'm almost finished here. The wog has just gone off to knock up a diamond merchant to make double-sure he's buying the genuine article. We've got a bottle of whisky. Come and wait with me down here.'

Adam followed him down the corridor to a little office with a table and a sofa covered in grimy brocade. A thin Egyptian was sitting on the sofa, smoking and reading an Arabic newspaper. On the table was a round brass tray with a brass coffee pot and three tiny coffee cups, and a bottle of whisky. Rob Roy, it said on the smudgy label, a brand that Adam had never heard of. The room smelt of cardamom, cigarettes and dirty bodies.

Koski collected some glasses from the sink and poured two measures of Rob Roy.

'Where did you go?' he asked.

'Nowhere in particular. I just went for a drink.'

'You could have had a drink with us. What was the matter? Was it something to do with the Englishman?'

'He's Irish really. Not that it matters. I didn't want to see him particularly, it's true.'

Koski brightened up. 'Tell me about it.' He stopped. 'No, you don't have to. I think I know.'

Adam had told Koski the story once, late one whisky-sodden evening, and had assumed Koski had been too drunk to remember it. Koski tipped his glass to his thick lips. 'Oh well, it was best that you didn't come along then. Though he seemed very friendly for an Englishman. Or Irishman.'

He had just replaced the glass on the table when the door crashed open and the room was suddenly full of shouting, uniformed men. For a second or two Adam thought bemusedly that they were members of the audience angry about some aspect of the performance. Then he saw the red covers on their caps. Koski jumped up from the table and moved back a pace, holding up his arms in an abject show of submission. Adam was pulled out of his chair and pushed against the wall.

'You're under arrest,' said a squat, muscular man with a thistle tattooed on his forearm and sergeant's stripes.

'What for?' Koski sneered.

'Diamond smuggling,' said the sergeant.

'Where's the proof?'

The sergeant jerked his head to the door, where a small Egyptian in a European suit was standing flanked between two soldiers. Koski lunged at him and managed to punch him on the side of the head before the MPs intervened.

'No need for that,' said the sergeant. 'He wasn't the one who grassed on you.'

They were led down the corridor and out of a back door into a courtyard, then up some steps to where a Jeep was waiting to drive them away. Koski sat hunched up against the cold slipstream, looking angry and and miserable.

'I'm sorry, Adam,' he said. 'I'll make sure they know that it had nothing to do with you.'

They drove to a barracks by the river where they were marched in to see a desk sergeant, who wrote down their names on a series of forms. Then they were led down to a basement. They locked up Koski first.

'Good night,' he said as they pushed him into the cell. 'We won't be here long, don't worry.'

Then Adam was led inside a cement chamber with a narrow bed – not very different, he thought, to his quarters in Takoradi. He lay down on the bunk and heard the door bang shut and the key being turned in the lock.

24

He was given scrambled eggs and tinned ham and fruit salad for breakfast. The guard who brought it was friendly.

'You'll be out of here soon,' he said as he laid down the tray. That's what Koski had said. But an hour passed and nothing happened. He banged on the cell door and no one came. He shouted for Koski but the doors and walls were thick and there was no reply. He began to panic. Lying awake in the night he had thought that he might be able to slip back into headquarters by mid-morning, just another hungover reveller who had found a friendly bed in town. The longer he was locked up, the more time the gears of military justice had to mesh, and the harder it would be to disengage them.

It was noon before he heard boots clattering outside and the door unlocking. Two silent military policemen took him up to the reception desk where he had been signed in the night before. Koski was already there. He winked when he saw him. The sergeant behind the desk pushed a yellow form towards him.

'We're satisfied that you weren't involved in last night's business,' he said. 'Just sign this and you can be on your way.'

Adam scribbled his signature without reading the form.

'Oh, and this was left for you.'

He handed him an envelope. Koski took him by the arm and led him out of the front door. They hailed a taxi.

'Well, you're in the clear,' Koski said. 'I'm supposed to report back to them later in the day. I think it's just a formality. That's the last I'll see of those bloody diamonds, though. What's in the letter?'

Adam tore open the envelope. The letter was in ink, written in a tight, cramped hand.

Poor Old Tommy,
I heard about your plight this morning and have managed to smooth things over for you. I can't say the same for your pal who has a few questions to answer. What strange company you are keeping these days! Do give me a bell if there's anything else I can do for you (within reason!). I can be contacted at Tel Cairo 738 – at least for the next day or two.
Yours, aye
Gerry

He felt a flush of humiliation. 'Fuck you, Gerry,' he murmured.

'What's that?' Koski asked.

'Nothing.'

They sank back into the sagging seat of the taxi and let their private anxieties close over them. At headquarters there was a message saying that Squadron Leader Zaborski wanted to see them as soon as they got back. There was no time to wash and shave. He was waiting for them in his cabin. Koski went in first. He came out ten minutes later, smiling. Then Zaborski called Adam in. Zaborski was a silent man, with woolly grey hair, whose mildly martyred air had irritated Adam on the rare occasions he had been forced into his company. Adam looked at him wearily.

'Don't worry. There will be no further action taken against you. You were just unlucky in having chosen Koski as a companion. Although that, it seems to me, was a misfortune of your own making.'

He pushed away the papers in front of him. 'What's going to become of you, Tomaszewski?'

'I don't follow you, sir.'

'Koski I can understand. He's a peasant. You, though, are a gentleman, or at least you were brought up as one. I've watched you. You seem not to want to fight this war any more. You were a fighter pilot once and now you're a delivery boy.'

'There are medical reasons for that, as you know,' said Adam quietly.

'Not very good ones.'

Zaborski leaned back and turned away to examine a portrait of General Sikorski that hung, slightly askew, on the cabin wall.

Adam felt a surge of anger.

'Are you telling me I'm a coward?'

Zaborski turned back, his damp eyes full of concern.

'No, no, of course not. But don't you ever think that you could be doing something more useful? The war isn't over, Tomaszewski. Perhaps you should ask yourself whether or not you are doing your duty.' He sighed and stood up. 'You're dismissed. There's a flight back to Takoradi tomorrow. In the meantime I should keep away from Koski.'

Adam went back to his cabin and stripped off his uniform. His tunic smelled of beer and smoke. He stood in front of the small mirror over the basin and looked into his bloodshot, yellow-tinged eyes, as if they belonged to someone else. Then he shaved and changed and went and knocked on Koski's door. They went to the bar and ordered Bloody Marys. Then they took a taxi into town and spent the afternoon in an officers' brothel. In the evening they got very drunk, moving methodically from club to bar to restaurant. In the morning, feeling surprisingly well, he travelled as a passenger in a converted bomber back to Takoradi. The morning after his arrival he went to see his commanding officer and requested a transfer back to operational flying.

PART THREE

25

As spring turned to summer that year, the southern half of England filled up with men and machines. In country lanes, exhaust fumes smothered the smells of the hedge-rows and the fields disappeared under ammunition dumps and fuel farms and tank parks. Country pubs that had rarely seen a Londoner were filled with Americans, a species the local drinkers had only encountered previously in films. The invasion was coming, everyone knew it, but nobody knew when, or where.

Adam watched the build-up from the flat lands of the middle of England. He was a flight lieutenant in a special duties squadron at Warneford, a small town in west Cambridgeshire. He flew a Halifax bomber over Holland, Scandinavia, France and sometimes Poland, dropping agents and supplies.

He was twenty-six years old. He had slept with less than a dozen women and been in love with one of them. He did not know how many Germans he had killed, but it was probably fewer then ten. He worried vaguely that it was not enough. He had no expectation of returning to his own country and no notion of what would happen to him if he survived the war. For the moment, it was enough to live. Something told him he would go on living. The war had taught him the art of survival, physical and psychological. He felt hardened, fit and confident and – despite the danger and uncertainty – content. He had not advanced far up the promotion ladder, or won much glory. He had stood on the edge of disgrace and come near to losing his own respect. But it seemed to him in the rare moments that he thought about it that he had come through each crisis more strengthened than damaged. By and large he was happy. It may not have looked much like it, but in his own way he was having a good war.

'Won't be long now.'

'Do you have to keep saying that?'

Outside the dusty windows of the pub, a convoy of American lorries were grinding round the square of the market town.

'Any minute now. Got to be.'

He was drinking with Hennessy, his fitter from the Kingsmere days. The rest of the squadron was scattered or gone. Bealing was a flying instructor in Scotland. Buxton was a prisoner of war, somewhere in Germany. Whitbread was dead – killed over Sfax in Tunis the year before.

Hennessy was a navigator now, and flew in Adam's Halifax. He was also Adam's friend, if going to the pub once in a while or a film show in Warneford qualified as friendship.

'Drink up,' Adam said. 'We'd better be getting back for the briefing.'

They tipped up the thick glasses and set off through the Georgian streets of the town to the road that led to the base. As they walked, Hennessy talked once more of his plans. He was engaged to a girl he had met when home on leave in London. Her father had a small building firm and had offered him a partnership in the business when the war was over.

'It's the only game to be in,' he said, repeating an observation Adam had heard many times before. 'Think about it. All those bombed-out families that need roofs over their heads. We're going to make a bleeding fortune.'

'Don't talk about it,' Adam replied, as he always did. 'It's bad luck.'

They lodged with the rest of the squadron in a big, redbrick house on the edge of the base, a few miles outside Warneford. It had been built for a Victorian businessman, an amateur horticulturist, and the grounds were planted with alien trees and shrubs. All around the house, stuffed birds stood trapped inside glass domes with dust dulling their plumage. It was big enough to double as the staff headquarters for the Warneford wing. The agents that Adam dropped would often stay there the day before the mission.

The briefing room was crowded and smoky and noisy with chatter. Wing Commander McCoy rapped on the desk in front of him and called for silence.

'I haven't got much to tell you,' he said. 'But what I can say is important. From tomorrow night on you must be at maximum preparedness, ready to move at a moment's notice. You all know what's going on, so you can guess what this means. As soon as I have something to tell you I'll do so. But in the meantime, try and relax. It will be the last chance you get for a long time.'

'So, that's it then,' Hennessy said as they filed out of the briefing room. 'The beginning of the end.'

The news leaked across the base like spilled ink. The pub was full that night, the babble almost hysterical as speculation raged over whether the landing would fall in Normandy or the Pas de Calais. They were drunk when they rolled home, on beer and the prospect, distant but real, of peace.

The following morning Adam went to Mass as he sometimes did these days. The church in Warneford was large and gloomy, built of brick like everything else in the town. He stood at the back. There were about thirty people in the congregation, mostly elderly women and men. It was cold and smelt of damp and wax and stale incense. His mind wandered as he listened to the Irish priest plod through the Latin. *Credo in unum Deum* . . . Did he? Really? Yes, he did, in a childish, superstitious way. Today, his belief was stronger than usual, as his mind strayed to dangers ahead.

He was called back by the bells jangling from the altar as the priest lifted the host in his veiny hands. The worshippers rose stiffly and shuffled, heads bowed, to the altar rails, lowered themselves down and raised their heads and extended their tongues, eyes shut like sleepwalkers, to receive the wafer.

A solid bar of sunlight broke suddenly through a high window, splitting the gloom, gilding and warming the cold plaster walls, bringing a reminder of the life outside the dank bricks of the church. The last communicant returned to her pew. The priest tidied away the communion things and pronounced the last words of the Mass. *Ita Missa est . . .*

Adam stepped out into the porch and through the iron-studded wooden doors and into the warm light of the morning. He had an hour to kill before he had to be back. He didn't feel like a drink. He sat on a bench outside the church and lit up. He half closed his eyes and enjoyed the luxury of doing and thinking nothing.

'I thought it was you.'

A woman was standing in front of him who looked just like Moira. It was Moira.

'Christ,' he said.

'No, just me.'

They looked at each other for a few moments, dumbly. In the days when he had dreamed that they would meet again, none of the scenarios had been like this.

Then she chuckled, that dark brown sound that he had loved.

'You look different,' she said. 'Grown up.'

'You don't.'

It wasn't true.

She looked worn, he could see now. Her features were sharper and there were faint lines at the corner of her mouth. Looking at her standing there in the revealing light, he knew what she would look like as an old lady.

'I stopped thinking I'd ever see you again,' he said.

'Did you want to?'

'Of course.' He paused.

She sighed. 'I'm feeling sad now,' she said heavily. 'Do you want to, I don't know, get a cup of coffee . . . ? I'm staying just over there.'

She pointed with her chin towards a hotel, an old coaching inn, on the far side of the square. They walked across the cobbles and into a low-beamed bar with round tables and hoop-backed chairs. They sat for a moment in silence, then the quiet was broken by a shout of masculine laughter coming from the far side of the bar.

She groaned with irritation.

'We can't talk here,' she said. 'Let's go up to my room.'

The bedroom was small and stuffy. There was barely space for the bed, an armchair and a chest of drawers. He stood by the door as she sat down on the bed, snapped open her handbag and retrieved a packet of cigarettes. She waited for a moment, as if expecting him to extend a chivalrous, lighter-bearing hand, but he stayed where he was, leaning awkwardly against the wall, and she lit the cigarette herself.

'You haven't told me what you're doing here,' he said.

'Neither have you.'

'I'm at Warneford now. Just up the road.'

She lit the cigarette herself and blew out a plume of smoke the way he remembered, and then looked up at him, embarrassed.

'Well I'm here because of Gerry,' she said. 'I'm here to say goodbye. They're dropping him somewhere. France, I imagine.'

He said nothing.

She sat with her knees pressed together, looking at the worn carpet.

'We're married, you know.'

'I didn't,' he said quietly. 'When?'

'Four years ago, nearly. Nineteen-forty. October the thirteenth.'

They hadn't wasted much time then.

'I see.'

A ringing silence closed in. She got up abruptly from the bed and ground out the cigarette in the ashtray on the tallboy and swung round on him, her eyes flashing.

'Don't stand there looking like some bloody martyr! What was I supposed to do? He was going away. I didn't know if I would ever see him again. Blame it on the bloody war.'

She sighed and shook her head and went over to him and took his hands in her long, strong fingers. He smelt her lemony scent and the tobacco on her breath.

'Let's not fight,' she said wearily. 'I want you to know what happened,' she said. 'Do you want to hear it or not?'

He nodded. She let go of his hands and clenched her fists and lowered her head, speaking in a slow, deliberate, voice, like a witness being asked to remember the details of a crime.

'After you left me that day, I felt happy. It all seemed so simple. Gerry had betrayed me. I thought I was in love with you. We were going to be together. Even after you telephoned and told me that Gerry was on his way over, I still had no doubts that everything would work out. But when I saw him, something happened. He didn't try and charm me back. He was crying and talking about killing himself. I actually believe he meant it. For the first time I was convinced he really did love me, but that wasn't why I did what I did. I didn't go back to him because he loved me. I did it because he needed me.'

'And I didn't?'

She looked at him and shook her head.

'No, Adam, I don't think you did. Not really, not in the end.' She went over to her handbag and lit another cigarette.

'After he found me, I told him I needed time to think. He said he would stay there in the hotel as long as it took. I walked for hours, round and round that bloody churchyard. I thought about everything that had happened that day and all the things you had said to me. And of course the things you hadn't said, too.'

She drew slowly on the cigarette. 'If things were normal I would have waited. But you can't afford to be patient when there's a war on. There isn't the time. You've got to seize the moment because you never know what's coming. Who knows whether I'll see Gerry again after tomorrow.'

She went back to the bed and sat down and patted the shabby counterpane. He joined her, feeling the mattress sag and the pressure of her thin thigh against his.

She took his hand and turned her blue grainy eyes on him.

'There's something I learned from all that which is probably the only bit of wisdom I'll ever acquire,' she said. 'You see, love is the most precious thing we will ever possess. I sound like a silly song. But it's true, it is. You know it too, Adam, because you hung on to your love when you could have given it to me. When you saw I wanted it, you thought it must be worth more than you thought it was and you would be a fool to give it away so cheaply.

'But you're wrong, you know. As wrong as it's possible to be. The point about love is that it's the most precious thing you have, but it's worthless unless you give it away.'

She paused. 'What a speech,' she said, smiling at him. Her eyes grow serious again. 'You will remember what I said, won't you?'

He nodded.

'Promise?'

He nodded again.

He tried to smile at her. He had forgotten how earnest she could be. He thought of protesting, but he knew she was telling the truth. Even in their most delirious moments, he had always hung on to something. Did that mean he had not loved her?

He could think of nothing more to say. She did not seem to expect anything. He saw them both framed in the mirror on the chest of drawers: him sullen, her used and worried-looking. He wanted to go but it did not seem right to leave. He had to salvage something.

He leaned towards her and pulled her close. Their lips brushed and for a second her tongue darted against his. Then, abruptly, she stopped and pushed him away.

'It's not right' she said. 'Sorry.' She got up from the bed and picked up her bag.

'I suppose I'd better go and find Gerry.'

The old priest was closing the church when he went past.

'Could you let me in for five minutes, father?'

'Sure, it's God's house, not mine, son. Go away in.'

Inside it was dark and the smell of snuffed candles hung in the air. He knelt at the back and offered up a brief, protective prayer. *Dear God. Please let me forget her quickly* . . .

He repeated it over and over until the order was lost and the words ran into one another. High up among the hammer beams, he heard a desperate fluttering. A small bird was beating against the leaded windows. He walked over to the wall by the tenth station of the cross, to where a cord hung down, and pulled on it. The window fell open and the bird flew free. He was smiling as he walked out into the sunshine.

At nine the next morning he was told to collect his crew and come to the briefing room in the house. Wing Commander McCoy and an intelligence officer were standing in front of a map of northern and central France.

'I'm sorry this is so vague,' McCoy said, 'but I want you to plot a route to west central France. At the moment I can't tell you more than that.'

There were four in the crew with him: Hennessy navigating, Hawkins the engineer, Mount, the dispatcher who supervised the jumps, and Johnson the rear gunner. They spent a few hours with the maps, charting a course due south to London, then east over the bulge of Kent and east Sussex, turning south again over the Channel, avoiding the heavy concentrations of flak along the Atlantic Wall. Then it was due south all the way, following the railway lines and the rivers that marked the path to their destination. He had flown the route a few times before. The biggest problem would be the night fighters lying in the darkness of the coastal airfields. Halifaxes were strong and dependable. If all went well they could be over the drop zone and back in under five hours.

Before lunch they drove over to the hangar to talk to the ground crew. The chief fitter wriggled out from a hatch in the aircraft's belly and came over to him. They climbed inside. The bomb racks had been adapted to carry cylinders packed with arms and supplies. At the back, a hole had been cut in the floor for the passengers to drop through. They called their mysterious passengers 'Joes'. The hatch they went through was the 'Joe hole'. They finished the checks, then climbed out again. There was nothing more to do.

The rest of the crew went to the mess for lunch. Adam went to his room and tried to sleep. He was restless and nervous. He read a book but his eyes kept slipping off the page. He went downstairs and out into the garden and walked for a while among the groves of strange trees and shrubs, past the weed-choked Chinese garden.

When he got back, he found the crew playing cards in the mess.

'Where did you get to?' Hawkins asked. 'McCoy wants to see us.'

He was over at the base. They took a Jeep through the lanes across the railway line and down the grove of lime trees that led into the aerodrome. It had been built, quickly, at the start of the war, and a few old brick farm buildings were still marooned between the hangars and workshops.

McCoy led them into the briefing room.

'It looks like you'll be leaving tonight,' he said, 'so I can tell you a bit more about the mission.'

They leaned forward in their chairs as he pulled down a map.

'You'll have five passengers. Two are chaps from a special operations unit you don't need to know anything about. The other three are agents engaged in business that is no concern of ours. You'll have a chance to meet them at dinner, but please, don't bother them with any unnecessary questions. You'll also be dropping a dozen supply containers. The drop zone is here,' he tapped at the map with a pencil 'about fifteen miles east of Châtellerault. Your main problem will be the night fighters at the Châteauroux base where the Germans have supporting radar. You'll be leaving at twenty-two hundred hours.'

They drove back in silence. It was a strange sort of day. There was a fresh breeze blowing and banks of clouds were rolling restlessly overhead. Back at the house, Adam joined the card school. They played pontoon for stakes that started out small but grew bigger as they became absorbed in the game. Hennessy played like a child, exulting in his wins and making loud accusations of cheating whenever he lost. Mount's luck was in. As the afternoon wore on, a pile of half-crowns and florins grew in front of him.

Eventually they tired of the game. A WAAF brought in a tray of tea. They were bored and nervous. The grown-up thing to do, they knew, would have been to retreat to their rooms, but they were reluctant to move away from the warmth generated by their huddled companionship. It was a relief when a WAAF came in and announced that a film show was about to take place in the library. It was a cowboy picture from before the war. For an hour they lost themselves in the drumming hooves.

At seven thirty they were called to dinner. Agents were sure of a good supper before they left, and the crews often ate with them. The housekeeper bought meat, game and cheese from local estates and farms, and some Cambridge colleges had donated wine from their cellars. Adam rarely enjoyed the dinners. There was too much on his mind and someone always made the same bad joke.

'I suppose you could call this the last supper,' they would say as pudding was served. For some of the anonymous men and women who had passed through the dining room, it was.

Before dinner they went into the library for a glass of sherry. Three of the passengers were already there, standing awkwardly in front of the empty fireplace. A bald civilian in glasses, the oldest among them, came over and began chatting. He did not introduce himself. They talked for a while about the weather and the neighbourhood and the progress of the war, then conversation died away and they stood in semi-silence, fiddling with the sticky stems of their sherry glasses.

Adam wondered why he had gone to dinner, or why the meal had been arranged in the first place. The Joes seemed green and nervous. He doubted if they had ever been in any real danger before. By rights they should have been writing a last letter home, or on their knees praying for luck or forgiveness. On the other hand, perhaps they drew some comfort from the sight of him and the crew, to all appearances casual and good-humoured, relaxed about a trip they had made many times before without mishap. He tried harder to make conversation. Finally a WAAF appeared and said that dinner was on the table.

As he was taking the passengers towards the arch that led into the dining room, he heard the door knob turning and an orderly's voice saying, 'You'll find them in there, sir.'

Heavy boots thudded over the carpet. Adam turned round. Gerry was wearing a parachute smock and canvas webbing loaded with pouches, scabbards and bandoliers. His hair was longer than before and he had grown a moustache that made him look like a nine-teenth-century poet.

'Hallo brother,' he said softly. 'Wartime is full of surprises. Not all of them this pleasant.'

He slipped off his webbing and smoothed his hand through his hair.

'Do you two know each other?' A young man, eager and nervous, was standing behind him.

'Course I do,' Gerry said brightly. 'Glover, this is Tommy, our chauffeur for the evening.'

They shook hands.

'Tommy and I go back years,' said Gerry in a light, slightly menacing voice. 'We share a lot in common. When did we last see each other?'

'Summer of forty.'

'That's right,' said Gerry. 'Summer of forty. Although we nearly bumped into each other in Cairo, but I don't suppose you want to go into that. By the way, you could at least have dropped me a line to thank me, you ungrateful bastard.'

Glover looked at him to see if he was joking. He decided he was and gave an uncertain laugh.

'Still,' Gerry continued boisterously, 'you can repay the favour by getting us safely to where we're going tonight.' He looked around at the rest of the company. 'I don't know about you, but I'm starving.'

They went into the dining room. Adam sat as far away as he could from Gerry, but it was a round table and Gerry did most of the talking. He spoke with apparent authority about the coming invasion and predicted that the war would be finished before the year was over. The others listened, absorbed, laughing at his jokes and nodding at his glib, reassuring analysis.

Adam watched him, fascinated at the easy way he carried people with him, and despising him for his need for admiration – or at least attention. Tonight he was getting both.

The food was as good as always. They had potted shrimps from Yarmouth and lamb with mint sauce, then treacle pudding and cheese. The crews were supposed to go easy on the wine, but the warning was unnecessary. Anxiety acted like amphetamine on the way out, and by the time you were heading back, the alcohol had long worn off. Gerry seemed to know all about the vintages and was particularly admiring of the Gevrey-Chambertin that was served with the lamb. In the end it was the bald agent who made the 'last supper' remark.

They pushed back the chairs and moved into the library for a synthetic coffee.

It was time for Adam to take charge. He got up from his armchair.

'Gentlemen,' he said. 'Your attention for a few minutes. Our vehicles will be coming for us at twenty-one hundred hours. From here we'll go to the airfield where we are scheduled to take off an hour later. That means we've got half an hour to relax and finish our coffee.'

Before he sat down, Gerry came over, all joviality gone.

'Come over here,' he said. They moved towards the bookshelves. He looked straight at him, the first time he had done so all evening.

'Let's not pretend nothing happened,' he said. 'You and me should talk.'

'There's nothing to say, is there?'

Gerry sank down onto a leather Chesterfield and pulled out his cigarettes. Adam joined him reluctantly.

'There's always something to say,' said Gerry, pushing his cigarette case towards him. 'Besides, we'll probably never get the chance again.'

The flame of the lighter trembled slightly as he lit his cigarette and Adam's.

'I have every reason to be sore at you and I suppose you should hate my guts. The fact is I don't really think that much about the episode. There are no hard feelings. I think I demonstrated that with the helping hand I gave you in Cairo. Playing the injured party isn't my style. Perhaps it's because I won. Or maybe I just think life's too bloody short to waste time brooding on its little setbacks.'

'It didn't seem like a little setback at the time, did it?'

Gerry looked at him more closely. 'What do you mean?'

'You were going to kill yourself. That's why she took you back.'

'Who told you that?' His voice was low and violent.

'Calm down. Moira did.'

'Moira?' he said stupidly.

'Moira. I saw her in town this morning.'

'She never said . . .' For a moment he looked confused, like an actor forgetting his lines. Adam had never seen him like that. Then he recovered.

'Well you're wrong. It wasn't emotional blackmail that did it, if that's what you're saying. The best man won. It was as simple as that.'

He dragged heavily on his cigarette.

'She was bound to come back,' he said. 'You stick with what you know.'

Adam could see Hawkins coming towards him, pointing at his watch. 'The cars will be out the front, skipper,' he said. 'We ought to get moving.'

Gerry stood up abruptly and smoothed back his long hair.

'He's right,' he said sharply. 'Let's get this over with.'

26

The wind had strengthened during the evening and was pushing tattered clouds fast across the dark pewter sky. Adam circled the airfield, then lined up on the railway to give himself a southward heading. The wind was behind them and would speed them along on the outward journey.

The dark mass of London showed up ahead; then they were over Kent and he could see the waves of the Channel glinting in the moonlight. The Kentish ports were dense with shipping. Over Sussex, Hennessy's voice broke into his earphones telling him to swing a few degrees to the south. He kept the Halifax low, skirting the known airfields and flak batteries lining the Normandy coast, and then the fields and forests of France were slipping beneath the wings. He picked up the twisting track of the Seine as it wound past Rouen. From there it was about an hour to the target area.

The agents were to jump first, over a site about fifty miles south of Tours. After that it was the turn of Gerry and Glover. It was blowing hard. He would have to bring the Halifax down yet further, to a thousand feet, if his passengers were not to be carried miles away from the drop zones by the wind. He handed over to

Hawkins and clambered back through the cockpit and into the fuselage. The passengers were asleep or dozing, lulled by the drone of the engines. They lay curled up under their sleeping bags on the floor of the aircraft, heads propped against rucksacks, strangely innocent-looking. Then Mount, the dispatcher, looked towards him questioningly. Adam shook his head and gave him a thumbs-up sign and climbed back into the cockpit.

Somewhere south of Chartres, a flak gunner heard the engines and opened up, but the shells exploded in clusters of dirty smoke at least a mile away. Then they were over the Loire. Hennessy moved over to him, tapping on the map with a gloved forefinger to show their position. He pushed the nose of the Halifax down and they began a shallow descent towards the first drop zone. Over the intercom, he told Mount to wake up the agents.

A layer of cloud came up to meet them, streaming over the cockpit, then they were through it and the ground was unrolling fast below. He saw copses and woods and a scattering of small lakes he recognised from the reconnaissance photographs. Hennessy nudged him on the shoulder and pointed ahead and to the left. He saw a clearing and a line of yellowish lights. He pushed on the controls, forcing the aircraft downwards. The altimeter showed a thousand feet. He looked at Hennessy who nodded, then switched on the green light that was the signal to jump. They were over the drop zone. He could see the ploughed corrugations of the field and the smoke rising from the signal fires, then the field was behind them and he pulled back on the stick to gain height. Mount came over the intercom. The agents had gone through the Joe hole cleanly. All their parachutes had opened.

The next drop was less than ten minutes away. He kept the speed as low as he dared without risking a stall. He concentrated on finding the main road and railway line that would lead him to the next destination. Then he heard a rattling from behind, the noise of the rear guns being fired. He flicked on the intercom.

'What's going on?'

Johnson's frightened voice crackled in his head-phones.

'Two fighters. Behind us.'

'Hang on,' Adam said uselessly. 'We're almost there now.'

They made an easy target silhouetted against the pale, grey ground. Cannon shells punched holes in the starboard wing. Behind he could hear the clatter of Johnson's machine gun shooting back. Then it stopped.

Mount's voice came on the intercom, strangely calm. 'I think Johnny's copped it.'

'OK,' Adam said.

With Johnson dead they had no defences. They were finished, he was sure of that. Cannon fire was pounding the starboard engine now. Flames jumped from the engine, then smoke. He pulled back hard and the Halifax strained upwards. He flicked on the intercom.

'We're baling out,' he said. 'Mount, get the passengers out first, then the crew. I'll follow.'

He motioned to Hennessy and Hawkins to move into the back. They hesitated for a moment, then scrambled to the rear. The second engine on the starboard wing was now on fire. He watched the propeller slow and struggled with the controls in an effort to keep the bomber steady.

Then Mount was speaking again. 'All passengers and crew gone. Your turn.' He pulled back to gain a last bit of height and slid down the gangway into the back of the plane. The fuselage was filling with smoke. The aircraft was yawing and rolling and he stumbled and fell, pitching forward to the edge of the Joe hole. Mount was clutching a bulkhead, braced against the side. He hauled Adam up, steadied him, then pushed him down into the rushing void below.

Adam was caught off balance. He felt a jab of pain as his knee banged against the metal lip. Then he was falling and the dark shadow of the plane slid over him. He scrabbled at the toggle on his harness and pulled, hard. For a moment nothing happened and he held his breath. Then his chest was gripped by the har-ness and he was swinging in the cool night air with the departing drone of the bomber's two remaining engines fading overhead.

He looked around. Ahead he could see the Halifax flying on, the burning struts and hoops of its body making a fiery cross against the sky, a ghost ship carrying Johnson to Valhalla. Away to the left, two parachutes tilted gracefully like jellyfish in a sea-swell. The dark mass below him looked like a group of trees. They were coming up quite fast. He felt a branch tearing at his calf, then a jarring shock that raced up his spine, and he was flung on his back on the cold ground and was rolling over. The shrouds of the parachute pulled at his shoulders. He got upright, grateful to feel his legs holding up underneath him, and pulled the cords towards him until he had gathered up the silk into an untidy bundle. He had landed on a field at the edge of a copse. He moved into the cover of the trees and sat down on the bundled parachute. He ran his hand over his leg and felt wetness. He touched the cut. It was about four inches long and did not feel too deep. The earth was soft and loose. He scooped out a shallow pit and pushed the parachute inside it, then heaped dirt and dead leaves on top. Then he sat with his back against the bole of a tree and listened.

The Germans would arrive soon. The night fighters would have alerted the ground to the parachutes. He would try first to find the others. If that failed he would make off on his own. All he could hear was the wind rustling in the tops of the trees and a dog barking in the distance. He got up and set off towards where he thought he had seen the parachutes falling, running and walking, hugging the side of the field so that his outline would be absorbed in the trees. He came to a hedgerow and found a gap and scrambled through. There was a wheat field on the other side, animated by the night wind. He stopped and looked, carried away by the strange beauty of what he saw. The wind stroked the wheat ears of the stalks, brushing them this way and that, making the field sigh and whisper.

Something was moving in the middle of the field. A figure was struggling through the waving wheat, swinging his arms from side to side to keep himself upright, like a swimmer wading ashore through the shallows. Adam moved forward cautiously. The figure bent over, disappearing beneath the rippling surface, then emerged again holding a bundle, which he raised above his head before setting off again towards the trees standing at the edge of the field.

Adam crouched down and made his way stealthily along the track that ran by the trees, and as he got closer he saw that there were three or four dark shapes gathered on the fringe of the wood. Just as he noticed them they turned towards him and he heard a murmur of alarm and the figures disappeared, melting into the trees. He heard an English voice, low but carrying, coming out of the greenish gloom.

'Who are you? Identify yourself or we shoot.'

The voice sounded so pompous and cross, he had to stifle a giggle.

'Don't do that. It's me, Tomaszewski.'

'Oh. It's you.' It was Gerry's voice, he could tell now. 'Come forward, but slowly.'

Adam advanced down the track, pacing deliberately, like in a children's game. Then Gerry stepped out from the trees. 'You shouldn't creep up on people like that,' he said. 'You're liable to get hurt.'

He had blackened his face so that the whites of his eyes stared madly out of their sockets. 'Where's the rest of your crew?' His voice was cold and professional now.

'I don't know. Everyone but Mount jumped before me.'

Gerry grunted. 'Well, we can't hang about looking for them. The Germans will be here any minute. That plane made a spectacle like bloody Guy Fawkes night.'

'That's hardly my fucking fault . . .' began Adam, but Gerry had slipped back between the trees and he followed behind. There were three of them, he could see now: Gerry, Glover and a young man, more of a boy really, wearing shorts and sandals and a jersey that was too small for him. They were joined after a few seconds by a fourth man in civilian clothes, who was sweating and panting, carrying a bundled parachute attached to a padded, canvas sack. Laboriously, he began detaching the sack from the harness.

'Give it here.' The older man looked up with uncomprehending eyes as Gerry snatched the bundle and slashed at it with a broad-bladed knife.

'Leave the parachutes. Let's thin out.' Gerry turned to the man.

'*C'est loin d'ici, votre camp?*'

'*Comment?*'

'*Où est votre commandant?*'

The man looked hopelessly around.

'Oh, fucking hell. You talk to him, Tommy!'

Adam spoke to him clearly and slowly. The man understood and moved a little way into the trees, beckoning for them to follow.

'Thank Christ for that,' Gerry said. 'Let's get a move on.'

They moved in single file through the belt of trees and onto a track that led across a field and onto a narrow road. Gerry and Glover were loaded down with rucksacks. Their webbing belts bulged with ammunition pouches and they carried short-nosed Sten guns. Soon, they were breathing heavily.

After half an hour they came to a lane that led to a farmhouse and a huddle of outbuildings. A dog started barking as they approached, but the boy ran on ahead to quiet it and the noise died away. At the entrance to the farmyard, the older man motioned them to wait. They saw him pad away and rap on the door. There was a muffled conference and he returned. He led them over to a barn, pushed open the creaking door and pointed to a mound of straw banked against a wall.

'This looks like our kip,' Glover said, trying to sound cheerful. 'And very welcome too. I'm bushed.'

'No more than three hours' sleep,' Gerry said. 'We'll have to be ready to be away from here as soon as the *maquis* blokes show up.'

Adam burrowed into the straw, feeling the cold now. He looked around the barn and found a bundle of sacking which stank of cow dung. He pulled it over him and soon fell asleep.

When he woke up the sun was poking rods of light through the chinks in the wall of the barn. There was no sign of the others. He went to the door and pushed it open. His watch said it was six o'clock. The farmyard was deserted. He looked around, then walked quickly across to the back door of the farmhouse. He could hear voices coming from inside. He knocked on the cracked paint and the voices stopped. The door opened slowly and a woman's face appeared. She looked at him blankly.

He told her who he was and she pulled the door open. He stepped into a low, beamed room with a stone floor and a big fireplace. In the middle was long table. Gerry and Glover were sitting at the table with their Sten guns trained at the door. Between them was a big-boned man in a baggy suit.

Gerry glanced indifferently towards him. 'You'd better sit down,' he said.

Adam did as he was told. The woman placed a bowl of hot milk in front of him and a plate of fried eggs and crusty bread. He ate and listened.

Gerry was doing the talking. 'If what you say is true, then we have to get moving immediately,' he said. 'We're expecting the rest of the gang to drop in tonight. But we don't know where until we get the radio working. I suggest that we move out of here and find a secure location near a decent dropping zone then contact HQ to arrange the rendezvous. After that we can look around for something to blow up.'

He seemed boisterous and businesslike.

'What's going on?' Adam asked.

Gerry glanced up at him. 'It's happened, apparently.'

'What has?' said Adam, knowing the answer immediately.

'The landing, you idiot.'

The Frenchman broke in. 'It's true,' he said smilingly. 'They went ashore all along the Normandy coast at dawn this morning.'

'How do you know?'Adam asked.

'There was a coded announcement on the *messages personnels* broadcast on the BBC just over an hour ago.'

Happiness pumped into Adam, buoying him up like helium. In all the time of fighting he had often wondered whether this thing would ever end. Now it seemed that one day it would. Some sort of finish was in sight. Not next month, perhaps, or even next year. But some time.

'But that's wonderful,' he said.

'Don't get carried away,' Gerry said. ' This is just the beginning.'

He looked over at Adam, apparently coming to some decision.' I suppose we are all in this together, at least for the time being,' he said. 'I'd better explain what's going on.' He leaned forward.

'Now that the landing is under way, the Jerries will be in a hurry to move their reserve units up to try and stop us breaking out of the beachhead. To the south of us there are some big concentrations of troops, including a division of SS who have been resting up after their time on the Eastern Front. When the rest arrive, our job will be to work with the local Resistance to try and slow their advance north by whatever means come to hand.' He turned towards the Frenchman. 'This is Alain. We'll be operating alongside him and his men. Alain, this is Flight Lieutenant Tomaszewski.' They leaned across the broad table and shook hands.

Gerry stood up. 'Let's get moving,' he said.

Outside, a low-slung car was waiting. The young man who had met them the night before was at the wheel. He nodded to Adam as he climbed in the back with Gerry and Glover. Alain sat in the front. They set off through a landscape of fields and spinneys and small lakes and ponds. The only other traffic on the road were occasional carts, drawn by horses. 'Petrol is precious,' Alain said in English. There was no sign of the Germans.

They drove through villages and small nondescript towns, each with its square containing church, mairie, hotel and café. There were propaganda posters warning the population against fleas and Communists, many of them torn and defaced. Here and there, someone had followed the instructions broadcast by Free French radio from London and daubed a V-for-Victory sign on a wall. After a while they crossed over a railway bridge and passed through a hamlet, then pulled off down a farm track and bumped along for ten minutes until they came to a flat field fringed with beech and oak trees.

'I thought this would do for the drop zone,' Alain said. They got out of the car and Gerry paced around. He turned towards Adam. 'What say you, Tommy?'

Adam looked around. 'It looks ideal. The pilot can get his bearing from the railway track and the church tower in the village.'

'Right-oh,' Gerry said. 'We'll take it.'

They drove back to the road and continued for five or so miles until the boy driver pulled into the driveway of a house on the outskirts of a village. It was built of brick and had chimney stacks twisted like barley sugar.

'This will be our base until tomorrow,' Alain said. 'Then we'll have to move on.'

He went over to the house and the boy led them into a large stone stable block at the back. Inside it smelt of hay and engine oil. A handsome car was jacked up on wooden blocks in a corner. Gerry and Glover undid the canvas bag and pulled out out a chunky wireless transmitter, which they placed on a trestle. Gerry stood back while Glover fiddled with it, then climbed up into the rafters seeking a high point for the aerial. When he was satisfied, he crouched by the apparatus and twisted a switch. A faint light glowed orange inside. Gerry rubbed his hands together with satisfaction. Glover donned a pair of headphones and began tweaking the frequency knob, delicately, like a bank robber cracking a safe. For a few tense minutes they listened in silence. Then Glover smiled. He motioned to Gerry who sat down next to him.

'Just tell them Bellona has landed,' he said.

Glover dabbed dots and dashes with the signal key.

He paused to listen and then started jotting notes on a pad with a stub of pencil.

Gerry snatched it from him.

'OK,' he said, 'now here's the fix for the drop.' He pulled out a map and dictated some times and grid references. As Glover translated the message, Gerry swung round to face them.

'They're dropping in another fifteen blokes tonight, and lots of equipment and explosives. That gives us all day to make some mischief.' He went off to the house to find Alain and left them in the stable block.

'What's Bellona?' asked Adam.

'The goddess of war, apparently,' said Glover. 'It's the name of the operation. They give them these funny names. Major Cunningham chose it.'

Glover lay back on a pile of straw.

'Do you think it's true?'

'The landing? Yes, I'm sure it is. It had to happen sometime.'

'So that means it will all be over pretty soon.' His voice could not disguise a note of hope. He paused before he added, 'I'll just catch the tail end of it.'

'It could be a long tail.'

'What do you mean?'

'It's a long way from Normandy to Berlin. '

Glover made no reply and Adam wished he had stayed silent.

'Have you been with the unit long?'

'The Special Operations Service?' Glover sat up. 'No. I volunteered a few months ago. Just finished my training and I was sent off here.'

'What were you up to before that?'

'Nothing much. After call-up I was commissioned into an artillery outfit, but it never went anywhere.'

'So you've never been in action?'

'No. Half the blokes in our mob haven't. It's grown a lot since the early days.'

Adam smiled at him. 'Well, don't worry about it. The thing is that when it happens there's so much going on that you don't have time to think about it.'

'Thanks,' said Glover. He offered Adam a cigarette.

Gerry came back looking businesslike.

'Got some good news for you, Tommy,' he said. 'One of Alain's boys dropped by. He said that a couple of types answering the description of your crew turned up at a farm about twenty miles away. He'll give you someone to take you over there to pick them up.'

Somehow Adam had assumed they would be all right.

'That's a relief,' he said. 'What are you doing?'

'I'm going off with Alain to find a camp where we can base ourselves when the rest of the blokes turn up. Then, if there's any time, I thought we might go and create a bit of mayhem.' He set off for the door then turned back.

'What's up, Glover? Aren't you coming?'

Glover got to his feet and hurried after him.

Outside, the low-slung car was waiting. Alain was leaning over the window talking to the young driver. He smiled as Adam came over.

'You're going on another tour of the countryside,' he said. 'Jump in.' He spoke English easily, without bothering too much about the accent. He handed him a blue cotton jacket. 'Put this on. I'm sorry I haven't got any trousers.'

Adam got in the front passenger seat and the boy set off. He had changed out of the shorts and jersey of the previous night, and had on baggy flannel trousers and a blue short-sleeved shirt open wide at the neck. But Adam noticed he was wearing the same childish buckled leather sandals, the sort that Adam had worn to school during the summer. He drove well.

'What's your name?' Adam asked in French.

'Jean,' said the boy briskly.

They followed long straight roads, through fields dotted with sheep and large, pale cattle. The country-side seemed benign, bucolic, empty of Germans.

'They stay in Montcharles mostly,' Jean said. 'In the country, most of the trouble comes from the Milice.'

'How many of your schoolfriends joined?'

'The Milice? Not many. The scum. More than joined the Resistance, though, but that's changing.' He spoke without looking at Adam, concentrating on the road. Adam noticed the reddish bristles on his chin. He was older than he had thought. Nineteen perhaps.

They turned down a lane, past a rusting abandoned car, and pulled up outside a shabby house shaded by some fruit trees. 'Wait here,' Jean said, and went inside. He came out a few minutes later and motioned him over. Adam ducked through the low door. After the bright sunlight outside it was difficult to see at first. Then he made out two figures crouching in a corner.

'Who is it?' a voice said.

'Pat?' Adam bent into the shadows. 'Is that you?'

There was a burst of laughter and Hennessy stood up. He came forward and shook Adam's hand. 'Am I glad to see you.'

Adam searched the gloom. 'Who else have you got there?'

'It's me, Hawkins.'

'Is Mount with you?'

'No. Didn't he bail out with you?'

'No, I went before him.' Adam felt a stab of guilt as he remembered the smoke-filled fuselage and the fiery cross in the sky. 'Maybe he'll turn up,' he murmured unconvincingly.

He led them out to the car. They stripped off their tunics and ties and stowed them in the boot, and climbed into the back seat. Adam swivelled round.

'Let's hear it then. What happened to you?'

They had landed in a wood and Hennessy's parachute had caught in a tree, leaving him hanging helplessly until Hawkins found him and cut him free. They had walked all night across fields until dawn broke, when they hid in woodshed. A farmer found them there a few hours later, took them into his house, fed them, and sent word to the local *maquis*.

'Neither of us speaks any French,' Hawkins said. 'When he sent his boy off, we thought for a while he might have gone to tip off the Germans.'

Adam suddenly remembered the extraordinary news.

'You'll never guess what's happened,' he said, grinning.

They looked blank.

'They've landed.'

'Who?' Hawkins asked.

'Us. The Allies.'

Adam watched their faces brighten with joy and they started to whoop and jump up and down.

'That means we won't have to bother about making our own way back,' said Hennessy. 'We'll just wait for the brown jobs to come and liberate us here.'

'But really, though,' Hawkins said. 'What are we going to do next?'

'I don't know,' Adam said. 'I suppose we could request a pick-up, but it would be a pretty tricky operation and with the landings in full swing I imagine we come a long way down the list of priorities. Or we could make our way south across the Pyrenees to Spain. Or we could do what Pat says, just stick with the SOS blokes and wait and see what happens.'

'That gets my vote,' Hennessy said. 'From what I've seen, there are worse places to hang about. Who are the SOS?'

'They're the blokes we dropped,' Adam said. 'They go around behind the lines blowing things up.'

'Sounds a bit keen to me,' Hennessy said. 'But I suppose they've got to do it while they've got the chance. The war will be over pretty soon.'

The straight road began to twist as they reached some higher ground. The bright light dimmed suddenly as a lone cloud floated across the sun. At the crest of the rise the lush foliage gave out, and they passed through a stricken forest of dead pines as grey as old bones. When they emerged they were on the side of a low hill that sloped down to a valley with a river winding along its floor. A small town was clustered around the ends of a bridge. The road took them through it. It was a small town like many others. They rumbled over the cobbles, between rows of terraced houses that opened onto narrow pavements, past small, neat shops, then into a square planted with amputated plane trees. There was a cross in the middle mounted on a granite slab. A bronze plaque was fixed on it, engraved with the names of those who had died in the last war. In a corner of the square, the striped awning of a café flashed through the trees.

'What about stopping for a drink?' Hennessy said, jovially. 'Have you managed to get hold of any of the local ackers?' They turned down the long side of the square. The awning was blue and white and it shaded a small terrace. Half a dozen drinkers were sprawled in the metal chairs, dressed in the field grey uniforms of the German army.

'Don't look at them,' Jean said sharply. He drove past purposefully, neither fast nor slow. Out of the corner of his vision, Adam glimpsed the eyes of the Germans lifting towards them at the sound of the motor, then shifting back to the company. They drove out of the square and across the bridge. He glanced at Jean and saw a grim smile flicker on his face.

Hennessy stayed quiet for the rest of the journey. When they got back, Adam took them into the stables. The others had not returned.

'Any chance of some grub?' Hennessy asked.

Adam was feeling hungry himself.

'I'll see what I can scrounge,' he said.

He crossed to the house and knocked at the back door. It was opened by an adolescent girl with a round, solemn face who showed no surprise at seeing him.

'Wait here,' she said. 'I'll get my mother.'

He was in the kitchen. It had tiles on the walls and steel pans hanging over the stove and gave an impression of efficiency.

'I expect you and your friends are hungry.'

He looked round. A tall, lean woman was standing in the doorway. She had light brown hair swept back in a bun and intelligent eyes that sloped down at the sides.

'You are right, madame,' Adam said. 'I'm sorry to bother you, but there wasn't any other choice.'

She smiled and moved across to a cupboard, her stiff dress rustling. She brought out a sausage and slices of ham and a cylinder of soft, white cheese, and some tomatoes and onions which she sliced up deftly on a chopping board. Then she mixed some oil and vinegar. Finally she reached into a bin and handed him a long stick of bread.

'You'll have to make do with water for the moment,' she said. 'You'll find a pump behind the stable.' She wrapped the food in cloths and put the salad and dressing into a bowl and put it with the bundles in a wicker basket. 'Please stay inside,' she said, handing him the basket. 'My neighbours can see into the yard.'

Hennessy and Hawkins fell on the food. Adam went round the back of the stable and worked the handle of the iron pump until the water came. He glanced up at the house behind but there was no sign of life behind the dusty windows. After they had finished eating, Hennessy suggested going outside to sit in the sun, but Adam told him of their hostess's warning. They sat in the dusty cool of the stables chatting, talking about the end of the war, and waited for the others to return.

27

It was early evening before they heard a car draw up and Gerry, Alain and Glover came through the creaking door of the barn laden with bottles.

'Where did you get those?' asked Adam.

'We liberated them from a wine merchant,' Alain said, winking.

'From some bloody collaborator,' added Glover as he tugged at a corkscrew. The cork came out with a wet pop and he raised the bottle to his mouth, taking a long gulp before offering it round.

Gerry sat down at the wireless set.

'Frank, come over here and get this thing cranked up, will you?'

Glover obeyed, crouching over the transmitter and delicately turning the dial. 'There you go.'

Gerry began dictating while Glover stroked the signal key.

'Don't forget to tell your people that we're with you,' Adam said.

Gerry nodded and held up a silencing hand, then carried on his report. He was about to end when Adam waved to get his attention and pointed to himself. Gerry rolled his eyes apologetically.

'Finish up: "We're in the company of three airmen from the crew of the Halifax that dropped us. Tomaszewski . . ."' He looked around for help. Hennessy and Hawkins supplied their names. 'OK,' he told Glover. 'That will do.'

He turned away from the radio and raised his voice. 'Attention please, everybody.' They stopped talking. 'The drop's still on. The weather forecast's good so there shouldn't be any problems, touch wood. We're getting fifteen blokes and a heap of supplies, and also, they tell me, some Jeeps.' He turned towards Adam. 'I'm glad you and your boys are here, Tommy, because you'll be able to give us a hand clearing the site.'

'Glad to be of assistance,' said Hennessy.

Gerry ignored him and carried on, outlining the arrangements for the rendezvous.

'Now we might as well relax for a bit,' he said finally. 'We can't get moving for another two hours.' He started studying a map and scribbled notes in a little book.

Alain went to look for food. Glover opened several more bottles and they passed them round. The wine was musty, past its best. The vulnerability Adam had noticed in Glover earlier in the day had gone. Now he was confident and hearty, a reflection of Gerry.

'What have you been doing all day?' asked Hennessy.

'We went to recce a new camp,' Glover said. 'I think we've found one. I'm not sure where it is exactly. It's hard to tell when you're driving around – they all look the same, these places. But it's in a wood near a village called Vercourt. It's well hidden and there's running water nearby.'

Since waking up after his siesta, Adam had felt a burning in his leg from the wound gouged there by a tree branch when he landed. It was hurting quite badly now. He rolled up his trouser leg to take a look at it. Flesh glinted red from the lips of the wound. The blood on the torn skin had dried black.

'Don't like the look of that,' Glover said. 'I've got a first-aid kit somewhere.'

He rummaged in his rucksack and pulled out a canvas wallet marked with a red cross. He took out a bottle and a bandage and scissors. He splashed some iodine onto a piece of cotton wool and cleaned carefully around the wound, wiping away from the cut. He had to crouch close to work. Adam felt his breath, sweet from the wine, in his face. He pressed on a dressing, bandaged it neatly and tightly and leaned back.

'There you are,' he said. Adam thanked him.

The stable door creaked open and Alain came in with a tray stacked with plates and glasses. He was followed by the woman of the house holding a heavy casserole. She put it down on the floor then left.

Alain ladled steaming pieces of chicken onto the plates and handed them around. 'She doesn't say much, does she?' Hennessy said.

'It's better that way,' Alain replied. 'Better if you don't know her name, better if she doesn't know yours. She's been in enough trouble already.'

'What happened?' Hawkins asked.

'Her husband was the head of the local school. He was arrested by the Milice and deported to Germany.'

'There seem to be some shocking bad hats among the local populace,' Gerry said. He had finished his preparations and was ready to take his place at the centre of the conversation. He poured wine into a mug and took an exploratory sip.

'Mind you, who knows how we would behave if we found ourselves in the same position? There are plenty of bastards I've come across in peacetime who I'm sure would make first-class quislings.'

'In war the scum rises,' said Alain. 'For most people around here the occupation has just been another thing to endure, like sickness, or a bad harvest. They put up with it, praying that one day it will end. But for others it's the best thing that happened to them.

Gerry nodded agreement as Alain went on. 'There are the resentful ones, the people who feel that before the war they didn't get enough respect. Of course no one is going to respect them for taking the side of the Germans. But people will fear them, which for them is the same thing. Then there are those who are doing it for money. For them the war is a great opportunity – it's business without the constraints. Some of them don't seem to feel they are doing anything wrong. They seem genuinely surprised when we threaten them.'

'Still, it can bring out the best in people too,' Gerry said piously, 'can't it?'

'Perhaps,' said Alain, 'but it's better not to be put to the test.'

'Who was the wine merchant whose wares we're drinking?' Glover asked.

'His name is Duchet. Before the war he was in competition with another merchant called Vincent. When the Germans arrived, he told them that Vincent was a Resistance sympathiser; which was the truth, as it happened. They closed down Vincent's shop and Duchet became a wealthy man.'

'Aren't you worried that he will inform on you?' Glover asked.

'It's too late now. Most of the *collabos* are frightened. Nowadays they're very keen to help. They know the Germans will be leaving them sooner or later and the settling of accounts will begin.'

Later Hennessy produced a pack of cards and they began a game of poker. Adam joined Alain, who was sitting a little away from the group, reading a newspaper and smoking. Alain made room for Adam and offered him a cigarette.

'You're not English?'

'How did you know?'

'Your manner. Your accent.'

Adam smiled. 'No I'm not.' He had stopped thinking of himself as Polish, yet he had not become anything else. The nearest he could come to categorising himself was as a man of the war, one of millions, sharing kinship of experience that would always be stronger than the bonds of class or nationality. He told Alain a short version of his story.

'What about you?' he asked at the end.

'I was studying to be an engineer when the war started. I was called up, captured a year later and taken off to a prisoner of war camp in Germany. When they let me out I came back here to work on my father's farm. I tried to stay out of trouble at first. Then I saw what they were doing. I joined the Francs Tireurs et Partisans.'

'The Communists?'

'I suppose so. I don't know how many of us believe in it. When I joined, they were the only ones doing anything.'

'You must be glad that it's nearly over.'

Alain laughed grimly. 'Where did you get that idea? No, for us it's only just starting. There are a lot of scores to settle. First we'll deal with the Germans; after that, our own.'

At ten o'clock, Gerry told them to get ready to go.

'Take all your gear with you,' he said. 'If it all goes well we won't be coming back here.'

It was dusk when they climbed into the cars and set off into the summer evening. In the fields old men and women bent over their crops, making the most of the fading light. When they reached the drop zone, *maquisards* were waiting for them. They looked like peasants in their stained and tattered suits and frayed shirts, yellow cigarettes stuck on their lower lips. They seemed poorer and dirtier than anyone Adam had seen in Britain; more like Poles. They stood under the trees, chatting quietly and smoking. Through the foliage he saw the dim outline of a cart, with a horse between the shafts. The light faded and died and the last warmth left the air. It was a clear night. Shortly after midnight the *maquisards* dragged straw and bundles of wood into the field and started building bonfires.

Just before one o'clock, Adam heard the drone of aircraft. He quietened the others and strained to hear. Gerry gave an order and the flames from the bonfires jumped into the night. They were definitely Halifaxes, two or three of them. He surely knew the pilots and crews. He imagined them staring down on to the black floor of France, matching the rivers and roads and railways to the lines on their maps, scouring the earth for the glow of the fires. The drone changed to a throb. He could see them now. They were slightly off course, half a mile to the west of the field. The men around him were staring up into the sky, as if trying by telepathy to drag the bombers back on course.

But the three dark shapes crawled past them and the noise of the engines faded.

'Fuck, fuck fuck,' chanted Gerry under his breath. 'That's it then. We might as well call it a night.'

'No, listen.' Adam could hear the pitch of the engines rising slightly, as if they were changing course.

'They're turning round,' he said. 'Maybe they'll see us on the way back. The *maquisards* splashed fuel on to the dying fires so the flames leaped up in a final spurt of light.

'They must be bleeding blind if they can't see that,' Hennessy said. And it seemed the lead pilot had noticed them, for now the bombers were heading straight for the field.

'Here they come everybody,' shouted Gerry. The first Halifax passed overhead and a stream of parachutes blossomed in its wake. Then the sky was full of canopies, swaying down through the night. Some of them were arranged in groups of four, each harness holding up a corner of a vehicle – the Jeeps that Gerry had been talking about.

The *maquisards* ran out of the trees and over to the parachutes, bundling them up and cutting the harnesses from the supply cylinders, then trundling them back to the corner of the field where a cart was waiting.

Gerry was grinning with pleasure. 'What about those Jeeps then, Tommy? Never seen that done before. Now we'll be able to get around the place in proper style.'

Four Jeeps were scattered about the field. Gerry hurried over to the nearest vehicle. It had hit the ground hard but seemed to be undamaged. He climbed behind the wheel. 'Will you look at that?' he said. 'You can't beat the old SOS service. They've left the keys in the ignition.' He turned the engine. The starter motor whinnied briefly then caught. He revved the throttle then let the engine subside into a burbling throb.

All over the field, men were picking themselves up and freeing themselves from their harnesses. Gerry drove the Jeep to the side of the field and went out to greet the arrivals. They retrieved the other Jeeps and supplies and prepared to move off. The men wore parachute smocks and were loaded down with equipment and their blackened faces gave them a desperate, piratical look. Gerry stood up in the Jeep and they turned towards him.

'Are we all here? Is there anyone missing?'

There was a low, uncertain murmur.

'Good. And we're all in one piece. We're heading to our base where we'll spend the night. It's a good hour away. Now the roads are pretty dead at night but you never know. If there's any trouble we want to try and get out of it without shooting if that's at all possible. Is that understood?'

The soldiers nodded and murmured.

Adam climbed into the back of Gerry's Jeep. Alain and Glover sat in the front behind a machine gun with a drum magazine that was bolted to the bonnet.

'Hey ho,' said Gerry cheerfully, and moved carefully off down the farm track and into the road. They drove for half an hour. The Jeep engines sounded dangerously loud in the quiet of the night. Alain was showing Gerry the way. They came to a crossroads, one of many that looked the same. Alain told him to turn right. A hundred yards down the road he changed his mind.

'I'm sorry,' he said. 'We should have gone the other way.'

'Don't worry,' Gerry replied airily. 'We all make mistakes.'

The convoy turned round in a cacophony of clashing gears and revving engines and set off in the opposite direction down a narrow twisting lane. Adam was leaning back in the seat, his head thrown back, looking up at the cold points of light scattered across the darkness above his head. Then he was thrown forward onto the floor as the Jeep came to a complete stop and there was a clash of metal striking metal behind. He pulled himself back on the seat.

Now he could see what Gerry had seen. In front of them, on the main road no more than fifty yards away, a river of light was flowing past. The Germans were moving north. For fifteen minutes they rumbled past, tanks, their hulls cluttered with bags and boxes and strapped-on oilcans, armoured troop carriers and lorries. From time to time the headlights of one lorry shone into the back of the truck in front and Adam glimpsed rows of dozing troopers, lolling against each other, hands folded gently around the barrels of their rifles. He half expected one of the sleepers to feel his gaze and look up and see them and shout the alarm, but they slept on, oblivious, rolling north to their rendezvous with the armies of the Liberation.

Then the last red lights crossed the mouth of the lane and the sound of the engines seeped from the night. In the front, Gerry giggled. 'Fuck me. That was a close one. Christ, it was a good thing we took that wrong turning when we did. I take it that was the SS boys moving north?'

Alain nodded.

'Where do you think they will be tomorrow? The least we can do is try and track down where they're lying up and call up the bombers to have a go at them.'

'I don't know. They could be anywhere. A long way from here, at any rate.'

Gerry gave a grunt of disappointment. 'Oh well.'

They darted quickly across the road and down another lane that crossed several broad fields before it descended into a wooded valley. They passed some elaborate wrought-iron gates, behind which an austere château glowed pale across a park. They turned off into a tunnel of trees that wound through the wood. Then Gerry pulled up and switched off the engine and the Jeeps behind stopped. For a moment there was only the rustle of the wind in the treetops. Then Gerry said, 'This is it, gents. The Vercourt Ritz. Make yourself comfortable. This is going to be home for a little while.'

28

When morning broke it was clear that Gerry had chosen the camp well. They were on the edge of a forest of oak and pine that sloped down to a narrow valley which had a stream running through it. The trees were thin and loosely planted so that from deep inside their cover you could watch what was going on in the fields outside, while a passer-by peering into the wood would find it hard to focus beyond the first few yards of waving branches and flickering, greenish light.

Adam woke up to the smell of wood smoke and frying bacon. A little way away, a soldier squatted by a fire, poking with a stick at the bacon to stop it sticking to the pan. He was stripped to the waist, and hard muscles stirred under his skin as he shook the pan. Adam wriggled out of the sleeping bag he had been issued with from the dropped supplies, and went over.

'Where did you get hold of that?' he asked.

The soldier looked up from under a fringe of brown hair. 'Scrounged it, sir. From a farmhouse, just over the way.' He flipped a couple of rashers on to a tin plate. 'There you are. Dig in. There'll be some eggs coming in a minute.'

'What's your name?' asked Adam, picking up the hot, crisp bacon in his fingers.

'Sar'nt Richards. Ron Richards.' He put down the pan and gripped Adam's hand. He was in his early twenties, with the cocksureness that comes from belief in your own luck.

'How long have you been with the outfit?' asked Adam.

'Long enough. I was in the desert for a while. Then we moved on to Italy.'

'So you know Major Cunningham quite well?'

'Oh, yes.' His eyes glowed as if he had heard the name of a lover. 'He was the OC on my first raid. I've been with him ever since.'

Some of the troopers came over to the fire having finished their ablutions at the stream, bare-chested and smelling of coal tar soap. They were young and happy and shone with health. Adam realised how dirty he was. He finished his breakfast, thanked Richards and went looking for Glover. He followed a faint trail that led down to the stream. The wood was old, carpeted in ancient depths of leaf mould and littered with mossy branches that snapped with a powdery crack when you trod on them. Just before the stream the ground fell away steeply, exposing a band of white limestone. He found Glover crouched at the water's edge, peering at a metal mirror and scraping a razor over his chin.

'Can I borrow that when you're finished?' he asked. 'I didn't think I'd be needing mine.'

Glover smiled. 'Of course. Won't be a sec.'

He finished shaving and wiped his face with a small square of towel. Adam took off his shirt and caught a gust of his own stale sweat.

'Some soap would come in handy too.'

'Help yourself,' said Glover. 'I'll leave everything. Just give it back when you've finished.'

The stream was narrow and lined with grey clay. He washed his face and under his arms. Then he took off all his clothes and crouched in the shallow water, enjoying its chilly purity. He rubbed the soap in his wet hands until he had worked up a thin lather. The razor snagged on his beard.

Glover had gone off with the towel. He rubbed himself down with his shirt, then put his dirty clothes back on and climbed back up the slope. The men were standing near the fire listening to Gerry. It was the first time he had seen him with his men. He looked strong and full of sense and energy. Death seemed far away from him. Just the man, thought Adam, you wanted to lead you into battle. Adam wondered if the crews he had flown with felt the same about him. Probably not. He distrusted instinct and believed in calculating risk. This caution only seemed to emphasise the likelihood of things going wrong. Gerry gave the impression that everything would turn out fine, even when the odds were unfavourable.

'Today we're splitting up the duties,' Gerry told them. 'Half of you will form up into pairs to recce for sabotage targets. You know the kind of things we're interested in. Ammunition and fuel dumps, railway switching points and bridges. You're to do what your

French guides tell you – within reason – and to avoid contact with the enemy. The other half will stay behind and take care of the camp.'

He ran through the company, calling out names and detailing duties. It was clear at a glance who were the veterans. They had a way of standing, of smoking their cigarettes, of answering back, a loose confidence that set them apart from the nervy eagerness of the novices. Gerry gave the scouting tasks to the veterans, the guard duties to the newcomers.

'What are you planning to do with with us, then?' It was Hennessy speaking. His voice sounded apprehensive.

'Nothing for the moment,' Gerry said curtly. 'I've got other things to worry about.'

He looked over to Adam. 'I need you. Could you come over here a moment?'

They walked away and he started talking in a low voice, as if someone was listening.

'Look, I know this isn't your department, but there's something I thought you might be prepared to help us with. There's a possible target that needs to be checked out. It needs someone who can speak good French, pass himself off as a Frog if he runs into any bother. Like I say, you're under no obligation. Just say if you don't fancy it.'

Adam knew he had no real choice. He was mildly surprised that Gerry had put the request so politely.

'OK,' he said.

Gerry grinned approvingly. 'Well done. Now come over here. Alain knows all about it.'

Alain was sitting under a tree studying a map. Next to him was a thin, middle-aged man in blue overalls, whose eyes darted nervously around. Alain gave a big, open smile when he saw Adam.

'I knew you'd help,' he said. 'Sit here for a moment please.' He pointed at the map. 'This here is a map of the marshalling yards south of Montcharles. We've received some information from this man that there are scores of petrol tankers sitting in the sidings. It's fuel for the SS troops you saw last night.'

Gerry broke in. 'Your job is to get there as soon as possible and do a recce, check on how heavily guarded it is and whether it will be possible for us to do the attack. You need to pinpoint the exact position of the trains, so if we can't do the job, the RAF can.'

He had not expected this. 'But Montcharles is full of Germans,' he said, regretting the alarm in his voice.

'Don't worry,' said Gerry, smiling. 'We've got a guide to hold your hand, haven't we Alain?'

Adam felt a twinge of panic at being pitched into the plan so quickly.

'When do you want me to go then?' he asked reluctantly.

'Now,' said Alain, getting to his feet. 'Come with me.' He led him off through the woods along a path that dipped down to the stream and climbed up the facing side of the valley. The undergrowth thickened, and several times they had to climb over fallen timber. Then the trees thinned out again and he glimpsed through the foliage the pitched red slope of a tiled roof. The house stood on its own at the edge of the forest. They arrived at the back entrance. It was a solid, homely looking place with dark green shutters and faded lemon walls. There was a big stone oven near the back door and pigs grunted unseen inside a row of sties.

'Wait here,' said Alain, and went inside. The sun was getting up. It was hot now, and clouds of insects hummed among the leaves. He smoked a cigarette. When it was finished he shredded the butt, the way he had seen the SOS men do it, letting the breeze carry away the paper so as not to leave any trace of an alien brand. The back door opened and Alain emerged carrying a bundle of clothing. He took him over to a shed and they went in.

'Put these on,' Alain said, and handed him a dark, dirty-looking suit. It was too long in the legs and the jacket was tight, but from what he had seen of the clothing of the local men this would make the disguise all the more authentic. When he had finished dressing, Alain handed him a beret.

'Now for your transport.'

He dipped into the gloom at the back of the shed and emerged wheeling a bicycle.

'This is it,' he said. 'There's a chance you'll be stopped, by the Milice or the Germans. If you are you should let the guide do the talking. If you're asked your name you're Georges Melin. It's the name on the *plaque d'identité* on your bicycle. Now I'm going to take you into the village to meet Claude – that's the code-name of your guide. Just do everything you're told and you'll be all right.'

They walked the few kilometres to the village, Adam wheeling the squeaking bike. Vercourt was bigger than a village, smaller than a town, with a cobbled square, a church, a *salle de fetes* and a café with a terrace and a sign over the door painted in a flowing script: L'Espérance. Dominating one side of the square was a solid stone building, half covered with ivy, bearing the name of the Auberge de la Vienne.

They sat down outside the café. The proprietor greeted them and Alain ordered glasses of bitter aperitif for both of them as there was no coffee. Occasionally a housewife went by, towing a child and a shopping bag, but there was no one who looked like Claude. Then they heard the ripple of rubber over the cobbles and a woman rode into the square on a bicycle.

'Here she is,' Alain said.

'Who?'

'Claude.'

'I thought Claude was going to be a man,' Adam said, 'but then of course you knew that.'

'It's a woman's name as well,' Alain said. He smiled. 'Gerry and I did think there might be a bit of confusion, I have to admit.'

She leaned the bike against a plane tree and came over. She was quite small and slim but looked athletic and strong under her plain blue dress. She had black wavy hair brushed straight back from a broad forehead and gathered in a clasp at the nape of her neck, high cheekbones and pale, clear skin. As Alain introduced them she looked at him neutrally, with brown, solemn eyes. When they shook hands she barely bothered to return the pressure of his grip.

Alain was in a hurry to go.

'You should be all right on the roads,' he said to her. 'The Germans are moving out and the Milice are too worried about what's going to happen to them to cause much trouble. Once you're in Montcharles you'll be less conspicuous. If you do get stopped, you know the story. You're brother and sister on your way to visit your parents.'

Claude nodded and looked to Adam to see if he had understood. Then Alain shook hands with them both and set off up the street. They mounted their bicycles and pedalled out of the village side by side.

'How far is it?' he asked.

'About thirty kilometres,' she said.

'You're joking,' said Adam. 'I'll never manage that.'

'You will,' she said, firmly.

A haze hung over the fields now and he found it hard work pedalling. The chain was rusty and squeaked with each turn of the cogwheel. It was hard to keep up and soon she was fifty metres ahead of him.

'Oy,' he called after her, 'wait for me.'

She turned and stopped. When he caught up with her she had a vexed look on her face.

'You'll have to do better than this,' she said.

'It's the bike,' Adam said feebly

She grunted and dismounted. 'Show me.'

She wheeled the bike experimentally back and forth then handed it back to him. She undid a little satchel slung at the back of the saddle and brought out a tin of oil.

'Hold my bike,' she commanded. She squatted down, exposing brown, pointed knees, and squirted some oil over the rusty chain, working the pedal back and forth to spread it evenly.

'Try that,' she said. They set off again and this time he could keep up. He looked over at her as she stared resolutely ahead, propelling herself steadily along. She couldn't be more than twenty. The sun was behind her, highlighting the tendrils of hair that had escaped from the clasp at the back of her neck.

'Why are you looking at me?' she asked suddenly, taking him by surprise.

'You're more interesting than the countryside,' he said boldly, deciding she had bossed him enough. 'Any objections?'

She did not answer.

'Anyway,' he added more gently, 'I thought all French girls liked being looked at. Admired, should I say?'

'I'm not all French girls,' she said discouragingly, in a way that made him smile.

'Who are you then?'

She grunted. 'Never mind, *M'sieur L'Anglais*. Let's try and go a bit faster.'

He grinned. 'But I'm not.'

'Not what?'

'Not English. I'm a Pole. Adam Tomaszewski.'

She looked at him closely for the first time.

'You look English, though. Blond hair and blue eyes. Isn't that what English men look like?'

'Not many that I've seen,' he replied.

She gave the merest suggestion of a laugh.

'Sorry for my ignorance,' she said. 'I've never gone further than Montcharles.'

He took his chance.

'What were you doing,' he asked casually, 'when all this started?'

'I was still at school. Then I went to university at Montcharles, to continue my studies, but I had to leave after two years.'

'Why was that?'

She hesitated. 'There was some trouble with my brother,' she said. 'He ended up in prison.' She paused, making making it clear the conversation was closed.

Later she pointed across a field.

'Look, there are some prehistoric stones, behind that clump of trees. Do you want to see them? We can eat at the same time. Are you hungry?'

'Not really. More thirsty if anything.'

The stones were unimpressive: seven irregular granite slabs arranged in a loose circle. He sat down in the middle of them. She went to her saddlebag and retrieved a paper bag and a bottle, which she handed to him. He pulled out the cork and lifted it to drink, but the contents had been shaken up by the ride and fizzed out, bubbling up into his nose and making him sneeze. When he looked up she was laughing. She took the bottle from him and tilted it back slowly, opening her lips wide, showing square, white teeth. The cider gurgled tamely in.

'That's how to do it,' she said. Their eyes met as she handed the bottle back. She turned away quickly and took a halved stick of bread smothered in white cheese from the bag and began slowly chewing.

The road rose on the next part of the journey. It was the hottest part of the day. He took off his jacket but his shirt was soon patched with sweat. She did not seem to notice the heat. She had put on a straw hat that hid the top of her face in shadow and threw into relief her strong, rounded jaw.

It was mid-afternoon by the time they reached the outskirts of Montcharles. They pedalled past new, Norman-style, half-timbered villas, and a concrete sports stadium, then began climbing the hill that led up to the old, medieval heart of the town. The cobbled streets were too steep even for Claude, and she agreed when he suggested dismounting. At the top of the hill the narrow road opened out into a wide square dominated by an ornately ugly town hall. Cafés lined one side of the square, and the tables on the terraces were crowded with grey uniforms. The soldiers looked up to eye the girl as they went past, then returned to their beer.

They left the square and freewheeled down a road flanked with tall stone houses with blank façades that curved down to the railway station. The tracks lay like a broad steel river between two high rocky banks hung with houses. There were four or five lines running between the platforms and a shimmering complex of marshalling yards and sidings spread beyond.

The sidings were crammed with freight wagons, but at this distance it was impossible to tell what they contained. To get nearer to them they would have to cross the mainline tracks. They skimmed down the last stretch of road and past the station, looking for a bridge or tunnel that would take them to the other side. After ten minutes they turned round and saw a high bridge linking the two hillsides divided by the railway, which they had failed to notice when they made the sharp turn towards the station. They began along the long-rising gradient that took them back past the station entrance, which they could now see was guarded by at least a dozen Germans, up the steep incline and onto the bridge. There was a welcome breeze blowing down the valley. At the other side they turned left and coasted back down the hill. The road flattened out and took them along a metal fence overgrown with weeds, past rows of derelict-looking wooden wagons and grimy sheds. From across the tracks they could hear the clash of wagons being shunted and the hiss of escaping steam. A gap in the sheds revealed a small locomotive at work, about two hundred yards away, butting at a line of fat, cylindrical tankers.

'Stop,' she said. They dismounted and wheeled their bikes along the fence. There were dozens of tankers, all painted olive drab and bearing stencilled signs saying BENZINE/ESSENCE. They could see now that several engines were pushing and pulling the wagons out of the sidings and towards the main lines. There was an opening in the fence leading onto a concrete path that ran along the embankment. They went through it, walking slowly, trying not to look too eagerly towards the scene of the activity. Then they heard the sound of German voices drifting towards them in the intervals between the clanking and rattling of the rolling stock. They stopped and looked around. About 150 metres away a group of soldiers stood by a parked wagon overlooking the sidings, smoking and chatting. As they watched, one of them turned away and walked towards them, stopping a little way away from the group. He looked down, then hunched forwards and undid his fly and began pissing against a pole, humming as he did so and looking around him.

They stood there immobile, as his gaze moved steadily towards them. Then Adam reached forward and clasped Claude by the wrist, pulling her to him. He felt an initial tug of resistance, then she understood and submitted, laying her arms gently around him, moving her head sideways so he could rest his head in the crook of her neck in the semblance of an embrace. He felt the German's eyes on him. He glanced over to the post. The soldier was buttoning his fly looking straight at them. He moved his head back into the crook of her shoulder, waiting for the yelled challenge. But none came. Instead, the soldier chuckled. He shouted something to his mates. Adam saw them turn slowly towards them, with indulgent smiles dawning on their faces.

But then the smiles gave way to looks of consternation, and he heard words being spoken that even at this distance sounded spiked with caution and suspicion.

'Let's go.'

He hooked his arm around her waist and led her back to the entrance, smiling and looking down at her, rigidly fighting against the desire to look back, waiting for the crack of rifle rounds.

They went through the fence and mounted the bikes and pedalled casually on. As they drew parallel with the soldiers Adam stole a glance from the corner of his eye. There were six or eight of them staring towards them.

Beyond the goods yard they came to a footbridge that took them back to the other side of the tracks. They had to get back and radio the sighting back to Britain as fast as possible if the fuel wagons were to be bombed before they were moved down the line. But they were tired now and the bicycles felt heavy and slow.

As the dusk thickened he asked, 'How much further is it?'

'About fifteen kilometres.'

'We might as well stop then,' he said thankfully. 'There's no point in carrying on. It's too late to organise anything now. We're better off getting some rest and setting out at dawn.'

She looked doubtful. 'Where are we going to sleep?'

'We'll find somewhere.'

They rode on. She showed no inclination to stop. The cut in his leg was hurting now. He wondered whether he could use it as an excuse to call the halt, but he did not want to seem weak. Then she pointed into a dim field to the right.

'Over there,' she said. Through the gloom he could see a narrow house at the end of a row of poplar trees. The shutters were closed and it seemed deserted.

'It looks empty to me,' he said.

'It is. I know the people who live there. They've closed up the house and moved into Montcharles.'

She turned into the driveway and he followed her round to the back. There was a padlock on the door. She went over to one of the shuttered windows. There were diamond-shaped holes cut in the wood.

'Give me a leg up,' she said.

He made a stirrup with his hands and she put her foot in and hoisted herself upright. She slipped her arm through the hole and groped around for the catch, giving little grunts of effort as she reached downwards. He had adopted a sort of crouch in order to keep his face from pressing against her breast but, even in this self-denying posture, he could feel the soft curve of her hip against his cheek. There was a click and she hopped backwards, almost tumbling as she landed.

'There we are.' They pulled back the shutters, revealing cobwebbed windows.

Adam felt it was his turn to take the initiative. He picked up a stone.

'Stand back,' he said, and threw it briskly through the glass. He put his hand through, wrenched open the handle and climbed in over the sill. She followed him in, holding on to his hand. The room was pitch black and smelled of damp and rotten wood. He struck a match and caught a brief impression of heavy furniture and a high ceiling before the flame guttered out and the dark folded in.

'There'll be a candle on the mantlepiece,' she said. He struck another match and saw that there were four candles, stuck in a candelabra. He held the candlestick up and looked around the room. It was furnished in the provincial bourgeois taste of the last century. The light

glowed on the varnish of the clumsy portraits on the
wall and the wax polish of the dark furniture.

'Let's not stay here,' she said.

He led the way upstairs, turning the handles of each
bedroom door and pushing them open for her inspec-
tion. At the top of the house they came to what looked
like a children's room, light-painted with a bare wooden floor and two iron bedsteads covered with patch-
work counterpanes. There was a window set into the
slope of the roof and the branches of a tree were
silhouetted against the glass.

He felt a stirring of excitement as she went over and
sat on one of the beds and looked up at him.

'I'll take this room,' she said. 'You can find another.'

'Oh.' He had expected they would take a bed each.
Brother and sister.

'Something wrong?' She seemed genuinely concerned. 'Have this room if you want it, I don't really
mind where I sleep.'

'No,' he said. 'Please, you take it.'

He advanced towards her. 'Well, good night, then.'

She stood still, arms by her side, waiting for him to
go. 'Goodnight Adam,' she said, as he retreated. 'Don't
worry about oversleeping. I'm sure to wake up in time.'

29

She acted like a stranger in the morning, barely saying a word to him when she came into his musty bedroom to wake him before slipping outside to wash in the pump in the yard. Cocks were crowing as they rode down the bumpy drive and out onto the main road. They had not gone far when they heard a rumbling, elemental noise in the distance, like thunder. It got louder and more menacing as they pedalled on. Adam realised that another convoy was coming their way, heading to the Normandy beachhead, more than two hundred miles away.

They pulled off the road and waited in the cover of the trees. The hull of the first tank ground past them, fifty metres away, followed by more armour, Jeeps, and trucks towing artillery pieces. He glanced at Claude lying flat in the bracken, watching intently the clanking cavalcade. She noticed his look and mimed firing a bazooka.

'Vlan!'

They grinned at each other.

When they reached the camp, the troopers were already awake and Gerry and Alain were standing by a campfire drinking from mugs.

'Home is the hunter,' Gerry said when he saw him. 'How did it go, brother?'

'Pretty good. The railwayman was right. There are hundreds of petrol wagons sitting in the yards, or at least there were late yesterday afternoon. The thing is, they were beginning to shunt them out of there, so we'll have to move fast if we're going to catch them. If you ask me it would take too long to organise a raid. Even if you managed to get into town, you'd never get out again. The best thing would be to call in the RAF.'

Gerry took him over to some camouflaged tenting stretched between two oak trees. The radio had been set up inside and an operator, one of the new arrivals, was squatting on a log beside it.

'OK Kelly,' Gerry said. 'Work your magic.'

He turned to Adam. 'What information can you add about the location of the target?'

'Anything I say about the tankers is probably out of date by now. They've got the coordinates of the station. They're just going to have to plaster the whole junction.'

Kelly signalled that he was through and Gerry sat down alongside him while his message was translated into dots and dashes. He described the position of the fuel trains, then made arrangements for a further drop of men and supplies to take place that night. When he had finished he got up.

'With any luck they'll get there in time to bomb the bejesus out of the place while the stuff is still there. The trouble is, everything's moving so fast.'

'I know. We spotted a big column of armour moving north on our way back this morning.'

'Why didn't you say so before?' Gerry asked crossly. 'What road were they on?' Adam told him and he ducked back under the canvas to the radio.

A few minutes later Gerry joined Adam and Claude by the fire. He looked at her with interest, fussing to make sure she had been offered sugar for her tea.

'Anyway,' he said, more to her than to him, 'you two have done a bloody good job, whether the RAF boys get there in time or not.'

He shifted his stance, angling himself obliquely towards Claude before continuing. 'We had a bit of fun ourselves last night.'

'Oh yes?' Adam said dutifully.

'Caused a bit of mayhem on the mainline south of Montcharles, blowing up bridges and points and what-have-you. We managed to thin out the Hun ranks a bit, too. We ran into a patrol on the way back. We were a bit quicker off the mark then they were. About five nil to us, I should say.'

He glanced at Claude for approval but she appeared not to have understood.

'Oh well,' he said cheerfully. 'Got to press on.' He walked away through the trees.

Claude turned to Adam and held out her hand. 'I'm going off now,' she said. 'Goodbye.'

He felt a sudden pang of disappointment as he realised he might not see her again. He tried to think of something to say to keep her there but nothing came.

She turned away, and picked her way through the fallen branches towards the light at the edge of the forest.

'Wait!' he shouted. She turned round. He jogged over to her, tripping on a log in his hurry.

'What is it?'

'Won't you want to know what happened? With the air raids, I mean.'

'I'll probably know before you do.'

That was true.

'Yes,' he said, 'I suppose you will.'

He reached out and put his hand on her firm upper arm.

'What I really mean is, will I be able to see you again?'

She flinched slightly, and for a moment he thought that he had offended her by his touch. But then she pointed through the wood.

'Over there, if you walk straight, you come to the road that leads to the village,' she said matter-of-factly. 'Just before the end of the forest you'll see a path that leads off to the right. At the end, you will find a cottage.'

'I know, Alain took me there this morning.'

'Good,' she said. 'I'll be there at six this evening. You can come then, if you wish.'

'OK.'

She held out a slim brown hand and he shook it. He watched her walk away, pick up her bike from where it was propped against a tree and pedal away. He walked back to the campfire where the men were squatting down, listening to Gerry, and took his place next to Alain.

Gerry was shifting his gaze around the company as he talked, fixing each one with a look that seemed to bind the recipient to him by an invisible bond of allegiance.

'This is a historic moment,' he said. 'You've heard from the wireless that the invasion is going well. From what I've learned from HQ this morning, this is not the usual bull. We're ashore and they're not going to push us back. But in the meantime we've got to do everything in our power to slow up the Jerry reinforcements before they can get to Normandy. Some of them have shipped out already. That's all the more reason to hammer those that are left behind. At the moment, our job is to concentrate on holding up the German movement northward for as long as we can. That means carrying on with the sabotage work: cutting lines and points and so forth. Even if the troops have moved on we can still mess up their resupply. Now here's how we're going to divide up the work.'

He detailed the duties. There were seventeen in the SOS team now. Half of the force would form groups of three and set off with a local guide to scout out targets for demolition, which they would then return to attack under cover of darkness. The rest would stay and guard the camp and make preparations for that night's drop. The rearguard was to post sentries – and no one was to leave the forest. He read out a list of names.

'Any questions?'

A voice came back, Cockney and aggrieved.

'That's the same list as yesterday. Why can't the people who stayed behind yesterday go out today?'

Gerry smiled bleakly. 'Nice to see you're so keen, Shirley. The fact is you blokes haven't any experience of this kind of work. The other blokes have. You'll get your chance, though. I promise you.'

He dismissed them and walked away, chatting to Alain.

Adam dozed for a few hours on the soft leaf mould until he was woken by the sound of the soldiers getting ready to set off. They were taking three of the Jeeps, leaving one behind in case of emergencies. They wore khaki battle-dress, making no attempt to disguise themselves.

The burble of the engines died away and the silence of the forest closed around the camp. Hennessy and Hawkins came over to join him. They had scrounged some sleeping bags and set up a bivouac of their own below a rock outcrop a little apart from the troopers. They went over to the bivouac and lit a fire. Adam collected water from the stream and brewed up some tea. One by one, the soldiers drifted over. Shirley, who had a single stripe on his sleeve, seemed to be the group's unofficial leader. There were eight of them altogether. They seemed hesitant and bewildered, with none of the pride in the unit that Adam had seen shining from Sergeant Richards.

'How long have you been with this mob?' Adam asked Shirley.

'Two months,' he replied. 'I volunteered, didn't I? Wanted to see some action. That's turning out to be a right bleeding joke.'

'You've never been in action before?'

'Nope.'

Adam looked round at the others. Reluctantly, they shook their heads.

For a while they talked about the drop that was due to take place that night. 'I don't know why they're bothering to send any more,' said a morose trooper called Maslin. 'There's not enough for us to do.'

They killed an hour stripping and oiling their guns. Then they retrieved some tins of steak and kidney pudding from the cache of rations and dropped them into a dixie bubbling on the fire. Adam's status as a foreigner and officer ensured that he was barely included in the conversation. He listened to the soft, bantering chat. They paid out information about themselves in careful instalments. With each detail, another plate fell from their armour, exposing their youth and softness.

At two o'clock someone remembered the radio and they turned it on and found the BBC News. The newsreader's tone was confident, almost triumphant, as he listed the continuing victories in Normandy. When he spoke the troopers leaned hungrily towards the radio.

'Is it really true, sir?' a Scot called Chisholm asked when the broadcast finished. 'Are we really doing that well?'

Adam looked at Chisholm's anxious, chubby face, and suppressed the cynical remark he was about to make. He nodded. 'It's pretty accurate, I think.'

He noticed the others smiling with relief. The good news made them restless.

'It's bleeding boring sitting here,' said Shirley. 'How about a shufti at the village down the road?'

Some of the others agreed, looking to Adam to gauge his reaction.

'Forget it,' he said. 'Your orders are to guard here until the rest get back.'

'Just a suggestion,' Shirley said grudgingly.

The conversation trickled on for a bit as they spooned the rubbery kidneys and soggy pastry from the tins, then petered out into silence.

Adam went for a walk, over the uneven ground of the forest floor down to the stream, where he lay on his back smoking cigarettes and looking up at the scraps of sky that showed through the branches. It was hot and still and peaceful. He thought about what he should do next. He had Hennessy and Hawkins to worry about. Their duty was to get back to their unit as fast as possible, but the landings had changed everything. There was little chance of being picked up until the invasion activity had slowed down. Maybe Hennessy was right and the Allied forces would soon arrive to liberate Vercourt. The most sensible thing would be to stay where they were, he decided, at least for another day.

A breath of wind stirred the tops of the trees and the branches waved and whispered, and for a moment he was back with Moira on the top of Hanger Hill. The outline of the memory was clear and sharp but something had happened to the colours. They had bled and faded. He realised that since leaving Warneford he had scarcely given her a thought. That was what he had prayed for and his prayer, without him noticing it, had been answered. The momentous meeting he had dreamt of so often in the early days had taken place and ended in a flat anticlimax. She was still beautiful and might fascinate him again if the opportunity arose. But the years had brushed away the magic dust of infatuation, revealing her to be merely human.

The breeze dropped. He got up and walked over to the edge of the trees and looked out over the fields that stretched down to the village. He heard voices, and saw, a few hundred yards away, two men moving along a row of vines, clipping and pruning, chatting as they went, doing what they had always done. The sight made him curiously happy. He watched them for a while, then moved back deeper into the concealing shadow of the forest. It took a minute for his eyes to adjust to the gloom. Dead branches splintered under his feet as he walked back to the camp.

The first Jeep arrived back halfway through the afternoon bearing Glover, Sergeant Richards and Kelly the radio operator. It was followed shortly afterwards by another, driven by a corporal called Schofield and carrying two troopers.

'The place is lousy with Germans,' Glover said. 'We had to leg it twice, didn't we Spider?' Kelly nodded. 'They didn't seem in a hurry to come after us, though,' he said. Glover looked around with flickering, nervous eyes. 'Any sign of Gerry?' he asked casually.

It was another hour before Gerry returned. He drove the Jeep, Alain by his side, and two troopers in the back, down a half-defined track that twisted through the trees and came out almost at the edge of the camp. He climbed down and called out to Glover and Schofield.

'Move the vehicles in here. They're sticking out like a dog's bollocks.'

They hurried off to obey.

He and Alain waited for them to come back, then he called everyone to him.

'All right, listen to me.'

Gerry perched himself on the Jeep's bonnet and the troopers gathered round. 'The situation is this. At around noon today the RAF attacked the sidings at Montcharles and made a hell of a mess. We could see the smoke from five miles away and Alain's people say that all the targets were destroyed. That petrol was destined for the SS, so we've delayed their arrival in Normandy by a few days at least. It's a great start. The trouble is that the Germans now know we're here. We had a brush with them last night and Frank was spotted today. It won't take them long to come looking for us if they're not doing so already. In the circumstances it's unsafe for us to hang around here much longer, especially as our numbers will double after the drop tonight. I'm going to look around for another camp. But in the meantime I want everyone to be extra careful. Do you understand?'

There was a rumble of assent. 'We're going to have a busy night. There will be an orders group at six o'clock. No one is to stray from the camp.' He dismissed them and called Adam over.

'Come and have a drink,' he said, smiling at him properly for the first time. He reached into the back of the Jeep and pulled out a bottle of champagne.

'Where did you get that from?' asked Adam.

'We've been levying a sort of tribute on the local shitbags as we've been doing the rounds,' said Gerry, winking at Alain. 'It's amazing the stuff that people have tucked away. Let's sit down.'

They rested their backs against a bank of moss-covered stone. Alain released the cork and passed the bottle to Gerry, who raised it in Adam's direction.

'Here's to you, Tommy. It was bloody good work this morning.'

'Don't thank me, thank Claude.'

'Ah yes, the charming Claude.' He took a gulp of the wine. 'That's really what I want to talk about. I think from now on it's going to be much too dodgy for us to swan around in broad daylight. What we need is someone who can move about relatively unobtrusively to spot targets that we can go back and hit later. Alain's people can come up with a lot of intelligence, of course. But frankly they're pretty useless when it comes to making any proper military assessment.' He fixed Adam with a serious look. 'Now, I know I've prevailed on you once. But it would be bloody valuable to us if you could do another recce – the same sort of thing you did yesterday. You know the military side of things, and you speak French. We'll give you a list of things to look at. All you have to do is take a quick butcher's and report back on whether or not it's worth having a crack at.'

He handed over the bottle. Adam sipped at it and thought. He had no wish to hang about the camp. He imagined more days like yesterday, pedalling along with Claude through the summer fields. It was supplanted abruptly by another vision, of German uniforms, arrest, torture, death. He glanced towards Gerry, who was pretending to ignore him while he chatted to Alain. He could imagine his contempt if he turned him down. Then he thought of all the Joes he had dropped at night, out into the black emptiness, and the guilt that he had felt nagging at him as he turned away from the swaying parachutes and headed back to home and safety. The success of the fuel train attack made him feel quietly proud. He made up his mind.

'OK,' he said. 'Tell me what you want and I'll tell you whether I'm prepared to go along with it.'

Gerry looked triumphantly at Alain, as if he had won a bet. Alain leaned over, smiled and shook his hand.

'Good for you,' Gerry said, placing a hand on his shoulder. He turned businesslike. 'Now listen. To start off with, we'd like you to do a preliminary recce around Montcharles. It's the headquarters of the Wehrmacht's Ninety Corps. At the moment their duties are security – keeping the lid on the *maquis* from the Loire to the Gironde. The chances are that sooner or later they'll be withdrawn and thrown into the fighting in Normandy. Just mosey around a bit, see what you can see. Anything you pick up will be valuable.

'But there's also a specific target. The Sicherheitsdienst have got an office in Montcharles. They're the SS intelligence people. It would help us enormously if we knew what they know about the *maquis* operations here. They could be planning operations, reprisals before they pull out. It could save a lot of lives.

'We're thinking about mounting a raid on the building. We know where it is. What we need is detail on how well it's guarded, routes in and out, that sort of thing.'

He paused and took a swig from the bottle. 'Are you still interested?'

'Yes,' Adam said, 'but with a few conditions. First I'll need a guide.'

'That's easy,' said Alain, encouragingly. 'You could have Claude again if you like, if she's agreeable.'

'OK. Why not?' said Adam as casually as he could. 'If she's agreeable, as you say.' He looked at Gerry, expecting to see a gleam of mockery in his eyes, but he smiled reassuringly back.

'The other thing,' Adam went on, 'is that I don't like the idea of going around in civvies. I know I can hardly wear a uniform. But dressed up as a Frenchman I'm automatically a spy if I'm caught. I'm going to take some identification, to prove that I'm a serving officer.'

Now he heard derision in Gerry's laughter. 'Much good will it do you, brother,' he said. 'Frankly, it wouldn't make any difference if you were dressed up in your mess kit. We're commandos, operating behind the lines. As far as the Germans are concerned, if we're caught we're to be killed like vermin, whether we're in uniform or out. Order from the boss himself, apparently.'

'Who told you that?' Adam asked.

'They did!' Gerry said. 'When I was in Italy I went into the bag, albeit briefly, after unsuccessfully trying to blow up an airfield. I was captured by some Wehrmacht types, regular army, not as beastly as the SS boys. They said as I was special forces I couldn't be treated as a regular POW. They were going to have to hand me over to the SD or the Gestapo. They didn't leave me in much doubt as to what would happen to me when they did. I managed to escape after that – I sometimes think they let me. I told our int. blokes about it when I got back, but they chose to regard it as an attempt to put the frighteners on me. As far as I know, it was never passed on.'

'Do your troopers know this?' Adam asked.

'Hardly,' Gerry said. 'I suspect there would be a dearth of volunteers if they'd advertised that detail.' He chuckled cynically. 'Still game?'

Adam thought. 'Well in that case I want some civilian identification. At least that might give me a chance if I'm stopped.'

Gerry looked at Alain again. 'Could you knock something up?'

'Have you got a photograph?'

He had. Everyone was issued with small portraits, taken out of uniform, for just this eventuality in case they were shot down. He fished it out if his tunic and handed it to Alain.

'I'll see what I can do,' he said.

Gerry went over to his Jeep and came back with some maps of Montcharles and its surroundings and they looked over them.

'You'll have to memorise this as it won't do to be caught carrying maps,' he said.

It didn't take much remembering. Montcharles had barely broken out of its medieval boundaries, an old city on a hill, and much of it was already familiar to Adam from the tour of the previous day.

Gerry went off to brief his men on the evening's operations. He was leading a demolition raid, leaving the supervision of the drop to Glover. When he had gone, Alain got to his feet.

'I'll contact Claude and see what she says.'

'Don't bother. I'll see her myself this evening.'

Alain widened his eyes.

'If she doesn't want to do it, I'll come back to you. Otherwise we'll set off as soon as it's light.'

'As you wish,' he said. 'Good luck.' He winked and flipped his yellow cigarette into the undergrowth.

He found Hennessy and Hawkins lying by the patch of ground they had made their own and explained what he was doing.

'That's nice,' said Hennessy with a strained smile. 'You leave us here while you go off with some French bint.'

'I'll be back, don't worry.'

'You'd better be,' Hawkins said. It was meant as a joke but the words were blurted out, revealing something that was better concealed.

Adam picked his way over the fallen timber, down the slope and over the narrow stream. It was hard to see more than ten yards ahead through the leaves and tangled branches, but then he made out the red slope of the roof and the yellow walls and green shutters of the cottage.

She was sitting, reading, at a round table in the garden at the front of the house. It reminded Adam of gardens he had seen in England, enclosed by hedges and with a circular bed planted with roses cut in the middle of the lawn. Across the fields, the village glowed in the evening sun.

'Hallo.'

She looked up and saw him. There was a slight frown on her face.

'Am I disturbing you?'

She stood up. 'Come over here.'

She plucked at the front of his shirt, once white, now grimy and creased.

'You look like a tramp. Wait here.'

He sat down and she went into the house. He heard voices. Then she returned with a bundle of shirts and underwear.

'Take these. They belong to my uncle.'

'Won't he mind?'

'He's got plenty more. He's got money now, thanks to the war.'

There was a bottle of cider on the table and two glasses. She poured a glass for him and he raised it to her.

'Thanks.' They drank in silence for a few minutes.

'So this is your uncle's house?'

'My aunt's. They don't live here. They stay in Limoges.'

He wondered about the voices he had heard coming from the house. He was about to ask when he heard someone calling from the side of the cottage. He looked up to see a young man, wearing schoolboy shorts, pushing a bicycle towards the garden gate. He waved and mounted the bike. 'See you soon,' he shouted.

'I know him,' said Adam.

'I know you do,' she said. 'He told me he'd met you. He's my brother.'

'I thought you said he was in prison.'

'He was. He escaped about two months ago. I didn't want to tell you because I didn't know you well enough.'

'And you do now? To trust me, I mean?'

'I think so. You have to make your mind up quickly these days. I haven't been wrong yet.'

'Tell me the story, then.'

She poured another glass of cider for him.

'There were five of them,' she said, 'studying at the university. There was Jean, my brother, and his friends: Marc, Didier, Bertrand and Jacques. They were interested in the usual things – sport, girls. When the Germans came they had no idea what to do. Their elders weren't much use. They were all busy trying to make their own lives fit in with the occupation.

'Like a lot of the students they felt they had to make some sort of protest. At first it was silly little things. We all used to go to a cinema called the Castille. Before the film they would show newsreels about how well the war was going and how good things were between the Germans and the French. We would all whistle and stamp our feet until the manager put the lights on. One day he announced that the lights would be kept on during the newsreel so the troublemakers could be identified. So the following day everyone arrived with newspapers and read them during the propaganda films. That went on until some of the students were arrested.' She smiled.

'Anyway, those were just games. Jean and his friends were more serious. They stole pistols from German officers when they were swimming at the bathing station by the river. They would go through soldiers' kitbags when they were doing PT in the park. One night, Jean climbed up onto the roof of the Hôtel de Ville and tore down the swastika flag.

'One day they went further. No one told them to. They were operating on their own and had nothing to do with the Communists or the secret army or any organised Resistance groups. The plan was that they were going to teach a lesson to one of the big collaborators in town.'

She leant back, and took a sip of her cider. From the edge of the lawn, a frog croaked.

'There was a policeman called Coudrin. He was nothing much before. The war made him a big man. He got on well with the Germans and was better than the Nazis themselves in tracking down their enemies. One night they waited for him outside his house in Montcharles. One of them went to the door saying he had some information for him. The idea was to kidnap him and give him a fright – show how easy it would be to assassinate him. Before they could overpower him, he pulled out his gun and started shooting at them. They stabbed Coudrin to death on the doorstep.

'The police and the Germans had no idea who did it. Nor did the Resistance. It was the Communists who found out first. They persuaded them – or blackmailed them – into joining in some of their actions. Once they helped them derail a train, which blocked the Paris–Bordeaux line for two days. That really upset the Germans. Anyway, one day the police caught some Communists setting fire to some wagons. My brother and his friends weren't there. The Communists were tortured and told everything they knew – including who killed Coudrin. It didn't take them long to find my brother and his friends and hand them over to the Section des Affaires Politiques.'

'What's that?' asked Adam.

'The political department of the police. Coudrin was one of their own. They wanted their revenge. They beat them and tortured them. The boys confessed to everything. The only thing they said in their defence was that they hadn't meant to kill Coudrin.

'Eventually they were put on trial. It was a crime against a Frenchman, so French magistrates presided at the hearing. The boys had lawyers – honest ones. They argued that it was a political crime and that France had abolished the death penalty for political crimes in 1848. To everyone's surprise the judges agreed. They sentenced four of them, including my brother, to life in prison with hard labour. Bertrand had only been the lookout when Coudrin was killed. He got twenty years' hard labour.'

She paused. Her voice was harder when she spoke again.'This wasn't enough for the collaborators, though. The press started screaming that if they were allowed to live, then no loyal follower of the Maréchal would be safe.

'It was the Germans who came to the rescue. They held their own hearing against them. The main crime this time was not the assassination of Coudrin but sabotaging the train. They were all found guilty and sentenced to death except Jean. A policeman gave evidence that he hadn't been present. The others were shot last September. Jean was sentenced to life in prison with hard labour. He was sent off to Paris first, to the Santé prison. He jumped off a lorry when he was being moved down south. He turned up here in May.'

Adam thought of the unsmiling boy in the childish shorts and sandals.

'Why did he come back? Why didn't he just run away and hide?'

She shrugged. 'He has scores to settle. If Jean had wanted to run away he would have done it at the beginning. Or he could just have ignored the occupation or gone along with it and joined the Milice. Some of his schoolfriends did. I suppose there are always people in any generation who aren't content with just surviving. Maybe they were born with consciences that were too big. Maybe they are just awkward and contrary, or they don't mind too much about dying. Jean is one of them.'

She looked at him. 'What about you? Surely you could have found somewhere quiet to wait for the war to go away.'

'I thought I had, once,' he said. 'But the war has a way of reaching out and grabbing you.' They both laughed.

'And you?'

'I don't know,' she said. 'It wasn't much of a struggle to make up my mind. I didn't really see that there was any choice.' She finished her drink. 'Anyway, what I'm doing is not very heroic. Riding my bicycle around the district on nice summer days.'

A breeze crept over the garden, shaking the rose trees.

'I have to talk to you about that,' he said.

'About what?'

'Well, Alain wondered whether you were prepared to go with me again tomorrow. Back to Montcharles.'

'Alain wondered?'

'Well, Alain and me.' He paused, embarrassed. 'Of course it's up to you.'

'Sure,' she said nonchalantly, getting up from the table. 'Why not?'

She turned back on her way to the cottage door.

'Are you hungry? You had better be.'

He nodded. He felt happy.

'Very hungry?'

He nodded.

'Good. Come inside. I've made us something.'

They had crayfish from the stream that ran just past the end of the garden, then slices of salty ham with waxy potatoes.

They sat at a table in the kitchen. The room was low-beamed and primitive, hung with iron pots and pans that looked as if they had been in use for centuries. Even with the shutters open to the setting sun, it was dark.

He praised the cooking.

'Anyone could do it,' she said, slightly ungraciously. 'It's just a matter of heating up hot water.'

'That's nonsense,' he said. 'French women have the gift. That's what they say, anyway.'

She laughed.

'Who says I'm a Frenchwoman? Well I am, I suppose. But maybe not a proper one. I hardly ever cook, I don't dress up. I'm not looking for a husband.'

'No shortage of candidates, I'm sure.'

She made a short, contradicting noise and moved to clear away the plates. She came back with an apple pie on an earthenware plate and a jug of cream.

'What will you do when it's all over?'

It was the question he never asked himself and stopped others answering. The bad luck question. She pushed her plate away.

'Medicine,' she said. 'That's what I was studying, at Montcharles, before I had to leave.'

'It's gloomy in here,' Claude said when they had washed up the plates. 'Let's go for a walk.'

They went through the garden and over the fields to the edge of Vercourt. The evening was warm and dry. They reached the church. It was simple and solid with a square bell tower and a slate roof shaped like a pyramid.

'It was built in the eleventh century,' she said. 'It's very plain but I like it. All the churches around here look the same.' There was a weather-stained board outside announcing the times of the Masses.

'The Church of Saint Radegonde,' he said. 'Is that a local saint?'

'Yes, there are lots of things named after her. People too.' She paused. 'My real name is Radegonde.'

'Ra-de-gonde,' he said, trying the hard consonants against his tongue. 'Who was Ra-de-gonde?'

'She was a Merovingian queen who lived in the sixth century – very holy, unlike the rest of her family. She founded an order of nuns and built a convent in Montcharles. She spent all her life trying to stop the wars that her relations started. Very holy and very clean. She had baths installed in the convent and made all the sisters wash three times a day.'

She held out her hand. 'Got a cigarette?'

'You smoke?'

'Sometimes.'

He struck a match and the flame jumped in the dark, illuminating her oval face and the black eyes that glittered under her thick, neat eyebrows.

'Thanks.' She inhaled cautiously.

'It was my mother's idea, Radegonde. She was a history teacher. A romantic. Not like me. She's dead now. And my father.'

She saw his look.

'No, nothing to do with the war. Come round here.'

She led him to the front of the church. Above the door was a row of arched windows, framed by roughly carved pillars. Above and below ran stone beams, decorated at regular intervals with crude gargoyles.

'They're not very beautiful, are they?' she said.

The gargoyles were primitive caricatures of dog-faced men and melon-headed demons. The carvings on the arches were more elaborate. One showed a cow with one body and two heads. Another showed a grinning devil holding up an infant in each hand, one by the leg and one by the arm. He felt a premonitory flicker of disquiet. He did not want to ask what they meant. He took her by the arm.

'Shall we go?'

She nodded and he led her out into the lane. The path sloped gently down into the village. From where they were standing they could see the entrance to the little square and the Auberge de la Vienne, glowing in the dying sun.

'What about a drink at the hotel?'

'It's not very safe,' she said.

'Nothing is.'

She smiled. 'You're right. We'll have to be careful though. Don't talk to anyone.'

The hotel smelled of woodworm and stale wine. The bar was surprisingly crowded. Most of the customers were middle-aged or elderly men who looked up at them as they sat down. A melancholy waiter in a black waistcoat and apron came over and they ordered glasses of white wine. At the next table a man was speaking rapidly and nervously to four or five others. He had a strong accent and Adam had difficulty understanding him.

'What's he saying?'

'Shh,' she said.

The audience listened raptly. From time to time they muttered and shook their heads. When the man finished they immediately started to ask questions.

'It all sounded very dramatic,' said Adam.

'It was,' she said. She looked uneasy.

'He's just got back from Montcharles. He saw the raid this morning.'

'Gerry said it was a great success. All the targets were destroyed.'

'Maybe. They managed to destroy a lot of other things as well.'

'Go on.'

'A lot of houses around the station were hit and some bombs fell in the main square. The stationmaster was killed, railwaymen too. They got some Germans. One bomb hit a cinema they were using as a barracks. He had a look inside. There were bodies everywhere.'

'Shouldn't he be pleased about that?'

'Maybe, but he isn't.'

Adam looked at the man more closely. He was small and skinny and still shaking with the shock of what he had seen. He realised that for most of the people in the area, the bombs would be a terrible novelty, their first experience of the everyday violence of the war.

Now that the recital was over, Adam was attracting some glances from the other table – curious, not hostile, but not friendly. She tugged at his sleeve and they got up to go. She placed some coins on the table and they walked out into the square. They walked along the lane back to the cottage, smelling the wild garlic and the spicy scent of sun-baked earth.

Cautiously, he reached for her hand. Her dry palm pressed back, assenting. When they got to the cottage he asked if he could come in for a last drink.

'No,' she said. 'You have to go back to the camp. Otherwise they'll think you've deserted. We need to start early tomorrow.'

'I'll come and wake you up.'

'No need. I'll be waiting.' She leaned up and brushed her lips against his cheek. 'Goodnight Adam.'

30

They reached Montcharles in the middle of the morning. Cycling past the stadium and the half-timbered suburban villas, everything seemed normal. Then they rounded a corner and suddenly there was a gap in the row of neat dwellings lining the road, and instead of a house there was a mound of blackened bricks and charred timber and the smell of wet charcoal.

In the main square, Place des Canons, torn curtains hung from the smoke-stained windows of the Astoria Hotel. Inside and out, a team of civilian workers were hauling away shattered masonry.

They wheeled the bikes through the debris to the other side of the square and swooped down the long road that led to the station. He could scarcely believe it was the same place they had visited the day before. The ordered rectangles of sheds and depots and water towers, the station hall, the platforms and offices had been swept away, and the tracks twisted up into tangles of steel, warped by the fires that still burned feebly in the rubble. The rows of sturdy bourgeois houses that perched along the banks overlooking the defile through which the line passed were now mostly roofless and scarred by shrapnel.

They cycled onto the bridge that linked the two sides of the valley and stopped to look down on the scene.

'We did this,' Radegonde said.

He had been thinking the same thing.

'You can't say that,' he said. 'This was planned before. It was obviously a much bigger operation than just bombing a few petrol tankers.'

He did not know whether he believed himself or not. Families pushing handcarts filed past. They wheeled them into the ruined houses on the hillside, picking around inside among the smashed bricks and fallen joists, emerging with a washstand, an armful of books, a blanket; anything that had escaped the devastation. They had the same hard, immobile look, numbly concentrated on survival, that he had seen four years before on the faces of other Frenchmen and -women as they trudged away from the German columns.

They wheeled their bikes back up the hill to Place des Canons. She seemed to have accepted his explanation of the scale of the raid.

'Your people had good information,' she said, nodding in the direction of the Astoria. 'The German officers used that place as their mess.'

Adam wondered whether it had been luck or judgement that had determined the hotel's fate.

The headquarters of the SS security police was in another hotel, the Flèche d'Or on Rue Wilson, which ran off Place des Canons. There was a terrace-café opposite where they could take a coffee and look the place over. The hotel was solid and Flemish-looking. It had a wrought-iron balcony on the first floor, with big windows, behind which they could see clerks and secretaries working listlessly in the heat. Stacked up along the walls were rows of filing cabinets.

The front doors were pinned open, revealing a high-ceilinged lobby with a black-and-white marble floor and a reception desk manned by two soldiers. Two SS troopers leaned against the wall on either side of the entrance, sagging with boredom.

'Where does this road go?' he asked.

'Rue Wilson? Down the hill. Then it joins up with the main road south.'

'Towards Vercourt?'

'Yes.'

That was useful. For the next half-hour they watched the comings and goings at the Flèche d'Or. He felt glaringly conspicuous. His hand kept going to his jacket pocket and the identity card Alain had provided for him in the name of Georges Melin. The photograph had been cropped tight. To his eyes, the document looked dismally unconvincing.

Most of the visitors wore either the field grey of the Wehrmacht or the black of the SS Panzergrenadier division who were based twenty-five miles to the north-east. Alain had said that the SS had left a garrison of two or three hundred troops when the rest had gone to join the fighting in Normandy. They arrived by foot or motor, parking in a space in front of the hotel. The guards barely looked at the visitors.

Just as they were about to leave, a long elegant car, a dark green Mercedes, drew up diagonally opposite and a man got out. He had a broad, strong face and brownish hair, cropped short, and was wearing a blue suit that made him look prosperous and important. A fair-haired woman, in a blue and white-striped silk dress, stood proprietorially by his side. For a moment Adam thought they were going into the hotel. Instead, they walked twenty yards down the street and into the front door of a stone town house.

Adam turned to Radegonde. 'Who are they?'

Her face had turned hard. 'That's Raymond de la Haye. The bitch with him is his mistress.'

'You don't like them, then.' There was something about her hostility that amused him.

'I hate them.'

'Why?'

'Raymond de la Haye was a lawyer before the war. To be fair to him, he was always on the right – Maurras, Action Française, all that. When the Germans came he was delighted. He started writing a column in the local paper denouncing Communists and Jews and Freemasons. He even attacked Vichy officials for not being hard enough on them. Naturally he loved the Germans. The only argument he ever had with them was over who should get the credit for inventing anti-Semitism. He felt it should be the French.

'Anyway, he became friends with the officers in the Feldkommandantur. He spent some time in Germany before the war and speaks some German. They helped him with business. Now he controls most of the black market in Montcharles.'

'I see.'

His curiosity was satisfied but she wanted to carry on.

'It didn't stop there. He started organising political meetings around the area to rally support for Vichy and the Germans. One day he was speaking at a hall in a small town near here and some people in the audience booed him. The local police were there but they did nothing. He complained to the Germans about them. The following day two policemen, respected men, were arrested and sent to prison.

'Then he took revenge on old rivals from school and university. He denounced a philosophy teacher who taught at the university, said he was a Communist sympathiser, and he was deported to Germany. When he thought that one of the Miliciens was getting too interested in his girlfriend, he arranged for him to be transferred into the Légion des Volontaires Français and sent off to the Russian front.'

He could see now that there was more than patriotism behind her animosity.

'But you hate him for something else, don't you?'

She paused. 'Yes. It's because of my brother. When he and the others were arrested, de la Haye used his newspaper column to call for the death sentence. When their lives were spared he did everything he could to get the judgement changed. It was because of him the other boys were shot. It must have bothered him that they let Jean live.'

'Why was he so concerned about Jean?'

'He wanted to get at my father. He was a lawyer. De la Haye came to him for a job and he turned him down. I think it's as simple as that.'

'And the girl?'

'Her name is Lucille. I was at school with her. She's stupid rather than bad. And weak. There are plenty like her.'

He was feeling nervous now. They had been sitting there too long. They paid for their coffee, mounted their bicyles and freewheeled down Rue Wilson, descending the slope of the town until it met the road south.

As they rode steadily back, he constructed a plan of attack on the Flèche d'Or. The idea was to capture or destroy the SD records, which Alain had said contained all the German intelligence on the area.

He was sure an attack could succeed if it was done quickly enough. There were only two sentries. Judging by their performance today, they took barely any notice of the comings and goings in Rue Wilson. The inside was unlikely to be any better guarded, if it was guarded at all. Getting into Montcharles presented a problem. A military operation, in daylight, using the Jeeps, would be suicidal. The place was full of garrison troops. Surprise might get them into town before the Germans realised they were there, but they would never get out alive.

If they tried the same operation at night they would have to negotiate checkpoints at the entrances to the town. Adam's advice would be to launch the operation in daylight, in civilian disguise. De la Haye had shown it was possible for a civilian to park by the Flèche d'Or without attracting the guards' attention. They were used to him, perhaps. But everything suggested that they would be able to drive up to the entrance without being challenged, at least not immediately. All they needed were a few seconds of grace. Then it was simply a matter of shooting down the guards, seizing as many documents as possible, and setting fire to the rest.

He looked at Radegonde, pedalling solidly alongside him. The violent pictures in his head faded. She felt him looking at her and smiled.

31

Adam kissed Radegonde goodbye at the cottage, saying he would come back later when he had some news. It was the middle of the afternoon and splintered sunlight was falling between the slim boles of the oak trees. When he got to the edge of the camp he was surprised to find there were no sentries. The ground was littered with rucksacks and sleeping bags and shirts and underwear hung drying on the trees. He heard laughter coming from the valley and walked down the slope, towards the noise.

A dozen soldiers lay sprawled about on the far bank of the stream. Some of the faces were new, arrivals from the previous night's drop. Hennessy and Hawkins were with them. Two young women sat in the middle of the group. No one noticed him as he approached. Then one of the men looked up.

'Hallo, sir,' he said. 'Come and join us.'

It was Shirley. He held up a bottle.

'Want a drink?'

Adam stopped where he was. He looked at the slack faces of the soldiers and the stupid smiles of the girls and a coal of fury glowed inside him.

He ignored Shirley, who had got to his feet now and was waving the bottle invitingly.

'Hennessy and Hawkins. Get over here, now.'

They got up, bemusement on their faces, and reluctantly made their way across the stream.

'What the hell are you doing?'

'What do you mean?' asked Hawkins looking perplexed.

'You heard Cunningham. They're supposed to be guarding the place. It's meant to be fucking secret.'

'Steady on,' Hennessy said. 'It's nothing to do with us. And you shouldn't have a go at the other blokes either. The girls turned up this morning. They wandered up from the village. Shirley and Maslin went back with them to fetch some wallop. It's so bloody boring here I don't blame them.'

A gramophone had appeared from somewhere. *Maquis* loot, Adam supposed. Someone cranked the handle, releasing scratchy music. Shirley got up, reached down and pulled one of the girls to her feet, and started to dance with her. She laughed as they stumbled over the uneven ground. She had a round, empty face and was wearing smudged lipstick. Chisholm took hold of the other girl and the two couples shuffled around to the music.

'Turn it up, I can hardly bleeding hear it,' Shirley called, and one of the troopers obliged. The other soldiers watched the dancers, clicking their fingers to the beat, dragging on cigarettes and tilting bottles to their mouths.

Adam walked over to the gramophone and snatched away the stylus. Quiet flooded back. Then a voice, childish and disappointed, broke the silence.

'Oh, sir! What did you do that for?'

'Shut up, Shirley. Get these women out of here. Clean up the mess and send some men up to the road to guard the approach to the camp.'

The women looked up at him, scared by the harsh edge to his voice. Without being spoken to, they crept away back through the trees. Grudgingly, the men stamped out their cigarettes and started collecting up the bottles. Shirley spoke quietly to two of them who detached themselves from the group and slouched up towards the road.

'Come over here.'

Shirley approached warily.

'You didn't have any right to do that,' he said. 'You're not in charge of me.'

Adam pretended he had not heard him.

'You had orders to guard the camp.'

'Yes,' said Shirley sulkily.

'Why did you ignore them?'

'We didn't. We were keeping an eye out. Anyway, it's as safe as houses here. There are no Germans for miles.'

'Don't fuck me about, Shirley,' Adam said wearily. 'I don't give a shit if you get killed but I do care about me and my men. Now you've endangered the whole camp. I'm telling Major Cunningham about it when he gets back.'

Shirley's sulky look vanished and he looked alarmed.

'Do you have to, sir? I can explain what happened.'

Anxiety had wiped the craftiness from his face. Adam started to feel sorry for him.

'Go on then. Explain.'

He started a rambling story about the arrival of the girls in the camp and how they had seen no harm in chatting to them and then going with them to the village to buy drink. As for the sentries, they had just joined them for a few minutes before going back to their posts.

As the explanation went on he got more confident, so that by the end he was chatting to Adam as if he was a comrade rather than an officer.

'So after all that, there's no harm done, is there?' he concluded.

Adam shook his head. 'Oh yes there is,' he said. 'What do you think those girls are going to say when they get back to the village? How do you think they knew we were here in the first place?'

Shirley looked puzzled. 'But they're all friendly types in the village, aren't they? They're on our side.'

'We'll find out soon enough,' said Adam. 'Anyway,' he repeated, 'I'm going to have to tell Cunningham that the girls were here. Sorry.'

Shirley looked unhappy but resigned.

Adam held out a cigarette.

'Thank you, sir.' The gap between them had resumed a familiar, comfortable width.

They puffed in silence for a while.

'How did the drop go last night?' asked Adam eventually.

Shirley brightened up. 'Went like clockwork. We've got twenty new blokes and three more Jeeps. Half of them went out this morning. The rest have been hanging around here with us.' He blew out a stream of smoke, looking dejected again.

'What do you really reckon?' Shirley said.

'About what?'

'About the war. I mean, how long is it going to go on? Now that we're ashore, the Germans can't win, can they? They're bound to give up sooner or later. And if that's the case, what are we doing frigging about here?'

'You're asking the wrong person. I'm here by accident. I'd much rather be somewhere else, believe me.'

Shirley laughed. 'I believe you. But the major and some of these other blokes . . .' He shook his head.

Hennessy and Hawkins joined them and listened while he described the trip to Montcharles. Then there was nothing more to say and boredom settled on them like fog. It was a relief when they heard the engines at the edge of the forest.

Gerry was driving one Jeep with Alain and a soldier as passengers. Glover was in another, with two soldiers. Gerry's passenger looked familiar. They parked the vehicles and covered them with branches. Gerry saw Adam and came over.

'Back so soon?' he said. 'Tell me how it went.' They walked across to Gerry's tent. He called Alain and they sat in silence while he gave his report.

'How would you do it?' Gerry said at the end.

Adam felt flattered. He ran through the plan he had made on the journey back. Gerry nodded as Adam listed the disadvantages of a full-scale military raid, by day or by night, and grunted at the idea of an infiltration in civilian disguise. Adam raised another idea he had thought of since returning – the raiders could dress up in German uniforms.

Gerry looked at Alain.

'What do you think?' he asked.

'It depends on how quickly you want to do it. We could get hold of some uniforms but it would take a few days.'

'Forget it,' said Gerry. 'We have to hit them now while they're still off balance from the air raid.'

Adam was pleased at this dismissal. He had only thrown it in to show he had thought of everything.

'I think with the element of surprise you could be in and out of there in a few minutes,' he said. 'Especially if you set fire to the place instead of carting all the documents away.'

'It would be a bloody sight quicker,' Gerry said. 'We've got some of the Lewis bombs we used in the desert. They'd do nicely.'

'No,' said Alain firmly. 'We need the documents intact. They're vital. They contain all their own intelligence and everything that's been given them by the Milice. They'll be able to tell us exactly how much they know about our networks and what they plan to do about them. If we capture them, we save a lot of lives.'

Gerry sighed. 'Well, if you put it like that. But let's not hang around there forever. And we'll take a few of the old bombs along just to be on the safe side.'

For the next hour they worked out the plan. There would be three cars, each carrying three passengers, soldiers and *maquis,* all dressed in civilian clothes. They would attack just after eleven in the morning.

Adam and Radegonde were to go on ahead and sit in the café to act as lookouts. At eleven o'clock the cars would be waiting at the corner of Place des Canons and Rue Wilson, within sight of the café. If the situation looked normal and there was no obvious change in the security, Adam was to stand up from his table and light a cigarette. Then they would leave immediately. If a stronger guard had been mounted, or there was any other indication of danger, he was to walk up the street towards them, arm in arm with Radegonde, and the raiders would slip away.

'You must be exhausted with all that cycling,' said Alain. 'We've got a van that can drop you and your bicycles off in the morning.'

Now the plan was a reality and, without being asked, Radegonde had become part of it. He felt a touch of alarm.

'Can't I just go on my own?' he asked.

'No,' Alain said. 'You're more likely to be picked up. You'll look less obvious if you're sitting with a woman.'

'What if she doesn't want to?'

'She'll want to.'

They went back to their planning, making it clear that Adam's part in it was over. The soldier from Gerry's Jeep had been waiting for the conference to end. Now he approached Adam and held out his hand.

'I'm Mark Minto. In fact we already know each other, though you may have forgotten it. It was in Cairo a few years back.'

Adam remembered the confident young man he had met in Cromarty's flat.

'Of course I do,' he said. 'This is a coincidence.'

'Not really,' Minto said airily. 'My experience is that people are always running into each other in wartime.'

The memory of that evening came back to him with unwelcome clarity. No doubt Minto would have heard the story of what had happened to him and Koski after they had parted company.

'How's Major Gibson?' he asked, pre-emptively. He imagined that the belligerent Ulsterman was long dead by now.

Minto laughed, managing to sound jovial and cynical at the same time.

'Dougie? He's gone up in the world. Head of the whole bloody outfit. Got more gongs than he can fit on his chest. He's very annoyed that they wouldn't let him come along with us, though I must say, personally speaking, it's a great relief. Poor old Dougie. Christ knows what he's going to do when the war's over.'

There was something Adam had forgotten. He went back to Gerry, who was still huddled with Alain, apparently planning the detail of the attack. They stopped talking and looked up when Adam interrupted.

'What's up?' Gerry asked impatiently.

'There's something you ought to know,' Adam said. 'While you were away a couple of girls showed up at the camp. Apparently they wandered up from Vercourt. Whether they heard we were here or whether they just stumbled upon us isn't clear. Either way it means word will get round.'

Gerry seemed to regard the news as a distraction.

'I wouldn't worry too much about it,' he said. 'We'll be moving on from here pretty soon. There's too many of us now to stick in one place and we may have to split up. We found a couple of spots today which might do.'

'Don't worry about the girls,' said Alain. 'I'll find out who they are. They won't talk, believe me.'

They turned their backs and resumed their discussion.

Adam went down to the stream and washed, then put on one of the shirts that Radegonde had given him. He took his time walking to the cottage, thinking of the days ahead. Tomorrow's operation would be the last, he decided. It was time to leave, to get away from France and from Vercourt wood. The forest was beginning to oppress him. The ground cracked and snapped as he trod down on the ancient debris of leaf and branch, releasing the mushroomy smell of rotten wood from the cushioned ground. The forest was revealing itself to him. He could feel its presence at his shoulder, always a step behind. He was glad when the trees thinned out and he was out in the early evening sunshine.

The shutters were open but there was no noise coming from the cottage. He walked round to the front and saw the door was open. He thought of knocking, but something stopped him and he stepped into the dim parlour. He could hear the noise of splashing water coming from a room off to the right, of a jug scooping into a bucket, being lifted and poured. She was bathing. He was seized by embarrassment and was turning to go when he heard the scraping of a latch lifting and her hesitant voice.

'Adam?'

He turned round slowly. She was wearing an old tartan dressing gown and was holding a towel to her hair, wet and shiny from the tub.

'I heard a noise,' she said. 'I'm glad it's only you. Sit down.'

He pulled up a chair at the long table and she went into the pantry and came back with a jug and two glasses and filled them with lemonade. He told her the plan for the following day and she listened without speaking. She seemed amused by Alain's determination to get hold of the documents.

'Are you sure you want to go?'

'Of course.'

She looked surprised that he had bothered to ask the question. She smiled, showing her white teeth.

He looked around the parlour. The cottage was very small, just this room and, he supposed, a couple of poky bedrooms upstairs. He wondered if she lived here on her own. He imagined her climbing the steep wooden stairs, pulling the bedclothes over herself in the narrow peasant bed. Did she sleep in it alone? Or was there a man who shared it with her? He hoped, very badly, that there was not.

'Let's sit outside,' she said. She went to the larder again and brought out a bottle and two small glasses. They sat at the round iron table and sipped apple brandy and watched the sun glowing on the gable walls of the houses at the edge of the village as it sank into the west.

For the first time he talked at length about himself, about his childhood and his escape from Poland and adventures on the way to Britain. He told her about his days as a fighter pilot, modestly, but hoping a little that the story might impress her, but she just listened and nodded.

When he had finished she said, 'You've left something out.'

'What?'

'Women.' She smiled, narrowing her black eyes.

She had caught him off balance. What could he tell her? The story of Moira? He was not sure how to tell it. It came out anyway. It was a fair version of the truth though he avoided revealing that Gerry had been his rival. It sounded to his ears as if he was describing a film he had seen, or telling a story about something that had happened to someone else.

'She sounds like she was a good woman,' she said when he finished.

Was she? Part of Moira's attraction had been her streak of amorality. He had assumed she was good, underneath the cold gloss. Otherwise he would not have loved her. Now he had no idea.

She lifted the little glass and stuck her tongue in to lick out the last drop of brandy and looked at him.

They turned to other, easier things. It was dark now and the moon was rising. He smoked a last cigarette and got up to go. He bent down to brush his lips against her cheek but she pulled him to her, too sharply, so that his nose poked into her eye and she stepped back with a little grunt of pain. Then he put his arms on her shoulders and drew her to him and they kissed, slowly and thoroughly. He felt her body, springy and supple under her cotton dress. His heart was thumping and the blood was singing in his ears, but then her hand slid between their bodies and pushed him back gently but decisively and they broke off the embrace. He felt breathless and slightly sick with desire. He moved forward to take her in his arms again but she stepped away, holding up a warning finger. Then she reached out and traced a line down his cheek, sending an icy flicker of pleasure through his synapses.

She waited as he walked away down the path that led to the back of the house and into the woods. He turned back three times and she was always there, her white dress growing dimmer and dimmer in the dusk.

There were fires burning all over the camp. The sound of laughter and conversation drifted through the wood and somewhere the radio was playing dance music. From a distance it looked like an operatic set, brigands making merry in their mountain hideout. Gerry was sitting cross-legged by one of the fires, in the middle of a semicircle of troopers, a bottle in his hand. His face glowed in the flames. He had found a leather jacket somewhere. With his moustache and dark, swept-back hair he looked more than ever like an artist from the wild fringes of nineteenth-century Bohemia.

The laughter died down as Adam approached.

'Here, shift up and make some room for Tommy,' Gerry said to Minto, who moved over to make a space for him. Adam squatted down.

'Been seeing your little friend?' Gerry asked insinuatingly.

'I have, as a matter of fact,' Adam said. He added lamely, 'I had to tell her about the arrangements tomorrow.'

'Of course, of course.'

Gerry handed Adam the bottle. It was covered in dust, and when he tipped it into his mouth the red wine tasted ripe and voluptuous. He waited a moment.

'You decided not to post any sentries tonight, then?' he asked lightly.

'What?'

'I walked right through the forest without being challenged once. If I had been the Germans or the Milice I could have crept in and killed the lot of you.'

'But you're not, are you?' Gerry said thickly. 'You're not a fucking German. You're my old pal Tommy and you wouldn't hurt a fly.'

There was menace in his voice. Adam realised he was very drunk.

'No,' Gerry went on. 'If the Germans knew we were here we'd be dead by now. But they don't, or not yet, so we're fine.' He put an arm round Adam's shoulder. 'You leave the thinking to me, Tommy boy. I'll take care of you.'

The others laughed deferentially. Gerry sighed and lay back, drawing up his knees, flinging out his arms, signalling his withdrawal from the conversation. He lay there while the others talked on, more quietly, as if anxious not to disturb him.

Then he turned on his side and looked up at Adam. His voice was soft and warm.

'What's the matter with you, Tommy? You've treated me like a bloody leper since we met up again. You can't still be angry with me over Moira. Christ, man, it's me that should be mad at you. After all, it was you who took her away from me in the first place if I remember the story correctly. Anyway, it was all long ago and far away and a lot has happened to us since then, and who knows where we'll all be twenty-four hours from now.'

He sat up and tilted on the bottle.

'It's too bloody boring to sit around and sulk.'

Adam thought for a moment.

'I don't understand you,' he said. 'There was a competition. You won. Why aren't you happy with that? Why do I have to like you as well?'

Gerry laughed. 'I suppose because I like you.'

'But you like everyone.'

'I pretend to. It's the way I was brought up. When you've no money, and you hail from dear old Ireland, and all you've got going for you is your charm, that's what you have to do. You're a bloody Pole, for Christ's sake, you should know that . . . But with you, I mean it.'

Gerry put his hand on Adam's shoulder and fixed him with clouded, slightly bloodshot eyes. 'I like you, brother, really I do.'

Adam found he was smiling. Gerry looked absurdly dramatic with his leather jacket and desperado moustache and cascade of greasy hair, sprawled in the firelight. He couldn't help laughing.

'That's better, Tommy,' said Gerry, clapping him on the shoulder. 'That's better. Always better to smile than to sit around looking miserable, which you've made something of a speciality of over the last few days.'

He lay back, weary again. 'Can't stand suffering,' he said distantly. 'It bores me.'

The bottles went round, the radio played softly. Gerry fell off to sleep for a few minutes then woke up with a jerk.

'We'd better be getting to bed,' said Adam. 'Big day tomorrow.'

'Don't be such a bloody wet blanket,' said Gerry. He raised another heavy bottle and recited:

'Where the rose blows along the river's brink
    With old Gerry, the ruby vintage drink . . .'

He lit a cigarette and gestured around at the dying fire and the slumped troopers.

'I'm going to miss all this. People say war is hell. Frankly, I've had the time of my life. So have most of the blokes in our mob – the original ones, that is. After this, everything is going to be a gigantic anticlimax.'

'It isn't finished yet.'

'It is for the likes of me. There won't be much room for us special forces types in the next phase. It will be armour and artillery all the way to Berlin, with us stuck on the sidelines. No, as far as we are concerned, the best of it is over.'

'What will you do afterwards?'

'I haven't yet worked that out. But I won't have to worry for a bit. I'll be pretty well set up by the time the war is over.'

'They pay well, do they, the SOS?'

Gerry smiled. 'I've managed to augment my earnings here and there. In fact I've found one or two interesting opportunities around this neck of the woods. Alain has been most helpful in pointing them out.'

'You seem to get on pretty well with Alain.'

'Difficult not to. We're cut from the same cloth, you see.'

From the fire came a sound of escaping steam and they looked up to see a swaying soldier pissing extravagantly onto the embers.

'Jesus Christ, Sampson, do you have to do that?' Gerry said disgustedly. The trooper appeared not to hear him and carried on, dousing the warmth from the fire.

'I suppose it's some sort of signal,' Gerry said with a touch of sadness. He tried to get up, leaning on Adam's shoulder for support, staggered, righted himself, then set off on a surprisingly steady course towards his tent.

32

Just before eleven, Adam and Radegonde sat on the terrace of the café opposite the Flèche d'Or drinking coffee. Rue Wilson was quiet. A housewife passed by, carrying her shopping. A delivery van rumbled over the cobbles. Then the street sank back into its mid-summer, provincial torpor.

Opposite, the SD headquarters seemed as somnolent as it had done the day before. In the twenty minutes since they had been sitting there, no one had arrived and no one had left. Two SS guards in black uniform stood at the door, leaning back against the wall to take advantage of the narrow band of shadow cast by the balcony above. The large windows on the first floor were open and, behind them, clerks in shirtsleeves were stooped apathetically over their desks.

Adam glanced up and down the street.

There were three minutes to go. His mouth was dry with anxiety. He took a sip of the muddy coffee and looked towards Radegonde. She smiled back. She seemed perfectly relaxed. If everything had gone right, Gerry and Alain and the *maquisards* and troopers should have arrived by now and be sitting in three cars at the corner of Place des Canons and Rue Wilson, waiting for the sign.

When the bell of the town hall struck eleven, if everything looked normal he was to stand up and light a cigarette. If they left the café and walked towards the square it meant something was wrong.

The street was now completely deserted. He pulled out his cigarettes in readiness. As he did so he heard a car engine and looked up. A long green Mercedes saloon appeared at the top of Rue Wilson from the direction of the main road. It pulled up outside the Flèche d'Or and Raymond de la Haye and his girl-friend Lucille got out. The guards saluted as they walked past, up the steps and into the lobby.

Adam looked at Radegonde questioningly. She shrugged. The air shivered as the iron bell in the square sounded the first stroke of eleven.

'Go on,' she hissed.

He got up and stepped onto the pavement and, turning towards Place des Canons, made an exagger-ated mime of lighting the cigarette. At once, three black cars moved stealthily into Rue Wilson. He looked round the café. The waiter had gone and the place was empty except for an old couple sitting in the back.

They had already worked out the best vantage point from which to watch the action. Next to the café there was a small garden square with a bronze war memorial in the middle, which showed bare-breasted Victory hauling a *poilu* from the Flanders mud. They stood behind it as the cars drew up, unhurriedly, at the door of the hotel. The SS guards looked up at the sound of the engines. Alain and Gerry were wearing civilian suits with wide trousers and short jackets and had their hands jammed into their jacket pockets. They looked ludicrously like film gangsters. They walked purposefully over to the guards, as if intent on asking them something. But the guards barely looked at them as they grudgingly disengaged from the wall and leaned forward to hear what they wanted. Then Alain and Gerry pulled their hands from their pockets. There was a glint of gunmetal and two sharp cracks. A look of astonishment spread across the faces of the guards. They put their hands gently to their stomachs, where glistening patches had magically appeared on the black of their tunics, and slid gracefully to the ground. As they settled, Alain and Gerry raised their arms in unison and there were two more bangs. The heads of the guards jerked back then dropped forward onto their chests.

At the sound of the first shots, the others emptied from the cars and rushed through the front door of the hotel. In the lobby Adam could see the two soldiers manning the reception desk, standing with their hands in the air while two raiders held guns to their heads. A *maquisard* shouted something to one of them and he babbled a reply and nodded towards the stairs. Then the pistols jolted in the raiders' hands and the soldiers jumped as if startled, and flopped to the floor like puppets whose strings had been cut. A woman screamed, over and over. A clerk ran out onto the first-floor balcony, climbed over the wrought-iron railing and dropped to the pavement. He fell over as he hit the ground and gave a yell of pain, picked himself up and hobbled away down the street. A raider emerged from the front door carrying cardboard boxes overflowing with papers and threw them in the back seat of one of the cars.

Radegonde tugged his arm. 'Let's go and help them,' she said.

He hesitated but she stepped out from the shelter of the statue, pulling him behind her. They heard a short burst of gunfire coming from the building. Inside, burnt gunpowder hung on the air, mixed with the smell of furniture polish. There was a broad wooden staircase to the left, leading to the first floor, and they ran up it. It opened onto what had once been a reception room and was now a large office crowded with desks and cabinets. Along the wall stood a line of uniformed clerks, quivering hands held high, faces clenched in fear. In the middle of the room, Alain was pointing a pistol at the head of an SS officer.

The raiders had divided into two teams. One group were wrenching open cabinets, scooping out files and stacking them on the desks, from where the second group collected them, hurrying off down the stairs and out to the cars which sat at the kerb with doors open and engines running.

Gerry was standing at the window looking out onto the street, keeping watch. He saw them crossing from the staircase and shook his head. They went over to him. Despite the gunshots, the street was quiet and empty. Gerry was sweating and trembling slightly.

He turned towards Alain. 'OK that's enough, let's get going.'

Alain ignored him and urged his men to work faster. There were dozens of filing cabinets in the room. Emptying them would have taken half an hour. Gerry ran across the room and took Alain by the arm.

'Enough, I said. Let's get out of here.'

Alain shook him off angrily but he called to his men to stop. He pulled the SS officer in front of him and hustled him down the stairs. Adam and Radegonde followed. Out in the street, sheets of densely typed papers lay scattered on the pavement. The car doors were open. Alain pushed the German into the back seat of the nearest vehicle and handed Adam a pistol, then ran back into the building. The remaining *maquisards* and soldiers came stumbling out of the front door and climbed into the cars. Adam and Radegonde squeezed in beside the German.

Gerry appeared at the door.

'Is everybody here?' he shouted. He looked around. 'Where's Alain?'

'Isn't he with you?,' Adam asked. 'I just saw him go back inside.'

'Oh Christ.'

Gerry darted back through the door. A few seconds later an explosion sounded inside the building, sending a shower of glass cascading from the first-floor windows, tinkling onto the pavement and roofs of the cars below.

'What was that?' Radegonde asked.

'An incendiary bomb, I think,' Adam replied.

They were sitting on either side of the German, who stared sullenly ahead. Adam pressed the pistol into his side. The bomb must have been heard all over the city. Yet here they were sitting in a driverless car. He handed the pistol to Radegonde.

'Here,' he said. 'I'm going to get them.'

Before he got out of the car, Alain appeared at the top of the steps, holding a pistol to the head of Raymond de la Haye. The lawyer's girlfriend stood beside him, shaking with terror. Alain shuffled them onto the pavement and looked around.

Gerry emerged from the hotel, coughing and blackened with soot.

'What in Christ's name are you doing now?' he yelled. 'Let's go.'

'They're coming with us,' said Alain calmly.

'There's no room, you fool,' Gerry screamed. 'Shoot them or leave them be, but let's get out of here.'

For a long second Alain did nothing. He raised the pistol to de la Haye's head. Then de la Haye spoke.

'I've got a car,' he said reasonably. He put his hand in his jacket pocket and produced a key.

'There.' He pointed to the green Mercedes.

'OK, take it,' said Gerry. 'But for Christ's sake let's go.'

He slipped behind the wheel as Alain pushed the couple down the street to the car. The engine was running. He revved the throttle and jammed the car into gear. They shot out into the road and down the hill and the others followed. Adam twisted round to look through the narrow rear window. Smoke was pouring from the upper storeys of the Flèche d'Or. He could see a few astonished faces in the windows of the houses lining the street, but there was no sign of any pursuers.

The three cars barely slowed down at the junction at the foot of the hill, and swerved right with a squeal of tyres onto the main road. Behind, Adam could see the Mercedes catching them up. Gerry had his foot to the floor and was talking to himself as the car lurched along the bumpy, patched road, urging it to go faster. After five miles they came to a small crossroads and Gerry swung off to the right, down a lane that had grass growing in a strip down the middle of the crumbling tarmac.

'We can get back to the camp by back roads from here,' said Gerry. He was calmer now. He glanced round. 'Better put a blindfold on our friend.' No one had a suitable length of cloth.

'His shirt,' said Radegonde. She yanked the cloth from the German's waistband and tore a strip from the tail. Then she wound it tightly round his eyes, jerking his head to and fro as she did up the knot.

He was quite good looking in a dull way, with light hair shaved away at the sides, tanned skin and white teeth; a good SS specimen.

'Do you know what will happen now?' He spoke in French.

At first Adam thought the German was inquiring about his own fate. Then he realised he was making a threat. He did not reply and let the German continue.

'When they find I am gone they will take hostages. They will seize people and if I am harmed they will kill them.' He spoke in a monotone, plodding and matter-of-fact.

'What's he on about?' Gerry asked.

'He's saying they will kill hostages if he's harmed.'

'It's a bit late to worry about that now,' Gerry said. 'God knows why Alain grabbed him.' He smashed his fist on the dashboard. 'Shit, shit, shit.'

The German started to repeat his words, patiently, laboriously, as if he was explaining something to a child. Gerry cut him short.

'Tell him to put a fucking cork in it, Tommy,' he said grimly.

Adam told him. The German grunted and settled back into the seat. They drove on in silence.

33

A dark bank of cloud was stacked up over the forest as they rounded the corner and descended the last stretch of road, past the château, to the track that led to the camp. The convoy drew up at the edge of the wood and everyone got out. Alain emerged from the green Mercedes and went over to Gerry. Then he called his men to him and they got back into the black cars and drove away.

'Thanks a lot, chum,' Gerry said, watching them depart.

He told Minto to drive the Mercedes into the cover of the trees, then ordered the prisoners to march into the wood ahead of him with their hands up. The German blundered and stumbled behind his blindfold, so that Adam had to grab his belt and steer him past the branches.

They stopped at the fire pit by Gerry's bivouac.

'What do you think?' Gerry asked. 'Should we tie them up?' He laughed softly. 'Our mob doesn't have much experience of taking prisoners.'

'I don't think so,' Adam said. 'They can't get very far.'

De la Haye settled back against a fallen tree and patted the ground next to him, signalling to his girlfriend to join him. She sat down carefully, folding her long legs modestly under her. He put an arm around her shoulder and pulled out a packet of cigarettes and offered one to her. They sat there calmly, smoking and whispering to each other.

'What are we going to do now?' asked Adam.

'I don't know,' Gerry said. 'I'm leaving it to Alain. He's gone off somewhere with those bloody documents. We'll have to wait for him to get back.'

He nodded towards de la Haye, who was now whispering in his girlfriend's ear. 'He seems like a cool customer,' he said approvingly. 'What's his story?'

Adam repeated what Radegonde had told him. Gerry listened with interest.

'What's this about the black market? What's he dealing in?'

Adam looked at Radegonde. 'Everything,' she said. 'First of all food and drink. Then he stole the stuff of people who had been killed or deported, Jews and Resistance. Then he grabbed their homes.'

'He has been busy,' Gerry said, neutrally. 'I'm going to get out of these civvies and find out what's been going on.'

He told two troopers to stand guard and walked over to where the radio set was hidden under a tarpaulin.

Radegonde turned to Adam. 'I'm going back to the house,' she said.

'I'll walk with you.'

Since the start of the raid they had hardly spoken to each other, and now when he tried to coax her into talking she seemed detached. Somehow, the day's violence had put a distance between them. They walked slowly, past small groups of soldiers who sat or lay on the ground, smoking, playing cards and dozing. They looked up as Radegonde went past, assessing her body. She did not seem to notice or, if she did, to mind.

He said goodbye to her at the edge of the forest.

'When shall I see you?' he asked.

'I'll have to come back to talk to Alain,' she said. 'Will you come and get me when he arrives?' He nodded. She waved and darted away.

Hennessy and Hawkins were sitting by the side of the stream when he got back.

'What happened to you?' Hennessy asked. Adam told the story.

'Sounds exciting,' Hawkins said.

'Too bloody exciting,' Hennessy said. 'How much longer do you think we're going to have to stay here?'

'I don't know,' Adam said. 'What about the landing?'

'They don't seem to have moved very far,' Hennessy said. 'It will be weeks before they reach us. When do you think the SOS boys will be pulled out?'

'They've only just got here,' Adam said. There was no point in raising hopes.

They were not good, he thought, at concealing their uneasiness. The forest was working on them too, stretching their nerves. It was, he saw now, both a refuge and a trap. The forest hid you from your enemies. But it also hid your enemies from you.

'What's on your mind?' he asked.

Hennessy spoke first, slowly as if he had prepared what he was saying. 'The longer we stay here, the more danger we're in. This group is far too big. There must be forty of us now. You can see for yourself, half of them haven't got anything to do. I would be amazed if the Germans aren't on to us already.'

'And?'

Hennessy glanced around. 'Well, we're thinking, the others can do what they want. I'm for legging it now, head south towards the Pyrenees and the Spanish border.'

'Maybe you're right,' Adam said. 'Cunningham's found another campsite, but they don't seem to be in a great hurry to move.' He paused. 'If you really think you want to go, I'm not going to try and stop you.'

'But will you come with us?' Hawkins asked anxiously.

'I'm not sure.' It sounded lame.

There was nothing to stop him now. He had done his bit. The longer he stayed, the bigger the danger. He felt no guilt about abandoning the soldiers. This was Gerry's show. But Radegonde . . . Why did it bother him, the thought of leaving her behind? Since their clumsy first embrace, nothing had happened. If anything, she was cooler to him now than she had been before. He was a fool to think that there was a chance of something between them. But when he tried to imagine leaving her behind, he realised he could not do it. He would have to persuade her to come with them.

'I may do,' he said cautiously. 'I have to work some things out.' He felt a swell of irritation as he looked at their despondent, anxious faces. 'Anyway, my decision doesn't matter. You have to do what you think is best.'

He stood up. 'Cunningham's on to London,' he said. 'Maybe there's some news. I'll come back when I know what's going on.'

When he reached the centre of the camp, Gerry was dressed in his khaki fatigues and leather jacket and was sitting on a log, smoking a cigarette and watching de la Haye and his girlfriend.

'What did London have to say?' Adam asked.

'Quite a lot. They don't seem too impressed with what we've done so far. They want us to step up the action. More derailings, more sabotage. It's no use explaining to them that it's easier said than done.' He tossed away his cigarette. 'Maybe Alain has some ideas.'

Alain got back in the late afternoon with a group of *maquisards*. Adam went over to the cottage to fetch Radegonde. He found her in the parlour, dozing in an armchair. He shook her gently and she woke up and yawned and smiled at him, and reached out and put her brown paw on his wrist. For a moment he held on to it and pulled her towards him, but she made a mild mewing noise of protest and tugged her hand away. They walked back slowly, saying little.

At the camp the atmosphere had changed. De la Haye and his girlfriend were half sitting, half lying on the ground, with their hands tied behind their backs and cloth gags cutting into their mouths. The girl's eyes were bright with fear. The SS officer had been trussed with rope so that his arms were bound tight to his sides, and a bandage had been wrapped round his mouth and another round his eyes. Five of Alain's men stood over the captives pointing rifles to their heads. Alain was talking intently to Gerry, who was swaying slightly, a cigarette in one hand and a bottle in the other, nodding as Alain spoke. They looked up as Adam and Radegonde approached.

'Hallo, you two,' Gerry said heavily. 'Maybe you can help with our little problem. We're trying to decide what to do with the guests. Alain is all in favour of hanging on to them as hostages. I want to turn them loose. The trouble is that they know where we live now.'

'The German doesn't,' said Adam. 'He's been blind-folded since we left Montcharles. We could just drive him back and dump him on the Montcharles road.'

'Then what do we do with the other two?' Gerry asked. Adam could see the difficulty. He felt uneasy. Gerry looked half drunk. All Alain's old casualness had evaporated and he seemed to be gripped by some malign energy.

He shook his head emphatically at Adam's sugges-tion. 'No,' he said, 'we can't let the German go. He knows too much about us already. We keep him or we kill him. There's no other choice.'

'What about reprisals?' Adam said.

Alain laughed. 'If we worried about that, we'd never do anything. Anyway, they'll hold off as long as they think there's a chance of getting him back. He seems to think he's someone of importance. We don't even know who he is.'

He moved over to the German, who sat against the log, immobile, blind and dumb.

'At least let them breathe,' Adam said.

Gerry looked at Alain and nodded. One of the *maquisards* bent down and untied the gags, jerking their heads this way and that. The woman's lipstick was smeared over her face and her chin was trembling. The German's mouth was set in a stoical, patient line.

Alain knelt down by his side, undid the buttons of his black tunic and reached inside and pulled out a wallet. He opened it and removed a stiff card with an identity picture stapled to it with a brass ring.

'Fehn, Werner,' he read. 'Obersturmführer. Born Karlsruhe, second September nineteen-seventeen. You've got the same birthday as me.' Piece by piece, he pulled out the contents of the wallet. There were a couple of creased letters, a piece of ribbon; a portrait of a lumpy, middle-aged couple staring warily at the camera, with the name of a studio in Pforzheim printed diagonally across a corner in curly script; a square of folded paper, which Alain opened, revealing dry, stained flower petals.

'Very touching,' he said.

He gave a last exploratory poke of his finger into the lining of the wallet. 'Ah, what's this?' he said, extracting a pasteboard oblong, a photograph of some sort. 'The girlfriend?'

He held it up and examined it. There was a sudden silence that seemed to fill the forest.

'No,' he said, quietly, 'not the girlfriend.'

He handed the picture to Gerry, who glanced at it and whistled, then passed it to Adam.

The girl in the photograph was about eighteen. She had thick blonde hair and she was standing on a stool in a loose cotton dress in the middle of what looked like a hay field. She was holding her head delicately to one side while a man in a black uniform slipped a noose around her neck. There was a look of polite forbearance on her face. The sun was shining. The camera was a good one, sharp enough to pick up the fuzz of down on her neck and the fibre of the rope. The girl was framed by other figures, an old man, two young women, a boy of sixteen or so, their swollen faces lolling on their shoulders, thin cords connecting their necks to the rough crossbar above. The man in the black uniform was smiling at the camera. Werner Fehn.

'Where was this taken?' Alain asked conversationally. 'It looks like Russia to me. It must have been a few years ago. You haven't had much time for fun like this there recently.'

'They were partisans,' the German said in his patient, correct French. 'They knew the rules.'

'Yes,' said Alain. 'The old man looks particularly dangerous.' He glanced down at the toothless scarecrow dangling from the gibbet.

'But why the photograph? Why did you have to take the picture?'

He kicked Fehn hard in the stomach. 'Why do you have to look as if you're enjoying it so fucking much?'

Fehn lay on his side, fighting for breath. One of the *maquisards* drew back his boot, a heavy farm boot studded with nails, and struck it hard into his face, as if he were kicking a football. Bright blood welled in Fehn's mouth and he rolled onto his front. Very slowly, like a tortoise righting itself, he struggled onto all fours and started methodically spitting out blood and saliva.

'Oh for Christ's sake stop that,' said Gerry. He looked around them with tired, red eyes. 'I don't know why you dragged him off with us in the first place.' He gestured at the lawyer and his girl. 'Or them. You've got a lorry-load of documents. What more do you want?'

'The German I took for insurance. Finding the other two there was just a bit of luck. He can tell us every dirty deal that has been done in the town since the Germans arrived.

'Anyway,' he continued, 'these things are for us to decide, not you.'

'That's where you're wrong, brother. I have to think about the safety of my men. I have to think about the safety of Gerry Cunningham. Both of those have been severely jeopardised by this bullshit.'

'Excuse me.'

They turned round. De la Haye was looking at Gerry with shrewd eyes.

'Don't listen to him,' he said in English. 'If you let us go, I give you my word there will be no reprisals. And I'll make sure that you're given enough time to get away. I have influence with the German authorities. They listen to me. This soldier on his own won't make any difference. He's nobody. They will come for you anyway. But I can stall them. I can make a bargain so there are no reprisals. Ask him.' He jerked his head towards Alain.

'Don't flatter yourself, bastard,' he said. 'The Germans have plenty more like you to lick their arses. Nobody's going to miss you if you disappear.'

De la Haye smiled. 'Give me a cigarette, please.'

Gerry hesitated. Then he leaned forward and shook a cigarette from his packet and and put it between de la Haye's lips, lighting it with his gold lighter. He reached behind his back and tugged at the knot in the twine binding his hands until he was able to work a hand free.

'Go on,' Gerry said, 'I'm listening.'

'Not in front of him,' de la Haye said, jerking his thumb towards the German.

Gerry looked at Alain, who nodded and murmured a few words. Two *maquisards* half dragged the retching German away from the fire pit over to a clearing ten yards away. There was a a yell of pain as they threw him to the ground, and the thud of rifle butts on muscle.

'So let's hear it,' Gerry said.

De la Haye licked his lips. He was thinking fast. 'Or in front of her,' he said, looking bleakly at his girlfriend. Gerry raised his eyebrows and motioned to two troopers who took her by each arm and led her away.

De la Haye hunched forward, eager and persuasive. 'Now. You take me and the soldier to a main road, the nearer to Montcharles the better. Time is important.'

'What about the girl?' asked Gerry.

'The girl will stay here. I'll explain why in a minute. I'll see the commandant. He's a friend of mine. I will say that we were kidnapped but that you let us go, on the condition that there were no reprisals. I will explain that you are still holding Lucille and that if anyone is harmed you will kill her.' He looked at Alain. 'I'm sure he would enjoy doing that.' He turned back to Gerry. 'They know me well. I have done them many services. The commandant is not a brute. He will have some sympathy for me.'

'And what about us?' Gerry asked.

'I'll say that you were already preparing to move on when I left you. I'll give some bad information about where I thought your camp was. I'll say that you handed over the girl to the French. That will give you some time to get away.'

Alain broke in. 'Why are you listening to this?' he asked wearily. 'Why do you believe him? This is a man who loves betrayal. What do you think he was doing in the SD offices this morning? As soon as he sees them he'll tell them everything he knows.'

'But we've got his girl,' Gerry said. 'That might be worth something.'

'He'll be quite happy to sacrifice her,' said Alain. 'You must see that.'

De la Haye's eyes were darting between the two as they spoke.

'There's something else,' he said.

'What?' Alain sneered.

'Not for you. For him. I want to speak to the Englishman alone.'

Gerry sighed. 'All right then.'

He waved his arms, shooing away the others, and they fell back, leaving the two of them huddled together by the fire pit.

Adam took Radegonde's arm and they moved away. The forest was getting dark. Adam looked at his watch. It was only six o'clock, long before dusk. There was a rustling in the top of the trees and the breeze eddied through the woods, stirring the spindly branches. Radegonde shivered and Adam put his arm around her. She didn't stop him. There was rain on the air.

The voices drifted over from the fire pit: de la Haye's fast and eager, Gerry's careful and sceptical. At one point de la Haye picked up a twig and traced a pattern in the ground. Eventually Gerry got up and walked over to Alain. He put his arm around him, but Alain shook it off. Gerry spoke quietly, one fist clenched in front of him, the way he did when he was giving a pep talk to his men. Alain seemed to be barely listening, shaking his head and twisting away as if he was being accosted in the street. But gradually he grew more interested, edging closer, dropping his head in concentration.

The forest was getting darker. It was barely possible to distinguish between the two of them in the gloom. Then the discussion ended and they walked back to the fire pit. Gerry whistled to call Minto and Glover.

'OK, we've worked something out,' he said. 'We going to dump the Frog and the German outside Montcharles and hang on to the girl.'

'What about us?' Minto asked. 'Won't he tell them where we are?'

'We've got his girl,' said Gerry. 'She's our insurance until we can move out of here.'

The matter seemed to be settled. They squatted down to plan moving de la Haye and Fehn to Montcharles.

Adam was leading Radegonde away when they heard a shot coming from the clearing where the *maquisards* were guarding the German. At the sound, everyone dropped to the ground and scrabbled for their weapons. A long, sobbing noise came from the clearing. Gerry and Alain got up and ran over. When Adam arrived the German was crouched, doubled up, with blood bubbling from his mouth and nose. He was making a rhythmic moaning noise as if he was praying to some primitive deity. Then he rolled over and the sound stopped.

'You fucking fools,' Gerry said, looking down at the silent body. 'Well, that's the end of that little scheme.'

Alain shrugged his shoulders. 'The problem has been solved.'

'No it hasn't. It's been made ten times worse,' said Gerry. 'This changes everything.'

Their eyes moved to the log where de la Haye and Lucille were sitting, looking apprehensively in the direction of the commotion. There was a heavy silence.

'Someone's going to have to tell them the bad news,' said Gerry. 'It's a shame. She's a good-looking girl.'

They walked towards them. The man and the girl sat there, tense and expectant.

'What's happening?' de la Haye asked.

'The German's dead,' said Alain.

'Ah,' de la Haye said softly.

'I'm sorry,' Gerry said. 'It's just one of those things.'

The wind was blowing more strongly now and the first drops of rain were pattering on the leaves, making them rattle like parchment. Off to the west the sky flashed white and they heard the rumble of faraway thunder. Adam took Radegonde's arm to lead her away.

'You don't want to watch this,' he said, but she shook him off.

'Yes,' she said, 'I do.'

They started with de la Haye. Two of the *maquisards* pulled him forwards onto his knees and pinned him between them, then bound his hands, winding the rough string carefully round and round his wrists. As they worked he twisted his head round to look at Alain. He was smiling.

'What's funny?' Alain asked warily.

'I'm just wondering if your English friends know what kind of people they have mixed themselves up with,' he said.

'They know we're loyal Frenchmen. That's all they care about.'

'And I'm not?' de la Haye asked, shaking his head. 'You call yourself a patriot. So do I. You claim to be an idealist. So do I. You have allied yourself with a foreign power to save France, just like me. We both can say we're loyal Frenchmen. I'm just loyal to a different idea of France.'

De la Haye smiled. 'I'll be sorry to die. Not because I'm afraid particularly – I'm as much of a soldier as you. But I'll miss the coming battle. I wonder if the British and the Americans have any idea of what is lying ahead. Yes, we spilled blood – but it was the blood of traitors and we did it to save France. It will be nothing compared to what will happen when the time comes for the Communists and the Jews to take their revenge. Everyone will be the enemy, every person who ever spoke to a German or sold him a loaf of bread. There won't be many whose hands are clean enough for these patriots.'

His eyes settled on Gerry.

'Well, I'm sorry our deal didn't came to pass,' he said in English. 'It would have worked, I promise you.'

The *maquisards* finished tying him and jerked him to his feet. They moved over to truss the girl.

'Do you have to?' Now there was no cynicism left in de la Haye's voice. 'She's guilty of nothing except being with me.'

He turned to Radegonde. Tears had started in the corner of his eyes and were sliding down his face.

'Can't you do something? Please?'

She looked at him unwaveringly.

The girl had been whimpering while her lover was tied. When the men took hold of her she began shrieking and struggling with them.

'Lucille, Lucille,' de la Haye said tenderly, 'hold on, sweetheart.'

By now most of the soldiers had drifted over to the fire pit and were standing, watching, in a silent semi-circle. A few of them started muttering, protesting that someone should stop it, but Gerry silenced them.

The girl gave up struggling and allowed her hands to be tied. The *maquisards* hustled the pair together so that they were standing side by side, as if on parade. Alain stepped in front of them and cleared his throat.

'You are being executed for your crimes against the French people. Long Live France!'

A crack of thunder sounded overhead and the rain began falling in heavy drops, tumbling through the branches and beating a tattoo on the soft ground. Soon the girl's dress was soaking and transparent. It clung to her, showing the curve of her breasts and the swell of her belly. The men stared at her, ashamed, but unable to look away.

The *maquisards* turned the couple round and pushed them forward, as if they were leading them off on a long march. But as soon as they started walking, the executioners' hands moved to their waistbands and they brought out pistols. The couple walked on, keeping in step. The executioners raised the guns to the back of their heads and fired. The girl stumbled forward slightly, as if she had caught her heel in a crack in the pavement. Then she toppled forward, bouncing infinitesimally as she hit the ground. De la Haye slithered to the side, twisting his knees neatly as he fell. The executioners leaned over them and fired a further shot into each of their heads.

'Oh dear, oh dear,' sighed Gerry.

He was standing with his legs apart, the rain glistening on his leather jacket, with a bottle of apple brandy hanging loosely from his right hand. He raised it to his mouth and drank.

The troopers hurried under the cover of the trees, anxious to get out of the rain. The bodies lay face down in the soaking leaf mould. The *maquisards* bent over them, rummaging in de la Haye's pockets and removing his wristwatch. Alain joined Gerry. He prised the bottle from his hand and took a mouthful. 'Your boys can get rid of the bodies,' Gerry said. 'They're your responsibility.'

Adam looked at the man and woman lying in the drenched earth. He felt terribly tired. He wanted to be away from here, far from Gerry and Alain and the forest.

Hennessy was right. They could leave at dawn. How long would it take to reach Spain? A week? Two? How did you get over the mountains and what happened when you reached the frontier on the other side? His mind was too numb to attempt to answer. But anything was better than waiting here in the deepening atmosphere of madness and death.

They would leave tomorrow. Hennessy and Hawkins would need civilian clothes. Radegonde would help them. She was shivering inside her wet dress and he put an arm round her and felt the slippery skin of her shoulder. She had to come with them. They would make a plan and tell Gerry about it in the morning, take him by surprise, deny him the time to bully them into staying.

He was about to lead her away when Gerry called out to them. Alain was at his side. He motioned them towards his tent. Adam hesitated. She looked up at him then, seeing his reluctance, took his hand and pulled him behind her. They squelched over the sodden ground, ducked under the flap and crouched down, feeling the heat of their bodies building up inside their soaking clothes.

Gerry switched on his torch and hung it from a nail on the ridge-pole. The torch gleamed on his dark, slick hair and moustache, a pantomime pirate caught in the footlights.

'We're in the shit,' he said. 'We're going to have to do some fast thinking. As far as I can see we're stuck here for the time being. If they don't get any word from us about hostages, the Germans will come looking. It's not healthy staying here. But if we try and move forty men and vehicles across country, we're bound to be spotted.' He took a swig of apple brandy.

'So either we sit here and wait for them to come to us, which means we've had it, more or less. Or we can try and create some sort of diversion that will draw the Germans away and allow the blokes to make a run for it to a new site. What do you think, Alain?'

'I agree. We can't stay here. And you're right that it would be mad to try and move across country now. But a diversion. How would it work? A hit-and-run raid is not going to draw many troops away.'

'You have to select the target,' Gerry said. 'You have to go for something small, but something they care about.'

'Like what?' Adam said.

Gerry paused. The rain tapped hard on the taut canvas.

'There was something that our collaborator friend said to me. As I understand it, the German commander has his headquarters in a house just outside Mon-tcharles.'

'Yes,' said Alain. 'Westendorp's HQ is at Saint-Sulpice, a few kilometres to the south, Château des Pierres. It's by the river.'

'How tough a target is it?'

'I've never really thought about it. As I say, there's a steep bank down to the river on one side. It's about two hundred feet high and covered with trees. The approach to the house is flat. I don't know how heavily they guard it. We'd have to take a look. I can think of plenty of easier targets, though.'

'Maybe. But this would be a bit of a coup, wouldn't it?'

Adam could see Gerry's enthusiasm kindling.

'Generals don't expect to be attacked in their own homes – or someone else's in this case. It would certainly shake the Germans up and take the heat off the camp for a day or two.'

'I suppose so,' Alain said doubtfully. 'What sort of thing do you have in mind?'

'It would have to be very much our show. Real SOS style – drive in, shoot the place up, plant a few bombs and fuck off. That way they would know it was a proper military op rather than a *maquis* affair, and pour troops into the area, pulling them away from the camp.'

Alain shook his head. 'We don't know anything about the strength of the guard, or the routes in and out of the place. It would take time to set it up.'

'But we haven't got time,' Gerry said forcefully. 'We'll have to move fast if this is going to work.'

No one spoke for a while and the raindrop tattoo slackened off.

'Tommy,' said Gerry.

'What?'

He knew what was coming.

'I know it's a pretty tall order. You've already stuck your necks out, both of you, but I'm asking you if you're prepared to do one more job for us?'

He managed to make the request sound simultaneously like a challenge and an entreaty.

'What we need is a recce of the house and the grounds – the sooner the better so that with any luck we can pull off something tomorrow.'

Adam felt an awful hollowness open up inside him as he looked at the pair of them: Gerry's face glistening from the rain, eager and demanding; Alain, brooding and watchful, weighing everything, but just as dangerous, he knew, as Gerry.

They were reaching out to him, pulling him back into the lethal pit they had dug for themselves.

Gerry shifted towards him, smiling.

'Well?'

'No,' Adam said. 'No, I'm not doing it. I've done enough. So has she. Anyway, the idea's bloody stupid. It would take us a whole day to get there and back. You couldn't do anything until the day after tomorrow, which would mean it was too late.'

'Not if you left now,' Alain said. 'The bicycles are still in Montcharles. If we dropped you in Montcharles tonight you could pick up your bikes and ride by the château tomorrow, and be back here by noon.'

There was another silence. Then Gerry spoke with a sudden, conclusive weariness.

'No, he's right,' he said. 'It's a stupid idea. Let's forget it.'

Adam felt relief coursing through him. He squeezed Radegonde's arm and felt an answering pressure back.

'Fuck it. Let's all have a drink.'

Gerry handed the bottle to Adam, and gave him half a smile. For a moment he saw the old Gerry, sitting in the evening sunlight in a Sussex pub, tipsy and melancholy, and he was brushed by a feeling of nostalgia, as sweet and mournful as the note of a hunting horn sounding far off in the forest.

'Poor old Tommy,' Gerry murmured. 'I've brought you nothing but trouble.'

'That's true,' said Adam. 'Do you remember the first words you ever said to me?'

'I can't say I do.'

'"You're out of luck, brother." That's what you said. It was in the ballroom of the Bristol Hotel at Alberton, when I was trying to sit down with Pam and Moira and I couldn't find a chair.'

They both laughed.

'What a memory!' Gerry said. 'But I was right, wasn't I? As far as you and I are concerned. I haven't brought you much luck. Quite the opposite.'

Gerry leaned over and slapped him on the shoulder and took the bottle back. They sat on the damp floor and the brandy went round. The tent filled up with cigarette smoke. Alain relaxed for once, talking about his life before the war, the wife he had sent to the south.

He spoke mainly to Radegonde, reminiscing about friends in Montcharles and the villages round about. Gradually Gerry said less and less. He settled back against the tent-pole, smoking and tilting the brandy bottle.

The rain had stopped. Now water was falling in plump drops from the soaking branches, landing with an elastic thud on the roof of the tent. It was time to go. He had to find Hennessy and Hawkins and prepare them for an early departure. And he had to persuade Radegonde to come with them. He got to his feet, rubbing his knees to ease the stiffness. He pulled Radegonde onto her feet. The batteries in the torches had faded and the tent was now dim and smoky. Gerry's voice came out of the gloom. 'Don't leave just yet.'

'Why not?'

As soon as he said it he regretted it.

'Because I've been thinking. There's a way we could do this.'

Adam felt a premonitory flutter of fear in his stomach.

'Oh yes?' he said faintly.

'Yes, listen. As the plan stands, you're right. It would never work. It would take hours for you to get yourselves from . . . what's the place called?'

'Saint-Sulpice,' Alain supplied.

'Right, from Saint-Sulpice to Vercourt. By the time we were ready to go it would be mid-afternoon and who knows what might have changed in the meantime. Then we'd be faced with a long overland journey in the

Jeeps in broad daylight. That would hold true even if we managed to get a car to pick you up and bring you back here as soon as you'd done the recce.'

'Yes,' Adam said cautiously. 'That's right.'

'But what if the raiding party moved to a position much closer to Saint-Sulpice beforehand? What if we were only a mile or so down the road? You could be with us twenty minutes after you'd done the recce. We could be on our way as soon as we'd made a plan.'

'But how are you going to find somewhere to hide at such short notice?' Adam asked. 'It will be impossible to arrange something now.'

Then Alain spoke. 'Not necessarily,' he said carefully. 'Saint-Sulpice is a suburb of Montcharles but it's countryside really. There are a couple of farmers nearby who support us or who owe us favours. They could hide us in a barn until we were ready to go.'

'There,' Gerry said, 'I knew there was a way. But if we're going to do it we'll have to start moving now, under cover of darkness, so we're all in place in the morning.'

They were dragging him back again, back to the pit. He felt giddy with desperation and tears of anger pricked the corners of his eyes. He had to stop them.

'No,' he said.

'No, what?' said Gerry mildly.

'No to the whole fucking thing. I'm not doing it. I've had enough. So have my boys. I was going to tell you later but you might as well know now. They're leaving and I'm going with them, first thing tomorrow morning.'

'You're going?' Radegonde clutched at his arm.

'Don't worry, I'm taking you with me.'

'But how can I go? 'she demanded. 'I can't just leave here. I can't just run away.'

'You wouldn't be running away. The war's nearly over. You've done enough. There are plenty of others who can finish the job off.'

'Looks like you've hit a snag, brother.' Gerry could barely keep the amusement out of his voice. 'It sounds to me as if you're going to have to change your plans. Unless you're happy to bugger off out of it and leave her to do the recce on her own.'

He looked at Radegonde, expectantly. She stared back at him and said nothing. So, she was on Gerry's side. He felt angry tears creeping under his eyelids again. Once again he was cornered. Gerry had him. If he left now he would regret it for the rest of his life, whether it was days or decades.

'All right,' he said sullenly. 'What do you want us to do?'

'Good old Tommy,' Gerry clapped his hands. 'I never doubted you for a moment. Here's how I think we should play it.'

Adam listened numbly as he ran through the plan. Alain would get a van to drive them to Montcharles where they would spend the night in a hotel. Meanwhile Gerry and the team would take the Jeeps in the dark to a safe farmhouse near Saint-Sulpice where they would lie up. The following morning, Adam and Radegonde would collect their cycles where they had left them in Montcharles and ride to Saint-Sulpice and carry out their reconnaissance of the Château des Pierres.

'We want to know all the obvious stuff,' Gerry said. 'The best way in and out, how many guards and what armament they've got. And the layout of the house. That's important.'

'Why?' said Adam. 'I thought you said it was a diversion. Shoot the place up and bugger off.'

'Fortune favours the brave!' said Gerry triumphantly. 'That's our mob's motto if you didn't know. If we're taking the trouble to do the job in the first place, we might as well do it properly. That might include having a go at old Westendorp.'

'And how the hell am I supposed to see inside the place?'

'Not you, her. She's a pretty girl. The Germans are flesh and blood after all. I'm sure she can find some pretext for taking a shufti.'

Adam was too miserable to argue. Gerry resumed the briefing. Once Adam and Radegonde were finished they were to cycle to the farm and tell them what they had found out.

'How will we know where you are?' Radegonde asked.

'I'll get a message to you at the hotel in the morning, before you leave,' said Alain.

'You see, it's simple,' said Gerry. 'Then once the job's done we'll race back here, pack up the camp and move onto the new site while the Germans are still chasing their tails at Saint-Sulpice.'

At that moment he hated them all: greedy Gerry and pious Alain with his closed, self-righteous face and talk of justice and patriotism. And Radegonde, how could she carry on this affair with death and danger when he was offering her life?

She whispered to him, trying to sound affectionate. 'I'm going to the cottage to pick up my things.'

He nodded. She pushed back the tent flap and he followed her out. The wind had dropped and the rain had stopped and the loudest sound in the forest was the dripping of the branches. He picked his way over the fallen branches, searching for Hennessy and Hawkins to tell them he would not be going with them.

34

The rain had washed the air, turning the night chilly. Radegonde sat in the front with the silent, unshaven *maquisard* who was driving them. Adam settled into the back of the van and tried to sleep, but each time he dozed off he was woken by a bump in the road or a clumsy manoeuvre by the driver.

He could just see her face in the gloom. She looked ahead, wide awake, expressionless.

What was wrong with her? The car drifted towards the high-banked hedge that flanked the road until the driver corrected course with a sharp twist of the wheel.

He stared at her, willing her to turn round, but she sat impervious to his telepathy, lost in thought.

Eventually he said, 'You could say something.'

She half turned to him.

'What?'

'You're very quiet.'

'Just thinking.'

'You've said nothing to me all day.'

'Oh, Adam. Leave me be. I've a lot on my mind.'

'Don't you think I might have too? The only reason I'm here is because of you.'

'You don't have to tell me that,' she said. Then she leaned back and squeezed his hand. 'Please. We can talk later.' She nodded her head meaningfully towards the driver.

He lay back against the wheel arch, feeling a little comforted.

'Who are we tonight?' he asked.

'Hmm?' She did not bother to look round this time.

'You and me, who are we?'

'I don't understand.'

'The first time we went out together we were brother and sister. Nowadays I'm Georges Melin and you're Claude. What's our relationship?'

'I don't know. What do you think?'

'Lovers?'

'No,' she said decisively. 'Cousins. Distant cousins.'

The van went slowly. Once, a hare ran out of the shadows into an open field. For a moment it kept pace with the car, then it bounded ahead, white scut fading into the gloom.

'Can't we go any faster?' Adam asked.

The driver shrugged and mumbled something and took his hands off the wheel to light another cigarette.

By the time they reached the edge of Montcharles the rain clouds had blown away, exposing the land to the moonlight. The old city gleamed on the hill. They stopped near the stadium at a neat, modern hotel that stood on a wide forecourt. The driver got out and pulled open Radegonde's door.

'This is it,' he said. He climbed back in and drove off with a clashing of gears. Then they were alone on the cold asphalt. The door was locked. He pressed the bell but it made no sound. He started knocking and after a few minutes there was a clicking of locks and the door swung open and a stout woman with dark curly hair and a kind face was standing there.

'We were expecting you,' she said.

She showed them into a dining room at the back of the hotel. It was bare except for two calendars, which hung behind a small bar in the corner advertising aperitifs.

'You must be hungry,' said the woman. 'I've got something ready.' She disappeared and came back with a thick-bottomed bottle of red wine and a basket of bread. She went away again. They heard sizzling from the kitchen and a few minutes later she returned with plates of glistening pale meat and fried potatoes. They had not eaten anything since the morning. The veal was greasy but it tasted good. They looked at each other. He raised his glass and she chinked hers against it. His spirits rose. Perhaps it would be all right after all.

The wine made him realise how tired he was. It was good just sitting opposite her, watching her eat, saying nothing. The woman returned to clear away the plates. She offered them pudding. Radegonde shook her head. 'I just want to go to bed,' she said.

'I'll be with you in a minute,' said the woman and took away the plates. She came back dangling several keys on coloured ribbons.

'How many rooms do you want?' she asked cautiously.

He looked at Radegonde.

'One,' she said. 'I don't want to be on my own tonight.'

The woman led them upstairs, her big bottom swaying as she heaved up the steps. The room was bare and smelled of lavender. There were two iron beds side by side. Radegonde went to the window and pushed open the shutter. The stars blazed in the fresh blackness. 'That way we'll wake up,' she said.

They fell into the creaking beds, not bothering to wash. As soon as he closed his eyes he felt a great weight pulling him down into the ocean of oblivion. He offered no resistance, raising his hands to make the descent easier. He twisted and rolled in the current. The water flowed over him, massaging him with strong fingers. He smiled to himself. He was asleep.

He dreamed he was on a bicycle, riding across a sunny plain, his shirt billowing out behind him in the slipstream. Then he was in a wooden rowing boot, surging on the surf towards a soft, sandy beach. Beyond it lay a forest of beautiful trees and the smell of fruit and flowers drifted over the waves. Then the events of the day came back. He saw the café and the old couple in the back; the slow, scraping noise the guards made as they slid down the wall; the documents scattered over the sun-splashed stone of the pavement; the terror in the faces of the clerks as they held up their hands. Then he saw the lawyer and his girl lying face down in the pelting rain and he walked over to them and rolled the girl onto her front and brushed the strands of blood-soaked hair away from her face and saw that it was not the lawyer's girl at all but Radegonde who opened her eyes and smiled at him. He sat up with a jerk.

'Adam? Are you all right?'

Across the narrow space between the beds her face was turned towards him, pale in the dark.

'Don't worry,' he whispered. 'It was a nightmare, that's all.'

He lay on his back fighting against the encroaching sleep, scared of returning to the forest and the dead bodies. He felt something at his side, disturbing the blanket. Then a warm hand was holding his.

'Come in here, next to me,' she said gently. 'There's just enough room.'

For a while they held each other. Her hot breath beat on his neck. She smelt faintly of almonds.

After they made love, they lay damply side by side. The bed was too small for the two of them. He dragged the other one alongside it and pulled out the bedclothes so they covered them both. He could barely see her in the darkness but he could hear her breathing and the sound of it filled him with a melting tenderness.

'Adam?' she whispered.

'I'm here.'

'Why did you want me to go with you? Away, I mean?'

He was about to reply, cautiously, circuitously. He was going to say that he wanted to get her away from danger because the war was almost over, at least in her part of the world, and that she had played her part, and that he didn't want her to die, which she might easily if she went on doing what she was doing. Instead he said, 'Because I'm falling in love with you.'

She sighed.

'That's nice,' she said.

It had been so easy to say. He lay there grinning to himself, stroking her damp hand.

He struggled onto an elbow and looked down at her. 'Do you mind?' he asked.

Her eyes gleamed up from the pillow and she smiled. 'No. It makes me happy.'

She lay silently for a while. Then she said: 'I thought about it. After you said it, I thought about how good it would be to walk away from Vercourt, away from the Germans and Alain and his men and the Milice and all the horrible memories and just keep walking until we reached somewhere where those things didn't matter. I thought how good it would be to be with you, sharing an adventure which we had decided on ourselves.'

'Why didn't you say something?'

'It was too late by then. Anyway, I wasn't sure. I knew what was happening between us and it frightened me. I had never felt like this before. I don't like what I'm not used to.'

'Are you sure now?'

She sighed.

'Of course I'm not. But I'm going to give it a try.' She stroked his face. 'This will be the last time. After tomorrow we'll leave here. We'll run south, east, as far away from the war as possible. Tomorrow will be the last time.'

'Do you mean that?' he said.

'Yes,' she said. 'I mean it.'

She leaned over him and kissed him, her hair falling into a cascade that tickled his forehead, then lay next to him, solemn and serene as an effigy on a tomb.

35

'Stop grinning,' she said.

'I can't.'

Adam and Radegonde were eating breakfast, milky coffee and crusty bread, served by the fat proprietress in the kitchen.

'Well try. She thinks you're mad.'

'You're doing it too.'

'Am I?'

She ducked to look at her reflection in the steel coffee jug.

'You're right. How strange. What's wrong with us?'

'I don't know. Maybe we're happy.'

She giggled and leaned over and kissed him.

There was a rap on the kitchen door and the proprietress went over and opened it. A thin, nervous-looking middle-aged man slipped in.

He ignored Adam and spoke quickly to Radegonde, giving the details of the meeting place. Then he was gone again. She tried to be stern and businesslike as they discussed the plan for the day, but was smiling too much to keep it up for long. Several times they sat in silence, just looking at each other. After today our real lives will begin, thought Adam.

Reluctantly she finished her coffee. 'Time to get the bikes.'

It was a fine morning. The town was stirring as they walked up the steep medieval streets, past the big doorways that led into the courtyards of the university's scattered faculties. In Place des Canons the bomb damage had been cleared away. The Hotel Astoria stood windowless and hollow. It had been absorbed into the antiquity of the town. It now looked as if it had been ruined by time rather than high explosive.

The bicycles were where they had left them, propped against a wall in the yard behind the café in Rue Wilson. The owner came to the back doorway and looked at them closely. They called a greeting but he did not reply and watched them as they wheeled the bikes out into the street and past the Flèche d'Or. The door was shut and the walls above the windows were black with smoke. They mounted the bicycles and pushed off down the hill, feeling the wind rushing past them and the cobbles rippling under the tyres, then swung onto the southward road leading to Saint-Sulpice. There was little traffic. They pedalled side by side, holding hands.

'They made a mess of the SD office,' he said. 'It looks as if it's closed down.'

'I imagine they've just moved it somewhere safer.'

'What will they do without their files? I never knew spying was so bureaucratic.'

'You know the Germans. They've probably got duplicates somewhere else.'

He had not thought of that.

'The raid was a waste of time, then?'

'Probably. But it wouldn't make much difference to Alain.'

'Why not?'

'It's what's inside the files that interests him – what they have on him and the other networks. And what it tells him about the relationship between the Germans and local people.'

'Why is that so important?'

'Alain's already concentrating on the next phase of the struggle – what happens when the Germans leave. The SD files are like gold to him. He can use them to put on trial the people he wants get rid of and to blackmail those he doesn't.'

'So you think de la Haye was right?'

'About a civil war? No.' She sounded emphatic. Then she paused and said more softly. 'I don't know. But I don't want to be here to find out.'

The joy of the early morning had departed. She began to pedal faster.

'I want this to be over,' she said.

Saint-Sulpice sat on a bluff above the River Brionne. Château des Pierres stood a little way away from the bulk of the town, on a spur road that linked up with the main highway to Montcharles. At the foot of the hill they dismounted and looked up to the crest, where the roof of the château poked out above the trees on the slope. In front of them, the brown river swirled past on its way to its meeting with one of the great arterial waterways of France.

They crossed the bridge and started along a path that followed the riverbank. The château was directly above them, about a quarter of a mile away. The woods were dense and tangled. A group of men could park the Jeeps off the road and creep up through them to within a few yards of the house without being seen. The drawback was that it would take time to scramble back down through the trees to the vehicles. Still, it was an option.

They went back to the road and wheeled their bicycles up the hill. Twice they were passed by lorries full of soldiers who looked at them with curiosity. They had decided on a plan that morning. It was simple and dangerous, Radegonde's idea. They would try and get into the house by pretending to be a couple looking for work – she as a domestic servant, he as a gardener or handyman. If they succeeded they could find out how the house and grounds were guarded and learn something of the the layout of the château. Then they would cycle to Les Marroniers, a farm five miles south of Saint-Sulpice, where Gerry and Alain and the SOS team would be waiting for them in a barn.

The road flattened out and they remounted their bicycles. A low flint wall bounded the grounds of the house. Beyond was a small park. Among the trees stood a row of tottering stone pillars – the remains, Radegonde said, of a Roman aqueduct. Ahead they could see a gate leading into the grounds. A metal pole, striped red and white, barred the drive, and a wooden guardhouse stood at one side.

As they approached Adam's mouth went dry and he tasted metal, the taste of fear. He had a sudden glimpse of the madness of what they were about to do. How could the Germans possibly believe their story? Who would be seeking work with them now, when their empire was crumbling and prudent Frenchmen and -women were shedding all links with the occupier? They had to call it off. But she was already ahead of him, swinging her leg demurely across the crossbar, scooting towards the gatehouse where two guards were sitting outside at a table, enjoying the sun, rifles across their knees.

They looked up as the couple approached. A mirror had been set up on one of the gateposts so that emerging drivers could see the oncoming traffic. He caught sight of himself in the dusty glass as he wheeled his bike towards the barrier: unshaven, hunched submissively inside his dirty suit. He looked what he purported to be.

The guards got up from the table. They held their rifles loosely at waist level, pointing towards them, casual but threatening. They could have been brothers with the same broad, pimply faces and cautious eyes. One of them held up a hand to stop them coming on. He pointed at Radegonde and waved her forward. She started talking, quietly and deferentially, first in French, which they did not understand, then in clumsy German. They took their time, saying nothing while she repeated the sentence.

'*Ich suche Arbeit in Küche oder Haus. Mein Freund wollen Arbeit in Garten. Bitte.*'

They looked at her with practised blankness. At any second they were going to raise their rifles and prod them down the drive towards the house and interrogation, torture and death. A trickle of sweat meandered down his back between his shoulder blades. Then one of the soldiers smiled. He clicked his fingers and stretched out his hand, demanding her identity card. He turned the document over and over as if he expected the text to have magically transformed itself in the time that it was hidden from his gaze. Then he motioned Adam forward. Adam shuffled up, fingering the grubby pasteboard and handed it over reverentially. The guard examined the tiny portrait, cropped so tight that it showed only his eyes, nose and mouth, as if he had his face pressed to a porthole. He looked hard at Adam before shifting his gaze back and forth between the image and the reality. Then he turned his back and ambled over to the hut and disappeared inside. They heard a telephone being lifted, a handle being cranked, German words. As he did so the other guard raised his rifle so that it was pointing unambiguously towards them. The back of Adam's shirt was soaking now. He set his features in an expression of dumb humility, as if this display might outweigh whatever damning flaw had been discovered in the document. But then the door creaked open and the other guard was jerking his thumb in the direction of the house. They could go.

'*Danke. Dankeschön.*'

They bobbed little bows of gratitude. The guards ignored them and sat down again in the sunshine, stretching out their legs, reaching into their tunics for their cigarettes.

They wheeled their bikes along the gravel drive towards the house. Three crumbling arches of Roman masonry stood marooned in the middle of a well-tended lawn. There was no sign of a machine-gun post or even any barbed wire. Apart from the gate-house, the château appeared to be undefended. It had been built some time in the previous century. It had two wings set at right angles to each other to capture the views across the river valley towards Montcharles, plaster walls and a steep slate roof. It wasn't a castle at all but the home of a prosperous businessman.

A square of raked gravel stood before the front door. A large black car was parked there, under the shade of a fir tree. The general was at home. The door was slightly open. They walked over and Radegonde pulled at the wrought-iron bell that was fixed to the lintel. They heard sure footsteps clopping over the floor-boards and the door swung open.

A tall, thin young man in a well-pressed uniform and shiny boots looked down at them and addressed them in French. 'Yes? What is it?'

Radegonde took a step forward. 'We're sorry to trouble you, mister. We heard that there might be some work going at the house. I'm looking for some-thing in the kitchen or around the house. My friend here has worked as a gardener.'

The door opened slightly wider, revealing a cosy room with an ornate plaster ceiling and Turkey carpets on the wood-block floor. Oil paintings stood stacked along the walls, three and four deep, gleaming lustrously in the dim light inside rich frames. Adam saw a pale, sorrowful Madonna nursing her child, an Annunciation scene, a classical landscape of noble ruins and rosy evening light. Then the German stepped sideways and blocked his view.

'Who told you that?' he asked sharply.

'Some people in Montcharles,' said Radegonde humbly.

A voice sounded from inside the house. The officer was being summoned.

'I know nothing about it,' he said. 'Go to the back of the house. Speak to the housekeeper.' The door slammed shut.

'Did you see that?' he asked as they followed the path that ran around the side of the château.

'What?'

'The paintings. It was like the Louvre in there.'

'Probably all looted,' she said. She did not seem much interested.

He took her by the arm. 'Why don't we just leave now? We've seen as much as we need to.'

She paused. 'No,' she said. 'We'll have to see the housekeeper now. They might be watching us. They might check.'

They walked past a vegetable garden to the back of the house. The kitchen windows were open and the sound of escaping steam and chatter drifted out. They propped their bikes against the wall and Radegonde rapped on the dark green door. It was opened by a wiry little woman in an apron who beckoned them into an anteroom with a passage off it that led into the kitchen.

'We're looking for the housekeeper,' Radegonde said. 'We heard that there might be work here.'

'I'll go and fetch her,' the woman said. They sat down on hard wooden chairs. A pendulum clock ticked sadly on the wall. An infinity separated each deep, portentous click. Laughter came from the kitchen, along with the smell of cooking. A maid emerged, looked at them closely, said nothing and disappeared through the padded, leather-covered door that marked the frontier of the servants' and masters' domains. The door flapped behind her and the clock ticked on, measuring out the silence.

'I wish she'd hurry up,' Adam said. 'This is driving me mad.'

Radegonde said nothing. He got up.

'Come on, let's go.'

Radegonde silenced him. 'We can't leave now. That will look even more suspicious. Anyway I can hear her coming.'

There were voices beyond the door, then it creaked open and the wiry maid came in, followed by a stout woman with a strong, handsome face and dark hair cut short.

Radegonde got to her feet.

'Good day, madame. We were just passing the house and we thought we would look in to see if you needed any extra help around the place, in the kitchen or in the garden.'

The housekeeper examined her closely with shrewd eyes.

'Who are you, miss?' she said eventually.

'Claude Arnoux, madame. I live in Montcharles. I heard there might be some work.'

'Really?' said the housekeeper. 'A Montcharles girl. And you want to work here?'

Radegonde nodded meekly.

'I wonder who told you there were any jobs? Never mind, you're here now. Tell me what you can do. Do you cook, sew?'

'A bit of everything.' Radegonde's voice was sullen.

The housekeeper looked at her for a moment. 'Show me your hands.'

Radegonde held out her arms, palms down. The housekeeper took them and turned them over. She trailed a finger across the flesh like a fortune-teller tracing a lifeline.

'Nice soft hands,' she murmured. The clock ticked, filling the silence.

'There might be something for you,' she said at last. 'I don't know about your friend. He'll have to talk to the gardener.' Her manner changed, courteous now.

'Come into the kitchen and Denise will make you a drink or something to eat while I sort something out.'

She turned to go and the padded door flapped behind her. The wiry maid led the way down the passage towards the kitchen. Radegonde held back.

'What is it?' he asked.

'She knows me,' she whispered.

Adam heard the clock ticking, very loud.

'She managed a clothes shop next to the university at the beginning of the war.'

'We're going. Now.'

Radegonde went to the kitchen door and spoke to the maid.

'We're just fetching our bicycles,' she said. The maid nodded. 'We'll be back in a few moments.'

They edged the back door open and stepped out onto the path.

He was desperately trying to think. The kitchen garden opposite where they were standing ran to the edge of the bluff. Below were the woods and the river. They would never get the bikes through the dense undergrowth. But the trees would provide cover for them as they scrambled down to the road below. Then they could make their way overland by foot to the rendezvous.

'Leave the bikes here. We're going down the hill.'

She understood. They crossed the vegetable garden and were just about to duck into the cover of the trees when Adam noticed something glinting among the foliage.

'Shit,' he said. A barbed-wire fence, ten feet high and nailed to concrete posts stretched along the lip of the bluff as far as he could see.

'It's no good,' he said. 'We'll have to go out the main entrance. But let's go round the other side of the house, away from the front door.'

They picked up the bikes and wheeled them cautiously along the path. Beyond the kitchen, the back walls of the house were blank. They turned the corner round to the château's gable end. Here, to his dismay, he could see that the wall was pierced by an arched window looking out onto a lawn. They stopped at the edge of it and Adam squinted into the room. He saw a grey-uniformed back standing behind a desk only two or three feet from the window. He could hear a woman's voice, cautious-sounding but indistinct. He signalled to Radegonde to lift her bicycle off the ground to stop the oily click of chain on flywheel. They darted across the gap. For a moment or two they stood frozen on the other side of the window, pressing against each other, hearts banging, but there was no commotion or alarm. They climbed onto the bikes and gently pedalled away out of the lee of the house and onto the drive.

The wheels made a crunching, pulverising noise as they ground over the gravel. It seemed impossible that they could not hear it inside the house. He strained to hear the sound of the door opening and the rattle of breech bolts. He imagined the strike of the bullet. It would be, he thought, like a hearty clap on the back at first. Then there would be an awful feeling of weariness before the pain set in.

They pedalled on. They could see the guardhouse. They rode up to the barrier and stood humbly, struggling to keep the fear from showing in their faces, waiting for the guards to bother to notice them. The Germans were reading now, newspapers in heavy Gothic script. One of them looked over without interest. A low, joshing argument broke out: whose turn was it to get up? They stood there, praying for someone to move. Then one of them levered himself out of his chair and strolled into the wooden hut. He came out and handed them their identity cards, then pressed down on the concrete block clamped to one end of the barrier, sending the striped pole swinging up to point at the cornflower blue sky. They pushed the bikes through the gate, murmuring their thanks. Then the telephone in the guardroom rang. They stopped. The guard looked at them, curious now. Something had changed. They vaulted onto their bikes, kicking clumsily at the pedals, and weaved away, bent over the handlebars.

Adam heard the ringing stop as the receiver was lifted. Someone shouted. He glanced over his shoulder. Both the guards were hurrying out onto the road, rifles in hand. He saw them drop to one knee and take aim. He bent lower over the handlebars, jamming his feet down harder and harder on the pedals. The leaden bike seemed hardly to be moving at all. It was an old familiar nightmare: he was running away from a band of pursuers but with each step he took his legs grew heavier and weaker and his breath shorter. Radegonde was ahead of him. Her legs were pumping fast taking her away from him. There was a bend ahead, after which the road dropped away, sloping sharply down the hill. If they could reach it they would be safe, at least for a time.

The first shot cracked past him and into the trees to the left. A second struck the road behind him and skipped away, whining disappointedly. He swerved across the road then back again – a useless precaution, he knew, if the guard's marksmanship was any good. The bend was reaching out to shelter Radegonde. She was almost there, white blouse billowing behind, brown legs pistoning. Then there was another crack and something red appeared on her shoulder. She glanced round with a look of annoyance, as if she had been stung by a wasp. Then she turned back and leaned into the bend and the bend shielded her and she was out of sight.

He was almost there now. The bullets were going high. He felt gravity taking hold of the bike and tugging it forward. Then he was thrumming down the slope, pedalling hard to catch her up. She was sitting straight up in the saddle, freewheeling, her dark hair tumbling behind her. As he got close he saw the patch of blood on her blouse, just below her left shoulder blade. He drew a little ahead of her and glanced round. There was a matching badge of red, the colour and shape of a poppy, just where her shoulder met the slope of her breast. It looked as if the bullet had gone straight through.

'Is it hurting?' he panted.

She shook her head. He knew she would deny it, even if she was in agony.

'We'll stop and take a look at it as soon as we get somewhere safe.'

'I'm fine,' she said stubbornly.

'No. We have to stop the bleeding.'

They reached the main road and turned to the south. The meeting place was eight kilometres away. There, they could find transport to take her to a friendly doctor. But the sun was hot and the bike was heavy and he had no idea of how bad the wound was. They rode on until he saw a track to the right of the road leading off into an avenue of poplars.

'Pull over there,' he told her. He sat her down under a tree. She kept her arms clamped tight to her side. He took her left arm and lifted it gently away. The side of her shirt was wet with blood. He undid the buttons of the blouse and pulled away the sodden cloth. The wound was neat and star shaped. He gently manipulated her shoulder, feeling for signs of a break, but could find none.

'The important thing is to get the bleeding to stop,' he said loudly, hoping his confidence would comfort her. 'You'll be fine, my love, trust me, you'll be fine.'

He pulled his shirt from his waistband and tore the tails into three strips, two short and one long. Two of the strips he folded into pads, which he got her to clamp hard onto the wounds. The other he tied over her shoulder and under her armpit, pulling it tightly so that he saw her shut her eyes in pain. She looked up at him and smiled, drowsily, as he buttoned up her blouse. He had to find a doctor. Did they dare to go back on the road? Too much time had passed. He took her face between his hands.

'We can't use the road now. Is there any way we can get from here to Les Marroniers by a back way?'

'Over the fields,' she said. 'There's always a path over the fields.'

He helped her up, then pushed her back down again. A hundred metres away, a convoy of three or four German Jeeps swished across the mouth of the tunnel of poplars. They waited a minute before setting off again, pushing their bikes to the edge of a stony field, then climbing on and pedalling jerkily along the track that ran along the side.

'We just keep pointing south,' she said. 'We'll get there eventually.'

He let her go ahead so he could watch her progress. For two miles they made their way painfully along rutted, weed-choked tracks. He could hear her breathing coming back to him, shallow and harsh, as she pressed down on the pedals, standing up on them to drive the bike over the deepest furrows. Then they came to a cornfield and the track got smoother and it was almost like cycling on a road. But gradually, her legs got slower and slower, and the bike wavered and faltered and she was barely going at walking pace. Then a handlebar trailed against the bank and caught in the hedge and the bicycle toppled over. He dropped his bike and hurried over to her. She was lying on her back, her lips parted, breathing in short, sibilant gasps.

'I can't go on,' she whispered.

He felt a surge of panic. About two hundred yards away were two low stone outhouses. He prayed there was a farmhouse attached.

'You have to get on your feet,' he said. She nodded slowly. He pulled her up and dragged her step by step along the path until they came to a stone wall with a broken gate that stood open, leading into a yard. A dog rushed at them, barking madly, then jerked back as it hit the end of the chain that tethered it.

Where there was a dog there would be humans. Her breath was getting feebler now and she kept lifting her head, as if the weight of it was too much for her.

'I'm going to carry you, my love,' he said. 'Put your arms around my neck.' She draped her arms over his shoulders and he hoisted her up onto his chest and felt her thighs gripping his waist. He staggered forward across the yard and there on the far side he saw a small, grey, mud-splashed cottage.

'Help!' he shouted.

Nothing happened.

He shouted again, loudly and wildly. 'Help me!'

Slowly a door opened in the wall and an old man stepped out. He looked at them cautiously, as if making a decision, then walked quickly over. Adam lowered her to the ground and the old man put her arm over his shoulder. Together they half carried her over to the back door and over the high step into a dark parlour.

'In here,' said the old man, leading them into a bedroom.

The broad bed had a scrolled head like the prow of a ship and almost filled the room. Above it was a dark wooden crucifix. A yellowish Christ, the colour of old wax, with protruding ribs and long, demurely crossed legs, was nailed to it. It was dim and musty. The tiny window barely let in any light. It looked like a room that many peasants had died in.

They laid her out on the plump quilt, then the old man took his arm and led him out of the room.

'Marthe!' he called. A woman instantly appeared from behind a door leading from the parlour, as if she had been waiting for his summons.

'Water for the girl.'

He turned to Adam. He had a thick grey moustache and bright blue eyes.

'She must have a doctor,' he said.

'I can bring a doctor,' Adam said. 'Once I get to Les Marroniers I can get a car and I can bring a doctor. I will be back here in less than an hour. Please promise me you'll take care of her.'

'You don't need my promises, mister,' the old man said. 'I'll do what anyone would do.'

'Thank you. She's been shot. She was hit once. She's lost blood. A lot of blood.'

The old man held up a hand to silence him.

'Save your breath,' he said. 'The less I know, the better.'

His wife emerged with a jug of water and a glass and walked silently across to the bedroom.

'You'd better get going,' the old man said. 'You know the way to Les Marroniers?'

Adam shook his head. The old man took him to the door and pointed.

'It's straight over there. Across four fields. You can almost see it from here.'

Adam ducked back into the house and went across to the bedroom. She lay there, sinking into the red quilt as if it was a tide of blood, with the dim light falling on her face, making it glow. He was not going to let her die here. He bent over and kissed her on the cheek and she opened her eyes and smiled.

'I'll be back in no time,' he said. 'I'll bring a doctor with me. Everything is going to be all right.'

She nodded. 'I know,' she said.

He kissed her again. 'You're beautiful,' he said.

'Thank you.'

She raised her hand for a second, then it dropped back on the quilt. He closed the door quietly behind him.

Adam ran back past the outhouses and into the field to the bikes. He picked up her bicycle – it was newer and faster than his – and set off along the track.

She was not going to die. It was only a flesh wound. Any doctor would be able to patch it up and she would have nothing to show for it save two little diamond-shaped scars that he would take care always to kiss during the numberless nights of lovemaking that lay ahead of them.

He stamped down on the pedals, driving the rattling bike over the rutted ground until he was choking for breath and a jumble of farm buildings came into view and a rusting sign told him he had reached Les Marroniers.

36

They were waiting for him in an old barn on the edge of the farmyard.

'Christ,' said Gerry. 'What happened to you?' He was lying on a hay bale surrounded by his men. Adam stood in the doorway, his torn shirt wet with sweat, empty of breath. The story came out in ragged bursts. At the end Gerry was frowning.

'That's buggered everything,' he said. 'The raid's off. What the fuck do we do now?'

'No,' said Adam, 'you haven't heard me. I don't care what you do. You have to get me a car and a doctor.'

Gerry was flapping distractedly at his tunic pocket, searching for a cigarette.

'Did you hear what I said?'

'Eh?' He seemed to come out of his trance.

'I'm sorry,' he said contritely. 'I hadn't forgotten the girl. Alain, quick, what are we going to do?'

'I've got my car. And I know a doctor who would help. But he's not around here. He's in Montcharles.'

'That will take too long,' Adam said desperately. 'There must be someone nearer.'

Alain thought. 'No one we can trust.'

Adam looked at him, hating his cruel serenity.

'Then we'll have to get someone we can't trust,' he said. 'And shoot him afterwards.'

Alain smiled. 'You've grown up,' he said.

Three of Alain's men were lounging in the shadows. One of them spoke.

'I know someone,' he said.

'Someone reliable?' asked Alain.

'He's married to my aunt. He lives near Saint-Sulpice.'

'Then let's go and get him.' Adam turned for the door. No one moved. He looked back. The *maquisard* was looking at Alain, waiting for his agreement.

'All right then,' he said, cautiously. He pulled some keys from his pocket.

'Take my car. We'll wait for you here. We haven't much choice by the sound of it.'

Adam drove. Out of the shadows, behind his cigarette and stubble, his companion was revealed as being not much more than a boy. He gave directions that took them down the farm track and onto a lane that led onto the Montcharles road. They drove for three miles along the highway, passing the poplar grove where only an hour before he had dressed Radegonde's wound, then turned left up the hill towards Saint-Sulpice. He was taking them past the château. The car toiled noisily upwards. The events of the morning had left no trace on the landscape. Even the château looked tranquil as it came into view. He slumped down in the driver's seat, staring ahead as they approached the drive and the guardhouse. Out of the corner of his eye he could see that there were now four or five guards on the gate, standing with their rifles trained on the road. He felt their eyes following the car as they drove past.

It was nearly two hours since since he had left her. He imagined her lying on the bed looking up when he walked through the door with the doctor, knowing then that she was safe, and the thought made him feel better.

'How much further?'

'Nearly there.'

A row of chalets standing along a railway line marked the start of the town. They drove past the mairie, through a small square.

'Down there,' he said, and they turned into a street of ornate villas. The boy told him to stop outside a house with a fir tree in the front garden.

'Wait here,' he said.

He ran up the path and rang the doorbell. A middle-aged woman appeared, smiled when she saw him, and kissed him on both cheeks. Then, to Adam's dismay, she shook her head. They stood talking unhurriedly for a while. Adam squirmed with frustration. The boy reached in his pocket, extracted a cigarette and lit it. Adam threw open the car door and shouted at him. The woman looked up and saw him and said something to the boy, who turned round and nodded. Then he waved to the woman and trotted back to the car.

'Where is he?' Adam demanded.

'He's on his rounds. But don't worry, I know where he'll be.'

'Where?'

'With an old lady patient. It's not far.'

They drove for a mile beyond the town until they came to a gloomy, creeper-covered house set back from the road.

'That's his car,' said the boy, pointing to a large Citroën.

'I'm coming with you,' said Adam.

They walked along the path, through the overgrown garden and up some mossy steps. Adam pulled a lever and a bell tinkled in the depths of the house. Faint footsteps sounded and a maid opened the door.

'The doctor, quickly,' Adam said roughly. The maid looked startled and shuffled rapidly away. He heard voices, querulous, questioning. Then a man came into the hall. He was plump and carefully dressed and wore tortoiseshell spectacles.

He looked at the boy, then Adam.

'Hallo Pierre,' he said. 'What's this about?'

The boy started speaking but Adam broke in. 'There's no time. Come with us to the car. The doctor looked at him with contempt. Adam realised how he looked to him: dirty, ragged, smelling sourly of sweat.

'Please,' he said more gently. 'It's an emergency. A girl may die.'

The doctor glanced to the boy as if for confirmation and the boy nodded.

For a moment Adam was sure he was going to refuse, but then he softened, perhaps afraid of the consequences of defying the desperate-looking man in front of him. 'All right,' he said grudgingly. 'I'll get my bag.'

When he returned his face was blank and hostile.

They walked quickly down the path. He turned towards the Citroën.

'Where are you going?' asked Adam

'I'm taking my car,' the doctor said.

'Oh no. You're coming with us.'

He sat the doctor in the front seat and put the boy in the back and they set off, driving fast.

'This girl's been shot. Do you have everything you need to treat her?'

'How should I know?' the doctor said sullenly. 'I can't tell until I've examined her.'

'It's only a flesh wound, I think.' Adam spoke encouragingly, as if by saying the words he could turn them into fact. 'There's no bones broken. But she's lost blood.'

The doctor said nothing and looked at his watch. They drove back through the town and past the château. This time there were more soldiers, moving briskly around the guardhouse. They sped down the hill. Adam was about to turn into the main road when he was forced to brake by a line of four open lorries grinding up the road towards Montcharles. In the back sat two rows of soldiers, helmets gleaming in the darkness, rifles propped between their knees.

'Where are they going?' the doctor asked.

'Maybe they're pulling out,' said Adam warily, anxious not to alarm him. 'Heading north to Normandy.'

'No,' the doctor said. 'Those are garrison troops. It's a local operation.'

The last lorry rolled past and they pulled out onto the road. On the way to Saint-Sulpice he had noticed a turning just before the avenue of poplars, which he was fairly certain would lead to the farm. They were almost there now. The fear that bubbled inside him was subsiding. It was going to be all right.

He took the turning and they bumped for a while down a lane pocked with potholes until some out-buildings appeared.

'There it is,' he said. He steered the car through the narrow gates and into the yard and pulled up sharply in a cloud of dust. He got out. The doctor sat where he was, staring ahead. Adam went round to the passenger door and pulled him out.

They walked over to the back door. It was shut. He turned the handle and it swung open. The room smelled of old cooking and unwashed bodies. There was no one in the parlour. The door to the bedroom stood ajar.

'Radegonde,' he called.

There was no reply. His heartbeat quickened as he crossed the floor and pushed open the door. The bedroom was empty. The only sign of her was a shallow dent in the red quilt. He stood there for a moment, taking in the dust dancing in the joist of sunlight slanting across the room and the dim yellow figure on the dark cross.

'There's no one here,' said a voice. The doctor was standing in the doorway. He sounded relieved. 'There's nothing for me to do here. You must take me back.'

'Shut up,' said Adam. His mind was slithering and floundering, searching for a purchase on reality. For a wild second he thought he was in the wrong farm-house, but he knew that could not be true. No, the most likely explanation was that she had felt well enough to try to make her own way on to the rendez-vous at Les Marroniers. But in that case where were the old man and the old woman?

He barged through the doorway, knocking aside the doctor, and pushed open the door in the opposite wall of the parlour, where he imagined the kitchen to be. The old woman was sitting in the corner, with her knees drawn up under her chin. She looked up when he came in, her eyes crazed with terror.

He helped her to a chair.

'What happened?' he asked gently.

She tried to speak but only a bleating noise emerged. She pointed to the window. He looked through the dusty glass. The old man was lying face down among the cabbages in the vegetable patch. The blood clotting the white hair at the base of his skull was turning black in the sun.

'The girl?' Adam demanded. 'Where is the girl?'

'Gone,' said the old woman. 'The Germans took her.'

She looked straight at him now and her face twisted in misery. 'Why did you bring her here?'

'I'm sorry,' he said, and laid his hand on her shoulder. She brushed it away. As he walked to the car he heard her start to cry.

37

Adam knew what he had to do. He was going to find her and save her. He would probably be killed in the attempt but that did not matter. There was really no choice involved. Guilt and shame would walk with him to his grave if he turned his back on her now. The meaning of the words 'life would be not worth living' came to him with a revelatory clarity that made his heart lurch.

'Where will they have taken her?' he asked.

Pierre, the boy, shrugged.

Now that his services were no longer required, the doctor tried to be helpful.

'They'll take her to the Wehrmacht Kommandantur in Montcharles, and get one of their doctors to examine her. If she's bad enough they'll move her to the Bon Secours hospital.'

'She's bad enough.'

Now that his mind was made up he found he was thinking coolly.

'You can go,' he said to the doctor. 'You'll have to walk back. If you talk to the Germans I'll kill you. You understand that, don't you?'

The doctor nodded vigorously.

★   ★   ★

They drove the few kilometres to Les Marroniers. The Jeeps had gone. He stepped into the barn but there was no sign of anyone. He called out and Gerry stepped out from the shadows.

'It's you. We were expecting the Germans. They were at the farm next door.'

'They're searching the area. They've got Radegonde.'

'Shit,' Gerry said. 'Now what?'

'We're staying here. You're going to help me to rescue her.'

'No can do,' Gerry said firmly. 'You've seen the situation. The place is crawling with Germans. We've got to shift – or at least sit tight until nightfall and leg it back to the camp.'

'I know where she is. They'll have taken her to the main hospital in Montcharles. They won't be expecting us. It won't take much. Just a car and a few men. It doesn't have to be you. Just tell Alain to give me the car and a couple of his men and I'll organise it myself.'

Gerry sighed and shook his head.

'I'd love to help you, Tommy, but it doesn't work like that. I run my show, Alain runs his. I can't tell him to do something he doesn't want to. I'll ask him. But I wouldn't hold out too much hope.'

He dropped his voice. 'The fact is, brother, that neither of us is risking our lives or those of our men so that you and your tart can live happily ever after.'

Adam hit him hard in the stomach. Gerry doubled over and coughed delicately. It was some moments before he spoke.

'Steady on, Tommy,' he gasped.

Adam hit him again. He took careful aim, placing the blow on the tip of Gerry's jaw and to the side so his head jerked back with a snap. Gerry tumbled forward and onto his knees. The others pressed forward, fascinated.

Gerry looked up at him. 'I'm getting fed up with this,' he said softly. One of the soldiers laughed uncertainly.

'Stand up,' Adam ordered. Gerry tried to obey but his legs were weak under him and Spider Kelly stepped forward to help him upright.

Adam glanced around the circle. Alain was hanging back. He seemed to be enjoying the drama. The troopers were looking at him with hostility and suspicion. Adam motioned them back.

'You all right, sir?' asked Kelly protectively.

'I'm fine, Spider,' said Gerry. 'Do as he says.'

They withdrew warily, keeping their eyes on Adam.

'Come over here.'

Gerry followed him over to a dark corner of the barn where the straw was stacked up in blocks. The bales made an alcove and he scrambled up into it. With some difficulty, Gerry hauled himself up behind him.

There was sympathy in Gerry's voice when he spoke. 'I feel for you, brother, honestly. She seemed – seems – like a good kid. But you have to face facts. They've got her now. If they're keeping her alive it's only because they want to . . .' His voice trailed off. 'You know what I mean. Anyway, she's as good as dead. You can't expect me to risk people's lives in pursuing something that's really a personal matter.'

'You did.'

Something had come to him, a bright shaft of revelation that lit up the darkness of the previous forty-eight hours.

'What?'

'You risked her life,' he said slowly, 'and mine as well, on a personal matter.'

There was a slight hesitation before Gerry answered.

'I don't follow you, old man.'

'The raid on the château. There was no need for that. No military need anyway.'

'Of course there was—'

'Shut up, Gerry.'

Gerry was listening to him now with an intentness Adam had never seen before. He fumbled in his tunic pocket and pulled out a cigarette and snapped on his heavy gold lighter.

Adam could see the picture now. The details were forming, steadily and inexorably, coming out of nothing like a photographic print in a tray of chemicals.

'It was supposed to be a diversion,' he said carefully. 'That's what you said. I believed you. But I wondered why you were so anxious to know about the layout of the château. Now I know. It looked like the Louvre. That's what I said to Radegonde.'

'What the hell are you talking about?'

'The paintings. That's what you were after. Westendorp's loot. Sitting there in the château waiting to go off with him when the Germans clear out.'

'Really?' His voice turned hard. 'And how the fuck was I supposed to know about that?'

Adam thought for a moment.

'Maybe because de la Haye told you,' he said. 'Maybe that's what he offered you when he was begging for his life.'

'I don't know why I'm listening to you,' said Gerry wearily.

'You're listening because you want to know what I know or suspect.'

'But you don't *know* anything,' Gerry said with exasperation. 'These are just fantasies. There isn't a speck of proof.'

'Proof doesn't really matter, does it?' said Adam. 'It doesn't even matter if it's true or not. The allegation will be enough to finish you.'

Gerry was propped up against a bale, blowing plumes of smoke that drifted up to hang in the dark rafters of the barn. 'Do you really think I'm such a shit?' he asked.

'I'm not thinking about you. I'm thinking about her. But, now you mention it, the answer is "yes".'

There was a silence. A bluebottle buzzed in the space between them before weaving clumsily away. Then Gerry spoke.

'You think pretty well of yourself though, don't you, Adam? There's no harm in that, I suppose. Most people do. The problem comes when you can't like yourself unless you hate other people. It suits you to hate me. It probably helped to cheer you up when you were wallowing in misery. After I persuaded Moira not to make a fool of herself and to come back to me. Did you ever wonder why she did that? Of course you did. All the bloody time. And the answer you came up with was that I'd tricked her, thrown dust into her eyes so she couldn't see who I really was and what I was really like. The trouble is, she knew all about me. And she knew you as well. And she decided she wanted me after all, bastard though I might be. You'll learn one day that I'm no better or worse than you are. I'm just different. I want some things, and because you don't want them you despise me for trying to get them. There are other things that you want Adam, but I don't hate you for wanting them. We're all in the same game. We'll all come to the same end. It's really a question of how you pass the time on the way.'

He leaned forward. There was a smear of blood on the corner of his mouth and his face looked old in the dim light. 'There's something in the scriptures, isn't there? About death. Well they're always going on about death. But there's a passage somewhere that says that Christ is a remedy for death. I remember it because it always stuck in my mind at school. Well, maybe he is, but most of us aren't satisfied with that, even the believers. We go through life looking for our own remedy: it's power or money or glory or a wife and kids. We find out soon enough, of course, that there isn't really a remedy. But we keep on looking just the same.'

Adam sat in silence. Gerry had escaped him. The great revelation that had glowed in front of him a few minutes before had dimmed and faded to nothing.

Gerry dragged hard on his cigarette and flipped away the butt. He got to his feet.

'I'm going to help you,' he said. 'Not because of that bullshit you've been spouting. You could never frighten me. Regard it as a present.' He gave a dark smile. 'Besides, we're fucked anyway. So there's no harm in doing the right thing for a change.'

He was back in charge again. Adam felt he had lost something, a power he would never have again. For a moment he thought of telling him he no longer wanted his help. Then gratitude took over.

'Thank you,' he said.

They climbed down from the bales and walked to the middle of the barn where Alain was sitting with the *maquisards*. Gerry took Alain by the arm and led him to the discreet gloom of a corner of the barn. He waved to Adam to join them.

'OK Alain,' he said briskly. 'Tommy's persuaded me. Only we can't do anything without your help. I think that's reasonable. She is one of yours, after all.'

He turned to Adam. 'Now this hospital.'

'The Bon Secours.'

'We don't know she's there,' Alain said. 'We'll have to check.'

Adam was about to protest but he saw that Alain was right.

'How long will that take?'

'A couple of hours? Who knows? I'll send someone down there now.'

He left them for a few minutes, issued instructions to one of his men and returned.

'What are you planning exactly?'

'A rescue operation,' said Adam. Now that he was confronted with the reality he had no idea how he would go about it. 'What do you know about the hospital?'

Alain thought for a bit.

'You've seen the Bon Secours? It's on the side of the hill to the north of the town. It's in civilian hands, though the Germans bring their wounded there from time to time. They even took some of ours there once, to get them well enough to be tortured. By the time we found out, it was too late to do anything about it. If she is there, everything will depend on how tightly she's guarded.'

'Will your men be able to find out?' asked Gerry.

'We can try.'

'OK, then do it. We'll stay here until things have quietened down. Then try and get back to the camp.'

There was nothing to do now but wait. Gerry had posted two more sentries to look out for any German search parties. The Jeeps had been parked out of sight in an outbuilding and a hiding place had been prepared in a storehouse below the floorboards of the barn. But time passed and there was no sign of Germans and it seemed likely that the discovery of Radegonde was enough to satisfy them and they had called off the hunt.

Gerry sat among his men playing cards. Adam had barely noticed them earlier. Now, as well as Spider Kelly the radio operator, he recognised Glover and Sergeant Richards. There were two others who arrived in the second drop whose names he had never learned. He wandered over. They looked up for a second then back to the cards, shifting round a little as though to exclude him.

'Don't be like that, boys,' Gerry said. 'Tommy's one of us. Here. Come and sit by me.' He shifted to make a space and Adam sat down. They were playing pontoon. Glover held the bank and he dealt him two cards along with the others when they played the next hand.

They played for the next two hours. Adam concentrated fiercely on the simple game, dragging his imagination away from speculation about what was happening to Radegonde. Now that Gerry had given his blessing, the others welcomed him into the circle. While they played they joked, ritual jabs of facetiousness.

Adam won with uncanny regularity. The pile of matchsticks in front of him grew large. He remembered the last card game at Warneford, Mount winning big and dying later that night in the fiery longship of the Halifax.

The SOS team fitted tightly together, he could see that: Spider Kelly with his mournful horse-face; Ron Richards, hard, cold and perpetually cheerful; Frank Glover. Glover. A few days before he had been a frightened boy. Now he was one of them. The nervousness had gone, replaced with the sardonic cockiness that seemed required of all SOS veterans, officers and men. Gerry was their model; Gerry was their lord. Adam noticed how their eyes always sought Gerry when they made a joke or won a hand, craving his approval.

Eventually, the game began to pall. Gerry yawned and examined his watch. The joking intensified as they strained to keep him in their company. But he rose and stretched and yawned again and went to lie down among the straw bales, where he lay picturesquely stretched out, a warrior in repose.

Adam lay down too. Now the game was over there was nothing to stop him thinking. The images invaded his head, competing with each other in awfulness. Then when he thought he could bear it no more, some switch was thrown and, quite suddenly, he was deeply asleep.

He was woken by Alain shaking him roughly by the shoulder.

'Get up,' he said. 'They've come back.' He turned on his side and rolled with a thud onto the floor. He got to his feet and two *maquisards* walked over to join them. One of them had been in the barn earlier in the day. The other was Jean, Radegonde's brother.

Alain saw that Adam had recognised him.

'I thought he'd want to be involved,' he said.

He gestured to a short dark-haired man in his twenties with a thick moustache.

'Tell him what you found out.'

'She's at the hospital,' he said. 'Apparently they took her there straight away. I spoke to one of the nurses there. She said she was not so good.'

He looked sympathetically at Adam.

'Go on,' Alain said.

'Well, they've put a light guard on her. Two soldiers who sit at the door of the ward. It's on the ground floor. The first one on the left after you walk in.'

'What about outside?' asked Adam. 'Are there any guards on the main gate?'

'None,' he said. 'You just walk in.'

Adam was elated by the news.

'Then it should be easy,' he said exultantly. 'All we have to do is drive up to the main entrance and walk in as if we're going to visit someone. Then we'll find the ward.

Two of us will hold up the guards. The other two will get Radegonde out to the car. Then we just drive away.'

He thought for a minute. 'That will mean we will need four people. Me and Jean . . .'

Adam looked at Jean, frowning and serious, dressed like a man now, in a blue cotton jacket and cloth cap.

The other *maquisard* held out his hand. 'Thierry,' he said. 'I'll come with you.'

'We need one more,' said Adam.

'Me,' Alain said.

'Then let's go,' Adam said.

'We have to tell Gerry what we're doing,' said Alain. They went over to where he was lying snoring softly among the bales. Alain nudged him and he jerked awake. He rubbed his eyes as Adam told him the plan.

'OK then,' he said. 'Good luck. Now, once you get away you should head to Vercourt by the back roads. Don't hang about, because we're going to move out tonight, to the new site, as soon as Alain's people show up with the transport.'

'What about a doctor?' said Adam suddenly. 'She'll need a doctor. Can we have one waiting for her there?'

'He's right,' said Gerry. 'Can you arrange that?'

Alain nodded cautiously. 'That might be possible.'

He left them for a minute to talk to one of his men. They walked over to the barn door. When Alain joined them Gerry shook hands with each of them and clapped them on the shoulder. They walked out into the hot afternoon sun and the smell of the farmyard.

38

They reached the edge of the town. The hospital stood on the northern slope of the hill, big and imposing. Inside the car, no one spoke. There were two entrances, marked by stone pillars. As the gates came into sight Alain took his pistol from his pocket and pulled back the slide, cocking the gun with an oily click.

Jean swung the car through the gates and parked just past the front door. Two nurses were struggling to steer an elderly woman in a wheelchair up a ramp that ran alongside the shallow steps leading up to the front door. Jean stopped just beyond the portico. They got out. Jean's blue cotton jacket made him look like a workman. Adam and Thierry walked over to the nurses and took hold of the wheelchair, propelling it firmly up the ramp and through the front door and into the lobby. The woman looked up and thanked them.

They stood for a moment in the lobby. It was a tall room with a wooden floor and it smelled of beeswax and disinfectant. There was a desk facing the door with a nurse sitting behind it. She glanced at them briefly then went back to whatever she was reading. They peered down the corridor to the left that led to the ward. The door was only ten yards away. It was glass but the view through was blocked by two large grey serge backs pressed against the panels.

Alain and Thierry led the way. They walked quickly, hands jammed in their jacket pockets, and pushed together at the swing doors. The Germans turned in unison to see who was coming in. Their look of irritation stiffened into alarm, then fear, as Alain and Thierry seized them by the lapels of their tunics and jabbed the square noses of their pistols into their cheeks so that their lips bulged comically. Alain motioned them to kneel and they fell to their knees with a thump. Without being told, they placed their hands meekly behind their heads. Alain waved Adam and Jean into the ward. It was a long, high-ceilinged room with ten beds on either side.

Adam hurried along the row of beds, the Browning that Alain had given in him in his hand, looking left and right. The patients were all old women with sunken faces and sparse white hair and they stared back at him, uncomprehendingly. She was not there. He started to panic. Maybe they had moved her. Then he saw that the last bed in the right-hand row had been curtained off. He strode over to it and found the gap in the heavy rubber drapes and slid his hand in it and pulled. The curtain slid back with a rasp.

She was lying there with her eyes closed, pressed to the mattress by the tight binding of sheets and blankets. Her body was outlined beneath the bedding, arms by her side, toes pointing upwards. He bent down and kissed her damp forehead. She opened her eyes.

'Hallo,' she said.

He smiled and kissed her again.

Jean had reached them now. Together they pulled back

the sheets and eased her upright and sideways so that her legs dangled down. She was wearing a long white night-gown. He lifted it back and examined the bandage that wound around her shoulders and across her breasts. It was reassuringly clean and white and smelled of antiseptic.

'Come on, quickly,' Alain yelled from the end of the ward.

They propped her up between them and trailed her to the door. The guards watched dumbly as they brushed through the swing doors and out into the corridors. They hobbled into the lobby. Radegonde seemed very heavy, heavier than she had been when he carried her into the farmhouse that morning. He glanced back. Alain saw him and waved him on impatiently.

They struggled down the steps to where the car stood with the back door open. Gently, they pushed her inside, and Jean slipped into the front seat. A few seconds later, Alain and Thierry ran down the steps and threw themselves into the car and Jean slipped the clutch and shot away. As they paused to turn right through the gates, Adam looked back. The two guards were standing at the top of the steps, watching mis-erably as the car moved onto the road and out of sight.

Now that they were in daylight, he saw that her skin had taken on a faint tinge of yellow and her lips were dry and cracked. She looked up at him. Her eyes were wet with tears.

'Where are we going?' she asked.

'To Vercourt,' he said. 'We're taking you home.'

'Good,' she said, putting her head against his shoulder. Soon she had fallen asleep.

She slept most of the way. Her breath was shallow and he felt its heat and wetness against his skin. Sometimes she shuddered and made small grumbling noises, like a child.

For most of the journey they bumped along narrow, high-banked lanes. It was a glorious evening. Over to the west, the sun slid earthwards, setting the fields on fire. The freshness was leaving the land. Now the earth would start to bake and the blue youth of the leaves and the grass turn into the parched green of high summer. They drove past farms, pursued by barking dogs and through deserted hamlets. The fields were busy, dotted with stooped figures, old men and women, bent over the soil, casting long shadows in the fading light. Occasionally one of them would straighten, stare at the car and the banner of dust that hung behind it, then stoop back to the earth again.

Once, when they stopped to work round a broken part of the road where a culvert had collapsed, she woke up and yawned and looked around.

'Where are we?' she asked.

Jean told her. She seemed satisfied.

'Not long now,' she said, and put her head against his chest and went back to sleep.

It was dusk when they reached Vercourt. The bell in the church tower struck the hour as they passed, the ponderous note filling the silence of the square. On the terrace of the Espérance, a few drinkers looked up as they went by. They left the town behind and saw the shadowy ramparts of the forest rising ahead of them across the fields. Then they drove into the hole that the road made in the forest and the darkness closed around them.

39

They stopped outside the cottage. Adam pulled Radegonde out of the back of the car. Jean opened the cottage door and she walked unsteadily towards it, holding tight to Adam's hand. She climbed the steep wooden stairs, lifted the latch on the bedroom door. Her narrow bed lay along the wall, beneath a window in the slope of the roof. She gasped as she lay down and put her hand to her breast. They pulled the counterpane over her and he bent down and kissed her dry lips.

'I'm going to the camp. There should be a doctor waiting there. I'll bring him back and I'll bring you some food as well.'

She shook her head.

'Not hungry,' she said. 'I'm thirsty, though.' She looked apologetically at Jean.

He clattered off down the stairs, and Adam rose to go. She caught his hand and squeezed his fingers.

'You won't be long, will you?' she murmured.

He shook his head. 'Jean will stay with you.'

He walked round to the back of the house and into the enveloping gloom of the forest. The twilight showed smudgily overhead through the black branches that swayed slightly in the dense air. Below, though, on the floor of the forest, the dark was deeper and he was no longer sure of the way. He walked fast, waiting to feel the ground falling away so he would know he had reached the lip of the valley, but the ground ivy and dead branches caught at his ankles and made him stumble. He stopped to listen for the rush of the stream but there was nothing except the harsh sound of his own breathing.

Then he heard voices, not near, but clear enough to give him a bearing, and he went towards them. Almost immediately the ground sloped away and a few minutes later he found the stream and the faint track on the far side of it that marked the path taken by the men when they went down to the water to wash.

He jumped across the narrow width of water, landing clumsily on the other side. Immediately he heard a frightened Cockney voice.

'Halt! Who goes there?'

'It's me, Tomaszewski. Who's that?'

'It's Shirley, sir. Thank God for that. I thought you was a Jerry.'

'Good to see you're on your toes.'

He could see him now, peering from behind a tree with the barrel of his rifle poking haphazardly towards him.

'What's going on?'

'We're moving, sir. As soon as the transport turns up, we're moving.'

He saw a concentration of flickering torch beams. Gerry was standing by the radio set with Alain, Minto and Glover. Spider Kelly was huddled by the wireless, head cocked, tapping the key, lost in concentration.

Gerry saw him and detached himself from the group.

'Hallo Tommy. I hear it went off OK. How's the girl?'

'Don't know until we get a doctor. Is he here?'

'Not yet.'

Gerry looked haggard and taut with strain.

'What happened to you?' Adam asked.

'We made a run for it just after you left. We ran into a patrol not very far from here and had to shoot our way out. The last bloody thing we needed.'

They joined the others.

'Where's the doctor?' Adam asked.

'He should have been here by now,' Alain said. 'Don't worry, he'll come.'

'That's what you said about the buses,' Gerry said, 'but we're still waiting.'

'They will come too. It's not easy.'

Gerry drew hard on his cigarette, and the tip glowed orange, lighting up his frowning face. The others hung back uneasily, anxious not to provoke him.

'They'll get here, I'm sure,' said Glover placatingly.

'How the hell do you know?' demanded Gerry. Then he added more gently, 'They better had. Otherwise we're all for the high jump.'

It was cool in the forest. Gerry shivered and pulled his leather jacket tighter around him.

'Is it my imagination or has it suddenly got darker?' he said. 'It's as black as midnight's arsehole in here.'

The men stood around in small groups, smoking cigarettes in the furtive way of soldiers, talking intermittently in nervous, bantering voices. Their equipment was stacked up around them, ready to go.

Adam walked away from the group and sat with his back against a tree. He lit a cigarette and ran over his plan. As soon as Radegonde could move he would get her away from there, to a quiet part of the countryside where there were no Germans and no *maquis*; out of the way of the war.

Where was the doctor? Anything could have happened to him. He tried to push the thought from his mind and lay back on the musty forest floor. He was desperately tired. As soon as his head touched the ground he dozed off, waking with a jerk when the cigarette burnt his fingers. He fell off to sleep again. This time he was interrupted by a hesitant voice, penetrating his dream.

'Adam. Is that you?'

He woke up with a jolt. Hennessy and Hawkins loomed over him in the dark.

'What are you doing here?' he asked numbly. 'You shouldn't be here. You should be on the way to Spain.'

'We thought we'd hang on for you.'

They were smiling, childishly relieved to see him. They think, thought Adam with dismay through the fog of fatigue, that I can save them.

'Where have you been?' said Hennessy anxiously.

Adam told them about the previous thirty-six hours. They barely listened to the account, willing him to hurry up so they could ask the inevitable question.

Hawkins said it. 'So what are we going to do now?' Adam felt his heart harden. He no longer felt responsible for them.

'The best thing you can do is go with them,' he said. 'Or if you don't fancy that, take your chances on your own, head for Spain like you said. I might be able to help you with cash and clothes.'

'But aren't you coming with us then?' Hawkins was almost pleading.

'Things have changed,' Adam said.

'The girl?'

'Yes.'

'What about us?' Hawkins sounded angry now.

'She's wounded. I have to take care of her. I haven't any choice.'

They looked down on him for a few moments in silence.

'I reckon we'll stick with the others then,' Hawkins said resignedly. 'I suppose there's safety in numbers.'

They walked slowly back to where they had come from, trailing a banner of disappointment. Adam was too tired to feel guilty. He looked at his watch. It was eleven o'clock. He had been gone from Radegonde for more than an hour. Where was the fucking doctor?

He climbed back up the slope. The men had moved in from the edges of the camp and were gathered round the wireless tent where Gerry stood, with Minto, Lockyer and Glover on one side of him and Richards and Schofield on the other. Alain sat with some of his men on a fallen tree next to them.

The soldiers had stopped talking and were standing

and squatting in a semicircle, watching intently. There was no light now except an occasional, wandering cone of torchlight, and their faces were pale smudges above the drab uniforms.

'This is no good,' he heard Gerry saying. 'If the buses aren't here soon it will be too late. We'll be on the roads in broad daylight.'

'They'll be here,' Alain said stubbornly.

The swagger had gone out of Gerry's cohorts. Minto, Lockyer and Glover, Schofield and Richards stood in apprehensive silence.

'Where's the doctor?' Adam demanded.

'He's on his way,' Alain replied. He sounded glad to have some positive news to relate. 'He should be here any moment.'

Gerry lowered himself to the ground, leaned back against a limestone boulder and closed his eyes. The cohorts took their cue from him and settled down among the scattered rucksacks. For the soldiers it was the signal to reach for their cigarettes.

They were too tired to speak. Silence settled over the forest. Then, at about midnight, Adam heard the note of an engine droning far off. Others heard it as well. Alain stood up and swivelled left and right, trying to locate the direction of the noise. Gerry opened his eyes and got to his feet.

'Is that them?' he demanded, but Alain only put his finger to his lips and strained harder to hear.

'It's coming this way,' he said eventually.

They were all straining to hear now, waiting for the thin drone to swell into the throb of a convoy of buses.

But after a minute it became clear that there was only one engine and one vehicle.

Adam heard one of the troopers behind him say, 'Maybe it's the first bus. Maybe the others will follow on behind it.'

'Another one directly behind,' called another soldier, 'Move right down the bus there, ding ding.'

There was a smattering of relieved laughter.

They could see the glow of headlights, briefly illuminating the sky over the forest now, as the vehicle swung towards them, then the light was flickering between the boles of the trees as it made its way up the track through the wood until it came to a stop and stood silhouetted at the edge of the forest. The engine died. There was a brief, echoing second of silence. Then the trooper behind Adam spoke.

'It's not a bloody bus,' he said. 'It's a car.'

They heard the doors open and two figures emerged and picked their way through the trees towards them. A torch beam danced in someone's hand.

'It's the doctor,' said Alain.

The doctor moved uncertainly to the side of the circle. He held his bag protectively in front of his waist. His escort went over to Alain and talked quietly. He nodded and walked over to Gerry. Adam saw Gerry's fists clench and he shook his head. Then he relaxed, as if in resignation, and turned round and walked into the circle.

'OK, listen everybody,' he said wearily. 'There's been a hitch. The buses won't be coming for us tonight.' There was a disappointed muttering from the troopers.

'It's not that bad,' continued Gerry reassuringly. 'We'll just have to sit it out here a bit longer.' He glanced over at Alain.

'That means everyone should turn in now. And the sentries must be extra vigilant.'

He stumped off to his tent. Alain came over to join them.

'This is Doctor Desforges,' he said. He was young, efficient-looking and, it seemed to Adam, surprisingly calm. They shook hands.

'Where's the patient?'

'Nearby,' said Adam. 'Come with me.'

'What happened?' he asked the doctor as they set off.

'One bus has broken down. The man who owned the other one said it was too dangerous.'

They walked past the muttering groups of troopers settling down for the night on the forest floor, then down into the valley, over the stream and up the other side. The gloom seemed to have lifted slightly and a half-moon shone faintly above the canopy of branches. Soon the dark bulk of the cottage showed through the trees. A light flickered in the dormer window of Radegonde's room. They passed the sty and the pigs shifted and snuffled within. Adam pushed open the front door and climbed the stairs. Jean was sitting by the bed.

'She's asleep,' he whispered.

A candle glimmered on the bedside table, casting huge shadows against the wall. In its light she looked as pale as a corpse. Jean stood up and the doctor took his place. He shook her gently by the shoulder and her eyes opened. She smiled when she saw Adam and reached for him with her hot hand.

'I'm sorry,' said the doctor gently, 'I'll have to examine your wound.'

She nodded and struggled to sit up. The counter-pane fell away. The front of her nightdress was dark with blood. The doctor leaned over her and pulled the fabric from her skin and then tore it wide open with a jerk of his wrists. The bandage was dark red in the candlelight, the blackish red of roses and wine. The doctor grunted and reached into his bag.

Radegonde lay back against the pillow with her arms spread wide, her palms upward. Her eyes were closed again and she seemed to be listening to a faraway voice. He wanted the doctor to say some-thing, any trite phrase of reassurance, but he was sunk in his work, stripping the blue paper off a dressing and splashing disinfectant into a bowl that he placed on the table. He opened a leather case revealing a slim syringe.

'Is there no more light than this?' he asked.

'I'll get some more candles,' said Jean, and left the room. He came back a minute later, handed them four candles and retreated again. They stood the candles around the table, fixing them in their own wax.

Desforges pushed the syringe into a glass ampoule and drew back the plunger. Radegonde's arm lay stretched out ready. She flinched slightly as he slid the needle in. He reached into his bag and produced another case, which held a long pair of scissors. He eased the blade under the sodden bandage and began, carefully, to cut. Adam moved away, but the doctor summoned him.

'Here, give me a hand. Go down and find a bowl or a pot. Anything will do.'

He found a deep earthenware dish in the kitchen. It was the same one they had used for the shells of the crayfish they had eaten on the lawn, only a few evenings ago. When he got back the doctor had cut away the bandage. He pulled it gently from the wound and draped it in the bowl. The puckered ring where the bullet entered had turned grey. He soaked a wad of cotton in the disinfectant and dabbed at the edges of the wound. Radegonde caught her breath as the brown liquid splashed onto the raw flesh and turned bright yellow.

He pressed a pad of gauze onto the entry wound and another over the red hollow in her back.

'Hold these,' he said to Adam.

Then he wound the bandage over and under her arm and round her chest in a neat chevron pattern. Her eyes stayed closed. When he had finished he eased her back down under the quilt and stood back. He looked at Adam and nodded towards the door. They stood in the gloom of the tiny landing.

'She shouldn't be here,' he said. 'She should be in a hospital. We shall have to move her tomorrow morning. If she lasts that long.'

'What do you mean?' Adam said, panic rising in him. 'You don't mean that she's going to . . .' He couldn't say it.

'I don't know,' said Desforges coolly. 'I think it's a clean wound. Without a proper examination I just don't know. I can't see any sign of infection yet. But she's lost a lot of blood. Anyway, I've done as much as I can for the moment. I've given her some morphine. She'll sleep now. I'll come back to see her in the morning.'

'Do you have to go?' asked Adam desperately. 'Couldn't you stay here? We could make up a bed downstairs.'

He shook his head. 'No. I must go. I'm out after midnight. I'm taking a big risk.' He made to go then hesitated.

'Here's my address. If she takes a real turn for the worse you can come and fetch me.'

He took a pen from his inside pocket and scribbled on a scrap of paper. He squeezed Adam's arm and climbed down the steep stairs. Adam stood for a while, listening to the shallow breathing coming from the room. There was nothing he could do now but sit with her, and pray. He heard footsteps on the stairs and Jean stood silhouetted in the doorway.

'What did he say?'

'He thinks she'll be all right.'

'Thank God.' He paused. 'I have to go back to the camp.'

'You go. I'm staying here.'

Jean crossed to the bed and planted a kiss on Radegonde's forehead. Then, 'Goodbye Adam,' he said. 'I'll be with Alain if you need me.'

After Jean left, the only sounds were Radegonde's breathing and the creaking of the old timbers of the cottage and the whispering of the wind in the trees outside the window. Adam sat on the frail chair by the bed. Her arms lay outside the counterpane. He took her right hand in his. It was hot and limp.

He sat for an hour watching. Sometimes he slipped into a shallow sleep, but he was never far away from her and any change in the tempo of her breathing brought him back to consciousness.

The heat of her blood had dabbed smudges of red high on her cheeks, and her hair was stuck in damp strands to her forehead. A memory of childhood came back to him: his mother lying exhausted in a giant bed, a red, pulsing bundle blinking in the tiny cot at her side. He had looked down and felt something stealing into his soul, an exalted wonder at the beauty of the being that lay there and a terrible fear at the completeness of its vulnerability. He felt a tide of tenderness flooding through him, dragging him out over the deeps and reefs of love.

She stirred and murmured in her sleep and her tongue flicked across her dry lips. He reached for the water jug and filled the glass and tipped a little water into her slightly open mouth. She opened her eyes a fraction.

'I've been dreaming,' she said. 'Really strange dreams. Did he give me something?'

'For the pain.'

'But I don't feel any pain. Whatever he gave me is taking me away, somewhere I don't want to go.'

'I'm here,' he said. 'I won't let you go anywhere. Not without me, anyway.'

She smiled at him. 'Thank you,' she said, and closed her eyes again.

He dozed off once more. This time he was woken by the sound of her coughing. She was wide awake and sitting upright, holding the quilt to her mouth. She was making a harsh, barking sound and with each cough her shoulders shook. He watched helplessly until the coughing subsided. She sat there clenched and immobile for a moment, clamping the counterpane to her mouth. When she took it away it was covered in bright red blood.

She looked up at him wildly.

'I'm frightened,' she said.

His mind searched uselessly for a remedy. There was nothing he could do. He could try and fetch the doctor again, but that would mean leaving her and a voice warned him that if he left her he would never see her again.

She coughed once more. This time there was more saliva than blood. It hung in pink strings from her chin. He leaned over her to wipe it away. This was no good. He had to get the doctor.

He waited for a minute. 'I'm going to have to leave you for a little while,' he said, as casually as he could.

She clutched his shoulders. 'Don't do that,' she whispered. 'Don't leave me here.'

'But I have to, my darling. I've got to find the doctor and bring him back here. Otherwise . . .'

'I know,' she said wearily. 'But at least I'd have you with me.'

He could not sit there as the lights went out, one by one. He bent over her and kissed her full on the mouth, tasting the metallic blood. Her hot tongue pushed back against his. He stood back and looked at her pale, scared face.

'I have to go now. You understand, don't you?'

She fell back against the bolster. 'I suppose,' she said quietly. 'Don't leave me long.'

She closed her eyes and her breathing was easy. He backed out of the room and lifted the latch.

'Adam.' Her eyes were open again.

'Come here. Come to me.' He went back. She reached up and touched his cheek with her hot fingers.

'I never told you. I love you.'

'There will be plenty of time to tell me that.'

She closed her eyes again. He slipped out of the room and down the stairs and out through the front door. As he reached the back of the house he heard the coughing start again.

40

He stood in the thick grass behind the house, fighting his panic and thinking what to do next. It was, he saw now, too late for the doctor. She needed a hospital. Alain must know one. He looked at his watch. It was four o'clock. It would be dawn soon. Already, a faint greyness was creeping over the fields. In the near distance he heard the drone of a heavy engine and the grinding of gears. A gust of wind stirred the trees and he thought for a moment that he heard male voices carrying to him, but the breeze dropped away and he listened again and there was nothing. He set off, running, through the wood. The forest seemed to have come malevolently alive. Roots came up to trip him and branches reached out to slash at his face. He came to the slope and stumbled down it, following a faint track that led down to the stream. He jumped, landed short and staggered back into the water.

He was making a lot of noise, enough to rouse the guards, but there was no challenge and when he climbed the clay bank he saw a sentry, lying against a boulder, rifle by his side, open-mouthed, snoring. On either side of the path, between the trees, troopers were curled in sleeping bags, clustered in twos and threes, sunk in the innocence of sleep.

He climbed the path, panting for breath, and reached the clearing where Gerry had his tent. More bodies lay scattered around the fire pit. An astral noise drifted from underneath the stretched tarpaulin that sheltered the radio transmitter. He ducked beneath it and saw Kelly crouched beside the set, his long face yellow in the glow from the valves. He looked round.

'Hallo, sir. What's up?'

'Where's Alain?

'In his kip, I should think.'

He turned to go.

'I picked up the BBC earlier,' said Kelly cheerfully. 'Have you heard? They've broken out of the beachhead. The Jerries are on the run. It won't be long now, eh sir?'

'No. Not long now.'

Bodies littered the ground around the campfire. Everyone looked the same asleep. They groaned and stirred as he peered down at them. He found Alain stretched out in a sleeping bag by the door of Gerry's tent. He put his hand on his arm and shook him. He mumbled but did not wake. He shook him again, roughly this time, and Alain's eyes opened. He looked at Adam blankly. 'What's happened?'

'She's much worse. I've got to have your car. I need to get her to a hospital.'

Alain shifted and turned away. 'Leave it till the morning,' he said.

'Don't you understand?' Adam said desperately. 'If I don't move her she's going to die.' Alain said nothing.

For a moment Adam thought he had gone back to sleep. Then he murmured, 'I've done enough for you. I'm sorry. Please let me sleep.'

Adam stepped away. He felt sick at his own impotence. He looked down with hatred at Alain who, judging by his deep, even breathing was unconscious again. His jacket was by his side. Cautiously he moved forward, dipped down and picked it up. There was a faint jangling from one of the pockets. He slipped his hand in and it closed round a set of keys. Gently he laid the jacket down again and crept away.

He found Jean in a clearing with some other *maquisards*, his blue cotton jacket draped over his shoulders. He woke with a jolt when Adam leaned over him.

'Why have you left her?' he asked.

'We have to move her. We have to get her to a hospital.' He scrambled to his feet, as Adam explained what had happened.

'Don't worry,' he said. 'I know somewhere. There's a convent at Saint-Maur, about fifty kilometres from here. The nuns will take her in. We can be there in less than an hour.'

They set off between the thin boles of the oaks towards the grey light that showed where the forest ended and the fields began. Birds were singing now and the leaves were turning blue in the morning light. The car sat at the side of the logging track that ran around the edge of the forest. Adam was opening the driver's door when he saw figures moving by the hedgerow that ran along the far side of the field opposite. There were four or five men coming slowly forward, shouldering heavy tools, farm labourers it looked like, on their way to the fields. There was something stealthy about their movements. They were all dressed the same, in clothing that matched the grey dawn light, and somehow they all seemed to have the same shape. Jean noticed him staring and turned to look.

'Germans,' he said.

As soon as he heard the word he saw them clearly. There were eight or ten of them, moving cautiously. Two of them held a mortar barrel between them and another cradled a heavy machine gun.

The car door was open. The Germans had not seen them yet. Even when they heard the noise of the engine they could do nothing at this distance to stop them. All they had to do was climb in and drive off. They could be on the road with Radegonde, on the way to the hospital before the attack began. He slipped into the car seat. Then the dead weight of his conscience settled upon him.

'I'm going back,' he said, trying to sound calm. 'Wait here. I'll be back in a minute.'

He slipped back between the trees and ran the fifty yards to the camp. He ducked into Gerry's tent and shook him hard. Gerry gave a gasp of fright and sat up.

'What the fuck?'

'Germans. They're advancing across the field to the north. They know we're here.'

'Shit,' said Gerry. 'How many?'

'Ten that I saw, but there are bound to be more, probably coming in from other directions.'

As he spoke there was a descending whistle and an explosion, some way off to the left. The tent wall rippled.

They fell out of the door. The mortar had galvanised the camp. Everywhere, men were hopping and wriggling to escape from the sleeping bags, swearing and reaching for their weapons.

Adam dodged back through the trees. Another mortar flew over, but this time it struck the trunk of a tree high up and exploded in the air. He reached the edge of the forest and found Jean lying in a shallow ditch by the side of the track, a few yards from the car.

'We're right in their line of fire,' he said. 'Do you still want to do it?'

'Yes,' said Adam.

'On the count of three, then. One . . . two . . .'

They ran to the car, bracing for a burst of fire that never came. Suddenly everything was quiet again. Adam opened the door nearest the forest and climbed over into the driver's seat. Fear heightened his senses. He could smell the worn leather seats, the scent of some wild flower. The birds were singing, louder now, and the gaps in their song emphasised the humming silence of the summer morning. He fumbled with the keys and tried to find the lock. His hand jiggled shamefully.

'Hurry up,' Jean pleaded.

The key slid in. Cautiously, he pulled back the starter. The motor emitted a hideous whinnying noise that swamped the air. Nothing happened. He released the knob and pulled it out again with trembling fingers, muttering and cursing. The motor whined beseechingly, even louder it seemed this time, on and on; then suddenly the engine caught and he threw the car into gear and they jerked forward. Then he was aware of a distant pattering noise and bright lights glittered across the windscreen. The car shook and a spray of splintered glass burst over him. Jean wrenched open the door and crawled out onto the grass. Adam scrambled after him and they fell together into the shallow dent of the ditch.

The Germans took their time with the car. It rocked on its springs as each short burst of fire hit, punching neat holes in the thin steel skin and clearing the glass from the windows.

He watched the bullets sparking off the metal. Radegonde's deliverance was disintegrating in front of him. Hope emptied out of him. He felt a terrible disgust at the injustice of what was happening. He hated everyone outside the little universe that they had been about to create. If only he could be with her now, holding her in his arms, filling her with his strength. He knew, with complete certainty, that his love could stop her dying.

The firing faded.

'Let's go,' he said to Jean. He rolled out of the ditch and pulled himself on his elbows into the shelter of the forest, with Jean following behind. They got to their feet and ran, crouching and stumbling, towards the camp. Almost immediately bullets cracked past them, coming from the direction of the camp, and they dropped down.

'Hold your fire!' he shouted. 'It's me, Tomaszewski.'

There was silence.

'Did you hear me?' he yelled.

This time a frightened voice said: 'OK. Advance slowly, keeping your hands up.'

They did as they were told. The troopers were lying in a line at the edge of the camp with their rifles trained towards them. He could see Gerry behind them, squatting by the transmitter.

'What's happening?' he called out. 'How close are they?'

'I don't know,' Adam shouted back. 'Maybe a quarter of a mile.'

Gerry scuttled over, bent double, and crouched beside him.

'They seem to be taking this slowly,' he said. His breath smelled sour. 'It looks as if they have got us pretty well taped. I imagine they'll try to drive us into a trap. They'll come at us from the north and east and try and push us south where there will be another lot waiting to shoot us down properly.'

He seemed calm, resigned to what was coming.

'I was thinking of standing and fighting but it would be pretty hopeless. If we stay we'll all be dead. The only chance is to head off to the west. The forest is thicker there.' He stared about him for a moment, as if trying to measure the dimensions of the approaching disaster.

'Listen everybody,' he shouted.

The troopers were crouched between the trees, staring around them. They turned their scared faces towards him.

'We're going to have to make a run for it. What you should do is . . .' As he spoke a rhythmic, bobbing din broke out and a stream of heavy bullets whipped and cracked between the trees. A shower of severed twigs drifted down, landing on Gerry's head.

He shouted louder. 'As I was saying, what we're going to do is split up into twos and threes and head off westward, using the cover of the forest. That means this direction . . .' He pointed.

The troopers were straining to catch his words. Those on the edge of the group were too far away to hear anything.

'Leave everything you don't absolutely need,' Gerry continued. 'Once you're clear you should make your way to the new campsite. You've all got the name. We'll regroup there. Good luck and keep your fucking heads down.'

He ran, bent double, back to his tent. Spider Kelly fired a burst from his Sten gun into the radio. Minto, Richards and Schofield shouldered their rucksacks. But the rest of the soldiers stayed where they were, squatting among the trees, as if Gerry's presence would protect them. He noticed the blank, frightened faces of Hennessy and Hawkins among them. They looked up and saw him and turned away.

Jean was crouched behind him.

'I'm going back to the cottage,' Adam told him.

'Good luck. I'm leaving with the others.' He smiled suddenly. 'Tell Radegonde . . .' He trailed off.

'I know,' said Adam. They shook hands.

He got to his feet, cautiously, and another burst of heavy machine-gun fire cut through the wood, scything through leaves and branches. The soldiers fell to the ground flattening themselves against the floor of the forest. Gerry looked around, trying to work out where the fire was coming from and saw them. He stood up and waved his arms frantically.

'Go! Go! What are you waiting for? Move!'

They stood up, nervously, clutching their rifles. Then Adam heard Shirley's Cockney voice shouting, 'Look! There!' and saw him pointing towards the edge of the forest where shadowy figures had appeared between the trees and were moving from trunk to trunk, their uniforms melting into the moss and ivy of the undergrowth, branches waving on their helmets like antlers.

Some of Gerry's men returned fire, but their single shots sounded puny against the gusts of machine-gun bullets ripping the air and smacking into timber. Soon they stopped shooting and lay flat, as chopped leaves and twigs floated down around them. The forest was quiet again.

Then, Shirley got up. He threw aside his rifle and ran, lifting his legs high to escape the undergrowth, stumbling over fallen logs, colliding with the thin tree trunks, down the slope to the stream. The others watched for a moment. Then they rose and followed him in a wild charge, hopping and slithering down the slope.

'No!' Gerry shouted. 'Wrong direction!'

But they were only listening to their instincts now, blundering on, down into the valley. Gerry stood watching their jerky, flailing figures, with his arms hanging limply by his side. He looked old and defeated. He turned to Adam.

'Come on,' he said.

'I'm not coming. I'm going back to the cottage.'

'You won't make it. Come with us. Not that it makes much difference. We're all going to die, here in the wood.'

'I know. But I have to try.'

'This is it then, Tommy. I don't suppose we'll be meeting again.' He held out his hand and tried to smile. 'I'm sorry about the way things have turned out.'

His hand stayed for a moment, in the space between them, then withdrew. Something seemed to die in his eyes, but then the old, cold sparkle came back and he shrugged and turned away. He bent to pick up his rucksack and his Sten gun then loped off through the trees, with Glover and Minto close behind.

A bullet struck the tree next to Adam. He started to run, down the slope, in the direction of the cottage. If Gerry was right, the Germans would be waiting in the fields beyond. But the cottage lay in between. He could still reach her, at least touch her again, even if it was for the last time. The ground dipped, giving some cover. Ahead, the straggling line of the fleeing soldiers rose and fell as they jumped over fallen branches. They splashed through the stream and laboured up the far slope of the valley. The firing behind seemed to have stopped. The noises now came from a different direction, off to the left. He saw a line of tracer bouncing off a tree trunk and accelerating crazily away. The Germans had entered the forest from the east, as Gerry had predicted. His men had stopped now. They looked around fearfully. Some of them stood upright, trying to hide behind the thin tree trunks.

The Germans moved methodically forward, taking cover, firing a burst, moving on. Those they hunted were running again, but back in the direction they had come from, towards Adam. They scrambled down the hillside. A soldier stumbled and fell and did not get up again. The others stopped. They stood looking back across the valley. Adam turned round. The Germans had reappeared at the lip of the slope behind him. Machine-gun fire sliced through the air over his head.

The desperate vitality that had driven those fleeing seemed to desert them. The few still holding guns threw them aside. They put up their hands. Shirley and Chisholm stood side by side, chests heaving, and behind them Hennessy and Hawkins were holding up their arms, rotating them slowly, displaying their harm-lessness to the Germans. But the machine guns started up again, pattering implacably. He saw Hennessy jump and fall. Hawkins started to run but was caught by an invisible force and sent spinning to the ground.

He launched forward down towards the stream, out of sight of the slaughter. It was his last chance. If he could get to it without being hit he could make his way along it to the road that led through the forest to the cottage. He reached the clay bank, dropped into the water and, crouching, crawled against the flow.

It took ten minutes to reach the road. From all parts of the forest now, the firing had started up again. He moved inside the tree line, parallel to the road, up the gradient where the valley rose from the stream until he reached a bend. He moved forward cautiously and stopped. Ahead of him, on the far side of the road, he heard a burst of gunfire and German voices. A few moments later a line of five men emerged from the trees. They were wearing mud-stained suits and caps. Their hands were folded over their heads. He could not see their faces. Six Germans were prodding them forward at rifle point.

Somone shouted an order and the men shuffled into a line at the side of the road. The soldiers unbuttoned their tunics, pulled tins of cigarettes from their pockets and lit up. The smell of the smoke drifted down to where Adam was lying. He felt the sun warm on the back of his neck and heard the lazy buzzing of an insect. The Germans chatted for a while, relaxed and good-humoured. Then they ground out their cigarettes under the heavy soles of their boots and raised their rifles. There was a volley of shots and the five men fell untidily to the ground. One of the soldiers, an officer it seemed, unbuttoned the flap of his holster and walked down the line, firing a single shot into each head. They set off back up the road towards Vercourt.

He waited for the footsteps to fade before getting up. The dead men lay peacefully in the sun. He recognised the nearest one, a silent *maquisard* who had been in the camp earlier with Alain. Amid the dark cloth of the civilian suits he saw a flash of blue; the blue of the cotton jacket that Jean had been wearing. He was lying on his back with his eyes closed. The stubborn set of his face had relaxed in death so that he looked almost contented.

Adam went through the pockets of the workman's jacket, not knowing why he was doing it or what he was looking for. There was a wallet in the inside pocket, small and worn. He pulled out a grubby envelope. There was a photograph inside. The football players stood with hands folded across striped jerseys, smiling proudly. Jean was crouching in the front row, holding a ball. On it, in a bold, optimistic hand, were chalked the numerals: 1940.

Adam ran back into the trees, over the broken ground, seeing the forest through a warm blur of tears. Then the red roof of the cottage showed through the leaves and he felt a swell of hope.

He saw the green shutters and the window of her bedroom, where she was lying, waiting for him.

He was almost there now. He stopped for a moment at the edge of the clearing. On the far side of the back paddock the warped timber of the back door stood half open. He ran across the springy turf and pushed at the warm wood, which swung open. It was dark inside after the sunshine. For a second he could see nothing. He peered into the gloom. He could make out two figures now, one standing and one sitting. The light from the door gleamed dully on high leather boots. Then he felt something hard poking into the back of his head and he was being hustled out of the kitchen and through the front door.

41

It had been her idea to go back. Make your peace with the ghosts, she said. Then you can find peace with yourself. Adam believed he was happy enough, with a life he liked and a wife he loved. The ghosts could only bring trouble. Better to leave them alone. But she had kept on in her gentle way, blaming his occasional bad moods and retreats into silence on the phantoms of forty-five years ago. To be released from the past he would have to return to it. She was younger than him and still believed in cures. He loved her, so eventually he gave in.

It was she who made the first inquiries, heard about the reunions, discovered the date of the next one, obtained the permissions, made the arrangements, saved up to pay for the tickets. They took the train on a warm, fresh June morning, across Germany, to Brussels where her sister's husband worked at NATO headquarters, and borrowed his car for the drive across France.

They stopped a night in Paris. The city delighted her, but made him feel shabby and provincial. He felt better in the countryside. They stayed off the motorways to save the cost of the tolls, rolling down the straight old roads, hearing the galley-oar swish of the engine washing back from the tall poplars that marched alongside them. The further he got from Paris the closer he felt to the past. They drove through identical little towns and large villages, barely changed since the war. Progress had left the blank fronts and heavy lintels of the little houses alone, and the same old enamelled plaques, rusty and faded now, hung on gable ends advertising aperitifs and engine oil. They took it easy, stopping one night on the way, like a diver halting on his journey to the surface to evade the fatal consequences of a too-rapid ascent.

The letter she sent to the Resistants' association had been vague, simply asking if it would be possible to attend the next commemoration. The reply had been welcoming and incurious: the time and place of the ceremony, an invitation to the dinner in the evening and a recommendation to book early at the Auberge de la Vienne.

They had arrived at the hotel just before noon. There were a few hours to spare before the ceremony began and they had driven into the countryside. She had wanted to see the old places, the scenes of the stories, but he was reluctant. Instead they had eaten lunch on the terrace of a little country restaurant. Then they had gone back to Vercourt, to the gathering in the square.

They stood in the corner with a few people from the village. He was moved by the sight of the veterans in their identical blazers and grey slacks, standing straight and dignified. He tried to put names to the faces but they all looked the same. All except Gerry. Even before he stepped up to the tribune, Adam recognised him. He stood a little more upright than the rest and his clothes fitted well, showing off his still-lean frame. Adam had thought about him from time to time. Lately, since he knew he was coming back, he had even dreamed about him.

And now here he was, sitting across the table, his hands flat on the cloth, staring at him through the candlelight, looking like a fraudulent medium confronted by a genuine apparition.

'Yes,' he said, faintly. 'It is you. I thought.' He winced slightly. ' I thought you were dead.'

Adam had known he would say that.

'I'm sorry to disappoint you.'

'I don't mean it like that,' said Gerry. 'It's just that it's a bit of a shock.'

A burst of male laughter drifted over from the long trestles that lay along the wall of the village hall.

The last time Adam had seen him, his hair had been long and dark. In the candlelight, it seemed almost as thick as before, though now turned grey, almost white. The bandit moustache had gone and there was a raspberry smudge of broken veins above his cheekbones.

'Why did you come back?' Gerry asked gently.

Adam did not reply.

'Maybe you should have a drink,' he said pouring Gerry a glass from a slender bottle half filled with straw-coloured spirit.

Gerry sipped thankfully and lit a thin cigar with a gold, oblong lighter that ignited with an electronic click. His hand was speckled with brown spots and it trembled slightly. The flame illuminated his face, highlighting his cheekbones and the dark sockets of his eyes, and for a moment Adam glimpsed the Gerry he remembered in the flickering light of a campfire. Then the blue flame died and he shrank back to his human proportions: a man, elegant, well preserved, but inescapably old.

There was another surge of hilarity from the tables nearby. A bench scraped back. Adam looked up. Two men were walking ponderously over. Adam tried to connect them to the men he had known in the forest, but time had blurred their features and thinned their hair so that behind the heavy glasses there was little to choose between their wide, pink faces. One put a hand on Gerry's shoulder and looked around pleasantly.

'We haven't finished with him yet,' he said. 'Mind if we join you?'

'No, Mark,' said Gerry quickly. 'I'll be with you shortly. This gentleman is an old friend of mine. We've got a lot of catching up . . .'

Mark Minto. The name and the face came back to Adam. How devastatingly ordinary he had become.

Minto shrugged and smiled, revealing suspiciously white and even teeth. 'OK,' he said. 'We know when we're not wanted. Well, don't go without saying goodnight. Come on Frank.'

They walked back to their table.

There were two French couples at Adam's table, the children of Resistants for whom the war was a dim memory and who attended the commemoration in a spirit of duty. They took the chance to leave, climbing out from behind the narrow benches, smiling and excusing themselves.

'That was Minto and Glover,' Gerry said. 'Of course you remember them. I'd have introduced you but I wasn't sure it was the right moment.'

'I'm glad you didn't. They survived then.'

'Yes, twelve of us got away in the end. Mostly the old and bold.'

'And the others?'

'The greenhorns. All shot. Ten in the forest. Along with the French, of course. The rest were held for a while, then taken off and executed in a field about twenty miles from here. Special forces, you see. No mercy, that was the Hitler order.'

He poured himself a drink. 'You didn't answer my question,' he said.

'What?'

'I asked you why you came back.'

Adam thought for a moment.

'To tell you the truth, I didn't want to. She did.' He nodded at his wife. 'She thought it would do me good.'

Gerry glanced at her as if for confirmation. She nodded and smiled.

'So you didn't come back for me, then?' he asked cautiously.

'No. Why would I do that? I wasn't even sure you were still alive until today.'

'I just thought . . .' He tailed off, then started again, more forcefully.

'I've never forgotten the last day. Some of the things you said . . . I can see why you might have thought what you did.'

Adam stayed silent. Then he said quietly, 'It was all a long time ago.'

Gerry seemed relieved.

'Too bloody long. I sometimes think it would be much better just to forget it all, but we come back, us lot I mean, again and again to hear the same speeches, then get drunk and tell the same old stories.'

He sipped at the pale liqueur and winced.

'Not much to commemorate, really, is there? Just a lot of young blokes getting killed for nothing. I don't know why I bother. Some of the others seem to enjoy it, though.'

He looked up, more confident now. 'What about you? Someone saw you being captured. We assumed the worst. Didn't try too hard to check up afterwards, I have to admit.'

'I was lucky,' said Adam. 'When they found out I was a Pole they didn't kill me there and then but sent me back to Germany for interrogation. It was a long journey. The RAF kept bombing the railway. We got there in the end, though.'

'Oh yes?' Gerry leaned across the table with something of his old retriever eagerness, keen to hear the rest.

Adam sensed his wife's tiredness and turned to her apologetically. 'You don't want to hear all this again, do you darling?'

'I don't mind.'

'Yes you do. Why don't you go back to the hotel? I won't be late, I promise.'

She was relieved to be released. 'Stay as long as you like. There must be a lot to talk about.'

She lifted her slim legs out over the bench and stood up, hand outstretched.

'Good night Mr . . .'

'Gerry.' He was on his feet too, elaborately courteous once more. 'Just Gerry will do.'

They watched her retreating, glossy brown hair bouncing slightly on the nape of her neck.

'She's a glory,' breathed Gerry. 'What did you say her name was?'

'I didn't. You wanted to hear the story.'

'Oh yes,' said Gerry. 'Do carry on.'

So he told him: of the shifting from camp to camp, of the constant expectation of death and the relief each time it brushed past him without quite connecting. The guards were frustrated by the setbacks to the smooth execution of their duty. He felt almost sorry for them. Then, one morning, in the piney camp in the sandy heathland north of Berlin, the guards ran away. They drove out of the gates firing a few last shots, then they were gone and a big silence folded in behind them.

Adam had been half conscious on his bunk. He tried to get up but he was too weak. He lay down and went to sleep. When he woke up the Russians were already there. There were three or four hundred prisoners in the camp. The Jews were turned loose. Stupidly, he told the liberators he was a Polish airman and they decided to hang on to him. He found himself in a new hell, where the indifference of his new captors threatened to be more lethal than the conscientiousness of the Germans. While they considered his story he got sicker and starved. Then one day he was told he could go. He walked through the gates past the barbed wire, smelling the pine needles and the damp soil, feeling the enormousness of the world before him and the gigantic beauty of his liberty, even if it was only the liberty to starve and die alone.

At the beginning of the story he tried to keep the details short, aware even after all these years of the brevity of Gerry's interest. But Gerry was listening properly, turned slightly to one side and bowed like a priest in a confessional, his eyes turned away, nodding solemnly at each new turn in the odyssey.

Adam paused. He needed a drink. He found a half-full magnum of red wine and poured a glass to the brim. He drank half of it, felt it warm him. Gerry turned towards him expectantly, wanting the rest of the story.

'And then?' he said, clasping his hands ecclesiatically. 'What happened next?'

Adam was suddenly weary. Why should Gerry care?

He carried on, but the drama of the account dried up and he filled in the rest of the story in short, unrevealing strokes. There had been a couple of years of destitution. The Communists mistrusted those who had served with the Allies, but his skills had some value and eventually he was given a job instructing at a flying school. When jets came in, he was phased out. He found a job in Warsaw, teaching English and French in a high school, and had stayed there ever since. He lived with his wife in a four-room flat on the sixth floor of a pre-war apartment building in Tarnowski Street. The two boys were nearly off their hands: one at university studying literature; the other working as an adviser in

Africa, teaching Socialist agricultural innovations to Tanzanians. He had three years to go to retirement. Then they would retreat to the holiday home they rented in the countryside east of Toruń, not far from Nowo Pole where he grew up.

The story was true, in the barest sense, as a technical account of a life. When he finished, he had told him almost everything. But nothing of importance.

Gerry's head was resting on his hand, and the smoke from his cigar curled around his fingers and coiled up from his grey temple. His eyes looked wet in the soft light.

'Your turn now,' Adam said.

To his surprise he saw Gerry's mottled hand move over the tablecloth like a crab traversing the floor of the sea, and settle lightly on his wrist.

'It makes me feel ashamed,' he said. 'All that pain. It makes my life seem trivial.'

'Tell me anyway.'

Gerry leaned back and half shut his eyes. The shock of the encounter was fading and the alcohol was reasserting itself again. We are just two tired old men who have had too much to drink, thought Adam.

'Well, as you know, I made it out of the forest,' Gerry said. 'I took my own advice and headed west. If only the other poor buggers had listened they might be here now. But they panicked, you see. Never seen action before.

'After that we kept going for a few more weeks, but without the Jeeps and the radio we were just going through the motions. We laid a charge here and there to keep morale up. Eventually, about a month after the debacle, a plane managed to get in and we were flown back home.'

He paused and withdrew his hand from Adam's.

'It was all a mess. A terrible bloody mess. But of course we couldn't actually say that. There was a move to dish out some gongs to try and make it look a bit better, but I put a stop to that. Yes me, who was always in the front row with his hand out when there was any glory going.'

He paused.

'Anyway, we managed to arrange it so the families can feel reasonably OK about it. The families of the dead, I mean. That's the best you can hope for, really.'

'And after the war?'

'I had the same problems as the other blokes settling down. I joined an expedition to the South Atlantic with some SOS chaps, including poor old Dougie Gibson, God rest his soul. Prospecting for oil, would you believe! But the conditions were awful and none of us had the faintest idea.

'After that I ducked and dived a bit until I got into the PR game. A surprising number of the old mob did. To cut a long story short, it all worked out fairly well – I had my own business until I sold out to one of the big boys. Moira and I stayed together. No kids, though, which has been a bit of a sadness. I don't keep in touch with the old comrades very much. Except Alain, of course. Are you staying at the Auberge? He's done a smashing job.'

Adam said nothing and Gerry took a sip of his drink.

'Of course you never liked Alain much, did you?' He sighed – a real sigh, full of weariness and regret.

'Still the same old Tommy,' he said. 'You always managed to make me feel guilty in some indefinable way and you're doing it again now. You can't blame me for everything that happened to you. Some of it, perhaps – some little things. But this was wartime, God damn it. I was as much a victim of it as you were. The big difference was I tried to make my own luck.'

'Which usually meant bad luck for everybody else.'

'What do you mean by that?'

'Nothing. Nothing.' Adam had no strength for a fight.

'I hope it's nothing.' He puffed on the cigar and looked away. 'I never forgot those accusations. They hurt me. It was so stupid. The paintings. What bloody use would they be to me? To Alain, perhaps. How would I have got the stuff home? To be perfectly honest you had your finger on something. There was something that interested me at the château – hard cash that the headquarters was carrying to pay the garrison costs. But that wasn't the reason for the raid. We attacked the place because we were at war with the Germans. It was as simple as that.'

He leaned back.

'I know it's difficult for you to understand, Tommy. We were different kinds of warriors. You fought because you had to. I did it because I wanted to. For me it was always fun. We were dropped into France to create bloody havoc, and that's what I tried to do. If I picked up some loot on the way, then so much the better. But that wasn't why I was there.'

They sat in silence for a while. The evening was ending. The blurred voices of the men and the shrill chatter of their women echoed around the hall. When Gerry spoke again his voice was soft and placating.

'I did feel bad about the girl, though. Just disappeared, I gather. Like so many, I suppose. The funny thing is that when I saw your wife, I thought for a moment that it might be her. I mean, the same hair, the same look, although she must be quite a bit younger. Stupid really.'

He looked at Adam expectantly. There was a hoot of laughter, loud and mirthless, that carried the length of the room.

'Radegonde's dead, Gerry,' said Adam. 'I'm certain of that.'

Gerry sighed and reached for his glass. 'I'm sorry. You may not believe it, but I know what that must mean to you, even now, however many years afterwards. There is only one love, no matter how much you bash it and dent it, no matter how much you deny the fact. There's only ever one that really matters. Most of us – even the most stupid – recognise it when we see it. But the funny thing is, instead of being happy, we're frightened. Your instinct is to try and kill it off. If you're lucky it fights back and survives and you come to see how mad and stupid you were. If you're unlucky you crush the life out of it and as soon as it's dead you see what you've done and spend the rest of your days regretting it or trying to find the same thing again, which can't be done.

'You knew what you had, Adam, and you fought like hell to hang on to it and you still lost it. That must be the hardest thing of all.'

Across the wine-stained tablecloth, Gerry dipped his head to the guttering candle to relight his cigar and Adam could see his scalp shining pink through the grey-white hair. He had sometimes hated him. He would never feel love for him, but now, as he puffed at the cigar and lifted a glass to his lips, Adam realised he was seeing Gerry for the first time as someone wholly human.

'Cheers, Tommy,' he said. 'Here's to what's left of our miserable lives.'

'Cheers.'

The glasses chinked and they held each other's gaze, sealing an understanding with their eyes.

The evening was finished. The hall was almost dark now and most of the people had gone. A woman emerged from the gloom and stood behind Gerry.

'Hallo, Moira,' Adam said.

She had kept her line and her elegance. Adam thought of an ancient bouquet of dried-out, dark-red roses that had once hung upside down behind his mother's bedroom door.

'Hallo,' she said. 'I've been watching you. I thought it was you. I wasn't sure.'

'You should have come over.'

'No,' she said firmly. 'Better to leave you two alone.' She laid her hand on Gerry's shoulder and he moved his hand up and squeezed her fingers.

'But I'm glad you came back, Adam,' she said.

'So am I.'

Adam and Gerry got stiffly to their feet. Gerry put his arm around Moira and the three of them walked through the now empty hall and out into the square. It was a clear night and yellow stars pricked the blue-black sky over the church tower. Their footsteps echoed as they crossed the square to the hotel. Adam stopped at the door.

'I'm going to walk a little,' he said. 'Sleep well.'

Gerry held out his hand and he took it.

'We'll see you in the morning then,' said Moira. 'At breakfast.'

And so Adam walked back across the square and up the road that led out of the village, past the blank façade of terraced houses and the little shops until he reached the fields. The forest lay on the earth like a dark bank of cloud. Behind him the church clock chimed the quarter. He could smell the dew as it gathered on leaf and blade, freshening the night air. He set off into the stillness. Far away a dog barked and a night bird called from the wood. Nothing had changed. He remembered every foot of the way. He passed the cart track that led off to the farm and the tiny, overgrown graveyard, filled with the long-forgotten dead. Then he was at the forest. It was cooler under the trees. He stood for a minute, as if daring the ghosts to come to him, but there was only the faint sigh of the wind in the branches and the subtle stirring of the leaves.

He found the path off to the right and followed it along the forest edge. The cottage showed dark through the thin timber. The iron gate groaned as he pushed it open. A frog croaked on the damp lawn. He walked up to the front door. The house was shuttered tight and weeds grew thickly in the cracks between the paving stones of the terrace. Beside the door sat an old metal table and two chairs. Was it here that she had served him crayfish and cider on the June night when he first realised he was falling in love with her? He sat down. This was where he had left her. This was where he had seen her last. Or was it?

One morning, on the last leg of the northward trek, the guards had halted them for half an hour at the gates of a compound on the edge of a pleasant town on a lake, the name of which was Ravensbrück, while they went inside to seek directions. He had sat on the ground with the other scarecrows, looking through the barbed wire at the rows of huts beyond. Between the huts a group of prisoners stood in ranks, while a guard counted them off into work gangs. At first he took them for men with their bony, shaven heads. Then he saw they were wearing rough, sacking shifts and he realised he was mistaken. The guard formed them into small groups and they walked away towards the wire to a path that led off to the workshops. They shuffled along the wire, looking straight ahead, starved and featureless, with only the sacking shifts to show they were women. He watched them numbly. One of the women stopped. She lifted her head and turned it towards him and for a second her black eyes – huge and liquid in the gaunt mask of her face – settled on him and he thought it was her. Then there was a shout of anger and a guard was shoving at her and she was stumbling on down the path. He staggered to his feet, waving, croaking her name, but she never looked back and the last thing he saw was the swaying back of the smock and thin, bare legs carrying her away from him.

The new camp was only a few miles up the road. In the weeks before his liberation he thought he was going mad. Sometimes he prayed that it was really her and that he would find her again. The rest of the time he prayed that it was a fantasy. The day they let him go he crept back to the women's camp, but the gate was barred and behind the wire it was empty. In the months that followed he did the rounds of the army head-quarters and relief offices searching for information. Then, one day, after about a year, he found a Red Cross official who had some news. Riomet, Radegonde had died three months after the Liberation, of typhoid, contracted not at Ravensbrück but at another camp.

He went over to the door and tried the handle. It turned and the door scraped back and he stepped inside. The house was bare and abandoned. He climbed the creaking stairs and stood for a moment on the landing, then lowered his head and ducked through the low doorway and into the tiny bedroom under the eaves. The narrow child's bed was still there, under the dormer window, and he lay down on it, burying his face in the musty mattress and imagined he could smell her and feel her body under him. Then he began to cry, a thin noise that seemed to be coming from another person.

He was woken by light falling through the dusty window. He looked at his watch. It was 4.50 a.m. on 21 June, the dawn of the longest day. He left the house and walked down the path, through the awakening earth, back to the hotel where his wife lay sleeping.

ACKNOWLEDGEMENTS

I would like to thank Nick Sayers for his enthusiasm and his meticulous and inspirational editing, and the rest of the Hodder and Stoughton team for the wonderful support they have given me, particularly Anne Clarke and Kerry Hood. I am also grateful to Richard Foreman for his crucial role in the genesis of *A Good War*. A number of friends have helped along the way in various valuable ways. Thank you to Mariann Wenckheim, Felicity Hawkins, Nick Farrell, Nina Watts, Viv Davidson, Ania Miers, Robin Gedye, Charlotte Eagar, Suzie Bell, Adam LeBor, Adrian Brown and Hugh and Rebecca Schofield.